ALSO BY MORGAN RICHTER

The Divide

THE UNDERSTUDY

THE UNDERSTUDY

Morgan Richter

Alfred A. Knopf
New York
2025

A BORZOI BOOK
FIRST HARDCOVER EDITION
PUBLISHED BY ALFRED A. KNOPF 2025

Published by Alfred A. Knopf, a division of
Penguin Random House LLC, 1745 Broadway, New York, NY 10019.

Knopf, Borzoi Books, and the colophon are registered
trademarks of Penguin Random House LLC.

Library of Congress Cataloging-in-Publication Data
Name: Richter, Morgan, author.
Title: The understudy / Morgan Richter.
Description: First edition. | New York : Alfred A. Knopf, 2025.
Identifiers: LCCN 2024029701 |
ISBN 9780593685709 (hardcover) | ISBN 9780593685716 (ebook)
Subjects: LCGFT: Thrillers (Fiction) | Novels.
Classification: LCC PS3618.I3637 U53 2025 | DDC 813/.6—dc23/eng/20240830
LC record available at https://lccn.loc.gov/2024029701

penguinrandomhouse.com | aaknopf.com

Printed in the United States of America
2 4 6 8 9 7 5 3 1

The authorized representative in the EU for product safety and
compliance is Penguin Random House Ireland, Morrison Chambers,
32 Nassau Street, Dublin D02 YH68, Ireland,
https://eu-contact.penguin.ie.

To Ingrid

THE UNDERSTUDY

1

Giddy Uncertainty

The first time my understudy tried to kill me was on the day we met.

We got off on the wrong foot, Yolanda and I, and while most of that was due to Yolanda being a very . . . complicated individual, some of the blame lies with me. Our difficulties started at our initial run-through, the first time the cast was assembled, and when Daniel introduced Yolanda to the group and announced that she'd be my understudy, covering me in the titular role of Barbarella, I felt a flash of irritation, uncharitable yet valid. She didn't need to be there. She *shouldn't* be there.

Back in July, before the original performance schedule had been torpedoed by the discovery of patches of asbestos in the theater, Daniel had cast Roksana Kahele as the lead in Astrid Busk's brand-new work, a two-act chamber opera based on the 1968 cult sci-fi film *Barbarella*. When he'd asked me to cover Roksana, I'd felt honored and excited. Early last year she'd starred in Astrid's attention-grabbing *Charlie's Angels* opera, and *The New Yorker* had published a short yet flattering profile of her in their Talk of the Town column; her popularity had only grown since then. Her presence would bring greater attention to the opera, and as her understudy, some of that attention would inevitably land on me.

From the start, Daniel had made it clear I wouldn't be needed until rehearsals moved to the stage. This is standard: Opera singers are paid per performance, whereas understudies are paid per rehearsal. As understudies rarely get a chance to perform, requiring them to show up to early rehearsals serves no useful purpose and bloats the budget. When Roksana was forced to drop out of *Barbarella* due to schedule conflicts created by the delay, Daniel quietly bumped me up to the lead. I expected him to pick someone who'd worked with the company before to cover me, maybe Akiko, the coloratura soprano who'd covered the role of Criside in his production of *Satyricon* the previous fall. I also expected not to see or hear from whomever it was until later in the process.

But here we were on the first day of rehearsal, and here was this complete stranger.

"Yolanda Archambeau," Daniel said, pronouncing her surname like he was sipping a fruity Beaujolais on the banks of the Seine. "She comes to us from New Orleans, and we are delighted to have her."

Voluptuous and radiating sexual confidence, Yolanda was gorgeous. Regardless of all the bad blood that would flow between us during our brief yet tumultuous acquaintance, I freely admit she was one of the most beautiful women I'd ever seen. She'd styled her platinum hair in soft waves, paired with eyelashes like crow feathers and lips so red and wet they looked like she'd dipped them in paint. She was probably aping Marilyn Monroe, down to the small black mole drawn above her lip in a precise eyeliner dot, but my thoughts immediately went to the late Anna Nicole Smith, model/reality star/tragic train wreck.

Years ago, before I was born, some tabloid ran a photo of Anna Nicole hanging out with my mom at a bash at the Playboy Mansion, both of them treading the line between glamorous and gaudy in low-cut evening gowns in glittery pastels. Soft white arms encircling each other's waists, ample bosom pressed to ample bosom, they looked like decadent sisters with matching smeared-lipstick smiles and shiny, unfocused eyes. Throughout my early childhood, that photo was taped to the refrigerator in our Pasadena home, probably to remind my mom daily of everything she'd lost by giving birth to me.

"Nice to be here," Yolanda said. She waggled the fingers of one hand at the group. All of us singers were seated in folding chairs arranged in a semicircle. Marla, our music director, sat at the upright piano; Astrid, who was pulling triple duty as the production's composer, librettist, and unofficial dramaturg, hunched into her battered silver motocross jacket and leaned against the wall by the door, like she was ready to slink off if we started to bore her.

Chamber operas are small, so there were only a dozen of us in the room: the eight of us in the cast, plus Yolanda, Marla, Astrid, and Daniel, who stood at a music stand in front of us, rocking from side to side like a fidgety child. The twelve-piece orchestra would join our group in two weeks when rehearsals moved to the stage.

Carlo looked up from the bound score in his lap and frowned at Yolanda. Sleek and handsome, Carlo was my leading man, the chaste winged angel Pygar. On the surface, the casting didn't make sense to me. I'd seen Carlo in Chelsea Opera's production of *Carmen* last spring, and he'd been glorious, sidestepping the expected path of playing Don José as a lovesick fool in favor of excavating the character's cruel and manipulative undertones. He'd let something dark and poisonous slither around the edges of his crystalline tenor, and it had been a masterful choice. Carlo was destined for a career built around a repertoire of beautiful and complicated villains; virtuous sylphs were a waste of his abilities.

"So Roksana's not coming back for any of the performances?" Carlo asked. "She'll be finished at the Met before our run wraps, right?"

"Correct. Her commitment to the Met's production of

La Traviata only overlaps with our first two weeks of performances, but she and I both agreed it would be simpler if she bowed out. Fortunately, Kit was available to step in." Daniel dipped his head in my direction.

Carlo's frown turned toward me. "Okay. That's cool," he said after a pause that was just long enough to make his feelings about the casting change clear.

Much as Carlo wasn't how I envisioned Pygar, I probably wasn't his physical ideal of Barbarella, the sweet-natured planet-hopping vixen made famous by a young and beautiful Jane Fonda. I wasn't worried about looking right for the part; clever costumes paired with heavy makeup would transform me from a mouse into a wide-eyed, big-haired, swimsuit-clad sex goddess. It could be problematic, though, if Carlo's frown indicated that he didn't think my voice was up to the rigors of the role. We'd worked together in *Satyricon,* but he'd been the lead while I was in the chorus, so I suppose I couldn't blame him for feeling ambivalent about me.

No worries, though. I had the ability. I had the training, the knowledge, the skills. I met Carlo's frown with a friendly smile and turned my attention to Daniel.

Somewhere in his early thirties, Daniel looked like a posh schoolboy, with a wardrobe consisting of shrunken blazers paired with vests and messily knotted neckties. He was tall and angular, with a great deal of black hair that managed to look both freshly cut and untidy. When he spoke, his diction was precise, words chosen with care. It surprised me during rehearsals for *Satyricon* to learn he'd been born and raised in New York; everything about him suggested dusty mansions and vast ancestral wealth.

"I want to thank all of you for having the patience to bear with this production despite some setbacks." Daniel's eyes darted toward Astrid, as though expecting her to chew him out for the exposed asbestos behind the crumbling walls backstage that had delayed the production. Astrid twitched one eyebrow skyward, but remained silent. "Barring further emergencies, we should have no trouble meeting our new performance dates. Thank you to Kit for stepping in to fill Roksana's shoes, and thank you to Yolanda for joining the Brio family." He gave Yolanda one of his signature tight-lipped smiles, prim and exact.

He didn't look at me, which stung. I didn't mind that I hadn't been his first pick; I wasn't in Roksana's league, not yet. But it was hard to shrug off the hunch that he'd dropped quite a ways down on his list of ideal Barbarellas before reaching my name.

It didn't matter. I was ready for this, my big debut. It was time. It was past time, honestly; my professional career thus far had consisted of back-of-stage ensemble parts mixed with long fallow stretches. Back when I was studying at Eastman—and even before that, back when the choir instructor at my boarding school had first guided me toward private lessons—I'd thought my future would be bursting with juicy prima donna roles.

Now? I'd turned thirty earlier in the year. No cause for worry, not yet; opera stardom often arrives late due to the years of training required to develop vocal skills worthy of a professional stage. Thirty was still a respectable age for my current level of accomplishment, but doors would close soon, and if I couldn't make the most of my opportunities, I'd find myself facing a lifetime of chorus work, perhaps interspersed with the occasional lucky comprimario role.

We warmed up as a group, Marla assembling us around the piano and leading us through a series of exercises. I didn't need the warm-up, as I'd arrived early to hole up in one of the practice rooms to get my vocal cords relaxed and flexible. Carlo had done the same, I'd noticed, as had Jerome, the portly baritone who'd be playing *Barbarella*'s villainous Durand-Durand.

Warm-up concluded, the official run-through began. Marla

pounded out an abbreviated version of the overture, then I rose from my chair and launched into the opening duet with Claudette, another *Satyricon* survivor, who was playing the President of Earth.

I'd worked tirelessly on the score since July. I'd badgered Gerard for extra lessons, asking for as many of his evenings as he could spare, even as he begged me to keep in mind that he was an elderly man of declining vigor who enjoyed his free time very much, thank you. I'd rehearsed daily by myself in my minuscule apartment, driving the retired firefighter next door mad with what he termed my "incessant warbling."

We sounded good. Better than good, really; Claudette's rich mezzo voice melded with my higher, lighter, more agile tones and created something magnificent and complicated. Since this was our first time performing for Marla and Daniel, I didn't bother with marking, the opera singer's time-honored tactic of performing at only a fraction of full volume during rehearsals to prevent wear and tear on the vocal cords. Astrid had written a series of complicated trills into this introductory duet, and I nailed them, every note distinct. When Claudette and I finished and sat back down, Carlo leaned over and silently bumped his fist against mine.

We progressed through the material. We were good at our craft, all eight of us, doing justice to Astrid's work. Astrid's native language was Icelandic, but her libretto was in English, her lyrics clever and complex. She hailed from a prestigious artist collective in Reykjavik; knowing her background, when I'd first looked at the *Barbarella* score, I'd expected it to be esoteric and experimental, the music atonal and calculatedly disharmonious. Instead, it was a bold crowd-pleaser, an opera singer's dream, overflowing with opportunities to dazzle. Even if *Barbarella* sank into obscurity at the conclusion of our run, I'd keep the music fresh in my repertoire, ready to perform arias from it at auditions throughout my professional career.

I didn't think it would sink, though. I had a hunch the production would do well. People would come for the gimmick of an opera based on a kitschy cult film, but they'd leave with the satisfied feeling that comes from an evening spent exposed to wonderful art. The show might get good reviews. I might be singled out by critics as someone to watch, a prima donna on the rise.

We reached my big aria, the climax of act 1, Barbarella's realization that she must return to the debauched city of Sogo to battle the Great Tyrant and rescue Pygar. This was a big showy piece, the one I'd spent the most time rehearsing, poring over the score to get every intake of breath right, to hit every note cleanly, to make certain my diction was precise enough so audiences could understand every syllable.

Here's what thrills me to my core about well-trained voices: precision. I once read a review of a performance of *The Magic Flute* where the critic praised the soprano playing the Queen of the Night for what he referred to as the "giddy uncertainty" of her voice; he claimed to be on the edge of his seat for the entire performance, heart racing, because he was never certain she was going to hit her infernally tricky high notes. I didn't understand that review, and I don't imagine I ever will. I love the confidence that comes from knowing that each note will be hit, that the technique will be flawless, that the entire experience will radiate artistry and professionalism.

I started the climb to the top. C6 and up to E, then all the way to G, nailing the high notes with confidence, knowing how much strength to give them so I wouldn't risk my voice cracking . . . I saw Marla, head bent over the piano keys, break into a smile; I saw Daniel exhale, his shoulders loosening in relief. I felt a sensation of triumph, which vanished as soon as I glanced at Yolanda.

Because Yolanda was yawning, right in the middle of my goddamned aria.

She tried to smother it, or pretended to try, covering her mouth with her hand. When my eyes met hers, she smiled prettily at me, her eyes wide and bright.

I finished, the final note echoing in the room. I waited.

Daniel cleared his throat. "That was very nice, Kit," he said. "It's clear you've been working hard on this. We'll get into the nuts and bolts this afternoon, but here's the big picture: The craft is there, but it's a little passionless right now. Marla and I are going to have to work on helping you find your spirit." He glanced over at the piano. "Marla?"

"The precision of your upper range is admirable, Kit. I can tell you've put in the practice. Please pass my kudos along to Gerard on his coaching." Marla smiled at me. "I think it'll be a matter of forging that connection with the audience, making it seem not quite so soulless. Precision is a wonderful quality, and we're so glad you're bringing that to the table already, but I think you could use more . . ." She considered her words, tilting her head from side to side as though ransacking her brain for the right way to phrase it. "Charm."

"I see. Thank you very much." I made sure to smile, though it probably looked as unnatural on my face as it felt. "I'll pay special attention to that." I'd trained myself to trot out that response whenever vocal coaches gave me critical feedback: Make eye contact, smile, thank them with every indication of respect and sincerity, looking nothing less than grateful to them for slicing and gutting my ego with a thousand sharpened blades.

I'm being dramatic. Obviously, nothing in that criticism was harsh or unjust. I'd done a good job; Marla and Daniel knew that. But I'd thought I'd done an exceptional job, one that deserved a soft round of applause from Daniel, or even a murmured "Brava" from Marla. Receiving praise for working hard is much less satisfying than receiving praise for being exceptional.

From her place near the door, Astrid caught my eye. Her

expression grim, she nodded once, her pointed chin dipping toward her chest. She was trying to communicate something, but I couldn't interpret what she meant. Agreement with Marla's and Daniel's consensus, most likely.

"We'll leave that for now and move on," said Daniel. "Beginning of act two, everyone."

Marla raised her hands above the keyboard, then paused as Yolanda spoke. "Can I try that?" she asked. For a Louisiana girl, she had no trace of a drawl. "Can I do that song before we move on?"

I almost gasped, my breath hitching in secondhand embarrassment at her lapse in etiquette. I'd been an understudy often enough to know that covering a role requires invisibility, unless the director or conductor specifically calls upon you to become visible. You learn the role on your own, then you keep close at hand during dress rehearsals, staying silent and out of the way until the director decides it's time to run through your blocking. I waited for Daniel to tell her, politely but with enough repressive emphasis to drive the point home, that she was overstepping.

Instead, he considered her request, pursing his lips in thought. "Yes, I think that would be a good idea, Yolanda," he said at last. He gestured for her to stand. "Whenever you're ready. Marla?"

Yolanda rose to her feet. She shrugged off her coat, which was fluffy and voluminous, made of faux fur the color of cherry pie filling. As Marla began to play, she squared her shoulders, inhaled, and sang.

I closed my eyes. In the moment before she hit her first note, I realized I was torn between wanting her to be great and wanting her to be terrible. On the one hand, there's nothing I love more than listening to world-class singing.

On the other hand? Bitch had yawned during my aria.

She was . . . fine. From her opening notes, her voice was sweet and clear. She started out softer than I had, slower, and it wouldn't have been my choice, but it made sense, built some drama. Slowly, slowly, she rose to a crescendo.

Oh. Her enunciation wasn't great; she'd have to work on that. One of my instructors at Eastman had lambasted several of my classmates—never me, never ever me—for what she called mushmouth. Yolanda had a bad case of mushmouth: a lazy tongue, sloppy consonants. Worse, she slid up and down between her notes on the trill instead of hitting each one dead on. Sliding around is fine, even encouraged, for many styles of singing—pop music careers have been built on well-deployed vocal scoops—but unless an artist really knows what she's doing, it's considered a bad move in opera.

She started the upward climb, and I inhaled, heartbeat quickening. I opened my eyes and gazed at her, so gorgeous and so radiant, her expression rapturous, her body vibrating with the music. I couldn't understand why it should make any difference, but when I looked at her, her voice sounded better, richer, more resonant.

She hit the C with strength, then went thin and strained on the E. Her G came out weak, more air than sound.

Okay. She had a lovely voice, but her skills weren't where they needed to be to perform a lead role. Still, she'd be an adequate understudy. Moot point, in any case; I wasn't going to let her replace me onstage. We were scheduled for twelve performances over four weekends in November, and I would be there, hale and hearty and in the best possible voice, for every single one.

She finished. She beamed. "How was that, Danny?"

Danny. Jesus. Nothing about Daniel suggested he'd enjoy being called Danny.

"Nicely done, Yolanda. The emotion in your voice gave me goose bumps at moments." Daniel looked thoughtful. "Those high notes weren't there for you today, huh?"

Yolanda shrugged. "I was close."

"You have a beautiful voice," Marla said. "You infused the lyrics with great depth of meaning. It's not there yet, but you and I, we'll get those top notes where we need them to be."

Yolanda laughed. "Thanks so much." She had a great laugh, light and musical yet somehow sophisticated. When she lifted one arm to push her hair off her face, her cropped jersey rode up well above her navel. Everything about her was voluptuous: those breasts, those hips, that provocative glimpse of her abdomen.

At her laugh, seductive and knowing, I felt a crude and spite-ful suspicion that Daniel wanted to sleep with her, that maybe he *was* sleeping with her, that maybe that was why he let her get away with calling him Danny. Maybe that was why he wanted her at the first rehearsal, and maybe that was why she gave him goose bumps while I failed to move him.

The most memorable divas tend to be larger than life in all ways: tall, shapely, powerful enough to project their voices to the back wall of a packed auditorium, beautiful enough to grab an audience's attention from the moment they swan onstage. That is . . . not me. I have the power, but not the size or beauty. I'm short, boxy, and plain. I have a wide rib cage with plenty of room for my lungs to expand, which is great for breath control and volume, but there are no curves anywhere on me. My hair is an indeterminate shade of beige; it grows out as thick and stiff as dried grass, so I keep it short to attract the least amount of notice. My face is unremarkable in all ways.

But my underwhelming appearance matters less on the stage than you'd think, thanks to the magic of costumes and makeup. It's only in rehearsals where a little imagination is necessary.

Yolanda, of course, had an advantage in that respect, thanks to her extravagant beauty. I could easily picture her as Barbarella, even in her street clothes, which already looked like a costume. So could Daniel, and Marla, and Astrid, and everyone else in this room.

Yolanda took her chair and swilled from her water bottle. She crossed her legs at the knee and sat back, radiating satisfaction. Her eyes darted over to me, and she grinned. It looked a bit like a smirk. I tried to grin back, hoping to appear friendly and relaxed and not at all threatened by her, not one tiny bit, but by the time I coordinated my reluctant facial muscles enough to come up with something resembling a smile, she had already looked away.

2

Oomph

We took our first break of the day immediately after that, just a short recess to stretch our legs and refill our water bottles. I headed for the restroom. By the time I exited the stall, Yolanda was there as well, leaning close to the mirror, carefully applying lipstick from a sleek gold tube. Her eyes met mine in the mirror.

"Hey," she said. "Kit, right?"

She showed no signs of budging from the mirror, so I wedged myself next to her at the lone sink so I could wash my hands. "And you're Yolanda," I said. I cleared my throat. "You did a nice job with the aria."

She turned her head to look at me. "Thanks," she said. "I'm so glad you thought it was *nice*."

The inflection was bitchy, breathtakingly so. She followed it up with a smile, natural and friendly, but I felt my cheeks start to burn. I covered my embarrassment by saying the first thing that popped into my head. "You're from New Orleans? Did you train at Loyola?" During my senior year at the University of Michigan, a recruiter from Loyola's music school had tried to entice me to join their graduate program. I'd been torn between Loyola and a couple of other rock-solid options before deciding on Eastman.

She shook her head, her hair swirling around her face once before settling perfectly back into place. "I've had some private instruction, but I'm mostly self-taught." It was said with a trace of smugness, which seemed unwarranted. "Self-taught" is not a phrase likely to impress anyone in the professional opera world.

"You haven't had formal training?" I tried to keep the judgment out of my tone.

"Singing shouldn't require a fancy degree," Yolanda said, like she was explaining an obvious concept to a slow child. Her eyes met mine in the mirror, and she laughed. "I can tell from your face that you have plenty of opinions about that."

I did, in fact, but I found myself shaking my head. "No, it's just . . . If it works for you, that's great." I picked my words carefully. "It seems like it would be a lot more difficult to pursue a career in opera in New York without completing an accredited music program. To me, it seems impossible."

She leaned closer to the mirror and applied another dab of lipstick, vivid red and very shiny, right on the shapely bow of her mouth. She pursed her lips together and examined the effect. "Yeah, well, you should probably let me worry about that."

Without shifting her attention from her face, she waved her lipstick in my direction. It took a moment to realize she was offering it to me. I shook my head.

"You sure?" She waggled the tube in the air. "Give it a try. A pop of color would do wonders for your face."

"I'm fine. Thanks."

"Suit yourself." It was frosty, like she'd been insulted by my rejection, and I found myself wondering if I should have borrowed her lipstick just to be polite. I wasn't sure the offer had been made purely out of benevolence, though. It seemed likely that she felt prickly about her lack of training, and getting in a small dig at my appearance could have been her way of settling a score.

Rehearsal resumed. We plunged into the second act. I half expected Yolanda to ask Daniel for another chance to sing, but she behaved herself, sitting quietly in her chair and paying close attention to the proceedings. Daniel and Marla still seemed a little underwhelmed by my performance, but if they had concerns, they kept them to themselves, apart from reiterating that I should focus on developing charm and appeal for my interpretation of Barbarella.

It was well after noon by the time we made it through the finale, and we broke for lunch. We'd been given a full hour, but I scrounged a fast bowl of chicken and vegetables from the Chinese joint across the street and was back in twenty minutes. I'd planned to slip into the rehearsal room and run through my big aria on my own, but the double doors were locked. I was about to head upstairs to the practice rooms when I saw Yolanda sitting by herself on the long bench that lined the hallway. She glanced up and gave a small wave. I paused, then headed over to her.

"You didn't eat?" I asked.

She shook her head. "Having food in my stomach while I sing makes me feel like puking."

I could relate to that. Still, I wanted to warn her that facing down a second block of rehearsal time without refueling was a bad idea: Opera is rigorous work, requiring a shocking amount of strength and stamina. I sank onto the bench beside her.

"I'm sorry if I sounded critical earlier when you said you were self-taught," I said at last. It came out halting and uncertain, because I didn't really know why I was apologizing, but I didn't want to get off on the wrong foot on the first day of rehearsal. "It just surprised me, that's all." Auditions for all of Brio's productions were by invitation only, and it was hard to imagine Daniel wasting his time on singers without basic credentials.

But here was Yolanda, undertrained and flawed, who was clearly in Daniel's—*Danny*'s—good graces. So what did I know?

"It's cool," Yolanda said. It was light, but she didn't look at me. "My self-esteem doesn't hinge on your approval."

Okay. She was definitely annoyed with me, but I'd apologized, and I had the sense that anything else I said would only make matters worse, so I kept quiet.

We sat. The silence was heavy. I got to my feet and tried the door handles again in the vain hope it had magically unlocked itself.

Yolanda spoke at last. "Hey, can I give you a suggestion?"

I paused. "Sure," I said, then immediately regretted it.

"Your singing is fine, but that lady in there—Marta? Maria? She's right. It's soulless. You need some oomph."

I froze. I believe, though I'm probably exaggerating, that a thin wash of red went over my vision. When I spoke, my voice sounded tight and prissy. "Her name is Marla. Marla Nicoletti. She's the music director of the entire company. Get her name right, or call her Maestro if you can't remember. 'That lady in there' is disrespectful."

She looked at me, eyes wide with what I was pretty sure was feigned shock. "Wow. Okay, sorry, I didn't know." She frowned. "Isn't Danny the music director?"

"He's the artistic director of Brio and the director of this opera in particular." How was it possible she didn't know that? "Marla will be conducting both us and the orchestra during performances. Daniel is in charge of the staging and our acting; Marla is in charge of everything relating to the music, including our singing. But you should listen to them both equally." I gave her a grim look. "And they're the only ones we should listen to. Performers don't criticize other performers during rehearsal."

"If you didn't want feedback, you could have just said so." Yolanda shrugged. "You shouldn't be so sensitive about criticism. Maybe that's what's holding you back."

I paused. "Holding me back?"

"I mean, who are you?" There was an open challenge in her

expression. "I looked you up online after your little lecture about the importance of proper training, because you clearly think you're hot stuff, and I was all prepared to be impressed, but there's not much out there. Unless you raise your game, I can see you doing back-of-stage roles for the rest of your career while I'm center stage at the Met. Watch and see."

The confrontational look faded, and her lovely face went vacant, lost in daydreams of satin gowns and velvet curtains in front of an adoring public. All of her predictions were pretty rich, because Yolanda and I were probably right around the same age, and I was willing to bet her professional credits were more lackluster than my own.

"Sure. I'll watch," I said. It came out as a snarl, which meant I was losing control. "But unless you radically improve your technique, the Met is a pipe dream. You missed those upper notes, your trills are sloppy, and your diction is a mess."

Her eyes narrowed. Her face shifted into focus, dark emotions transforming the fuzzy daydreams into something violent and visceral. "Did it sound like Danny was worried about my diction? Did it sound like Marla—excuse me, the *Maestro*— was worried about my trills?" She snorted, short and angry. "You heard them. You saw their reaction to my performance. Now compare that to their reaction to yours. Back in that rehearsal room, they were ready to replace you with me, and you know it."

It came out as a hiss, contempt fueling her words, and my cheeks burned like I'd been slapped. Insults only hurt if there's truth behind them, and Yolanda had landed a direct hit. While scarfing down my lunch, it had popped into my head that maybe I was in a precarious spot. I was already Daniel's second choice; maybe Yolanda's performance, or at least her Barbarella-appropriate beauty, had bumped me down to third.

"Like I told you before, you did a nice job," I said. It was a struggle to contain my temper. "But I can't possibly be the first to say you need more training before you're ready for a professional career. Get back to me about how I need more oomph after you've mastered the basics."

She frowned at me, then faced forward and stared at the wall opposite us. We fell back into silence, strained and awkward.

Eventually, she rose, and in a reluctant voice, she said, "I'm grabbing tea from downstairs. You need anything?" She picked up her purse. It was quilted black leather; I saw the interlocking gold Chanel logo on the clasp and calculated the probability of it being the genuine thing. Low, I concluded: Yolanda's appearance had a lot of polish, but I doubted she'd come from money. Her defensive anger seemed like a textbook sign of an early life filled with uncertainty and deprivation.

Ask me how I know this.

Her tone was sullen, but the offer was a promising sign. At least she was making an attempt to smooth things over. "I'm fine. Thank you," I replied, as politely as I could manage.

She headed off, leaving me to wonder how things had gone so terribly wrong. Almost without exception, I got along with my fellow performers, though I tended not to form lasting bonds. Opera is a stressful and unstable career, and singers can be mercurial; over the centuries, the word "diva" has developed distinct negative connotations, and there are many excellent reasons for that. Despite that reputation, I tried to stay calm and pleasant. People liked me, or at least they found me inoffensive. I showed up on time, I stayed focused on the work, I kept my personal drama far from the stage. I didn't lose my temper.

Except I *had* lost my temper. Yes, I'd been provoked; Yolanda had goaded me by insulting my voice and my career prospects, and I'd retaliated by criticizing her skills. That hadn't been my place, any more than it had been her place to attack mine. I probably should have let her buy me a cup of tea, or offered to buy her one as a peace offering.

She returned a few minutes later, clutching a lidded paper cup and about eighteen honey straws from the little café next door. She flopped onto the bench beside me and smiled, and I felt relieved. Like me, she'd had a moment to cool off. Probably she'd thought it over and realized we'd both been needlessly hurtful.

She raised the cup to her mouth and froze. She pried open the lid with one crimson-painted thumb and sniffed her beverage. She exhaled in a huff. "Damn it. The girl at the café gave me green tea. I asked for mint. I can't stand the taste of green tea."

"If you add all that honey to it, you'll obliterate the flavor anyway," I said.

"You want this?" She proffered the cup in my direction. "I haven't touched it. Otherwise it's going in the trash."

It was a cold October day, and the building was old and chilly. I'd been sipping lemon water from a thermos all morning to keep my throat clear, but hot tea with honey sounded good. "Sure," I said. "Thanks."

She passed me the cup. I added two of the honey straws and sipped. Yolanda stuffed the rest of the straws into her Chanel bag, which would make an ungodly mess if one of them burst.

We sat in silence, though it seemed less strained than before. I considered apologizing for our earlier spat, then decided to let it go. By the time I finished my tea, the rest of the cast had trickled in to join us, wrapped up in puffy coats and long scarves against the blustery chill of a New York autumn. Before long Daniel arrived to unlock the room.

The second chunk of rehearsal started with another round of vocal exercises, all of us thronged around Marla's piano as she took us through scales and tongue twisters. That concluded, we took our seats, and Astrid, who'd spent the morning in grim silence, came forward to explain her work to us. Lean and elfin, with keen gray eyes that glinted beneath her black-rimmed glasses, her silver hair short and spiky, she made eye contact with each of us in turn, confirming that we were paying close attention.

"This is not about tits and ass," she said, her tone crisp and exasperated, as though one of us had ventured forth the opinion that *Barbarella* was all about cleavage. "Drive that out of your head right now, if that is the baggage you are bringing into this room. As with *Charlie's Angels, Barbarella* is retrospectively viewed through a lens of kitsch, or is regarded as cheesy, even ridiculous, because audiences have difficulty reconciling the concept of women who are sexually appealing in overt ways with the concept of women who are also engaged in rigorous or heroic professions. If a work depicts a woman who embodies both of these concepts at once—if, for example, it features a heroine who looks like a centerfold model and is also an astronaut, or a soldier, or a scientist, or a crime fighter— such a work must be unserious. Campy. Worthy of derision, even contempt. My goal with *Barbarella* is to force audiences to reevaluate such a way of thinking."

I tried to focus on what Astrid was saying, though it was hard, because the room was distractingly warm. But Astrid's lecture was interesting, and I struggled to give it my full attention. To prepare for the role, I'd watched the *Barbarella* film, of course, and I'd found it cheerfully sleazy. Campy, certainly. I'd half expected Astrid's libretto to lean into the absurdity, to push it to the verge of parody. Instead, it had been witty yet sincere, *Barbarella* reimagined as a classic dramatic opera in which a brave, good-hearted heroine stands up to dark forces at great personal risk, like a Brünnhilde who forges a happy ending for herself.

Astrid continued. "Barbarella is a character designed to please the male gaze, of course, yet she also represents a very powerful and sexually vital form of feminism, and it is that dichotomy that my work explores. This opera is about Barbarella discovering the formidable power of her sexuality; she will take on many lovers, and in each encounter, sex will be a very appealing, very enlightening experience for her. In the face of peril, Barbarella remains a positive force: vibrant, triumphant, and sexually voracious."

I heard Yolanda, in the seat beside me, smother a giggle, maybe at Astrid's unsmiling delivery combined with her strong Icelandic accent while talking about sexual voraciousness. Astrid's chin pivoted in our direction, and the stern gray eyes focused on us; I hoped I didn't look like the guilty party, because I was sweating a lot more than I should.

Like, way more. Way, way more. So much sweat. Sweat gathered in sticky puddles in my armpits and the small of my back, and my skin felt like it was burning from the inside. My eyes were dry and scratchy; I blinked to clear them, and my vision blurred.

Someone had cranked up the thermostat, probably, and now it was too high; the boiler in the basement must be churning out too much heat. Or maybe it had broken, maybe it was flooding us with lethal levels of carbon monoxide. That had happened in my apartment building last winter, and I'd crashed on Gerard's sofa for two very long nights before it got fixed. I felt my heartbeat speed up, a staccato pounding. Maybe I was having a panic attack; I'd never had one of those before, but surely this was what one felt like, this combination of rising body heat and an accelerating heart rate, like I was having a heart attack . . .

Maybe I was having a heart attack.

Astrid finished her lecture and slouched off to the back of the room. Daniel stepped up to the lectern, and he was saying something I couldn't understand over the roaring in my ears. I should have left the room to address whatever was happening to me, but I didn't want to draw attention to myself, because maybe Daniel would decide I was problematic. Maybe he'd think replacing me with Yolanda was the best plan.

Ah, we were going to rehearse. At last, Daniel's words penetrated my brain, which felt like it was expanding from the heat, threatening to burst out of the confines of my skull. We weren't going to take it from the top this time; we were going to start with my duet with Carlo, Barbarella's first encounter with Pygar. I had it memorized, of course, but I flipped through my score to find it anyway because I didn't trust my recall at the moment. The musical staves and notes were a blur of lines and dots.

Carlo was on his feet, which meant I should stand as well. I did, and as I heard Marla's first chords on the piano, the world blurred and tilted, and then I was vaguely aware of the cold, cold floorboards against my cheek.

3

A Much-Needed
Soupçon of Drama

I woke up in the hospital. I'd been unconscious throughout all the wild drama that led to that point, which I pieced together later: somebody called an ambulance, I was whisked off to Mount Sinai, doctors initially suspected an overdose before revising their guess to some sort of poisoning. They administered activated charcoal through a nasogastric tube, which sounds like a delightful experience; I'm sure I would have enjoyed that, had I been awake for it. They also did a blood test, which, according to the doctor standing by my bedside, was how they figured out what had poisoned me.

"Tetrahydrozoline," he said. He pronounced the word crisply in a West African accent. He looked extraordinarily young, like a college kid, with rounded cheeks and a wide gap between his front teeth. He'd introduced himself, but I'd missed his name; I looked at the ID badge on his lanyard, squinting to focus through still-blurred vision. Dr. Seth Makinde. "Do you know what that is?"

Tetrahydrozoline. A memory stirred, some ad campaign from my childhood, but I couldn't come up with the details. I shook my head.

"Eye drops," he said. "Tetrahydrozoline reduces redness in

eyes. You ingested over-the-counter eye drops. From the severity of your reaction, it was probably close to a full bottle."

I blinked at him. "I did?" I tried to sit up, but the room tilted. "How bad is that? Am I going to be okay?"

"You're awake and communicating lucidly with me, so the answer to your final question is most likely yes." He smiled. He had a charming smile, relaxed and sympathetic. "But you're quite fortunate. You could have had a stroke, or your kidneys could have shut down. You could have died."

I stared at him. "I didn't . . ." The room tilted again, making my thoughts slosh about in my brain. I knew how this happened, surely, but I couldn't piece it together. "I didn't drink eye drops."

Dr. Makinde nodded. "The tetrahydrozoline might have been placed into your food, or in something you drank. It could be an accident, but . . ." Something placating crept into his smile, like he thought what he was about to say might upset me. "Often it's intentional."

"I didn't drink eye drops," I said again, louder this time. I sounded indignant. My brain was starting to work better now, albeit with a few crossed wires, and I thought Dr. Makinde was accusing me of ingesting eye drops deliberately, like maybe that's what kids were doing for a cheap high, the same way the problematic girls at my boarding school would huff nail polish remover for a brain cell–obliterating rush. "Why would I do that?"

"You are unlikely to do this intentionally. I understand that." He held up a conciliatory hand. "Tetrahydrozoline poisoning has an unwarranted reputation for being not very serious. It's sometimes seen as a prank, something that can make an unwitting target briefly yet embarrassingly ill. But it can be very serious indeed."

A prank. Well, crap.

Yolanda.

Yolanda and her tea. She'd dumped a full bottle of eye drops into her cup and handed it to me. Green tea is naturally bitter, and honey would further disguise the taste. Just a prank.

Dr. Makinde looked at me like some response was required, but I didn't trust myself to speak. He must have seen something in my face, because he cleared his throat tactfully. "Is there anyone who might wish to play such a prank on you?"

My first instinct was to sic everyone on Yolanda, immediately and en masse. Tell Dr. Makinde everything, get the hospital to bring in the police. Press charges against her for assault, maybe for attempted homicide. Get her ass thrown in jail.

I smothered those fiery, vengeful impulses. If I involved the police, I could be fired from the production. I couldn't rationally explain why I believed that so strongly; after all, if Yolanda was in jail and thus unavailable to perform, I'd ostensibly be more valuable to *Barbarella* than ever. But Daniel was regretting his decision to promote me to the lead; I knew that from his lukewarm reaction at rehearsal. My rock-solid reliability was one of my key strengths as a performer, and if I jettisoned that by becoming unstable—by interrupting rehearsals with sudden violent illness, by accusing my understudy of attempted murder, by bringing police scrutiny down on the production—Daniel would cut his losses and find someone to replace me. I was 100 percent certain of that. "I don't think I have any enemies," I said at last. "I'm just an opera singer."

Dr. Makinde smiled again, though his eyes remained alert. "You have no rivals who might wish to do you harm? I have heard that the New York theater world is very competitive." It was a joke, probably.

I forced myself to smile back. "Opera is highly civilized," I said, which was both snobbish and untrue, but right now it was a stereotype I was happy to perpetuate.

My statement hung in the air, and I figured Dr. Makinde knew I was bullshitting him, but didn't want to push me while I was weak.

He nodded. "Well. Think about it for a while, please," he

said at last. "In the interim, we will view this as an unfortunate accident."

"Is it okay if I go now?" I had no idea how much time had elapsed since I'd lost consciousness, but if I left immediately, maybe I'd be able to make it to the tail end of rehearsal.

Dr. Makinde shook his head. "We will keep you overnight for observation. If all goes well, I see no reason you shouldn't go home tomorrow."

"Can I get checked out early? I have rehearsal at nine."

"You will not want to go to your rehearsal," he said. His smile was as kind as before, but his eyes were serious. "After leaving here, you will want to spend the day in bed recovering from your ordeal. I recommend, very strongly, that you do exactly that."

I nodded. "That's a good idea. I'll do that," I said. "Can I still get checked out early in the morning?"

Makinde looked weary. He knew damn well I was blatantly lying, but the smile didn't waver. "We'll do our best," he said. "One of our healthcare aides will be with you soon to see if there's anything you need. In the meantime, rest. Your body has undergone a sudden trauma, and it needs time to recover." He scribbled something on the clipboard at the foot of my adjustable bed and left me alone.

I found my purse stuffed in the bottom drawer of my bedside table. I checked my phone and read a curt text from Daniel asking for a status report. I texted back that the hospital was keeping me overnight, but I'd be at rehearsal in the morning. I paused, wondering how much else to say, and then limited myself to asking if I could meet with him beforehand. Shortly thereafter, my phone beeped, alerting me to his response: 8:45 my office. Three minutes later, a second text came in: Glad you're feeling better.

It wasn't the most heartfelt sentiment, but his priority was the opera; my health was valuable to him only in the sense that it was important for me to be well enough to perform. Daniel wasn't inclined to form deep personal bonds with the members of his cast.

Except Yolanda had called him "Danny," and he hadn't seemed to mind.

Since I had my phone out already, I looked her up online. Yolanda Archambeau. The search results were scant and irrelevant; whatever Yolanda's professional credits might be, they weren't listed under that name. That wasn't noteworthy by itself, as opera singers sometimes perform under different, more exotic names. I'm Katherine by birth and Kit to all who know me, but I'm billed onstage as Katerina. That was Gerard's suggestion: He'd argued that a cool Russian stage name would give my professional image, in his words, "a much-needed soupçon of drama." I'd let him talk me into it, a decision that still gave me an occasional pang of embarrassment.

So Yolanda Archambeau might be known onstage by an entirely different name. It didn't matter; I didn't need to know her life story. Yolanda had poisoned me, so Yolanda had to go. Even if Yolanda had been a lot better at rehearsal, even if she could sing like the reincarnation of Maria Callas, no director would keep such a dangerous loose cannon in the cast.

Dr. Makinde was as good as his word, and I was able to check out in the morning, following a quick appraisal from a harried yet competent nurse, who dropped off a tray of scrambled eggs and bacon before taking my blood pressure and blitzing through a checklist of questions about my condition. I showered at the hospital and changed from my adorable backless polyester johnny into the sweater and slacks I'd worn to rehearsal the previous day. My clothes smelled a little ripe, thanks to the copious amount of sweating I'd done as the tetrahydrozoline coursed through my system. I didn't have enough time to get up to my Hudson Heights apartment to change, so I ignored the feeling of being stinky and headed straight to rehearsal.

The Tammany Performing Arts Center in Midtown, a six-story limestone building dating from the 1930s, was the home of one main stage, which served as Brio's opera house, and two smaller black box theaters. The Brio production offices were located on the second floor, down the hall from the rehearsal room; two dance studios and the offices of eight small theater companies occupied the upper levels. Daniel was at his desk, door open, when I checked in with his assistant, Julie, who sat in the reception nook just outside his office. Middle-aged and athletic, Julie propped her elbows on her desk and leaned forward to look at me, her chin braced on her clasped hands. "How are you feeling, Kit?" she asked. "I heard it was pretty dramatic when you fainted yesterday."

It hadn't been a faint. From what the nurse told me this morning, it had been a seizure followed by unconsciousness as my body tried to decide whether it should fight off the effects of the tetrahydrozoline or succumb to shock, organ failure, and death. While I was grateful to my body for opting for the former, I felt demolished, like I'd fallen from a great height to a concrete floor. I wished I'd followed Dr. Makinde's sensible advice about spending the day in bed. I had a blistering head-ache that no amount of ibuprofen could subdue. I was so sore it felt like my bones were trying to rip through my skin. "I'm absolutely fine now," I said. "I hope I didn't worry everyone."

"You've got to make sure you're eating enough on rehearsal days. Consider taking some B_{12}, too; it'll help you keep your strength up," Julie said. She held up one hand and ticked off a quick list on her fingers. "B_{12}, iron, zinc, ashwagandha. Take those every morning. Do you want me to write that down?"

Daniel approached the doorway, which saved me from having to respond. I wasn't entirely certain what ashwagandha was, but I was pretty sure it wouldn't have prevented my collapse.

"Kit, it's good to see you up and about." Daniel gestured for me to enter his office, which was small and tidy. The window behind his desk was wide-open, and a sudden breeze sent a blast of chilly October air into the room, ruffling the papers on his desk.

Daniel pointed at a chair. "Take a seat. I'm sorry about the cold air. The boiler's malfunctioning, and if I keep the window closed, I end up with triple-digit heat." He frowned. "If it's not asbestos or the wiring, it's the boiler. This is a beautiful old building, but sometimes I think it's not worth the constant hassles." He looked harassed and unhappy, and I suspected I was about to make his stress levels increase.

Before sitting down, I pulled his door closed. During the production of *Satyricon,* Julie had earned a reputation among the cast as an excellent pipeline of intercompany gossip, and while my news about Yolanda would probably leak out, I wanted to give Daniel the chance to control the information flow as best he could. "I have something disturbing to tell you."

He motioned for me to take a chair. His expression was neutral, but his jaw looked tight, and I knew he was afraid I had some serious medical condition that would force me to drop out of the opera.

"Yesterday I had a seizure and collapsed because I'd accidentally ingested tetrahydrozoline. It could have killed me. Somehow eye drops got into something I ate or drank. I don't use eye drops except during allergy season in the spring; I don't have them at home right now, and I don't carry them on me." I kept my tone neutral. I could veer off into explosive anger if I wasn't careful, and I wanted to keep this as coolly factual as I could. "During our lunch break, Yolanda and I got into an argument outside the rehearsal room. Afterward, she went downstairs for a cup of tea, which she gave to me. I drank it, then less than an hour later, I collapsed."

Daniel stared at me. His expression didn't change, but he

went pale, and deep purple gouges appeared under his eyes. "What did you eat for lunch?" he asked at last.

"I went to Lotus Pier across the street. I had chicken and steamed vegetables with rice. Same place I'd go all the time during *Satyricon*." Accustomed to the rigid and joyless eating habits of working opera singers, the owners were happy to adjust their dishes to leave out the oil, the sugar, the spice, anything that might irritate the throat, coat the vocal cords, or disrupt digestion. "It's possible someone in the kitchen laced my lunch with tetrahydrozoline, either intentionally or in some kind of freak accident, but it seems more likely it was the tea."

Daniel was perfectly still. "Do you think Yolanda tried to poison you?"

"I think Yolanda *did* poison me." I swallowed. I had to be careful about this. "From what my doctor said, putting eye drops in food is sometimes considered a prank. Maybe she just wanted me to feel so unwell that I'd do a lousy job and embarrass myself. But she could have killed me."

"A prank?" Some of the color started to return to Daniel's face, and I could see him grasping for that option like it was a life preserver after a shipwreck. Far easier to deal with a prankster in the cast than an attempted murderer. "What did you and Yolanda argue about?"

My cheeks grew warm. "Is it important?"

"It is if you're accusing her of poisoning you."

Fair point. "She told me my performance needed more oomph. I pointed out that her diction was sloppy and that she missed her high notes." Daniel frowned, and I could feel my flush deepen. "I know. I was out of line. It was a stupid squabble, and I regret my part in it."

"She missed her high notes in the morning. In the afternoon, she nailed them." Daniel's eyes were locked with mine.

I'd have to take his word on that. I hadn't been there in the afternoon. In my absence, Yolanda had stepped into my role and had apparently whipped out a bravura performance. I could feel my stomach twisting into knots, so I took a deep breath to compose myself before speaking.

"We exchanged some words, and then she left to get tea. We both behaved badly, but it was a childish spat, that's all. When she returned, everything seemed okay between us. Then later . . ." I spread my hands. "You saw what happened in the rehearsal room."

Daniel was quiet for a long time. "It's not conclusive that she put anything in the tea."

"Honestly, I feel pretty sure she did," I said. "Obviously, though, that's something that will need to be investigated."

Daniel's eyes widened. "Investigated by whom? By Marla and myself? Or do you mean the police?"

"I don't know. I'm inclined to think this is a police matter, because like I said, I could have died." I chose my words carefully. "I'm taking this very seriously. But I wanted to talk it over with you before doing anything. In the hospital, I told my doctor I didn't have any idea how this happened."

"I appreciate that." Daniel exhaled audibly, like he'd been holding his breath the whole time, and the tension in his jawline eased. "Before any outside parties become involved, I'll need to talk to Yolanda."

"Not with me in the room," I said. It sounded brittle. "I don't want to be around her."

"I won't dismiss her from the production without knowing more about this." Daniel sounded mild, but there was an undercurrent to his tone that unsettled me. He was shocked about what had happened, clearly, but he was also annoyed, and that annoyance was directed at least in part toward me.

If I brought in the police, Yolanda would be investigated, perhaps even arrested. In that event, she'd almost certainly be dropped from *Barbarella*, but I suspected Daniel would boot me as well. I was aware of the horror stories about the mezzo originally cast as Sabrina in Astrid's *Charlie's Angels* opera; she'd butted heads with Daniel during rehearsals, challenging his creative decisions, and he'd cut her without warning right before opening night. I hadn't heard a word about her career since then. I suspected rumor had spread throughout the insular community of small New York opera companies that she was difficult and not worth the fuss.

"I understand that." I tried smiling at Daniel, hoping I looked cooperative and easygoing. "I just don't feel up to facing her. Not today, at least."

"You shouldn't rehearse today, in any case. You look unwell." Daniel glanced at his watch. "Go home and get some sleep. I'll talk to Yolanda at the break and update you when I know something."

I shook my head. "I'm ready to rehearse," I said. That was a lie; I felt like I could collapse again at any moment. "If you're sending anyone home today, it should be Yolanda."

Daniel gave me a humorless look, then nodded. "Wait in here, please," he said. "I'll dismiss Yolanda for the day, and then rehearsal can go on as usual. I can trust you not to talk about any of this with the rest of the company?"

"I don't gossip," I said.

He examined me carefully, then nodded again. "Thank you." He rose from his desk. "Let me talk to her now."

It took him about twenty minutes, during which I sat alone in his office, listening to Julie scheduling an appointment with her acupuncturist over the phone while I stared at the OPERA IS MY ARIA OF EXPERTISE bumper sticker plastered across the back of Daniel's laptop. The cold air from outside felt good; it cleared my head. I gazed out his open window at the rickety iron fire escape and entertained wild notions of climbing onto it, dropping down into the alley, and never returning.

That was a new and unsettling line of thought. I loved singing. More, I loved the entire process of putting on an opera, from learning the score and practicing the music, to undergoing costume fittings and suffering through disaster-riddled tech rehearsals, to experiencing the electrifying thrills of opening-night triumphs and champagne-soaked after-parties. This was my life, or at least the only part of my life that I considered worthwhile. I'd felt deliriously happy when Daniel had called to ask me to replace Roksana as the lead, like the world was finally opening wide for me. And yet . . .

I didn't like this. I didn't like this at all. I was fine with being discreet about what had happened; discretion was my default mode. I always behaved appropriately; I avoided conflict and unnecessary complications. But Yolanda had complicated things, and if she remained in the cast, she could lead me into further messes.

Julie stuck her head through the door. "Kit? Daniel says you can join the rehearsal now." As I rose to my feet, she passed me a sticky note emblazoned with a scrawled list. "Here you go. B_{12}, ashwagandha, iron, zinc. It'll help you power through your day."

In the rehearsal room, Yolanda was nowhere in sight. Everyone looked at me in concern when I entered, and I doubt my unwashed hair and general aura of bone-deep exhaustion put them at ease. "How are you feeling, Kit?" Marla asked from her position at the piano.

"Pretty good. I'm sorry about all the excitement yesterday. I hope I didn't scare anyone."

"Food poisoning?" Carlo asked.

So that was Daniel's explanation. I caught his eye. "Seems to be the case," I said. Daniel bowed his head once, as though thanking me for playing along. "I've wasted enough of everyone's time already. I'm ready to dive in."

I did not sparkle during rehearsal, but I was fine. Marla and Daniel were kind to me, probably in deference to my recent ordeal, and while both of them gently reiterated their earlier notes about the lack of passion in my performance, they were otherwise complimentary. I'm a remarkably consistent singer, delivering the same level of quality regardless of internal or external circumstances, which is somewhat unusual in my chosen field. An interrupted night of sleep, a heavy meal, an inattentive audience: Any of these things might impact the performance of an opera singer. Not me, though. I'd trained myself to ignore all distractions and focus on the music.

It seemed I could add "murder attempt by an understudy" to the list of adverse conditions I could overcome through sheer force of will. That was good to know, though it seemed like the kind of thing that would surely happen only once in a career.

How little I knew.

4

Peace Offerings

When I finally returned to my apartment after eight hours of rehearsal on the heels of an overnight hospital stay, I felt exhausted and humorless, and I just wanted to stumble into the shower and go to bed early.

So of course I found Yolanda sitting on my doormat, hunched into her fur coat, leaning her back against my apartment door. When she spotted me, she struggled to her feet, tottering on the spiky heels of her ankle boots. She beamed.

"Scale of one to ten, how pissed off are you at me?" she asked.

My first thought was to wish, for not the first time, that the building management team would finally get around to replacing the broken lock on the exterior door. "Did Daniel give you my address?"

The smile widened. "He didn't want to, but I insisted, and he agreed that it would be nice if you and I talked. I'm here to apologize."

I had my keys in my hand, but there was no way I was going to give this monster access to my apartment. "So you admit you put eye drops in my tea."

"I did, yes." She raised her chin. "I had no idea it would send you to the hospital. It was supposed to be a joke. I thought it would make you shit your pants during rehearsal."

At first I couldn't speak. It horrified me to realize that she was serious. "You wanted me to shit myself. As a joke."

"Sure." She shrugged. "You'd been so arrogant and conde-scending, like you thought I was so far beneath your level that I shouldn't even have an opinion about your singing. So while I was putting my wallet away after I bought the tea, I saw my eye drops in my purse, and . . . look, it was a spontaneous urge. I regret it now, obviously."

"That's psychotic," I said. I was trying to keep my volume low; the walls in the building were thin, and I had no doubt my opera-loathing next-door neighbor, Costas, was eavesdrop-ping on our conversation. Costas was a bored and still-lively retiree from the FDNY who had a whole lot of time on his hands to pay close attention to my personal business. Sound traveled clearly in this building, and Costas didn't need to hear all about my understudy's weird scat-based revenge fantasies.

"I know! Totally. I overreacted." She held up a shopping tote. It was pale mauve and glossy, with rope handles and a promi-nent Bergdorf logo. "Can I come in? I brought peace offerings."

I didn't want to let her in, I really didn't, but I didn't want to continue this conversation in the hallway. Seeing no alterna-tive, I unlocked my door and gestured for her to enter.

"Thanks." She stopped in her tracks and looked around. I had to nudge her aside so I could close the door. "Oh, wow. So small."

My apartment was small, sure. It was also dark and claustro-phobic, built along the general proportions and aesthetics of the interior of a moving van. It had a galley kitchen at one end and a microscopic bathroom at the other. My twin bed filled up a big chunk of the remaining space, though I'd carved out a small area beneath the sole window for an armchair and a coffee table salvaged from the dumpster behind the building. I gave Yolanda the chair and sat on my bed.

"It's fine," I said. "It's worth it to live in Manhattan." Her reaction to the size made me feel certain she lived in one of the outer boroughs, or maybe in New Jersey, where rents were less astronomical and roomy apartments weren't a pipe dream. "Hudson Heights is barely Manhattan, though," she said. "I have my own place in the East Village, and it's not what I'd call huge, but at least I have a separate bedroom."

That made me do a quick reassessment. Living in the East Village without roommates meant Yolanda could afford to pay several grand in rent each month, which was not the norm for opera bit players and understudies, myself very much included. Maybe she was the spawn of wealthy music lovers, big donors to Brio; maybe that was why Daniel had cast her despite her lack of technical ability. "This is enough space for me," I said.

"If you say so." She looked around. "Looks like you really love opera, huh?"

I felt my face burn. I didn't get many visitors; my space wasn't designed for entertaining. I tried to see my decor through the eyes of a stranger: a keyboard on a folding metal stand, a bookcase crammed with battered scores and stacks of unbound sheet music, a coffee table topped with opened packets of lozenges, ginger chews, throat spray. "Don't you?"

"Sure, but it's not my entire personality." She twisted her torso around in my chair to take in the entire apartment, her nose wrinkled in distaste. "Don't you have any other hobbies?"

"What's the peace offering?" I asked.

"Right." She started pulling things out of the Bergdorf bag and placing them on the coffee table. A bottle of Veuve Clicquot. A baby blue box of what I suspected were confections of some kind. A handbag made of dark green leather, stamped in gold with the Hermès logo. I didn't know much about luxury goods, but I could identify a Birkin bag on sight.

She held it out to me. I didn't take it. I stared at it, then at her puffy Chanel purse, then back at the Birkin. "That can't be real," I said.

Sure, that would be an unpardonably rude thing to say about a gift under normal circumstances, but screw it, I was talking to my attempted murderer. I saw no benefit to civility.

"It's not. I'm pretty sure it's not. But you can't really tell from looking at it, can you?" She lifted the buckled flap to show off the interior. "Look at the work on that. You could take it to the Hermès counter at Bergdorf's, and it would take them a while before they figured out it's not the real thing. It's crazy how well-made knockoffs are these days. They're not cheap, either." She thrust it at me again and waggled it in the air until I took it.

"I'll be honest, I'm regifting it. This guy I know gave it to me today, and it was sweet of him, but the color is a deal-breaker. Green used to be my favorite, and then I had this terrible boyfriend who kept buying me green presents. Green panties. Green Jimmy Choos. Green vibrators. And I hate his guts now, so every time I see anything green, I feel my gag reflex kicking in." She scrunched up her face. "But if you don't mind the color, it's pretty cool, right? He probably paid five hundred bucks for it, easily."

I'd never owned any imposter goods, or any genuine high-end designer goods either, and the idea of shelling out five hundred dollars for a known fake was mind-boggling. But Yolanda was right: This was quality. Tight seams, a smooth satin lining, heavy-duty zippers and fasteners, the rich smell of leather that I always associate with luxury. I scrutinized the interior of the main compartment, searching for defects, and noticed an uneven seam along the bottom, the stitches irregular. Apart from that, though, the manufacturing seemed flawless.

I pulled out something from inside the handbag, a stiff cream-colored note card edged in gold. I found myself looking at a message meant for Yolanda, handwritten in small, precise letters: *Hey gorgeous, I hope you're wearing this next time I see you.* The following sentence launched into detail about the wild carnal adventures the writer hoped would take place at said encounter, so I stopped reading and handed the note card to Yolanda. "Your boyfriend hopes you're wearing a handbag when you see him?"

Yolanda snorted and stuffed the card into her own purse. "He also sent me some fancy underwear. La Perla. I kept that."

"Is he going to be okay with you just giving away his gift?"

"If it bugs him, I'll ask him to send me a replacement. Maybe the next handbag he buys me will be in a color I actually like." Her tone was teasing, but I suspected she was mostly serious. "And he's not my boyfriend, or at least not my *only* boyfriend. Don't get me wrong, he's pretty great, but I know a lot of guys who buy me gifts."

Guys used to buy my mother gifts all the time, perfume and jewelry and lingerie. Nobody ever bought me gifts, not counting the flowers Gerard would dutifully deliver backstage on all of my opening nights.

It was nice getting gifts, even castoffs from Yolanda. I stroked the textured leather exterior of the handbag, enjoying the feel of it under my fingertips.

"Anyway, I just wanted to say I'm sorry. It was an accident, but I know it hurt you," Yolanda said. Her tone was blithe, which pissed me off.

"You're using 'accident' wrong. You meant to poison me. Maybe you didn't mean for me to get hospitalized, but you didn't dump your eye drops in my tea by mistake. You're lucky I haven't gone to the police," I said. I sounded uptight and crotchety, the way Costas sounded whenever he'd pound on my door and order me to stop singing.

"I get your point." Yolanda bobbed her head in agreement. "I don't know how many times I can say this: I meant no harm. It was a lapse in judgment."

She hoisted the bottle of Veuve. "And now that that's behind us, let's have a toast to our new friendship. Where do you keep your stemware?"

It shames me to admit that as much as I loathed Yolanda, I also felt a sudden illogical urge to accept her offer. It would be pleasant to sit and drink champagne with a castmate while chatting about the production. Maybe I could forgive her earlier behavior.

No. No. Never. "I'm not having drinks with you," I said. I sounded snippy again. Yolanda had called me arrogant and condescending, which wasn't quite fair, but I could see how I might come across that way. I gestured toward the beribboned confection box. "You can take those away, too. After yesterday, I'm not going to eat anything you give me."

"Oh, come on." She laughed. "Isn't that a little dramatic? Do you think I've poisoned the champagne?"

"How should I know what you're capable of doing? You almost killed me," I said. "It's generally considered a good idea not to eat or drink with your enemies."

"Fine with me." Her eyes sparkled. "We can be enemies. I've had enemies before, and it usually ends up being pretty entertaining. And in our case, it's only natural: Don't understudies always wish ill on the performers they're covering? I bet you jumped for joy when that other singer quit so you could grab her role."

"You seem very confident that you're still my understudy. Don't be surprised if Daniel fires you for this."

"Danny's not going to fire me." Yolanda sounded cheerful. "No offense, but I bet I'm on that stage opening night instead of you."

I felt a little spurt of adrenaline. "What's that supposed to mean?" I asked. "Planning on poisoning me again?"

Yolanda batted my words aside. "Obviously not. I just mean Danny and Marla clearly think I'm a better Barbarella than you, and I don't see that changing anytime soon."

She smiled at me, a dimple flashing in each cheek. She rose to her feet and picked up her fuzzy coat and her purse. "See you at rehearsal tomorrow."

She sailed out of my apartment, leaving behind a lingering

cloud of jasmine perfume. I closed the door behind her, trying my best not to slam it.

The champagne was sealed, the cage and foil intact. There was no chance it'd been poisoned, not that I'd really found that likely. I stuck it in my fridge, where it looked glamorously out of place alongside my sad bagged salad greens and lemons with withering skins. I tossed the box of confections—macarons, according to the gilt cursive script on the label—in my kitchen trash.

I paused. Damn it. The box was decorated with painted flowers and tied with a satin ribbon. Sugar causes mucus to collect on the vocal cords, so I preferred to avoid sweets while preparing for a production, but the package was pretty, and it made me feel special to receive a gift.

I fished the box out of the trash, set it on my coffee table, and stared at it. Finally, I stuffed it into an empty cupboard, where it would be out of my sight until I sorted out how I felt about Yolanda.

5

Substantially Worse
than Dreadful

After Yolanda left, I abandoned my plans for an early bedtime. I felt agitated, so I called Gerard to ask if he could squeeze me in for an emergency session. He paused meaningfully before letting out a weary sigh. "Of course, Katerina. Do come over."

The doorman at his Park Avenue building knew me and sent me right up. Gerard met me in the doorway, wrapped in an enormous wine-colored smoking jacket with a satin paisley collar and cuffs. "You look dreadful," he said as he ushered me into the foyer, shuffling in his ancient house slippers.

"Do I? That's promising. I feel substantially worse than dreadful." I let Gerard help me off with my coat, which was black wool and durable and had seen me through a decade of hard winters. He hung it off the trunk of the brass statue of Ganesha that stood next to his door, then waited as I removed my boots. In socks, I padded across his thick Persian rugs into the plant-filled conservatory, a beautiful glass-walled room with French doors leading out onto the corner balcony.

The conservatory boasted a baby grand, which stood on the parquet floor beneath a chandelier shaped like tree branches tipped with sparkling dewdrops of light. Gerard arranged himself at the piano and held out a hand for my *Barbarella* score. "You aren't coming down with anything, are you? I've told you not to stop by if you're feeling poorly. I'm not young, and my immune system isn't what it once was." Gerard glowered at me, small dark eyes glittering in the middle of his soft, hairless face. His bald head was a perfect oval, as pale as an egg.

"I was sick yesterday, but nothing contagious. My cover thought it would be funny to dump her eye drops into my tea at rehearsal, and I spent the night in the hospital."

The small eyes widened. "My goodness," Gerard said, his tone mildly scandalized, like I had just burped in front of him. "Did you deserve it?"

I snorted. "No. We argued, but she started it."

"Katerina, 'she started it' is a debate tactic worthy of toddlers." He patted the piano bench next to him. "Tell me more about this understudy. Begin with why she was at the rehearsal in the first place. Does that mean what I think it does?"

"That Daniel wants to make sure someone is ready to step in if he decides I'm not cutting it? Yeah, I think it probably does." I sank onto the bench. "He hasn't said that, of course, but it's clear he prefers Yolanda to me."

"Yolanda." Gerard pronounced the name with dramatic emphasis, rolling the syllables around his tongue. "Tell me all about this naughty Yolanda."

"I don't know much. She's from New Orleans. Yolanda Archambeau."

"A bold name for what must be a bold young lady, if she's already poisoning her rivals on her first day," Gerard said. "As I'd rather not testify in some future lawsuit for slander, I should ask if you're certain she did the deed."

"She admitted it. She claims it was a dumb prank, which could be true. Of course, it could also be true that she wanted to kill me, or at least make me so ill I'd have to exit the production."

"That's one way of snagging a role, I suppose." Gerard smiled, though I knew he didn't actually find Yolanda's actions funny. "I assume she's a talented singer, at least?"

"Yes and no." I thought about it. "Bear in mind my perspective is biased. I don't like her very much."

"No, I don't imagine you do."

"She has a good voice. But she's sloppy. She slides all over the place, her diction is mushy, and she missed her top notes and didn't seem to care," I said. "She has a delusional view of her own ability. I'm not saying she's Florence Foster Jenkins, but she's clearly undertrained. She told me that she's mostly self-taught, and she doesn't seem to think that's a big deal."

Gerard's brow wrinkled. "But really, that's odd. Why would Marla and Daniel push a neophyte into a leading role, even just as an understudy? New York has no shortage of excellent and experienced sopranos to choose from." He examined the back of one wrinkled hand and frowned at his dark spots. "I should know; I train several of them."

"I don't know what Marla thinks. I suspect she sees potential in Yolanda. Maybe she views her as a fixer-upper. But Daniel's definitely a little funny about it. He knows about the poisoning, and he's clearly upset that it happened, but he has no intention of getting rid of her. She's convinced her position is unshakable."

"At this point, it could well be. Daniel might be loath to ditch her now that rehearsals have begun." Gerard took the *Barbarella* score from my hands and waggled it in the air. "This is a brand-new opera. Apart from you and that soprano who workshopped your role, the one who was so marvelous as Kelly in Astrid's preposterous *Charlie's Angels* piece . . ."

"Roksana," I said. "Roksana Kahele."

Gerard dipped his chin in acknowledgment. "Roksana, yes. Apart from you and Roksana, no singers have this role in their repertoire. If Daniel bans Yolanda from the production and you become incapacitated, your replacement would have to learn it from the ground up."

I hadn't considered that angle. "I guess that makes sense," I said.

Gerard gave my leg a firm, friendly pat. "Enough of Yolanda. How about yourself? Why do you think Daniel is unhappy with your performance? And what does Marla think?"

"'Unhappy' might be too strong. He's . . . underwhelmed, I guess you could say. I'm not entirely sure why." I tried to put my thoughts together. "I feel like I'm doing a good job. I've nailed my runs, hit all my notes, done everything right, but Marla and Daniel say I lack passion and charm."

"Yolanda has considerable charm, I take it?"

"Yolanda has considerable boobs. She's also beautiful and loaded with sex appeal, and the way I see it, Daniel is interpreting that as charm."

"Ah. Now we're getting somewhere." Gerard raised his chin and examined me. I found myself nervous about what he was going to say next. Despite his fundamental kindness, his approach to coaching tended to be unsparingly honest, genial banter softening his blunt assessments. "You do have charm, Katerina, though you do your best to disguise it. It seems as though, for this role in particular, Daniel sees special value in the physical, whereas you have prioritized the mental: your technique, your knowledge, your work ethic. I don't say that's the wrong approach, but to make Daniel happy, you might want to adapt to his way of thinking."

"Stuff socks in my bra, you mean?" I asked.

Gerard smiled. "That might be a bit too literal," he said. "You would say Roksana has sex appeal, wouldn't you?"

"Sure. Roksana is gorgeous. But she's also a lot better than Yolanda. She's onstage at the Met right now, you know."

"I know. *La Traviata*. You should send Ms. Kahele roses for handing you your first break." He waggled a finger at me. "And it's up to you not to squander it. Ignore Yolanda. Even if Daniel seems enchanted by her, he's no fool. If Yolanda isn't skilled enough, she won't appear on his stage. You, Katerina, are certainly skilled enough. But your task, as I see it, is to prove to Daniel that you are also a dynamic and beguiling performer."

"Yeah, but how do I do that?" I asked. It sounded petulant; Gerard pursed his lips, and I expected him to chastise me for whining. Instead, he seemed to give the question serious consideration.

"Do you remember the day I first heard you sing?" he asked.

"Of course." I'd been a miserable and near-feral adolescent, and Gerard had visited my music class at Macaulay, my new boarding school in Ann Arbor. Ms. Kapoor, our choir teacher, had studied under Gerard at Juilliard, and she'd invited him to drop by while he was hosting a lecture series at the University of Michigan. I'd sung the soprano solo in Mozart's "Veni Sancte Spiritus," and after our unpolished voices had chirped our way through to the end, Gerard had stared at me for a long moment, brow furrowed, then took Ms. Kapoor aside for a furtive conversation.

He chuckled. "I'd asked if there was an empty practice room you and I could use so I could coach you individually on that piece, and I was told there would have to be additional supervision. I remember thinking, Well, that's very good and responsible, they simply want to protect these young pupils from any chance of outside danger."

"And then you discovered they were protecting you from me." I couldn't keep the bitterness out of my voice. "That first year especially, they did stuff like that all the time. I couldn't be alone with anyone. I didn't have a roommate. They banned steak knives in the dining hall, and while no one ever said that was because of me—everyone was much too *nice* to say that, at least to my face—all the kids knew anyway."

No one went near me, not during that first year. I was the messed-up and violent kid who had stabbed someone. The ratty, surly girl whom this elite establishment had accepted into its ranks as a favor to the state, which otherwise would have placed me in a group home. At least I no longer experienced the acute shame I used to feel while talking about my past. My cheeks were warm, but it was from embarrassment compounded by a dull twist of anger.

"An overreaction on their part, certainly, but you *were* a furious little thing. You had that magnificent voice, high and clear and strong enough to cleave a heart in two, but it was always threatening to burst out of your control." Gerard tilted his head back and looked up at his chandelier, lost in memory. "It was exciting to hear you sing in those early years, though also a bit harrowing."

I winced. "I can imagine," I said. "Opera was crucial for teaching me control."

"It was," he said. There was something proprietary in Gerard's smile, but he'd earned that. He'd maintained close contact after that first meeting, pressing Ms. Kapoor to enroll me in private lessons, shepherding me through the tangled process of auditioning for elite music programs, helping me secure grants and scholarships to pay for it all. "But to gain that control, you extinguished that reckless spark. It may have been a necessary sacrifice, but in light of Daniel's response, you might wish to invite a bit of it back in, as long as you can do so without compromising all you've accomplished."

He looked at me like he expected me to say something, but my emotions felt dangerously close to the surface, so I just smiled at him instead, polite but noncommittal. He looked away first, flipping through the *Barbarella* score to my act 1 aria. "Well. We've gabbed long enough. Shall we begin?"

Upon leaving Gerard's place, I was consumed with nervous, gloomy thoughts, which lasted the entire subway ride uptown. I'd wanted to rehearse longer, but he'd kicked me out after half an hour, insisting that my voice was in perfect shape, that overtraining was as hazardous as undertraining, and that he needed his beauty sleep. For not the first time, I wished I had a dedicated spot where I could rehearse at night. Despite Gerard's assurances, I knew I needed to practice more. As soon as I made performing as Barbarella as intuitive as breathing, I could focus my attention on finding that elusive quality— charm, charisma, sex appeal, whatever—that Daniel and Marla thought I lacked.

I trusted Gerard, but his advice on that front seemed fundamentally wrong, even dangerous. Nostalgia colored his memories, making him recall all the dazzling potential of my young voice—that "reckless spark," in his words—while forgetting my rages over missed notes, my tantrums, my tears. I'd been barely human back then. It would be a mistake to try to recapture any of that misery merely because Daniel didn't think I was as pretty or as charming as Yolanda.

Something lay in a sad heap on the black mat in front of my apartment door. At first glance, I thought someone had dropped a glove.

No such luck. It was a rat. Dead, and the cause of death was obvious: A kitchen knife had been plunged all the way through its small body, the tip of the knife embedded in the rubber mat.

I wasn't squeamish, but this repulsed me. Of course I knew who'd left it. This was a threat. A childish one, sure: I didn't know if Yolanda had killed the rat herself, or if she'd spotted a predeceased one on the sidewalk and got it into her head to play another prank on me. The knife had a handle made of molded plastic; it looked cheap, the kind sold in open bins in discount stores. She'd probably had to use some elbow grease to drive the blade through the poor little creature.

I should know. I'd stabbed my aunt's boyfriend in the shoulder with a similar knife. I'd used all the adrenaline-fueled strength my twelve-year-old body could muster, and the blade had only sunk in an inch.

Still, the whole gesture was as psychotic as it was stupid. My fingers twitched on my phone in my coat pocket. Was this a police matter? Should I call the cops and point them in Yolanda's direction?

I took out my phone. Instead of calling anyone, I crouched down to photograph the rat. At first, my hand trembled so much I felt like my phone was going to slip out of my grasp. I had to squeeze my eyes shut and take several deep, shaky breaths before I felt steady enough to open my eyes, bend even closer to the rat, and take photos from multiple angles. Blood had pooled in the ridges of the mat, which indicated that Yolanda had killed the creature herself; surely an old corpse wouldn't bleed.

Inside my apartment, I grabbed a roll of paper towels. With each hand wrapped in towels so I wouldn't touch the corpse or disturb fingerprints on the knife handle, I held the rat steady. My stomach lurched ominously as I eased the knife out of the little body, and for a dangerous moment I thought I might vomit.

I wrapped up the corpse and tossed it into the trash chute down the hall. I stashed the knife under my kitchen sink for safekeeping.

I didn't have proof Yolanda was behind this. But I'd keep the knife and the photos, and if she did anything else to mess with me, anything at all, I'd go straight to Daniel.

The worst part of this? I'd found myself drawn to Yolanda when she'd stopped by with gifts and apologies. I'd been tempted to forgive her for the near-fatal poisoning because she was gorgeous and magnetic, and she'd filled my crappy apartment with dazzling color during her visit. But Yolanda, for all her beauty, was a menace. As I squeezed a long streak of dish soap on my rubber mat and washed away the rat blood in my sink with a healthy spray of hot water, I tried to decide which outcome was more likely: that Yolanda would once again try to hurt me, or that Daniel would replace me with her.

Maybe it didn't matter. Either possibility was unacceptable.

There were few advantages to having a grumpy neighbor who was always up in my business, but Costas's inherent snoopiness might come in handy if I needed an eyewitness. If Yolanda had left me the rat, there was a good chance he knew all about it.

I headed next door, then hesitated at the sound of voices inside his apartment. I was reluctant to disturb him while he was entertaining visitors, but this was something that couldn't wait. I rapped my knuckles against his door.

After a long moment, it opened. Costas leaned in the doorway and scowled at me.

"Ah, it's the warbler," he said. "If your question is whether it's too late for you to do your warbling, the answer is always yes."

He was dressed in a grimy tank top, and his arms, covered in fuzzy white hairs, were muscular. His chest was too broad for me to look past him to see who else was in his apartment. Costas had to be somewhere in his seventies, but he'd retained the wide-shouldered athletic frame that had probably served him in good stead as a firefighter.

I could feel myself flushing. I was a bad neighbor; all singers are. Even the most fervent music lover doesn't want to get stuck living next to an opera singer in a thin-walled building. I strictly adhered to reasonable practice hours—never before nine in the morning, never after nine at night—but even still, I could understand why Costas would get annoyed by his status as a perpetual captive audience member.

Didn't mean he needed to be such an ass about it.

"No more warbling today, I promise," I said. "I just got back from a lesson, and I wanted to check if a friend of mine had stopped by while I was gone. Did you hear anyone walk past your door? It would have been in the last hour or so."

"Sure. I saw her, too. Platinum hair and all the curves? Looks like the first runner-up in a Marilyn Monroe look-alike contest?" Costas gave me a grin that strongly resembled a leer.

"She was here earlier. But you saw her, didn't you? I heard you two girls chatting in the hall. From what I heard, she didn't sound like much of a friend."

Ah, yes, Yolanda yammering on about how she'd wanted me to shit myself during rehearsal. Of course Costas had overheard that. "Yep, that's her. We talked for a bit, and then I had to leave, and I think she might have come back while I was out."

"Didn't hear anything. But I could have missed her. I've had company." He stepped aside so I could see into his apartment. "We were talking about you, in fact. You should meet my guest; he might be your new neighbor."

He looked into the room. "I didn't get your name," he said.

A man with a lot of sandy hair and a suspiciously deep tan for October rose from the sagging plaid couch and joined Costas in the doorway. At first glance, I found him handsome yet generic—large brown eyes, a straight nose, a small cleft in a strong chin—but as soon as he turned his full attention to me, I felt a curious flutter in my chest. It was all in those eyes, which focused on me with alert interest, as though he'd instantly pegged me as someone worth knowing. When he smiled at me, my whole body felt warm. "Hi. I'm Patrick."

He extended a hand, and I made a split-second decision to operate on animal instinct. With Gerard's words about becoming a charming, beguiling performer still fresh in my brain, I tried my best to mimic Yolanda. I lowered my chin so I could gaze up at him through wide-open eyes, I tilted my head a bit to the side, and I took his hand in mine. "It's very nice to meet you, Patrick." I tried to add a hint of huskiness to my voice. "I'm Katerina."

At Patrick's side, Costas snorted. With effort, I ignored him. Costas had never, ever addressed me by name, but we'd been neighbors long enough that he surely knew I was a Katherine, not a Katerina, and he probably thought I was being ridiculous. Which I undoubtedly was.

It seemed to work on Patrick, though. His smile intensified, and he held on to my hand a teensy bit longer than necessary before releasing it.

"I mentioned to management a while back that I've been looking to sublet, and tonight Patrick came knocking at my door," Costas said. He gestured with his head toward me. "This is the warbler I was telling you about, the bane of my existence. The reason I've got to get out of this damnable place."

"You're moving just because of me?" I asked. It was awful to think that I'd been annoying enough to drive Costas out of his home.

Costas made a dismissive gesture with his hand. "My sister in Rego Park has been pestering me to come live with her. It's not all you, warbler. But Patrick here tells me he doesn't mind opera, so maybe you two will be a better match."

"I love opera." Patrick had a wonderful smile, warm and relaxed. "You're a professional singer? Are you appearing in anything right now?"

"I'm in rehearsals for a new chamber opera. It's based on an old film. Do you know *Barbarella*? I'm playing the lead," I said.

"*Barbarella*? Jane Fonda? That's crazy. I love that movie." The smile widened, and his eyes gave me a clear once-over, flicking up and down before returning his attention to my face. "That would be a perfect role for you."

It was flirty. Goddamn, that was flirty. I had flirted with him, and wonder of wonders, he was flirting back. He glanced down again. He looked like he was about to say something further, but then he inhaled sharply. "Are you *bleeding*?" he asked.

I was confused, and then I looked down. The rat had dripped blood all over the bottom hem of my beige sweater, and it looked for all the world like I'd been stabbed in the gut. I pulled my coat around me to hide the stain. "Oh. No. Sorry. There was a dead rat on my doorstep. It must have bled on me when I threw it away."

Costas barked out a loud, angry laugh. Mortified, I opened

my mouth, ready to explain that the rat had been imported to my front door from somewhere outside the building, then reconsidered. To a prospective tenant, a rat infestation wasn't good, but a harassment campaign from a psychotic understudy might be worse, so I closed my mouth and kept silent.

In any case, Patrick's mouth was now twisted in disgust, like he'd decided I was kind of gross. It was a shame; I'd already started to look forward to the idea of him as my replacement neighbor. As I muttered some words of parting and slouched back to my own apartment, I reassured myself that he probably wasn't actually interested in subletting anyway. In his camel overcoat and tailored suit, he'd been dressed too nicely for this dump of a building. He probably worked in something like finance, or real estate, and thus would want to live in a more upscale area. It seemed likelier he'd wormed his way into Costas's apartment on false pretenses. Maybe he was a property developer with an eye on the building, assessing whether it would be worth the effort to buy it up, tear it down, and replace it with shiny new condos. That sort of thing was happening all throughout Hudson Heights, more and more old buildings getting demolished every month and replaced with something bigger, better, newer.

That was bad news for me. Not that I was attached to this place, but it was all I could afford. I was counting on the success of *Barbarella* to lead me to steadier work, meatier parts, and a nicer apartment. That was still my plan, but it would be possible only as long as my understudy didn't rip the role out of my grip.

6

Not-Daniel

The doors to all four practice rooms on the third floor were closed when I went up there during my lunch break the following day, after I'd consumed an unproblematic yet grim salad of poached chicken and chopped vegetables. I hovered in the hallway and listened; the rooms weren't soundproof, so I could hear the thunk of piano chords and the trill of voices coming from inside three of them. The fourth was silent. I rapped my knuckles lightly against the door, then eased it open.

It was occupied. Daniel sat on the piano bench facing the keys, and Yolanda was astride him on his lap, arms wrapped around his neck, hands twined in the back of his hair. One of his hands rested on her hip; the other was up under her shirt. Yolanda looked over Daniel's shoulder at me, hair hanging in her face. "You should knock," she said.

Daniel twisted his neck around to glance at me, and I felt a rush of disorientation, because it was Daniel, and yet it wasn't.

Not-Daniel wore a suede coat over a black cashmere turtleneck, expensive yet casual, and his hair was swept off his face and held in place with some kind of product that glistened under the overhead light. He looked startled but not annoyed by my entrance, and it was that lack of annoyance that made me realize it wasn't Daniel at all, but a stranger who looked incredibly similar to him.

"I knocked. But I didn't think anyone was . . ." I swallowed, hardly aware of what I was saying, my brain occupied with the mystery of Not-Daniel. "Sorry. I'll leave you alone."

I started to back out. Not-Daniel shifted Yolanda off his lap. He gave her hip a firm pat, then got to his feet. "Wait, hang on. If you want the room, it's all yours."

He looked like Daniel. He *sounded* like Daniel, only friendlier, more casual. "I don't need it," I said. I hovered in the doorway, indecisive. "Are you . . . Daniel's brother?"

He grinned. "Older by two years. Genetics are strong in our family, huh?" He extended a hand. "I'm Niko. Are you in the opera?"

So Daniel had a brother named Niko, a brother who was apparently on *very* friendly terms with a singer who was covering a lead role despite being undertrained, a singer who seemed certain her position in the cast was unshakable. A lot of things were making more sense. I shook his hand. "Kit Margolis. Nice to meet you."

"We're sharing the lead role. She's the one I was telling you about." Yolanda smiled at me, unfazed that I had interrupted her cuddle time with her handsome friend.

Niko's eyes widened. "Oh, right!" He examined me, his brow scrunched in an exaggerated manner. Every time he spoke, or moved, or changed his expression, the resemblance to his brother faded. He was more expressive than Daniel, livelier. Better looking, somehow, even though they were close to identical in appearance. "Do we know each other? I'm pretty sure I've seen you before."

"I was in Daniel's production of *Satyricon*. Maybe you remember me from that?" It didn't seem likely. I was certain I hadn't met him at rehearsals. If he'd been seated in the audience, I doubt I would have made any impression on him; I'd been relegated to the back of the stage with the rest of the chorus.

"That could be it," Niko said. He sounded doubtful, but shook it off. "Hey, Yolo told me about the whole eye drop thing. You're doing okay now, right? No hard feelings?" He looked genuinely concerned, more worried than his brother had been, though I chalked that up to Niko's expressiveness versus Daniel's outer lack of affect.

Yolo. "It's okay," I said, which was a big fat lie, of course. But I was determined to play nice with Yolanda for now.

"If there are any hospital bills, or if your insurance hassles you, let Danny know, okay? We'll make sure you're taken care of."

It was a generous offer. My hospital visit had been a nagging worry; my healthcare coverage was meager, and past history suggested the higher purpose of my insurer was to hassle me. I'd been braced for a future filled with horrifying invoices, exasperating phone calls, and the threat of financial ruin. Assuming Niko's offer was sincere, it might come in handy.

Unless, of course, it was a veiled bribe to make sure I didn't involve the police or push Daniel to fire Yolanda. "I'll let you know," I said. "Nice to meet you, Niko." I nodded at them and started to back out of the room.

"See you at practice, Kit," Yolanda said. She sounded friendly, like she hadn't impaled a rat on my doormat the night before. My phone felt heavy in my coat pocket, daring me to whip it out and show the gruesome photos to Yolanda and Niko just to see their reactions.

I hadn't quite made it to the stairs leading down to the second floor rehearsal room when I heard Niko behind me. "Tonya Margolis!" he called out at my receding back.

Part of me wanted to pretend I hadn't heard him. Instead, I paused and twisted my head to look back at him. "Hmm?"

"Tonya Margolis." He jogged down the hall to catch up to me. He was beaming in what looked like delighted triumph.

"You're Kit Margolis. Tonya Margolis has to be your mom, right? You look just like her."

I frowned and wrinkled my brow. "I don't know who that is."

"You're kidding, right?" Niko looked incredulous. "Tonya Margolis. She was in all these cool films thirty years ago; I discovered her on cable a while back and got obsessed. She's great. *Sorority Ninjas,* that was a good one, and *Miami Steam,* and *Savage Rage Two.* She was on *Baywatch* for a couple of seasons."

My mother had been on *Baywatch* for six episodes, actually, playing a lifeguard who turns out to be an undercover FBI agent hot on the trail of a ring of beachfront drug smugglers. It's probably her best work. "Never heard of her."

"You have to be related. You look exactly alike. Except she's . . ." Niko held up his hands, palms facing each other, and I had the mortified feeling he was going to pantomime a curvy figure. He reconsidered and lowered his hands. "She's taller than you are. But your face is identical to hers."

"Sorry to disappoint you," I said, though I was dismayed to find I looked enough like my mom to be readily identifiable as her daughter. It was startling that Niko could detect any resemblance at all through the wild mane of teased hair and the expert layers of makeup my mother had donned for all her screen appearances.

"Huh." Niko scrutinized me. He looked like he was pretty sure I was lying, which confused him, because he obviously thought Tonya Margolis was awesome, and why wouldn't I want to stake a claim to her? "Hey, I really am sorry about what happened between you and Yolo. The eye drop thing was uncool, she knows that. She's horrified that it hurt you."

"She doesn't *seem* horrified," I said.

"She said she apologized." Niko's face looked open and concerned, like it really mattered to him whether I had forgiven his girlfriend for casually trying to murder me.

"She did. She dropped off some nice gifts last night after rehearsal, and I thought everything might be okay." I could feel my irritation growing, directed at Yolanda for attacking me, at Daniel for keeping her around, at Niko for thinking an apology was enough to make me move past what she'd done. "And then after she left, I went to a voice lesson, and when I got home, I found this."

I fished my phone out of my coat pocket, scrolled to a particularly attractive photo of the stabbed rat, and handed it to Niko. "This was on my doorstep."

Niko held the phone close to his face, like he was trying to make out all the gross details. "This couldn't have been her," he said at last, his attention fixed on the screen.

"Who else could it be?"

"I don't know, but she was with me last night. She came over after leaving you." He passed the phone back to me. "She was at my place by seven thirty."

She'd left my apartment a little after seven. I hadn't gone to Gerard's until almost eight. "When did she leave?" I asked.

"She didn't. We ordered in, and neither of us left until this morning." Niko looked earnest and sincere, but he could be lying to protect his girlfriend. "She did the eye drop thing, but not this. It looks like you've got another enemy."

The odds of that seemed so remote as to be not even worth calculating. Of course the rat was Yolanda's work, so of course Niko was lying to shield her, which meant I couldn't trust anything he said, including his impulsive promise to cover my medical bills. Arguing the point wouldn't get me anywhere, so I put my phone away and headed down the stairs. Niko called after me: "Tonya Margolis! You should watch her films. If you let your hair grow out, you could look just like her."

Just what I always wanted. I didn't turn around.

On the second floor, the double doors to the rehearsal room were closed. A tall woman with dark hair rattled the handles, then gave up when they refused to open. At the sound of my approach, she turned, then smiled in recognition, her face lighting up with what looked like genuine delight. "Kit! How's it going?" she asked.

She extended both arms toward me. A little surprised by her evident joy at seeing me, I took her hands in both of mine. She brought me in for air-kisses on both cheeks. Her perfume smelled like long-ago holidays, like roasted chestnuts and bayberry candles.

"Really well so far," I said. "How are you, Roksana?"

She smiled, flashing deep dimples in both cheeks. She wore a royal blue princess coat, the knee-length hem flaring out in soft pleats. "I had an appointment in Midtown this morning, and I don't have to be at Lincoln Center until two, so I wanted to drop by and say hello to all of you." She glanced around the empty hallway. "I should have realized it'd be everyone's lunch break."

"How's the Met?" I asked.

She let out a sigh of deep contentment. Her huge brown eyes grew wider and softer. "Magical. Kit, it's everything, absolutely everything. I've been on that stage before, of course, but not like this."

Yeah. I'd been on that stage, too, but not because I was playing a plummy role in freaking *La Traviata*. Five years ago, Roksana and I had found ourselves competing against each other for one of those heartbreakingly few elite spots in the Met's Young Artist Development Program. We'd each survived the grueling early audition rounds, both district and regional. The finals were held over an exhausting yet thrilling smattering of days, culminating in one last performance before judges on the Metropolitan Opera House stage. At the end of the process, she'd been invited into the program. I hadn't.

It still stung. I still thought the judges had picked incorrectly: Roksana had been excellent, but I'd been perfect. As part of her three-year apprenticeship, Roksana had performed small background roles at the Met while covering meatier ones.

She'd learned a great deal about the world of elite professional opera, and it had placed her in contention for some world-class opportunities. Like *La Traviata.*

"I keep meaning to get tickets," I said.

"Grab them while you can. We're selling out." Roksana flashed her dimples again. She rummaged in her leather shoulder bag and produced a three-ring binder. "I was hoping I'd run into you today. Here."

I took it from her and opened it. It was her *Barbarella* score, filled with her handwritten annotations. I flipped through the pages. "This is for me?"

"It's an earlier draft, so you'll notice a bunch of differences. But this is the score I worked from in the spring when Astrid asked me to workshop it with her. I wrote down everything she said about character motivations, themes, emotions. I don't know how readable my notes are, but it might help you to know exactly what she was thinking when she wrote the opera."

"This is amazing," I said. My own *Barbarella* score was thoroughly marked up with my own notes, but Roksana had worked one-on-one with Astrid for weeks, serving as a sounding board for her ideas when the work was in its early stages. Her score would be a treasure trove of information. "Thanks so much. But you'll want to hang on to this, won't you?"

"It's all yours." Roksana shrugged. "I won't need it."

"You don't want to do *Barbarella* again?"

"Never say never, but . . ." Roksana looked around. Even though we were alone in the hallway, she lowered her voice. "I did *Charlie's Angels,* of course, and I enjoyed it. And the process of workshopping a new opera, observing Astrid while she brainstormed ideas and rewrote bits that weren't working, I wouldn't trade that for anything. I have a huge amount of respect for her and everything she does, but I became a singer to do classic opera."

She gave me a small smile, laced with what looked like a touch of chagrin. "I know opera is a dying art, and I know it's vital to attract viewers who might avoid the classics because they think opera is stuffy and pretentious, but I worry that works like *Barbarella* and *Charlie's Angels* might be a little too . . . I don't know, too unserious. Goofy."

This attitude startled me. Sure, I'd rolled my eyes when I'd first heard rumors of an opera based on *Charlie's Angels*. It had seemed like an idea more suited for musical theater: Broadway was cluttered with lavish song-filled productions based on beloved films and television shows. Opera, though, was different. More respectable, more sophisticated, less preoccupied with attention-grabbing gimmicks.

But then I'd seen it on the stage, and I'd understood what Astrid was doing. How she was experimenting with classic opera tropes, the heightened emotions and the melodrama and the wild bursts of passion and violence, and placing them within the framework of a familiar pop culture property. It was clever and, considering Astrid's shrewd observations on sex and gender roles, actually sort of intellectual. Roksana had starred in *Charlie's Angels* and had workshopped *Barbarella;* surely she knew all this.

"I love *Barbarella*," I said. "I think it's really good."

"It is!" Roksana placed a hand on my arm. "Of course it is. I didn't mean to sound like I was slighting it. But . . ." She chewed her lower lip and appeared to be choosing her words with care. "I'm at the stage in my career where I have to think seriously about my choices. I don't want to get pigeonholed as the soprano who always stars in operas centered around a gimmick."

I wasn't at that stage, nowhere close. I allowed myself to wonder whether I'd mind being pigeonholed in that way, then decided I wouldn't. Like Roksana, my heart belonged to classic opera, but for me, Astrid's work qualified.

"I've been texting with Carlo this week," Roksana said. I nodded; it made sense they'd be friends. She'd been the Carmen to his Don José last spring, and the two of them had flooded the stage with their twin blasts of talent and beauty. "He says you're doing really well."

I perked up at this. "Yeah?"

"Hang on." Roksana took out her phone, scrolled through what looked like a very long text exchange, and handed it to me. I read Carlo's reply to Roksana's query about rehearsals: Kit is a pro. The new girl is . . . and at that point in the text, Carlo had inserted an emoji of a grimacing face.

What does that mean? Roksana had replied, and Carlo had replied with a series of three grimaces.

I tried my best not to smirk, but I couldn't quite extinguish the flicker of triumph I felt at the sight of those grimaces. Carlo thought I was doing a good job, and he seemed to share my assessment of Yolanda's skill level. Nice to think I might have an ally within the cast.

"He's talking about your cover, right? 'The new girl'? It sounds like there's a story there. Who is she?"

I wanted to answer that in detail and tell Roksana everything from the missed high notes to the eye drops to the dead rat to the newly revealed detail that Yolanda was dating Daniel's brother, but I'd promised Daniel I'd be discreet. "I don't know," I said. "I don't know anything about her."

Roksana turned her head at noises on the stairs, then squeezed my arm. "There's Carlo. Good catching up with you, Kit. I'm so happy everything has worked out so well for both of us."

She sailed off, and I was left alone, hoping she was right about everything working out for me.

7

Prickly and Uncompromising

The following Monday, Astrid asked me to skip the second half of rehearsal and join her for a private conversation. Daniel offered us the use of his office, but Astrid insisted on meeting me at the Scandinavian café in the lobby of the boutique hotel next door to the performing arts center. She was hovering near the counter when I arrived, shifting from foot to foot in her motorcycle boots, drumming her blunt nails on the counter while waiting for the barista to complete her order. The café was tiny, with a scary behemoth of an espresso machine taking up half the length of the wall behind the counter; it featured a daunting number of shiny chrome pipes and nozzles and emitted a series of ominous hisses and rattles while in use. The nervous teen boy working the controls looked relieved when at last it spat an inch of frothy blackish fluid into a demitasse cup.

Astrid collected her cup, then nodded at me. "Kit. Thank you for seeing me." She inclined her chin toward the espresso machine. "What will you have?"

"Ginger tea for me, please." I didn't want coffee. Late-day caffeine made me jittery, and I worried that it could adversely affect my performance. Not that it seemed likely I'd need to perform again that day; after our morning session, Daniel had sent me off to discuss the role of Barbarella with Astrid while

Marla focused her attention on Yolanda's high notes. I didn't care for that, because it meant Yolanda was squeezing in some valuable practice time while I was exiled here.

This was the café Yolanda had visited before giving me the poisoned tea. I found myself watching the barista closely as he poured hot water from an electric kettle over a tea bag. Satisfied he hadn't slipped anything into my mug, I accepted it from him, then perched on a high, skinny chair at a table across from Astrid.

Astrid sipped her espresso and replaced it on her saucer, her movements precise. She folded her hands on the table and leaned forward. "Before we start, I wish to ask how you are feeling."

Ah. Right. The last time I'd seen Astrid was in the rehearsal room a week ago when I'd collapsed in a heap. "I'm fine. Thank you for asking," I said.

Astrid unnerved me a bit. Back when rehearsals for *Satyricon* were underway, *Charlie's Angels* was at the end of its run, and Astrid was always hanging out in the performing arts center, looking artsy yet foreboding with her spiky hair and her leather clothes and her omnipresent scowl. A glowing profile in *New York* magazine had labeled her a neurodivergent genius, prickly and uncompromising, and had specifically mentioned her intolerance for fools. I wasn't a fool, but ever since my swoon at that first rehearsal, I'd felt chaotic and messy. Messiness and foolishness are close relations.

"Food poisoning, I have heard."

"Mm-hmm." I sipped my tea as an excuse to dip my head down, away from those piercing gray eyes.

She stared at me, bending over and around her espresso. Her ears had blunt points at the tops, which gave her the look of a malevolent elf from a fairy tale, one who could grant wishes and destroy lives within the same conversation.

At last, she spoke: "Daniel claims it was nothing serious, that you simply ate the wrong foods at lunch, but there are whispers." She twitched her nose. "I doubt Daniel is being honest. This is to be expected. He is more of a businessman than an artist, and he is always aware of the need to present his business in the best light. But I would like to know, and I would like you to feel you can tell me: Was it her?"

She didn't have to say the name. "Daniel asked me not to talk about it."

Astrid looked into my eyes, like she could see my thoughts, then nodded. "Why is she still here?"

It didn't seem like she expected me to know the answer, but it didn't seem like a rhetorical question, either. She clearly wanted to open up a dialogue, and despite my promise to Daniel, I found myself wanting to indulge her wish.

"She says it was a prank," I said.

Astrid shrugged. "It makes no difference what she says. Her intent was to incapacitate you so she could step into your place. That is not acceptable behavior."

She shook her head and turned her demitasse cup around in its saucer. I spotted a small tattoo in the fleshy bit between her thumb and forefinger. Crossed ax blades.

"Daniel and Marla and I met for dinner this weekend to conduct a postmortem on the first week of rehearsals," she said. Her eyes glinted. "Daniel asked us what we would think if he promoted Yolanda to your role."

I felt a sudden gut blow, like she'd hauled off and punched me. "He did?"

Astrid nodded. "He recognizes her vocal weaknesses, but he believes she might be more pleasing to audiences. More memorable, those were his words."

"Did Marla agree with him?" I asked. My voice came out as a croak; I took a drink of tea to moisten my throat.

Astrid shook her head. "Marla was against the idea. She believes Yolanda has potential to develop as a performer if she is willing to put in the work, but is currently suitable only as an understudy."

She leaned across the table, hunching far enough over that I worried her jacket lapels would dip into her espresso. "Marla raised the possibility of delaying the start of performances for two weeks."

The implications of that sank in immediately. "To give Roksana time to finish her run in *La Traviata*?"

Astrid nodded slowly. "So Roksana can step back into her original role."

This was a bad shock. Delaying performances would be a costly and disruptive move. It meant Marla thought it would be better to throw schedules into disarray than to have me appear on the stage. For a horrifying moment, I thought I might burst into tears.

I battled to keep my expression neutral. "Do you agree with them? Either of them?"

When she spoke at last, her words were slow and careful. "Yolanda is, to me, an unacceptable choice. Even disregarding her bad behavior, she has not had the right training, and that ends the discussion. Charm and charisma are no substitute for years of professional education and practice. A surgeon may have a pleasant bedside manner, and that may be nice for her patients, but without a medical degree, she has no place in an operating chamber."

It was good to know Astrid was immune to Yolanda's charms, but I remained quiet, waiting for her verdict on my suitability for the role. I still felt like crying. I drank my ginger tea, hoping it would settle my knotted stomach.

Astrid sipped her espresso, eyes unfocused. "Roksana has the training, of course. Her technique is impeccable, and she is a gifted performer. She infuses her voice with passion. She understands the meaning of words as well as the emotion behind them. Have you seen *La Traviata* yet?"

I shook my head. Astrid tapped the table with one finger. "Make that a priority. The production is excellent, and Roksana is worthy of it. She shines in classic opera, and she will go on to have a prominent career. But."

I didn't understand that "but." It hung in the air, though it seemed like Astrid had said everything she'd planned to say. "But?"

Astrid looked unhappy for the first time. "When Roksana performed in *Charlie's Angels,* I could sometimes sense her wink to the audience, as though she wanted to assure them she was in on the joke, that this subject matter, while treated with the outer trappings of solemnity, was fundamentally unserious. Perhaps this is my ego speaking, but if there is a joke in my work, I myself am not in on it."

I started nodding as she was speaking. "I know. Your *Barbarella,* it's not a joke at all. It's more like Wagner, isn't it? I love the *Ring* cycle, and I love singing Brünnhilde, but it's a role I'll never perform on a professional stage; it's all wrong for my voice and my physical presence. But I feel like Barbarella is my Brünnhilde, my warrior-maiden heroine. When I'm singing the role, that's how I feel, like it's my chance to perform Wagner."

Astrid's expression changed only subtly, but I thought she seemed pleased. "I argued for Daniel to make you Roksana's cover," she said, and though she said it casually, nothing she'd said during this entire unsettling meeting startled me more. "From the moment Daniel showed me the tape of your audition, I saw you as Barbarella. When Roksana withdrew, Daniel wanted to hold another round of auditions, until I convinced him you were more than up to filling her shoes. But it was not easy to persuade him. At one point, he considered spending a great deal of time and money to recruit a bold-name performer, someone audiences would find glamorous and exciting."

Astrid smiled for the first time. It was a surprisingly cute smile, impish and playful. "If I tell you that he asked if I knew whether Ariana Grande was classically trained, perhaps that will give you some idea of where his thoughts lay. But you were and are, to me, the obvious choice."

"Thank you," I said. I felt unnaturally warm, and if I hadn't watched the barista make my tea, maybe I'd suspect he'd slipped something in my cup. "Thank you so much."

"When you sing, I don't worry about you. You will hit every note. You will crescendo when you should crescendo, and decrescendo when you should decrescendo. You will sing as though you understand the meaning behind the words, as well as the words themselves."

"That's very good to hear," I said. "What do I do, though? Daniel and Marla say I need to find charm and soul."

"Yes, they do say that. What they say is different from what they mean. What they mean is that you need to be prettier. Sexier."

Yeah. I'd figured that was at least a part of it. "I'll be prettier onstage."

Astrid nodded, understanding my meaning. "Yes. This is true. Brio employs superlative backstage artisans. Ana in the costume shop and Veronique in hair and makeup are experts at what they do; they will transform you into Barbarella. But until then, it falls to you to change the minds of your detractors."

For a queasy moment, I thought Astrid was going to suggest a makeover, which was a nonstarter with me. I didn't move through life wishing I were pretty or sexy; my mom was both pretty and sexy, and there was nothing about her life or career I found worthy of emulating. I was fine with having a forgettable face. "How do I do that?" I asked.

"I always find it funny, the importance placed on sex appeal, as though it is something inherent and rare, a commodity accessible to only a privileged few." Astrid sipped her espresso. "It goes by other names, of course: star power, charisma, magnetism. Charm. Whatever it's called, it exists only on the surface, contrary to what some insist, and it can be manufactured.

So manufacture it. Look at Carlo when you sing to him; tilt your head to the side. Like this." She leaned her head until her ear almost touched her shoulder, and her stern features softened. She licked her lips and let her mouth part, glossy, rapt. It was the look of a woman in love.

And then she straightened her head, and the illusion dissolved. "You see? Do that. Do exactly that onstage. Manufacture the illusion of passion, and Daniel will be convinced. And then the audience will see it and likewise be convinced."

"You make it sound a little robotic," I said.

"It is," Astrid said, deadly serious. "Or it should be. People use 'robotic' in a pejorative sense, conjuring up images of ambulatory tin cans speaking in a monotone, but this is an outdated perception: Today's robots are complex. Artificial intelligence can feign human response to an impressive degree, and the technology expands daily. When the technology is equal to the task, I will write an opera to be performed by robots. A sophisticated robot will hit every note, it will nail its runs, its voice will be incapable of cracking. For the first time in human history, opera will exist as it was always meant to be: perfection in every moment. Until then, singers such as you are as close as we have to that ideal."

Astrid was my advocate, which was lovely and good, and it warmed me to know she had fought for me to get the role. And Astrid was quite likely a genius, so I had a great deal of respect for her thoughts and opinions. But this struck me as possibly falling on the wrong side of where I wanted to be.

Being comparable to a robot was, I felt certain, a bad thing for any rising opera singer.

Still, I understood what she was saying. I needed to fix the areas of my performance that Daniel and Marla considered weak. Astrid thought sex appeal could be feigned; for the sake of my job security, I hoped she was right, because Yolanda had sex appeal to spare.

—

I thought about Yolanda on the crowded platform at Penn Station while waiting for the uptown A. I was drained and exhausted from the emotional roller coaster of the meeting. In terms of the production, Yolanda had become an existential danger to me. If Astrid's account was accurate, Daniel was willing to endure the inevitable reviews that would sniff at Yolanda's vocal weaknesses, because at least as many reviews would laud her beauty and charisma.

What would those critics say about me? Nobody would rave about my beauty, but there'd be no digs at my voice. I'd hit the high notes, I'd maintain control over my vibrato, I'd execute flawless trills. I'd be reliable.

But was reliability actually more important than charisma? I turned that over in my head. Was it possible Daniel was right, that Yolanda was genuinely a better choice for the role because, in this instance, her skill set was more valuable than mine?

I heard a rumble in the tunnel and felt the crowd shift around me. I nudged closer to the edge of the platform, angling through the crowd without pushing or shoving.

All parts of Manhattan are congested, but subway platforms are a very special brand of overcrowded. As a whole, New Yorkers aren't nearly as impolite as our reputation suggests, but when trains arrive, it's not uncommon to be jostled to the side by someone anxious to be the first to board.

However, it's not at all common to feel a sharp, targeted kick against the back of the knee when the train is arriving, which is what happened to me. My right leg collapsed upon impact. I pitched forward off the edge of the platform, directly in the path of the oncoming train. It was coming fast, hurtling out of the tunnel, all bright lights and roaring sound, ready to obliterate me into bone fragments and gristle.

A yank, a jolt, a burning pain at the side of my neck, and I was hauled backward by mysterious means. The train blasted its horn, and I didn't know if it was meant for me or just for the crowd in general, warning us all to stay back, keep our distance, don't be like the damn fool woman who almost fell off the platform.

The train stopped. Doors opened right in front of me. Passengers disembarked, and the crowd surged and swarmed around me on all sides. I turned to face my savior.

I was astonished by how small she was. She was both shorter and slighter than me, but she'd saved me from obliteration by grabbing my messenger bag with both hands and pulling me back into the crowd. She'd saved my life, even though it felt like she'd almost decapitated me with the strap of my bag. She was a teenager, maybe fifteen or sixteen, dressed in an oversized Knicks windbreaker, the hood pulled up over her head for warmth. Short dreads stuck out like corkscrews from each side of the hood. Her eyes were wide. "She kicked you," she said. "Bitch kicked you."

My heart hammered in my chest; my knees were almost too weak to support my weight. There was a roar all around me, and it was probably the departing train, but it could have been the rush of blood in my ears. "Who?" I asked, but I knew.

"The bitch! That lady, she kicked your leg!" She was shouting, her adrenaline in overdrive, and I understood that feeling. "She kicked you, I saw her, she kicked the back of your leg absolutely on purpose."

I looked around, though it was a lost cause. Yolanda had boarded the departing train, or else she'd slipped through the crowd toward the exit, and in either case, she was gone. "Did you see what she looked like?" I asked. "Did she have platinum hair?"

The girl shook her head. "I just saw her back. She had a hood up. She was wearing a big red coat."

Red. With a hood. Yolanda's fake fur had a draped hood. "It was fur, right?"

She nodded slowly. "I think it was fuzzy, yeah." She must've seen something in my face, because her expression sharpened. "You know her, right? You and her, you got some issues?"

"Yeah," I said. "I know her."

I looked around the platform. Nobody was paying us any attention; maybe this girl was the only one who'd seen the kick, or maybe others had seen it but hadn't wanted to get sucked into someone else's drama. "Will you come with me? Can you tell a transit cop what you saw?"

She grinned at that, sharp and cynical. All her earlier excitement had faded away, and she looked older, smarter, more guarded. "Yeah, no," she said. "Hell, no. I ain't doing any of that. No police, lady. I saved your life, I figure that's enough."

I wanted to argue with her. She was a good eyewitness, someone unconnected to me in any way who could identify Yolanda and testify that she saw her kick me in front of an oncoming train. But I looked at her face, and I knew it was hopeless. If I called an MTA officer over to talk to her, she'd clam up, and I didn't think I could blame her for that. Getting her mixed up with the authorities was a poor way to repay her for saving my life.

Which . . . yeah, she had done exactly that, and in my adrenaline-fueled burst of horror and anger, I hadn't shown any gratitude. "Thank you," I said. "Thank you so much." I hesitated. "Can I do . . . What can I do for you?"

The girl grinned, suddenly charming. "Nah, it's all good." She gave me a nod and edged away down the platform. "Just sort your shit out with that lady. Whatever her beef is with you, you might want to think about apologizing."

I could follow her and talk to her some more, maybe find out her name, but she didn't want any of that. So I stayed where I was and watched the crowd swallow her up.

8

Unpretty and Boring

I stood on the platform for far too long. Another train arrived, and the crowd shifted around me once more, but I stayed in place. I felt furious yet indecisive.

I could find a transit cop and tell them all about what had happened. Surely the MTA had surveillance cameras trained on the platforms, and maybe one would show Yolanda kicking me.

Was I sure Yolanda was behind this? I'd said my farewells to Astrid and left the café at six, the same time rehearsal would have ended. Yolanda could have trailed me into the station, or maybe it was just happenstance that we'd ended up in the same place. Maybe she'd come over to chat, and when she'd seen me close to the edge of the platform, she'd lashed out on impulse. As with the eye drops, maybe she'd seen an opportunity to get me out of her way and had grabbed it.

The platform was suffocating. I left the station, climbing up the stairs into the crisp night air. I stood beneath the awning of a closed café, out of the heavy flow of sidewalk traffic, and called Daniel.

He picked up immediately. "What is it, Kit?"

"Are you still at the theater? I need to talk to you."

"I'm almost home. You're talking to me now."

"Yolanda tried to kill me." I had to raise my voice to be heard over the traffic. A pair of tourists struggling with gigantic Macy's bags stopped in their tracks to stare at me. They exchanged concerned glances, then continued on toward the Marriott.

"Yolanda kicked me in front of an oncoming train at Penn Station just now. Some girl yanked me back, or I would have been killed."

"Kit, calm down. Shouting is bad for your throat." Daniel's tone was sharp. "Did you actually see Yolanda attack you?"

I paused, aware that my instinct was to give him an unequivocal yes: Yes, I saw Yolanda on the platform behind me; yes, I glanced over my shoulder just in time to see her kick me. Such a small lie. Almost the truth, really.

"No. I didn't. The girl who saved me described her coat, that red fake fur she always wears. It had to be her."

There was a long silence as Daniel processed this latest emergency. "Have you talked to the police?"

"Not yet. I'm on my way to the precinct now," I said, which wasn't true, but I had the sense that Daniel was trying to gauge the gravity of the situation, and it seemed important to convince him I was serious.

"Come here first," he said. "My place. You remember where that is?"

"Sure."

"Text when you arrive." There was another long pause. "Thanks, Kit."

I'd been to Daniel's apartment once, for the cast party for *Satyricon.* He lived in a four-story postwar building in Chelsea; I couldn't face Penn Station again, so I walked there as fast as I could, the night air prickling my inflamed cheeks. At my text, Daniel came down and met me at the door, then led me up the stairs to his apartment.

He was still in his work clothes, a dark V-neck sweater over a crisp white shirt. "I just got in, so I haven't ordered dinner yet," he said. He sounded irritated. "Are you hungry?"

I shook my head. "Sorry to bother you at home. I won't take up much of your time." I hovered near the doorway, glancing around.

Daniel came from money. If his address hadn't established that, his decor would have tipped me off. His furniture leaned toward elegant midcentury pieces that looked like antiques, not replicas. In the corner by the bay window stood a Steinway baby grand, made of honey-colored wood that shone under the recessed ceiling lights. I coveted that Steinway like I've coveted few things in my life. When I'd been there for the *Satyricon* party, a couple of my castmates had sat down at that piano to plunk out tunes while Daniel watched, bristling with tension like a first-time mother watching visitors pass around her newborn. I hadn't dared to even touch the keys, but I worshipped that piano from afar.

"Take a seat," he said. He motioned toward the sofa. "I'm having a drink. Rye?"

"No, thanks." I sat. The sofa felt stiff and inflexible, like sitting on a block of wood. Daniel gave himself a small splash of rye and drank it neat in dainty sips.

He sat in a leather chair across from me. "So."

"Yolanda tried to kill me, Daniel."

His expression was hard to read. "And you have a witness."

"She didn't stick around. I don't know how to contact her. She saw a woman in a red hooded coat come up behind me and kick the back of my leg at the edge of the platform right as the train was coming." I examined Daniel for traces of surprise or skepticism, but his face gave nothing away.

He nodded again and sipped his rye, his eyebrows drawn together, his eyes distant and unfocused.

"You didn't see her do it," he said at last. "Your witness can't confirm it's her. She's not the only woman in New York with a red coat."

"She's the only one who would try to kill me, though." My voice sounded harsh. "My blood enemies are a pretty small club. In fact, there's only a single member."

"Okay. But . . ." He twisted his head to the side, staring at his beautiful baby grand, or maybe at something beyond it. "Think about it. The eye drops, that was one thing, and I'm not saying it wasn't bad, but pushing you in front of a train would be a drastic escalation of what seems like a minor personal conflict. You didn't see Yolanda, and your witness only saw a woman in a red coat. Step back a bit, and the whole idea seems absurd."

I wanted to refute this, and then I thought it over. "Maybe," I said slowly. In the moment, it had seemed obvious that Yolanda had tried to kill me, again. Now, though? I felt some uncertainty creep in. "But if it was her, it means she's dangerous."

Daniel didn't answer. I couldn't guess at his thoughts, but it seemed very clear that he wasn't going to take any action, just like he hadn't done anything after the incident with the eye drops.

"If you're not going to get rid of her, I don't want her at rehearsals anymore," I said. I sounded cross. I *was* cross. "That's the least you can do. She's attacked me twice. She can't be around me."

"That's unrealistic," Daniel said. "It's important for her to gain exposure to the rehearsal process."

"Even if she kills me?" It was sharp; Daniel looked startled by my angry tone. "I could have her arrested, you know."

Daniel's brow creased. "Kit . . ."

"That's not a threat. I already told you I wouldn't do that." I sounded childish and petulant, which wasn't great, but releasing a bit of my coiled anger felt good. Maybe too good. "But I'm doing you a favor by not reporting this, and you're not willing to do anything for me."

"She needs to be at rehearsal, and that's final," Daniel said. Something flashed behind his eyes, and I knew he was a heartbeat away from yelling at me. That was okay; like any professional opera singer, I was no stranger to getting yelled at by temperamental directors. I didn't want him to get angry enough to fire me, though, and it seemed like we were veering close to that territory, so I bit back my immediate reply and thought for a moment.

"I need something," I said at last. "You have to keep me safe from her. Make sure she stays away from me at rehearsal. Tell her not to talk to me. In fact, tell her not to go anywhere near me."

"Fine." Daniel still sounded terse and annoyed, but he was clearly relieved I'd taken the threat of the police off the table. "Anything else?"

For one moment, I was back on that crowded platform. The train rushing at me, lights in my eyes, horn blasting . . . In the safety of Daniel's warm apartment, I could feel a cold layer of sweat on my back. "I can't take the subway to and from rehearsal anymore," I said. "There are too many people and too many places where she could attack me."

"Then take cabs." Daniel pinched the bridge of his nose between two fingers. "Give your receipts to Julie. I'll make sure you get reimbursed."

"Thank you." It was a victory, of sorts, and while it might have made my shaky relationship with Daniel even more strained, I was glad I'd fought for it.

Daniel didn't reply. Into the silence, I asked the question that had been bothering me from my first exposure to Yolanda. "Why is it so important to have her at rehearsals? It's not usual for understudies to be around this early in the process."

"It's not customary, no, but I wanted her to be involved with the production from the beginning." Daniel's energy seemed to be seeping away as he spoke. "I thought it would be valuable to expose her to the process of putting on an opera from start to finish. She doesn't have much performance experience."

"Does she have *any* performance experience?"

"Are you questioning my decision to cast her?"

"No, but . . ." I considered, then decided to plunge ahead. "Look, I know she's involved with your brother."

Daniel raised his eyebrows, and I knew he was close to telling me to mind my own business. "Niko recommended her, which is why I agreed to let her audition." It sounded reluctant, like the admission was dragged out of him against his will. "If she'd come in off the street and presented me with her CV, I wouldn't have spent any time on her, not with her lack of qualifications."

I nodded. "She told me she hasn't had formal training."

"She says she's had years of private coaching. She has some technique that she couldn't have developed on her own." Daniel brought one hand up to massage the side of his neck. "She's not at the level of someone who's completed a full course of music education. But she's good enough to be an understudy, and in many ways she's ideal for the role."

I didn't answer. Opera singers can be snobby about our craft, but that's because training is such a prolonged, laborious process. It offended me that Yolanda could skip past all that and land right at my level simply because she was a physical match for the role.

Beautiful people already move through the world with advantages not available to the rest of us. Juicy parts in an opera didn't need to be another perk.

"You and I are participants in a dying art form, Kit. It's difficult to run an opera company; it's almost impossible to run a profitable one. Even the Met isn't nearly as stable as it's been in years past. They're working to attract new viewers, but it's an uphill battle."

I had no idea where he was going with this, so I just nodded. After a pause, like he was trying to get his thoughts in order, he continued.

"Thank god for Astrid; *Charlie's Angels* attracted people who might otherwise have never considered going to an opera. *Barbarella* will do the same. Give us a few years and a few more works from Astrid, and Brio will make a name for itself. But it's going to be expensive, and right now, Brio won't survive without Niko."

Ah. "Niko is helping out financially?"

"Niko's money built Brio." Daniel sounded grim. "The company is doing much better than most. Too many small opera houses have gone under in the past few years. But I still depend on his support."

"And in return for that support, you've given his girlfriend a starring role." I tried my best to sound neutral.

"No. I made his girlfriend an understudy. It was a request, not a demand, and after I met Yolanda and heard her sing, I was happy to do it." His shoulders slumped. "I'm less happy now, of course, after all the problems you've had."

"But you don't want to fire her because you think that might upset Niko, and you need his money."

"I don't want to fire her because I think the production needs her," he said. "I look at Yolanda, and I see my Barbarella. I see her perform, and I'm drawn into her world. I listen to her sing, and it's *almost* there. Her technique is flawed, and I don't feel confident about the top part of her range, but I think the obsession over vocal perfection can do more harm than good. This could be a transformational experience for her."

"And for me?" I asked.

He exhaled so deeply that he seemed to deflate, all the life seeping out of him. "I don't think you're working out," he said at last. Even though I'd prepared for the worst, I felt myself implode at his words, my rib cage crushed to bits, jagged shards of bone tearing apart my lungs. "I'm not sure why not. You have the voice, and even if physically you're not especially . . ." He trailed off, his face flushing. "What I mean is—"

"It's okay. I know I'm not as pretty as Yolanda," I said. "That's just a fact. But I'm a much better singer."

"That's true. Of course you are. But it circles back to what I was saying. Singing and performing are two different realms.

Your singing is close to perfect, but perfection can be boring. Your Barbarella is . . ."

"Boring," I said. I was boring. Unpretty and boring. "Are you going to give her my role?"

"I don't know." Daniel sounded unhappy, which was good, because he was making me miserable, and I saw no reason he shouldn't feel the same. "We'll start rehearsing on the stage next Monday, and maybe that will give me a better idea of where everyone stands."

"What can I do to improve?" I asked. I was pleased by how calm I managed to sound while my dreams evaporated around me. "How can I show you I'm right for the role?"

Daniel shook his head. "I'm not sure," he said. "Do you have any ideas? What can Marla and I do to help you with your performance?"

"Apart from getting rid of Yolanda?" Daniel looked annoyed at that, so I backed off. "Off-hours access to the practice rooms would be helpful. I can't rehearse as much in my apartment as I'd like. Thin walls and angry neighbors."

"That's no problem. I can give you a key to the building. Stop by Julie's desk in the morning and ask her for it."

"Thank you," I said. I got up to leave. "That would be useful. Thanks for listening to me. I'll try to improve."

He walked me to the door and waited while I pulled on my coat and boots. "I don't think more rehearsing is going to be the solution to the problem, Kit," he said at last.

I didn't think so, either, because I still didn't understand why the problem existed.

9

Crazy and Beautiful

I took a cab from Daniel's apartment. The odds of Yolanda lying in wait for me on the subway platform were small, but I reveled in this small triumph anyway. It had been an unsatisfying and borderline damaging meeting with Daniel, but at least this bit of special treatment made me feel like a star.

The driver dropped me off at the corner in front of a bodega next to my building. A pair of flimsy metal bistro tables rested on the sidewalk in front of the grates that protected the bodega's windows. On that chilly October night, a lone figure sat at one, hunched into his camel overcoat, his hands wrapped around his paper coffee cup for warmth. At my approach, he looked up at me expectantly, like he was waiting for someone. I recognized him at once from his thick mass of sandy hair. "Patrick?"

He stared at me blankly, no sign of recognition on his face, and I felt small and foolish. Before I could identify myself, his face cleared, and he smiled that warm grin that I'd remembered from the doorway of Costas's apartment. "Barbarella!" He was pleased to see me, and that gave me a silly burst of happiness. "Grab a seat." He motioned to the rusted chair across from him. "I forgot your real name."

"Kit," I said, and then cleared my throat. "Ah . . . Katerina, actually."

Patrick glanced helplessly around him. "I was supposed to meet a broker here so he could show me a few apartments in the area, but I think he stood me up."

Evidently I'd been wrong about suspecting he was some kind of developer. "You're looking at other places? So you decided against subletting from my neighbor, huh?" I asked. I felt a spike of mortification at the memory of his handsome face contorting in disgust at the sight of my blood-splattered sweater, but I smiled anyway, determinedly playful and carefree. "Was it the dead rat?"

He laughed. "The dead rat wasn't a selling point, no. What did you do to that poor thing, anyway?"

I considered dodging the question, then realized, surprisingly, that after Daniel's cool reaction, I desperately needed to vent about my troubles with Yolanda to a sympathetic outsider. "I found it on my doorstep with a knife through it. I think my understudy left it for me." It felt strangely cathartic to be so candid with a stranger.

He looked at me with a confused half smile on his lips, unsure whether I was joking. "What?"

"My *Barbarella* understudy is crazy and evil," I said. I kept it light, like I was just telling an entertaining story about a problematic coworker, but I felt a tightness in my gut that needed to be released. He looked both intrigued and sympathetic, so I plunged ahead. "The first day I met her, she laced my tea with eye drops and sent me to the hospital. And earlier tonight, I think she might've tried to shove me in front of an oncoming train."

He burst into incredulous laughter, which he immediately tried to stifle. He shook his head. "I'm so sorry, I'm not laughing at what she did. All of that sounds horrible. It's just . . . I mean, you hear wild stories about diva behavior, but she's taking that reputation to ridiculous lengths, isn't she?"

I laughed to show I could be a good sport, but the pain in my stomach intensified. Nothing about Yolanda's actions seemed funny to me. "We're not all like that. Most opera singers are very well-behaved."

"Why isn't she in jail?" Patrick asked. "How does she still have a job? Is she that talented?"

I shrugged. "She's that beautiful."

"Crazy and beautiful can be a potent combination," he said, and there was something a little wistful about it, like he was remembering all the crazy and beautiful women who'd breezed into his life on various occasions. For one fleeting moment, I wished I could be crazy and beautiful in a way that would anchor me in the memories of everyone who encountered me. Patrick hadn't remembered he'd met me until I'd spoken to him; no one who'd met Yolanda was likely to forget her.

I swallowed. I wanted to try something. I braced my elbow on the bistro table and rested my chin on my hand, leaning forward to make intense eye contact with him.

"So, with that said, do you have your tickets for *Barbarella* yet?" I asked. I tried to turn my natural speaking voice into a coquettish purr, but to my ears it sounded like I was nagging him. "Seats are going fast." That was probably a lie. Even performances of *Charlie's Angels,* which had generated a nice amount of press for Brio, had never sold out.

He looked startled. "No, but thanks for the reminder." He got out his phone and started typing on the screen. He glanced at me and grinned. "It's going to be you onstage and not your crazy, beautiful understudy, right?"

"It'll be me," I said. "Unless she kills me before opening night." I couldn't quite manage a laugh.

He frowned at the search results on his phone. "It's at Brio? Where's that?"

"That's the name of the company. We perform at the Tammany Performing Arts Center. Midtown. It's easy to find."

He flashed his nice smile at me. "Is that where you rehearse, too?"

"Every day until performances start." That was all he had asked, but the smile was still beaming at me, and the warm eyes were fixed on my face, and that combination was short-circuiting my brain. I kept talking, abandoning my attempt to be coquettish. "If we need it, we'll start adding weekends and evenings as we draw closer to our performance dates. Hopefully it won't come to that, but opera singers don't have much in the way of social lives. I mean, it's not like we have no lives at all. My evenings are free for the time being." Goddamn it all, I was babbling. Magnetic and charismatic women shouldn't babble.

"Great. I'm looking forward to it." He was still smiling, but he seemed distracted now, and the eyes had lost their keen focus, like my verbal vomit had made him lose attention. In desperation, I made one last stab at seducing him.

"Do you want to grab a drink? I could tell you everything you've ever wanted to know about crazy opera divas."

Something snuck into the edges of his smile then, something that made my chest tighten with a sudden sense of loss. It was amusement. He was amused by my attempt to flirt with him; I had made a fool of myself. "It's been a long day. I should be getting home." The eyes were sympathetic, like he felt a little sorry about rejecting the drab, weird girl who had tried to make a pass at him, and that made it far worse.

He rose to his feet, crushing his empty paper cup in his hand. "I'll see you on opening night," he said, and headed down the sidewalk in the direction of the nearest subway station. That left me sitting alone at the cold, cold table in the cold, cold night air, feeling like I wanted to fling myself down on the sidewalk, beat my fists against the concrete, and throw a full-scale tantrum for ever thinking I could be anything like Yolanda.

10

Somebody's Baby

"Lean into me more," Carlo said. He grinned. "Don't be so afraid to touch me."

This annoyed me, because I clearly *wasn't* afraid to touch him. I'd touched him plenty of times over the course of this rehearsal, and he was acting like I was a fangirl with a crush instead of his professional equal. I just nodded. "Sure. Of course." I looked at Marla. "Should we try it again?"

We took our duet from the top for the fifth time thus far in this endless rehearsal. Carlo and I crooned and trilled about our passion for each other while Marla pounded out the accompaniment on the piano and coached us through our movements, lifting her eyes from the score to check on our progress: "Move closer to Carlo, Kit. There you go. Rest the tips of your fingers on his shoulder. Delicate, yet seductive. Lift your hand as you go into the crescendo. Let it tremble in midair before lowering it to your side, as though you're reluctant to stop touching him."

Ordinarily it would fall to Daniel as the director to shape my performance while Marla focused on my singing, but he was away this morning attending to other company business. In any case, I suspected Marla and Daniel had been having multiple behind-the-scenes conferences about The Trouble with Kit, and thus they'd decided to coach me from all directions to try to make my performance as appealing as Yolanda's.

I followed Marla's instructions dutifully, miming my heartfelt love/lust for Pygar, hoping the emotion came through with every tilt of my head and flutter of my lashes. I moved closer to Carlo, I ran two fingers up his arm in what I hoped was a provocative gesture, I glanced coquettishly over one shoulder at him, my eyelids lowered.

We reached the end. Marla nodded. "Okay. Better. That's where we need to be. Do you feel the difference, Kit?"

"Absolutely. Thank you. That was very useful," I said, though I felt like my motions had been awkward and obvious.

"This is a very horny opera, Kit," Marla said. She wiggled her eyebrows provocatively. "Lots of touching, lots of stroking. I want you to make your Barbarella as overheated as you can get her, okay?"

It was true: *Barbarella* was horny. Despite its stodgy reputation, opera is surprisingly horny, what with all the epic tales of inflamed passions and extravagant seductions, and this particular role involved an even greater than usual amount of groping and fondling. I thought I seemed comfortable with this, yet apparently I was coming across as timid, if Marla's and Carlo's feedback was accurate.

It was just me, Carlo, and Marla in the room. Yolanda had been in earlier, but she'd been dismissed for lunch already, and I was fine with that. It'd been four days since she'd kicked me on the platform, or since some unidentified miscreant had kicked me, and my strategy for dealing with it had been to ignore her. She'd rehearsed first this morning at Marla's request, and Marla had done an admirable job of coaxing the high notes out of her during our—my—big aria. Hearing Yolanda at her best made my spine tingle. Beautiful music echoes in the soul; it's like listening to a heavenly choir, angels bending near the earth to touch their harps of gold. I'm not spiritual in any way, but opera is a religion for me.

And this was where I parted ways from Astrid, with whom I seemed to otherwise share a great deal of common ground. Maybe it was a foolish, sentimental thought, but I felt in my soul that I'd know the difference between opera sung flawlessly by a human and opera performed flawlessly by a sophisticated artificial intelligence, and I'd prefer the human version every time.

Or maybe I wouldn't know the difference. Maybe I needed to embrace my robot side and learn how to convincingly mimic emotion, charisma, sex appeal.

When we broke for lunch at last, Marla suggested that Carlo and I grab something to eat together. "You two should spend more time in each other's company," she said. "I'd like to see you build some chemistry. In your performances, you're coming across as strangers."

Carlo grinned. "What if Kit and I spend more time together and find we hate each other?"

Marla seemed unbothered by that idea. "That might be even better," she said. "Chemistry can be positive or negative, and either way, your audience will interpret it as sparks. Anything is better than bland neutrality. Right now, you two look nice together, but watching you perform is like eating unseasoned food."

After some debate, Carlo and I ended up at a sushi bar down the street. Sushi is a solid and inoffensive lunch choice for a long day of singing: fish, vegetables, rice, seaweed. We nestled at a small table and dug into lacquered bento boxes filled with exquisite sushi rolls, the raw tuna and vegetables glinting like jewels. I drank green tea; Carlo drank hot sake, poured from a small glazed decanter into a tiny matching cup.

We chatted about the chilly fall weather, our expectations for a freezing winter, our backgrounds and education, our respective neighborhoods. A Carnegie Mellon graduate, Carlo shared a row house in Crown Heights with his girlfriend and two college roommates, all singers as well. We didn't talk much about the opera until we'd finished our bento boxes and Carlo had ordered a second decanter. Above my protests, he dumped some sake into my empty teacup. "Drink up. You shouldn't be afraid to live a little. Unless you don't trust drinks from your castmates?" He winked at me.

I didn't reply. Carlo reached the correct conclusion from my silence. "She did it, didn't she? Wow." He laughed. "Eye drops, right?"

"How'd you hear about it?" I asked.

"You know Julie in Daniel's office? She likes me. Older women tend to like me." Carlo smiled. "She talks a lot."

I had no doubt that older women did tend to like Carlo, though it seemed pretty clear Julie had talked to Astrid, too, and very likely others as well. At this point, everyone involved in the production might have heard about Yolanda's eye drop escapade. "I can't talk about it," I said. "I don't *want* to talk about it. It's in the past."

"Sure." Carlo sipped his sake, then refilled his cup, his motions deft and elegant. He looked handsome and polished, like a menswear model on his lunch break; a cluster of well-dressed businessmen in a nearby booth kept shooting glances over at our table from time to time, and I wasn't the one who'd grabbed their attention. They were scoping out Carlo's sculpted features, his well-groomed hair, the expensive tweed coat hanging over the back of his chair. In his company, I felt plainer than ever. "But if she's a danger to you, she's a danger to us all. I don't know what back alley Daniel dragged her out of, but I'd be fine if she returned there."

I picked up my teacup and took a sip to avoid answering. Carlo's sake was warm and pleasant.

"At least . . . I have a general idea which alley, at least." He picked up his phone and scrolled through his photos before passing it to me.

I found myself looking at a picture of Yolanda—a screenshot from a video, it looked like—reclining against a stack of fluffy white pillows on a pink bedspread. She wore a cupless lace bra, her nipples huge and dark against her skin, with a matching garter belt and stockings. No underpants. The screenshot had been taken at a moment when she was between expressions, her glossy mouth half-open, her eyes half-closed.

"Where's this from?" I asked. I was aware of Carlo's eyes fixed on my face, the grin playing on his lips, hoping I was scandalized or shocked or aroused or whatever reaction guys hope to see whenever they ambush women with naked photos. I kept my reaction under wraps. I didn't feel like allowing him the rush of pleasure he'd get from knowing he'd forced an emotional response out of me.

The primary emotion I felt was anger, compounded by a hint of loss. Since my brief chat with Roksana, I'd felt optimistic that Carlo might be my ally because he thought I was better in the role than Yolanda. But Carlo had just revealed himself as a scumbag, and even though Yolanda had tried to murder me (twice, most likely), I couldn't ally myself with a scumbag. If I teamed up with Carlo against Yolanda, giggling at her photos or, worse, weaponizing them against her in some way, she'd have the moral high ground, while we'd be the bullies, the mean kids. The scumbags.

"You know Somebody's Baby, the website? Sexy webcams that lonely guys pay to watch? She's on it nightly. This was last evening. I spent half an hour chatting with her, telling her everything I wanted her to do, and she never figured out it was me," Carlo said. I passed the phone back to him, but he held it up in the air so I could still see the photo. "Look at that. She's had a tummy tuck. Look at that scar."

I'd seen the scar at first glance, a puckered pink line very low on her belly. I'd instantly realized it didn't have anything to do with cosmetic surgery. "How'd you find her webcam?" I asked.

My voice sounded flat, emotionless. He waggled his phone around, which probably gave the diners seated at nearby tables a good view of the screen. He obviously wanted me to try to grab it out of his hand or cover the image out of embarrassment, and there was no way I was going to do that. Instead I kept my eyes locked with his, my face blank.

"Like I said, Julie likes me. I was having a hard time believing anyone that undertrained could get cast, so she showed me Yolanda's audition file. Daniel scribbled something about her extracurricular hobbies in the notes he took during her pre-audition interview. So I did some investigating." He smirked. "She wasn't hard to find. She goes by the name Carmen Callas online, which is a whole wild universe of delusion."

"You should put your phone away," I said.

"What, are you embarrassed by naughty pictures?" The corner of Carlo's mouth crooked up in a smile, flirty and taunting, and I wanted to punch him in his handsome face.

"I don't care what Yolanda does in her spare time. But she didn't give you that photo, and she didn't give you permission to share it with me, so put your phone away."

He stared at me. "It's on the internet," he said, like I was a slow-witted child. "She did this *on the internet*. It's there for everyone to see. If she doesn't want people looking at her body, she shouldn't show it to anyone with a credit card."

"This is a bad idea." I still sounded composed, and I could tell from the confusion in Carlo's face that he couldn't get a handle on my reaction. Was I outraged, offended, embarrassed?

He lowered the phone at last. "You want some advice?" he asked.

I flashed back to the hallway outside the rehearsal room on that regrettable first day, Yolanda offering me feedback on my performance right before poisoning me. "Not really."

Carlo ignored that. "You need to loosen up. You can sing,

but I feel like I'm sharing the stage with a corpse. You're just so damned uptight. I'm sorry if sex and nudity offend you or whatever, but I thought you and I could relax and have a good laugh about Yolanda. You know you can't stand her either."

I caught our waiter's eye and signaled for the check. "Let's get back to rehearsal," I said. I rummaged in my messenger bag for my wallet.

Carlo tried to pick up the tab, but I insisted on splitting it down the middle, unwilling to be in his debt in any way. We walked back to the performing arts center together in strained silence. At the front stairs leading into the building, Carlo turned to me. "Hey, you're not going to be weird about this, are you?"

I looked at him, expressionless, and didn't reply.

Daniel and the rest of the cast, Yolanda included, joined us for the afternoon rehearsal block. We started from the top, a full run-through, with Daniel stopping us at frequent intervals to offer notes and corrections. Carlo was off his game, I was spitefully pleased to see. Me, I was ice. If an overnight hospital stay following a bout of poisoning hadn't affected my ability to perform, some clumsy assholery from Carlo wouldn't, either. I recalled every movement Marla had taught me in the morning session, every gesture, every facial expression. I parted my lips and looked at Carlo with soft eyes, I ran my fingers along his arm, and every once in a while, I caught a glimpse of panic in his face. He hadn't elicited a predictable response from me, and now he was viewing me as an unexploded grenade, pin pulled yet inexplicably dormant, and he was afraid I would detonate at any moment and take him down.

That gave me a small flare of satisfaction. For the health of the production, though, keeping Carlo off-balance wasn't a good strategy. Going forward, it would be best to smooth things over with him. I should pretend today's lunch hadn't happened; I should never mention his photo of Yolanda again.

It wouldn't be fair to Yolanda, who probably deserved to

know about this public violation of her private life, but what did I owe her?

Marla beamed at me. "Kit, I think that lunch did you a world of good. That was miles better. I can just about buy you two as a pair of passionate lovebirds."

"Thank you. Lunch was a great suggestion," I said. I didn't glance at Carlo.

After rehearsal ended, I stayed behind to consult with Marla about some feedback she'd given me on my breath control in Barbarella's big aria, and then I headed up to the third-floor practice rooms. The central staircase in the performing arts center had multiple twists and landings, and by the time I reached the second landing, I'd developed a prickly awareness that I was being followed.

I paused and listened. Everything was silent. I had no idea why the back of my neck was tingling, and then I had it. Beneath the usual smell of dust and mildew, I could detect a whiff of jasmine. It was Yolanda's perfume, something complicated and pervasive, which had lingered in my small, stuffy apartment after she had visited me.

If I'd stopped to think about it, I might have behaved differently. As it was, though, the sudden surge of adrenaline-fueled fear and anger hijacked my brain, and I swirled around. By the time Yolanda rounded the corner and reached the landing, I was on her. Both of my hands grabbed fistfuls of soft red fur, and I slammed her against the wall. "Stay away from me!" I yelled in her face. My nose bumped against hers; our foreheads touched.

Yolanda froze, her eyes very wide. Something dangled from one of her hands, and I glanced down, expecting to see a weapon. It was her heeled boots, which she'd removed. No wonder I hadn't heard her behind me.

After a startled moment, her shocked expression faded into anger. "What is *wrong* with you?" It came out as an outraged shout.

"Why are you following me?" I asked. She'd crept up behind me, shoes off, and god only knew what she'd intended to do. Maybe she'd planned to shove me down the staircase to my death.

"I'm not following you!" She wriggled around, trying to slide out of my grip, but I maintained my hold on her ridiculous coat while keeping her pressed to the wall. My fists were pushing into her shoulders with so much force it was probably hurting her, but I didn't care. "I was just going to use the practice rooms."

"You took your shoes off!"

"Danny says you don't want me around you, so I was trying to be quiet so you wouldn't know I was here." The outrage was fading, and now she was beginning to sound sulky. "Why are you being so weird?"

"Because you shoved me in front of a subway train, you absolute nutjob!" It felt good to confront her directly instead of hoping in vain that Daniel would take action.

Yolanda's response surprised me. Beneath my hands, she turned to wax, all color gone from her face. She looked cold and blank, like she'd understood my words but couldn't fathom why I'd said them to her.

"What?" she said at last. "What did you say?"

"Monday after rehearsal, somebody kicked the back of my leg at Penn Station, and I almost got hit by the arriving train. An eyewitness described you."

The blank expression didn't change. After a frozen moment, she shook her head once, like she was still trying to make sense of my words. "Monday," she said at last. "You left rehearsal early on Monday to meet with Astrid."

She sounded genuinely baffled, like she had no clue what I was talking about, and I felt my uncertainty grow. "So you're claiming you didn't . . ."

"No!" Her eyes opened wide in what looked like sudden panic. "No, of course not! I put the eye drops in your tea, and

I'm really sorry about that, but I'm not some cartoon villain who pushes people in front of trains!" Her horror seemed genuine, and with a growing sense of embarrassment, I thought I might believe her. If she hadn't attacked me on that subway platform, it meant I'd been acting pretty foolishly for the past few days.

I took a step back. I forced myself to unclench my fists and release my hold on her. My fingers ached from how tightly I'd gripped her coat. "You can't blame me for suspecting you," I said. It sounded weak.

"I know I'm messy," she said. "I get why you'd think it was me, thanks to how badly I behaved when we met. But . . ." The corners of her mouth pulled down. "I didn't push you. I know I said we could be enemies, but I was just trying to be funny."

"Why were you following me?" I asked.

"I wasn't! I swear I wasn't." Yolanda straightened out the hem of her coat and ran her hands over her hair to make sure it was in place. Color had returned to her face, and now she was starting to look flushed. Whether she was angry or embarrassed, I couldn't tell. "I just wanted to get in some extra practice. This opera is really important to me, and I want to make sure I'm as good as I can possibly be." Her eyes met mine, wide and sincere. "Your skill level is much higher than mine. I know that."

It was said earnestly, and that admission, coming from her, should've made me swell with pride. Instead I felt small and mean and spiteful. We were long past the point where I wanted Yolanda to respect me as a performer; now I just wanted to crush her.

"Shouldn't you be at home, taking your clothes off for strangers online?" The words tumbled out with no thought behind them, fueled only by a primal urge to inflict damage. I probably succeeded, because something in her face crumpled. Then her expression hardened, and she smiled, tight and humorless.

"Danny told you about that, huh?" she said.

I shook my head. "Carlo was one of your customers last night."

That surprised her almost as much as my spontaneous physical attack. Her jaw went slack, and her lips parted in astonishment. "Well, fuck," she said at last. "Hang on."

She plopped her boots on the floor beside her sock-clad feet and took out her phone. I saw her open an app—Somebody's Baby, had to be—and scroll through what looked like a long list of avatars and aliases within some kind of chat feature. "You said last night? Do you know what name he was using?"

Curious despite myself, I stared down at her screen. If that was all from one night, she'd kept up separate conversations with a lot of clients, maybe ten or twelve. As I pondered the kind of money she could be making from her seedy side hustle, I spotted a likely candidate on the scrolling list of aliases. "Don José. That's Carlo."

Yolanda kept scrolling. "Nope. That's not him."

"It has to be. It's an opera reference," I said. "Carlo played Don José in *Carmen* last spring."

She shook her head. "A bunch of my clients use opera names. I'm on intimate terms with a Figaro and a Falstaff." She glanced up and gave a half smile at my look of confusion. "In my bio on the site, I mention I'm an opera singer, so guys try to impress me by showing off their music knowledge. Like that'll make me think they're *so* sophisticated." It sounded bitter. "I've been chatting off and on with Don José since before rehearsals even began. Besides, he's a gentleman, and Carlo is an asswipe. Don José is the guy who gave me the Birkin that I gave you." She frowned at my utilitarian shoulder bag. "How come you aren't carrying it?"

I chose not to answer. "You meet these guys in real life?" I asked instead.

Yolanda rolled her eyes at me. "No, because I'm not an idiot," she said. "They know I'm an opera singer, and that's all. I have a post office box. I like receiving gifts, so I encourage my various gentleman friends to mail stuff to that address."

She stopped scrolling and tapped one impeccably manicured fingernail on the screen of her phone. I glanced down at the name she was indicating: TheDevilUKnow.

"There. That guy. That's Carlo," she said. She snorted. "Asshole."

She tilted her phone toward me. I looked at the screen and read fleeting bits of a chat dialogue. TheDevilUKnow's online interactions with Yolanda, who was using the Carmen Callas alias Carlo had mentioned, seemed to consist of a series of bold demands for performative sexual acts, his words laced with overt misogyny. For the first time since meeting her, I felt genuine sympathy for Yolanda. Whatever she was earning each night, it wasn't worth putting up with that.

"Yep. He's an asshole." I looked up at her. "He's also an idiot. He thought your C-section scar was a tummy tuck."

"Jesus." She snorted, dark and mirthless. "You're not going to ask?"

"I don't care enough to ask." It was impossible to picture Yolanda as a mother.

"That's fair." Yolanda shrugged, then tapped at the screen. "There. He's blocked." She glanced at me. "Thanks for the heads-up."

I felt a little guilty, because it hadn't been any kind of helpful impulse that had led me to tell her about Carlo. I'd wanted to wound her, and while I had good reason for that, shaming her for her sex work was low. "You really didn't push me in front of the train?" I asked. "Really?"

"Really, really. It was probably some crazy person. Is there anything I can say or do that will persuade you of that?" Yolanda returned her attention to her phone, backing out of her vile chat with Carlo and loading up another text conversation. "If I give you *La Traviata* tickets, is that enough to convince you I'm not your enemy?"

She sounded like she meant it. I stared at her. "Are you serious?"

"Sure. I have two tickets for tonight's performance that will otherwise go to waste. Is it supposed to be good?"

"It's supposed to be great. That's what Roksana left our production to do."

Yolanda gave me a wry half smile. "Lucky for both of us that she dropped out, huh?" She waggled her phone in the air. "One of my gentleman friends sent me a pair of tickets."

"Don José again?"

"Nah, this is someone else. Some nice old guy. He says I remind him of his daughter."

I wrinkled my nose. "That's gross."

Yolanda laughed. "He meant it in a nonincestuous way, I think. It was sweet of him, but I'm not going to go. You want them?"

I did. I did. I really, really did. "You mean it?"

"They're yours. I have plans for tonight." Some ice crept into Yolanda's voice. "I'll be taking my clothes off for strangers online."

I exhaled in a hiss, like I'd been punched in the gut. "Look, Yolanda . . ."

"The tickets are being held at the box office. I'm texting you the order number now." I was glad she interrupted me, because I really didn't know what I was going to say. The idea of apologizing to her was inconceivable, but now I felt I owed her something. "Grab a friend and enjoy."

My phone beeped. I looked down and saw the incoming text. I found it a little disconcerting that Yolanda had my phone number at the ready, but Daniel had given all cast members a contact list, so I guessed it was natural enough.

"I don't have a friend," I said, which sounded pathetic, but I didn't know anyone I could call at the last minute and invite to a fancy night at the opera. There was Gerard, of course, but he had another pupil scheduled for tonight, and anyway, he'd seen it already. "I'll only use one ticket. Give the other one to someone else."

Yolanda gave me an expression of what could be pity, but seemed more like sympathy, like maybe she understood what it was like to be essentially friendless in the city. "Have a good time," she said abruptly. She picked up her boots and continued up the stairs to the practice rooms, leaving me alone and conflicted.

11

Conversational Land Mines

The orchestra struck up the opening notes of the overture, the red curtain rose, and as soon as the performers moved onto the stage, all of the foolishness with Yolanda, all of Carlo's crude spitefulness, all of Daniel's and Marla's concerns about my performance, all of that evaporated. I settled back in my seat.

I'd performed as Violetta in *La Traviata* during my final year at Eastman, rotating the role nightly with another soprano, and this opera became one of my fiercest loves. Seeing it on the Met stage filled me with emotions. Hearing beautiful music performed live by world-class singers on a world-class stage is a transformational experience; I was tempted to close my eyes and lose myself in Verdi's score, but that would be a waste, because I also wanted to drink in the costumes, the sets, the performances.

The curtain fell after act 1, but *La Traviata* has two intermissions, so I stayed in my seat and scrutinized the performer biographies in the program, crunching the odds of someday seeing my name and photo among them. That brought me down to earth, and I felt the low dread of the past couple of weeks creep over me again. If I couldn't hack it in a small company like Brio, the Met would be forever out of my grasp.

The houselights flickered on and off, warning us that the

second act was about to begin. I straightened up and slipped the program into my purse—I was toting around the fake Birkin bag for the first time because it made my black slacks and plain button-down shirt look dressier—just as Yolanda slid into the unoccupied seat beside me.

"Hi," she said as she wriggled out of her fur coat and tossed it over the back of her seat. Beneath it, she wore what looked like a silver nightgown trimmed in sequins, and a truly incredible amount of cleavage was on display. She was attracting some sidelong frowns from the elderly couple seated on her other side, but she looked like a million bucks, and while I'd never worn a sparkly gown to the opera, I saw nothing inappropriate about her choice. She nodded at the stage. "What have I missed?"

"It's been fantastic. Everyone's fantastic," I said. "I thought you were going to stay home tonight."

"I was doing some of my cam stuff, but business was slow, and thinking about Carlo killed my mood." She shrugged. "That other ticket was going to go to waste, and I got to thinking about what you said about not having any friends . . ."

"Hang on," I said. "I didn't mean I don't have *any* friends."

"Yeah, you did, but it's okay, because I don't have any friends either." Yolanda's smile was bright but a little fragile, and I was shocked to realize she was telling me the truth. "No friends who'd be willing to go to an opera with me, at least. There's always Niko, but he loathes opera. How has whatshername been, the girl who was Barbarella before us?"

"Roksana. She hasn't appeared yet. Annina doesn't come onstage until act two."

The corners of Yolanda's lips curled up. "Huh. Must be a small role."

The houselights dropped one final time, and the second act began. I felt a momentary fear that Yolanda, the perpetual loose cannon, wouldn't behave herself, but she sat quietly in her seat, attention fixed on the stage, applauding politely when appropriate. When it was over, she rose from her seat when I did to join the ovation as the performers took their bows.

I applauded as vigorously as I could for Roksana, partly out of loyalty and partly because she'd been damn good as Annina, prim yet angelic in her formal maid costume, voluminous lace ruffles at her throat and wrists. Her eyes sparkled in the spotlight; her face was beatific, and her voice was flawless. During the second and third acts, I'd studied every detail of her performance, focusing on her movements, her body language, her facial expressions.

Was I honestly as good as Roksana? My singing was every bit as good as hers, and perhaps a bit better. But what about those nebulous areas prioritized by Daniel and Marla, those areas they felt I lacked? Sex appeal and charm were aspects of performance, not vocal ability. I'd always thought I was a decent performer, that acting was mostly a matter of understanding my character well enough to make all my onstage actions and reactions seem logical and genuine. No formal opera education is complete without acting lessons; I'd done well in those required courses.

But I was missing *something*, obviously, and whatever it was might cost me my first professional leading role.

I was ready to go home right after the performance, but Yolanda wanted to extend the evening. Since we didn't have rehearsal the next day, I let her talk me into wandering up Columbus to a brick-walled wine bar, where we settled into a leather banquette and ordered tasting flights of bold Italian reds. It wasn't until our table was covered with wine goblets that it dawned on me that less than two weeks ago, I'd made a big deal of refusing to drink champagne with Yolanda on the chance that she'd poison me.

It seemed very long ago. Much of my enmity toward Yolanda had faded, as though her gift of the tickets had forged a small alliance between us. She'd been convincing in her insistence that she'd had nothing to do with the subway kick; I sipped my wine without worrying she'd slipped something nasty into one of the goblets in front of me.

"Thanks so much for tonight," I said. "I had a great time."

"Sure. *La Traviata,* I'd never seen that one. I'd heard some of the music before, but I didn't really know the story." Yolanda smiled and shook her head at me. "Don't say it."

"Hmm?"

"What you're thinking. That I don't know much about opera. I know I have gaps in my education."

Yolanda had read my mind. I had indeed been feeling exasperated by her unfamiliarity with one of the world's greatest operas. I reminded myself to work on being less of a music snob. "Did you enjoy it?"

"Sure. Roksana was pretty good. It wasn't much of a part, just playing a maid, but she did a nice job. I would have done more with the role, but she was fine."

I stared at her. "Come on. She was flawless."

"I didn't say she wasn't. I'm just saying I'd be better." She winked at me, playful and self-aware, which neutralized some of the irritation I felt at her unbridled egotism. "I know I haven't had her training, but give me time to learn the role, and I could blow her away."

"Well, confidence is a good thing in our line of work." I raised one of my glasses and clinked it against hers.

Yolanda reclined against the seat. "So . . . Niko says your mom is a famous actress?"

The change in topic caught me off guard. My instinct was to pretend I had no idea what she was talking about, but that approach clearly hadn't worked with Niko, so I couldn't see much point in trying it with Yolanda. "If you stretch the definition of famous, sure," I said.

I tried to keep it light, making it sound flippant instead of sour. Often when I talked about my mother, a dark and ugly bitterness would creep into my tone.

"She's a B-movie star. Or was one, at least; I don't think she has any recent credits." I was in the habit of checking my mom's IMDb page about once a year to see if any new projects had popped up. I was sure that was more than she did to keep abreast of any new developments in her daughter's life. "She was a *Playboy* Playmate of the Month before I was born."

Yolanda's eyebrows went up. This impressed her, as I suspected it would. "Whoa, really?" she asked. "That's cool. I mean, *Playboy,* that used to be the big thing, right? What films has she been in?"

"Absolutely nothing that anyone other than Niko has seen," I said. I smiled. Keep it bouncy, keep it fun. "Straight-to-video stuff. Exploitation films, soft-core thrillers, that sort of thing. Honestly, I'm shocked that Niko has even heard of her."

"Well, that's Niko, right?" Yolanda said, rolling her eyes. Her tone was familiar, as though I should know all about Niko and his fondness for decades-old trash films. "Did you grow up in Hollywood?"

"More or less. I lived with my mom in a bunch of places around Los Angeles until she decided she'd had enough of me."

Yolanda's brows came together. "What does that mean?"

I considered backtracking or changing the subject, but something about the interest and compassion in Yolanda's expression made me feel safe continuing on this path, at least for a little while longer. "She thought I was ruining her career. From her perspective, I probably was." I shrugged. "I made her miss out on some opportunities. Having a kid got in the way of the kind of career she wanted. You can't drag your toddler along to the set of *Machete Girls,* right?"

"What about your dad? Was he in the picture?" Yolanda asked.

"No. Well, sort of, at first. Until I was five, my mom and I lived with this film producer in his mansion in Sherman Oaks, and I thought he was my father. Hell, *he* thought he was my father." I had only hazy memories of that house, and of that producer, but I remembered the pool in his backyard, a perfect square of azure that glittered in the bright California sun. "He and my mom fought all the time. At some point he demanded a paternity test, which he flunked, so he kicked us out," I said. "My mom has always insisted she had no idea who my father could be, if it wasn't him."

"Same story here. Well, not the part about living in a mansion, but I don't know who my father was, either," Yolanda said. "We should start a club. Opera stars of uncertain parentage." She held up her hand for a high five, and I wasn't sure the situation warranted one, but I gave it to her anyway.

"My mom tried raising me on her own, but it wasn't working out. So when I was ten, she sent me off to live with her sister in Michigan," I said.

"You were okay with that?"

"No. Not really." *Not at all.* My throat felt dry, so I took a drink of wine. "I don't have a relationship with my mom anymore. At first, she used to check in with me every few weeks, but she stopped after I . . . she stopped after a year or so. We haven't spoken since she signed over her parental rights."

Yolanda's expression was hyperfocused and intense, like she was paying rapt attention to what I was saying. It was flattering that she found me so riveting, but I was beginning to feel self-conscious. She nodded slowly, glossy lips parted. "I can see how that would hurt, feeling abandoned by your mom," she said. "But it was probably the best thing she could have done for you."

Her complacent assessment pissed me off. I almost snapped at her that abandoning me had been far, far from the best thing. I was too angry to speak, so I just made some noncommittal sound in the back of my throat and took another drink of wine.

"I don't know anything about your specific situation, obviously," Yolanda said. She opened her eyes wide, her expression conciliatory, like she realized she'd misstepped and was eager to make it right. "But everything has worked out for you, hasn't it? You're an opera singer in New York, how cool is that? It seems like your mom knew she wasn't the right person to give you what you needed, so she sent you to live with someone who could. If you look at it the right way, it was a generous impulse."

I still couldn't really speak, so I just nodded, struggling to keep my expression neutral. She was waiting for my reply, but that way lay madness, or at least explosions of anger and potentially dangerous confessions, so I just sipped my wine and let the silence drag on. Our server had given us a card describing each wine in our respective flights in effusive and borderline nonsensical detail—*a supple mouthful of tart cherry jam, with lingering notes of juniper, freshly cut asparagus, and green curry*—and I picked it up and squinted at it, trying to look like my attention was consumed by my deep and complicated thoughts about wine.

Yolanda leaned back against the banquette seat. The wall behind her was mirrored, and if I looked up I could see my plain and gloomy face, my nose blotchy and red from our walk in the night air, looming in the background of her own luminous visage. The contrast was painful, so I kept my attention fixed on the wine description.

"I have a daughter," she said at last. "You saw the C scar, right? That's all thanks to Violet; apparently she wanted to give me as much hassle as she could on her way out of my body. She's four, but I haven't seen her in two years. She's staying with this woman I used to work with. She's got her own daughter, and she's raising the girls like sisters."

I thought Yolanda might take out her phone to show me photos of Violet, because that's what every parent I'd ever met in my adult life had immediately done upon mentioning their kid, but she didn't. "I was dying in my old life," she said. "I had this horrible desk job at this horrible escrow company. It was located in some crappy corporate park outside the city. Just the bleakest place you can imagine. Everything was *beige.*"

I had a hard time picturing glamorous, vibrant Yolanda working in an office. "This was in New Orleans?"

"Sure. Let's say it was." Yolanda's mouth curved in a conspiratorial smile, like she was letting me in on a secret, tipping me off that I shouldn't trust anything she'd ever said about her past. "Anyway, I was singing on the side, mostly local bars, and it wasn't enough, not nearly enough. I was made for so much more. After I had Violet, everything got worse. I tried to be a good mom to her, but it's not in my genes. I wanted to head off on my own, but I also wanted to be a responsible parent, and I couldn't decide which path to take. Then all of a sudden, that decision was made for me."

"What happened?" I asked.

"My life started getting *super* complicated." She shook her head. "I like complications. Complications make life interesting. But at some point it got to be too much, and I had no choice but to split."

Knowing Yolanda, I could come up with some reasonable guesses about those complications. Deceptions and betrayals, wrecked relationships, maybe some dramatic feuds that escalated into violence. "I take it you burned a few bridges behind you?"

"Oh, yeah." She chuckled. "I doused those bridges in kerosene and took a flamethrower to them. Pretty much guaranteed that I could never go back, not that I would ever want to."

"Yeah? Who'd you poison?"

"Ha, ha," she said flatly. "Nothing quite at that level. I slept with my boss, which pissed off his wife. At her request, he broke things off with me in what I considered an undignified manner, which was a stupid thing to do to someone who knows where all the bodies are buried." She grinned. "He hadn't been keeping his nose clean. That particular escrow company is no longer in business, I'm just saying."

This sordid little tale was really no more or less than I'd expected from her. "You are an agent of chaos, Yolanda."

"That might be the nicest thing you've ever said to me." She swirled her wine around and scrutinized the legs that formed on the glass. She sniffed at it delicately before tasting it, the tip of her pink tongue dipping into the glass, her brow furrowed in deep thought, before taking a bigger drink and swishing it around in her mouth before swallowing. She held the glass up to the light and frowned at it. She looked like she knew exactly what she was doing, like she'd trained for years as a sommelier, but I had a hunch it was an act, that Yolanda was no more of a wine expert than I was. She was a good observer, though, and a good mimic, and she could bluff her way through new situations. This was how she was approaching the opera, I realized: She was faking her way through the role, covering the gaps in her training with an outer veneer of extreme confidence, helped along by her attention-grabbing beauty.

"I tell myself I had no choice but to leave Violet behind, and it's kind of the truth, but also kind of a lie. I could have taken Violet to New York with me. She could be living with me right now. But . . ." She looked up toward the ceiling, eyes unfocused. "I love Violet. I'm crazy about her; I want her to have everything wonderful in life. And that's why I know I'd be terrible for her. I'm too selfish to be a good mom. I pose nude for cash. I have too many boyfriends, usually all at the same time. I get into dumb feuds." She grinned at me. "I try to poison my rivals."

I almost smiled back. "Can confirm. You do."

"I do. I really do." Yolanda nodded. "Is that the kind of thing a good mom would do? No, it most certainly is not. Violet shouldn't be around me. I know my former coworker is struggling to get by, so I send her cash every month. A grand at least, more if I can get it. That's why I do the camgirl work, so I can provide for my kid. And I know people say a child needs her mother, but that's a bunch of crap. Violet is better off without me in her life. So maybe you were better off without your mom in yours."

"I don't know your situation, obviously. What my mom

did, though, it wasn't some self-sacrificing decision. She didn't make it with my well-being in mind," I said. I thought carefully about my next words, because I was heading into an area I should avoid. "And it turned out to be a mistake."

"Why? What happened?" Yolanda's beautiful eyes were filled with compassion.

I shook my head. "Just . . . a lot of things. It didn't work out well with my aunt."

"Your aunt must have done something right, though, getting you into all those schools with great music programs. Michigan for undergrad, Eastman for your MFA, right? I would have killed for those opportunities. It's why your voice is so good."

Considering how scornful Yolanda had been about my credentials during our first acrimonious conversation, her change in attitude came as a surprise. She seemed genuinely impressed, almost deferential, and I realized her early bout of trash-talking had been an act designed to make me feel insecure.

Or maybe this was the act right here. Maybe she was buttering me up because she'd made a calculated decision to position herself as my friend and ally.

Or maybe she genuinely wanted to be my friend.

"You could be right," I said. I kept my tone neutral. I picked up one of my glasses and busied myself with tasting. I frowned at Yolanda. "The card says this one tastes like pistachios, yeast, and leather, and I can't detect any of that. How's your palate?"

Yolanda stared at me for a moment, then smiled. "Okay," she said. "Message received. I'll drop the subject. But I think it's possible you don't fully appreciate all the advantages you've had in life."

There was a bite behind her words, and it made me feel defensive. I didn't think I could answer without snapping, so it was a relief when Yolanda picked up one of her glasses and went through her full swirling-sniffing-tasting-pondering routine again. "I can taste pistachios, definitely," she said. "I don't know about yeast."

"Maybe in the finish, at least a little bit," I said.

"Hmm. Maybe. I get a hint of malt; that might be what they meant." We devoted ourselves to our wines, chatting about the tasting notes, determinedly avoiding any further conversational land mines.

12

Angry Bumblebee

Apart from opening night, my favorite part of the process of putting on an opera is Sitzprobe, the first rehearsal in which the performers are joined onstage by the orchestra. Sitzprobe is German for "seated rehearsal," and thus we all sit, generally in uncomfortable folding chairs placed in rows on the stage, and we experience the electrifying sensation of singing together with a full orchestral accompaniment for the first time.

For those first two weeks in the rehearsal room, Daniel, as the artistic director, had been mostly in charge. Now that we'd switched to the stage and the orchestra was involved, Marla took the lead. She'd marked the occasion by swapping out her usual oversized velour tunic and stretch pants for a black ruffled blouse and tailored jacket, and she stood at the lectern, baton raised, conducting both the orchestra and the singers, her expression focused and serious. Last week she'd been the friendly lady at the piano helping us stay on pitch and remember to breathe; today she was the Maestro.

And today, at least, there was no splitting of the lead role. I was onstage as Barbarella, and Yolanda was seated in the front row, observing the proceedings while staying silent and out of the way. Instead of marking, I sang at full voice, because it was important to hear the way my vocals resonated throughout the theater. The main stage had a few hundred seats, which is small by the standards of opera houses, yet vast compared to the rehearsal room. Opera singers perform without any kind of artificial amplification; our voices must expand to fill every corner and reach every seat. It's what we train to do, and it's a joy. Singing at full volume in a big space with excellent acoustic design is one of the most intoxicating experiences in the world. It's far better than sex, at least any sex I've ever had.

While there's no formal blocking during Sitzprobe, it's both easier and better to sing while standing and interacting with other performers, and so that's what we did, rising up from our chairs as necessary and wandering about the stage. I did my best to recall every expression and movement Marla had taught me the previous week, pantomiming Barbarella's love, her lust, her wide-eyed delight in her surroundings. While caressing the shoulders of Gina, the raven-haired mezzo playing the Great Tyrant, I happened to glance at Yolanda in the front row. Her mouth was twisted in a grim smile, and there was something in her expression that gave me pause. She looked darkly bemused, like something I was doing was pissing her off, but in a way she found entertaining.

Ah. It should have dawned on me much earlier. The movements Marla had coached me on, all those little gestures, those calculated flutters of my eyelashes, those were Yolanda's. Yolanda had originated these movements in rehearsal, and Marla had stolen them from her and handed them to me, likely in the hopes of handing me some of Yolanda's sex appeal as well.

I worried this would anger Yolanda, perhaps justifiably, but when we broke for lunch, she came up to me right away, excited and impressed. "That was cool," she said as I gathered up my coat and purse from where I'd left them in the front row. I was carrying the Birkin bag again; I'd discovered at the Met that I liked the way it looked on my arm. "It sounds better with the orchestra, doesn't it? More dramatic."

"Singing with an orchestra is a whole different thing," I said, then wondered if she'd think I was flaunting an experience she'd been denied.

Yolanda seemed to take no offense. "You're doing really well," she said. It sounded abrupt, like she felt awkward about saying it. "I know I'm not supposed to comment on your performance, so I don't want to sound like I'm giving you advice, but I just wanted you to know . . . you were good today. You seemed more relaxed."

I glanced at her in surprise. "Thanks," I said. I suspected Yolanda meant it, and I suspected it had been hard for her to admit.

We walked down the long center aisle toward the theater doors. I wondered if she was going to ask me to go to lunch with her; I wondered if I wanted her to, or if I wanted to continue keeping her at arm's length.

"I've got this thing tonight," she said. "At Chanteur Malheureux in the East Village. It's a cabaret club. I've never performed there before, and it's just a two-song set, and they gave me a bad slot: I go on at eight when everyone will be at dinner. If you don't have plans, do you want to go? It's free; I just want someone there who'll clap for me."

The request surprised me, even touched me. I had a lesson scheduled with Gerard, but he'd been increasingly irritated by the number of extra sessions I kept requesting, and he'd be thrilled if I canceled. I didn't know if cabaret was my kind of thing, but . . . "Okay, sure," I said. "I'll try to make it."

Yolanda squeezed my arm. "Great. Thanks. It should be fun." She released me and headed off in the direction of the ladies' room, leaving me to wonder whether it was possible that Yolanda and I were becoming friends.

—

Chanteur Malheureux was located in the lowest level of a glamorously crumbling brick building on Avenue A, wedged between two other glamorously crumbling buildings. To enter, I descended a few stairs from the sidewalk level, passed beneath a brick archway into an unlit alcove, and had my ID checked by a leggy woman dressed like an old-timey cigarette girl in fishnets and a short ruffled skirt. After meeting her approval, I was allowed to enter the club, which turned out to have claustrophobically low ceilings. The walls were covered in peeling paint the color of black raspberries; low-hanging chandeliers with dusty bulbs lit the room with a dull glow. Yolanda's fears of a lack of an audience were unfounded: Dinner hour or not, the room was crowded with stylish young couples clutching martini glasses at small tables.

New situations leave me feeling awkward, so I hovered close to the door to get my bearings. On the stage at the far end of the room, a lean giant of a man dressed in a suit with thick candy-cane stripes pounded the keys on an upright piano while a brunette in a blue velvet catsuit gazed out at the audience through a sheaf of heavy bangs and crooned a slow-burning, torchy version of Depeche Mode's "Personal Jesus."

Opera singers can be insufferable when it comes to other forms of singing. I'm not proud of belonging to that category, but nonetheless, I thought she was the worst singer I'd ever heard. Instead of bothering with her high notes, she lapsed into breathy baby talk and whispered her way through them. Her pitch wandered; she inserted dramatic pauses at intervals that made no damn sense. She was captivating, though, with glitter-covered eyelashes and a wide fuchsia mouth, and she was a pro at interacting with the audience. She moved around the stage; she smiled and winked at the crowd, her face mobile and expressive. She seemed to be enjoying herself, and by the time she'd finished, I'd warmed up to her. I didn't want to hear her sing anything else, ever, but I had to admit she seemed lively and fun, like she'd be a blast to hang out with at parties.

She reached the end and took a bow. As the crowd applauded, I found my way to a tiny round table and grabbed a seat. A gauntly handsome waiter with long hair tied in a sloppy bun appeared at my elbow and thrust a menu at me. "If you sit down, you have to get a drink."

He seemed determined to take my order at once, so I scanned the options as fast as I could. The list was long and in French, and the prices were stupidly high. I wasn't a cocktail connoisseur, but I spotted "miel" and "citron" in the ingredient list of some concoction and figured anything with the vocal cord–friendly combination of honey and lemon would work. "Le Bourdon en Colère, please."

Like many opera singers, I like to think of myself as a polyglot, as I've taken extensive university courses in French, German, Italian, and Russian. In truth, my vocabulary in all languages other than English is pretty rudimentary: good enough to carry on a basic conversation, but a long way from fluent. My accent in all of those languages, however, is superb. In opera, pronunciation takes precedence over comprehension.

The waiter didn't move. "There's a two-drink minimum."

I looked at him in surprise. "Do I have to order them both at once?" I asked.

He made a noise that sounded like a huff. "No. But just so you know," he said. He remained where he was, staring down at me. As soon as the silence had grown awkward, he said, "I need a card to open your tab."

I fished through my purse and handed him my Visa. I could've been wrong, but I thought his look of bored exasperation lightened a bit when he spotted the Birkin bag, like he suddenly thought I might have been less worthless than he'd first assumed. He accepted my card and slithered off to another table.

My drink had just arrived by the time Yolanda, clad in a black sequined coatdress with wide satin lapels, took the stage.

Her hair was teased into an angelic mane, and her dangling earrings glittered in the low light. The man in stripes took his seat at the piano again; Yolanda consulted with him quickly, all charm and smiles, and then moved into the spotlight as he began to play the intro to "Bewitched, Bothered, and Bewildered."

I sat up in interest, curious as to how this would play out. Some opera stars can sing the blues to rival Ella Fitzgerald and belt out show tunes like they were raised backstage in a Broadway theater. I am not a member of that cohort. Everything about my voice that makes it ideal for opera makes it grotesquely unsuited to any other type of music. I turn down offers to hang out with acquaintances on karaoke night; I mouth my way through group sing-alongs of "Happy Birthday." I'm a coloratura soprano, which means I warble. My voice, capable of executing a wide array of sophisticated operatic maneuvers, makes me sound ridiculous when I sing any other form of music. It's bad; people laugh at me. So I wondered how Yolanda would fare.

She didn't get off to a promising start. She missed her entrance and skipped her first line. The accompanist paused, long fingers poised in midair over the keys as he realized she hadn't come in on cue. She stood in the spotlight, eyes wide, expression stricken, skin unnaturally pale, and I realized, with a fierce spike of sympathetic anguish, the kind you feel while watching a gymnast tumble off the beam during the Olympics, that Yolanda had stage fright.

Well. That was a deal-breaker. If Daniel had been here tonight, it would kill Yolanda's chances of ever performing as Barbarella. I wanted to feel smug at this evidence that Yolanda was fundamentally unsuited to replace me, but I felt gutted by proxy. I'd never frozen up onstage, and it seemed unlikely to ever happen, but if it did, I knew it would crush something precious and irreplaceable inside me.

With the next line, she recovered. She came in sure and certain, her expression softening into a relaxed smile. She started in a low croon, soulful and husky, and then her voice rose, volume climbing along with her pitch, until the room was filled with lush, vibrant sound.

I could have imagined it, but I thought a hush came over the room. Chitchat subsided as patrons began to realize they were in the presence of something remarkable. All the flaws I could hear in Yolanda's voice in rehearsal, the slurred words and the lazy slides up to notes, were now assets. She was sensational.

When she was done with Rodgers and Hart, before the crowd had a chance to applaud, she segued into a new song, something I hadn't heard before. It was gothic and melancholy, filled with a sense of burned-out hopelessness and despair. I made a mental note of the lyrics so I could look it up later, something about burying her heart in an iron casket to keep it safe, only to later find it contained nothing but ashes. When she finished, the audience clapped, and maybe it was the effect of my cocktail, my Angry Bumblebee, but I felt offended on her behalf that the applause wasn't louder.

She stepped down off the stage and scanned the crowd. I felt a thrill when I saw her expression light up as she spotted me. She made her way to my table, a wide smile on her face, and plopped down in the chair across from me. "How was that?" she asked.

"Yolanda, that was amazing," I said. "Forget opera. You should sing this kind of music all the time."

"You're just saying that because you won't have me as competition anymore." She smiled, but there was a trace of acid behind the words.

"I wouldn't have you as competition because I can't sing torch songs. I can't belt like you can," I said. "But you could be on Broadway. You could get a recording contract."

The gaunt waiter chose that moment to appear at Yolanda's

shoulder. "I can waive the two-drink minimum because you performed, but if you sit down, you have to order," he said. His tone was nakedly antagonistic, as though Yolanda and I had just picked a fight with him on the subject of two-drink minimums. He thrust a menu at her and turned to me. "You still need your second drink."

"I'll take another of the same," I said.

Yolanda scanned the menu, and I could tell by her expression that she was lost at sea. "If you need anything translated, my French is pretty good," I said.

She glanced at me. "Of course it is," she said. She passed the menu across the table. "Help me out. I'm in the mood for something dangerous."

I looked at the options. I wasn't sure what would fit Yolanda's definition of dangerous. "Ananas à l'absinthe? Do you like absinthe?"

"That sounds perfect." She smiled at the waiter, dazzling and seductive. "Ananas à l'absinthe, s'il vous plaît." Her accent was pretty good.

"I need a card to start a tab," he said.

Yolanda looked beside her chair, then twisted her head to look at the back of her chair. She laughed. "Right. I left my purse in the green room. My coat's there, too. Hang on, I've got to grab it."

"You can put her drink on my tab," I told the waiter. It was a brave offer, since each cocktail here cost more than I'd spend on a typical dinner, but Yolanda had earned it.

The waiter turned to Yolanda, who had risen out of her chair. "You were good up there," he said. He spoke in the back of his throat, like the words of praise were being forced out of him even as he tried to push them back. "Most of the performers here are nothing special, but you sounded great. You looked good, too. You're really pretty."

Yolanda laughed again, delighted, and patted him on the

arm as she moved past him into the crowd. Two strange thoughts occurred to me as I watched her head down a dark hallway, which was marked with a sign directing guests to the TOILETTES: One, I was starting to like Yolanda, and two, I was starting to envy her talent.

13

Ananas

Alone at my table, I watched as the man in the candy-cane suit played some ragtime, no sheet music in sight, long fingers flying deftly over the keys.

Yolanda had been gone a long while, but she'd mentioned a green room, so maybe she was changing clothes or fixing her makeup. Our dour waiter had vanished, too; I glanced back at the bar and saw our cocktails waiting on the top, forlorn and forgotten, my Angry Bumblebee resting beside Yolanda's absinthe concoction, which was a beautiful frosty chartreuse and came in a hurricane glass. I spotted our waiter at long last, sauntering down the hallway leading from the restrooms; when he finally deposited the glasses at our table, he smelled of night air and cigarette smoke. He brought my credit card, too, and stood too close to my chair as I signed for our tab, which I took as a pointed indication he wanted us to down our drinks fast and free up the table so a fresh batch of customers could fulfill their requisite two-drink minimum.

When Yolanda returned at last, her color was high, and her hair was mussed. "Sorry for the delay," she said as she draped her red fur across the back of her chair before sitting down. "My purse wasn't where I'd left it, and I was starting to freak out, and then I realized it had fallen behind a sofa."

"Is everything in it?" I asked.

She plopped the puffy Chanel bag on her lap and rifled through the contents. "Phone, billfold, makeup case. I think I'm good." She leaned back in her chair and looked at her cocktail for the first time. It was garnished with two chunks of fresh pineapple speared on a gold skewer, and I could see from her grimace that something was terribly wrong.

"Ananas à l'absinthe," she said. "I assumed 'ananas' meant bananas."

"Pineapple."

"I'm allergic." She shoved the glass a few inches away from her with two fingers of one hand. "I can't even have skin contact. I'll break into hives." She looked around for our waiter, who had vanished yet again.

"I haven't touched mine," I said. "We can trade if you want."

"Could we? Thanks." We swapped drinks. I wasn't sure I'd had absinthe before, but it seemed appropriate for a French-themed cabaret club, so I sipped. The cocktail was pleasant: herbaceous and fruity.

"So," Yolanda said. She rested one elbow on the table and leaned forward, propping her chin on her hand and looking up at me through her beautiful eyes, which were rimmed in glistening smears of burgundy. "You were in the middle of telling me how great I was tonight."

I laughed. "You were great. You absolutely were." I took another sip of my cocktail. "What happened at the beginning? Was that nerves?"

Yolanda shook her head with enough vigor to send her mane of hair swirling. "No! I was looking for you in the audience, and I thought I saw someone I didn't want to see, but then I realized my mind was playing games. After that, I was fine."

I liked the idea that she'd been looking for me, but I wasn't convinced. More likely she realized how dangerous it could be to let anyone involved with *Barbarella* know she suffered from stage fright. "You recovered well," I said. "That kind of music is really your forte. You could make a career in cabaret."

Yolanda smiled. "Thanks. But I can't help thinking you're flattering me because you believe I don't belong in opera."

It was playful, but there was something vulnerable behind it. I took a moment before replying, busying myself with my drink while I considered the best approach.

"The day we met, I said some nasty things about your lack of training," I said at last. "I apologize. The stuff I criticized you for, your high notes and your enunciation, I know you and Marla have worked hard on that."

"But?" Yolanda ran one finger around the top of her coupe glass, which was rimmed in a mix of sparkly gold sugar and red cayenne pepper, then raised it to her mouth and licked it. "There's a 'but' in this, I know it."

"But without the right training, you're going to reach a point where you can't go any farther in opera. It's just the way it works. But that doesn't apply to other kinds of music; nothing would stop you from pursuing a career in cabaret, or musical theater, or even pop, if that's what you wanted. I bet you'd be successful."

"But I want opera," Yolanda said, implacable and calm. Remembering how she'd flown off the handle during our first encounter, I'd been wary of her reaction to my advice, but she seemed untroubled by anything I'd said. "That's the difference between you and me, Kit, you're hung up on training and perfection. That might be the way opera used to be, but it's outdated, and honestly it's pretty elitist. If opera is going to survive, it needs to become more accessible."

"Okay." There was a germ of an idea in her speech that I agreed with: Due to the financial burden of training, many promising singers are blocked from pursuing a career in opera, and the opera world would clearly benefit from lowering the economic barriers. Sending undertrained singers onto the professional stage, however, seemed like a disastrous solution. I

didn't feel like ruining Yolanda's triumphant evening by arguing with her, so I let it drop. "I guess my point is that you
sounded amazing tonight. Like, you were almost supernatural,
like an angel. You met our waiter, our waiter is a total dickhead,
and even he fell in love with you. I bet everyone in this room
felt the same way."

Where had that come from? Expressions of gooey emotion
weren't at all typical for me. Yolanda was silent, staring at me,
the side of her mouth turned up, like she was both entertained
and a little concerned by my outburst. She lifted up her coupe
glass and waggled it by the stem. "How many of these have you
had tonight?"

"I'm not drunk," I said. It came out indignant and angry,
which did indeed make me sound drunk, which didn't make
any sense, because, for crying out loud, I'd just had one measly
cocktail and was maybe two-thirds of my way through my second. I took a long drink of the delectable absinthe concoction,
almost a gulp. "I just feel like I've spent a lot of time over the
past couple of weeks resenting and underestimating you, and
now I realize you're *super* talented. And you're nice, too, and
so beautiful, and I don't know why you say you don't have any
friends, because it seems like you should have all the friends in
the world."

The anger ebbed, and I felt warm, expansive. Yolanda kept
staring at me, still with that strange half smile, and that made
me feel indignant again. I was being heartfelt and sincere,
and instead of becoming sincere in response, Yolanda seemed
thoughtful. Calculating. Maybe a little wary.

"Something I've been wondering," she said, and her tone was
artfully casual. "What we were talking about last Friday, after
the opera. You started to tell me about your mom, or about
your aunt, and then we didn't finish the conversation."

"I don't want to talk about my mom," I said. There was nothing left in my hurricane glass, which was a shame, and I wondered whether I should flag down our terrible waiter and ask

him to reopen my tab. "My mom was a bad person. I know Niko thinks she's cool, but she was awful to me."

"Was she abusive?" The half smile had left Yolanda's face, and now her expression looked compassionate and sincere, and that was much better. It made me want to open up to her. So I did.

"Not like she'd hit me or anything. But she was just lousy at being a mom, you know? Lousy at being a human being." I tried to take another swig of my cocktail and was devastated anew by my empty glass. "When I was six, she decided I was fat, so she put me on a strict diet. My pediatrician kept telling her I was a normal-sized kid, but she didn't want a daughter who was normal, she wanted a daughter who was *pretty*. So she'd do stuff like give me celery sticks and Diet Coke for breakfast, and she'd refuse to send me to school with money for lunch. That kind of thing."

I could hear my resentment building at the memory, my voice growing louder and faster. "She got it into her head that it'd be cool if I became a child star, so she'd force me to go on auditions. She'd slather me in tons of makeup like one of those creepy child beauty queens. She'd curl my hair into ringlets— she made me wear my hair long, all the way down my back— and send me to open-call auditions for commercials for pizza rolls in, like, a tube top and leggings. I was eight or nine at the time. It was gross. I hated it, and I hated her. So I started acting out. I became unmanageable."

Why was I telling Yolanda all this? I felt compelled to speak, and it seemed weird but somehow right, and I knew I needed to tell Yolanda all the things I kept buried inside me. Yolanda was my friend, and telling my friend my secrets would free me from them.

"I'd tell her that I wished she were dead. I called the cops and told them where they could find her cocaine stash in the medicine cabinet. I ran away all the time. Finally, when I was ten, she gave up on me. Signed a voluntary relinquishment of parental rights." I had trouble with "relinquishment," stumbled over it and had to back up and try again, and from the flicker of confusion that crossed Yolanda's face, I think I ultimately botched the word beyond all comprehension. "She sent me to live with her sister in Dearborn. She'd mail a check each month to pay for my room and board."

Remembering how Yolanda said she sent money to a coworker to care for her own daughter, I scrutinized her expression, hoping she didn't think I was comparing her to my horrible mother. Her face was calm, filled with benign interest, so I felt it was safe to continue. "She knew her sister didn't want me living with her, and she didn't care. She was done with me. She was a bad mother, and I was a bad kid, but she was my mom, and she abandoned me."

My eyelashes felt wet against my skin when I blinked, and crazy as it seemed, I thought I might be crying.

Yolanda didn't say anything, so I kept talking, unable to shut up even as the tears rolled down my face, even as my nose started to drip.

"Even though my mom was awful, I still wanted to stay with her. My aunt made it clear she considered me an intrusion. Her house was small, so I slept on the couch while she shared the bedroom with her boyfriend. Glen." I used my cocktail napkin to swipe at my runny nose. "Glen was retired from the air force, and he was a bossy jerk, just this absolute dick, and he shouted at me all the time. I could never do anything right. I was messy, I didn't help with the housework, I didn't clean my plate, I talked back. So this one time I ran away, and the cops picked me up at the mall and brought me home. Glen yelled at me for causing trouble, so I told him I hated him, and he belted me in the face hard enough to break my jaw."

Yolanda blinked but didn't otherwise respond. I continued. "It was the first time in my life that anyone had hit me. I was so scared and so angry, I've never been that angry in my life, and when he went to hit me again, I grabbed a steak knife from the dish drainer and stabbed him in the shoulder as hard as I could."

"Whoa, really?" Yolanda looked riveted. "Wow. What happened after that?"

"My aunt took us both to the hospital. She and Glen tried to come up with some story to explain what had happened, but when you've got a twelve-year-old with a broken jaw, the hospital is probably going to draw the right conclusion," I said. I tried to sound breezy, but failed. "Doctors called CPS. I was removed from the home."

"Did you get arrested? For stabbing him?"

"No! Of course not." I was outraged by the question, offended that Yolanda could even think such a thing. "I was a kid. I was clearly the victim. No one *arrested* me." I sounded hostile, but Yolanda just twitched her eyebrows in response. "The state couldn't figure out what to do with me, and my mom refused to take me back, so I was placed in a group home while I finished out the school year. And then I got sent to Macaulay."

I tripped over the name, slurred it a little. I'd had two cocktails, two measly cocktails, and yet I was drunk and miserable and pouring my soul out. What the hell was wrong with me?

"Was that a reform school or something?"

I felt another burst of outrage, but that must be the drunkenness, because it was a decent guess; it just happened to be wrong. "No, not a reform school. Macaulay is a boarding school. Ann Arbor. Very fancy. Uniforms. Rigorous academics. Five percent of their students are charity cases. That was me." I was trying to speak slowly, because I kept stumbling over my words, and I saw Yolanda try not to smirk. "I didn't fit in. I was an angry kid. I hated all my classmates and they all hated me, but I got into music there, choir and then opera, and from there on out, everything was fine."

I tried to end my words with a smile, because I was aware I was being a downer, but it sure didn't feel like everything was fine. The striped-suited man had stopped playing ragtime, and the stage was being set up for another performer, and Yolanda and I should leave, but I felt a swirl of sudden panic, because I realized I was too messed up to make it home on my own.

Yolanda said something, but I couldn't hear her, because a sudden horrible thought had struck me. Two cocktails. I'd only had two cocktails. I wasn't drunk from that; I couldn't be. But I felt sloppy, sick, and emotional.

I'd been drugged. Poisoned, maybe.

A bottle of eye drops in a cup of tea. God knows what could be placed in a hurricane glass filled with ananas à l'absinthe. I'd switched drinks with Yolanda, but maybe not before she'd slipped something into her glass. Maybe she'd poisoned me. *Again.*

She couldn't have done it at the table, not without me seeing her, but she'd been gone for a long time while our drinks had sat unattended on the bar. The bartender had been busy all evening, and Yolanda could have put something in one of the glasses without anyone paying much attention. She'd picked the wrong glass, but maybe the ananas à l'absinthe had been easier to reach. Maybe she knew I'd offer to switch if she claimed an allergy.

I needed to ask if she'd poisoned me, but I'd have to ask politely, because Yolanda was now my friend. I lost track of that train of thought, though, because we suddenly were in motion. Yolanda hustled me to my feet, draping my coat over my shoulders and handing me the fake Birkin bag, and then we moved through the crowd, heading for the exit. I was getting some annoyed stares, maybe because I kept bumping into people. Yolanda put her arm around me to keep me upright, and it should have been comforting, and yet it wasn't.

Chilly wind whipped at my face. The night air restored a bit of clarity to my thoughts. "Yolanda, did you poison me again? I think my drink had something in it."

"You're just drunk, Kit," Yolanda said. "God knows how

many drinks you had before I joined you, but you are thoroughly plastered."

"One. I only had one," I said, or thought I said, but Yolanda didn't reply, so it was possible I hadn't spoken at all. "No. Nope. Naw. I don't get drunk."

We were heading in the direction of the water, which was bad news, because I needed to get home and there were no trains anywhere between us and the East River. "Where are we going?"

"My place is the next block over. I'm not going to walk you all the way to the subway," Yolanda said. "And I didn't put anything in your drink. Stop blaming me for everything that goes wrong in your life." The anger in her tone startled me.

She hustled me along the sidewalk, her gloved hand gripping my arm. My coat was still just draped over my shoulders, and I worried that it would slip off and that Yolanda wouldn't let me stop to pick it up, that she'd keep dragging me along and that I'd freeze to death before we reached her place. I worried she wouldn't care if I did.

We headed down a narrow side street, past a stretch of townhomes that looked like they'd seen better days but would nonetheless cost millions and millions, then came to a stop in front of a three-story brownstone, a relic of a bygone era. It had huge bay windows and an intricate carved arch over the doorway, and it was so much more attractive and interesting than my own prison block of an apartment building that my chest felt tight with envy. Yolanda released me and headed up the stoop.

At the front door, she dug through her bag, her brow wrinkled. "Goddammit," she said. She dropped her purse and crouched beside it so she could sort through the contents with both hands, her expression murderous. Eventually, she took out her phone and dialed a number. "Leo!" she said, her voice too loud on the quiet street. "Leo, I lost my keys. Are you here? Come down and let me in!" She continued to rummage around in her purse, muttering under her breath and paying no attention to me. She stood up when the front door opened.

I smelled Leo's aftershave before I saw him. He was young, tall, and exquisitely made. His damp blond hair was slicked off his face; Yolanda had apparently caught him in the middle of shaving, as there was a streak of white cream along his elegant jawline. His immaculate white shirt, worn untucked over his dark pants, was buttoned with a single button along the covered placket. He looked expensive. He smelled expensive.

"If you had used the call box, I could have simply buzzed you in," he said. "Please stop losing my keys."

"I'll find them tomorrow. Someone messed around with my purse backstage at the club I performed at tonight; they probably fell out then." Yolanda moved past Leo into the entryway, reaching up to wipe his chin with her gloved thumb. "Missed a spot."

"You're lucky I was home. I'm running late for a dinner appointment. I should have left already." He looked at me and frowned. "Is your friend all right?"

"She's just drunk." There was scorn in Yolanda's voice, and I wanted to insist again that I wasn't, but I didn't want to embarrass myself by slurring my words. I slunk past Leo into the entryway, too ashamed to introduce myself.

Leo headed upstairs, and Yolanda and I followed. The stairs were carpeted in thick black wool printed with gold fleurs-de-lis; the handrail was ornamental brass and looked like it could have been part of the building a century ago. Yolanda's apartment was on the third floor; I felt dizzy and out of breath by the time we got there. Leo produced a thick gold key ring bearing a series of keys labeled with numbered leather tags. When he started to unlock Yolanda's door, she stopped him with a hand on his wrist.

"Just give me the key, Leo," she said.

He worked it off the key ring, shaking his head. His nails were clean and perfectly rounded. "This is my only copy. If you lose it, I'll have to have the lock changed, and that will make me extremely irritated with you. More than I am already."

"Aw, did I make you angry?" she asked. She leaned her head to the side and batted her lashes at him.

"Yes, and you know why. Your mouth will land you in serious trouble someday."

"You love all the things my mouth does for you." Yolanda seemed unconcerned by Leo's irritation. "Is Niko still mad at you for blabbing to me about the box seats?"

Niko. I wasn't able to follow their conversation much, but the reference to Niko got my attention. If Leo was linked to Niko, he was linked to Daniel, and that meant I should probably behave in a professional manner instead of looking like I was a heartbeat away from puking on his shoes. If word got back to Daniel about how messy and erratic I'd been . . . I tried my best to stand up straight, but I could feel myself start to swoon, so I leaned against the wall near the doorframe. The wall was covered in deep red fabric that felt soft against the side of my face.

"Let's not talk about that," Leo said. He tilted his head in my direction.

"She's not going to remember anything we say." Yolanda unlocked the door, grabbed my arm, and pulled me into her darkened apartment. "You're a king, Leo. King Leopold."

"Save it. You know how I feel about you, but sometimes I think you're more trouble than you're worth. I could lease your unit to someone who actually pays rent, you know," Leo said. He hovered in the doorway and glanced at me, a flicker of concern crossing his pretty features. "You should check on your friend. She doesn't look good."

"That's just her face," Yolanda said, then burst out laughing. "Nighty night, Leo."

Leo shook his head. There was only one other door on this floor, directly across the staircase from Yolanda's, and apparently that was where Leo lived, because he headed straight for it, pausing once to look back at us with a small frown on his face.

Yolanda switched on a light inside her apartment and shut the door behind us. The Birkin bag seemed heavy, too heavy, so I dropped it next to the door. My coat kept slipping from my shoulders; I rolled it into a ball and crouched down to place it beside the bag. When I started to straighten up, Yolanda shoved me from behind, unexpected and rough. I pitched forward and collapsed onto a thick, plush rug in shades of pink and lavender.

"You're a mess," Yolanda said. "Don't puke on my rug." Her voice was thick with contempt.

My eyes couldn't focus on anything specific about Yolanda's apartment. I had an overwhelming impression of shades of soft rose and violet and red, accented with glints of antiqued gold. It was hot and stuffy, and it felt like the claustrophobic heat of bodies pressing against me from all directions in a rush-hour train. I wanted to stand, but my legs didn't work and my arms couldn't support my weight, so I stayed on the rug. It was soft, and I thought I could curl up on it and go to sleep.

Yolanda crouched down and examined me. "Did you really only have two drinks tonight? Really, truly?"

"Cross my heart and hope to die," I said, and then regretted it, because at the moment it felt like I really *could* die.

"Your pupils look funny," she said. "They're huge." She stood up, hands on her hips, and looked down at me. When she spoke, she sounded triumphant. "You've been roofied."

Roofied was better than poisoned, and while it wasn't good news, I felt a stab of relief that at least Yolanda knew I wasn't drunk. "That's what I've been saying. It was my drink. The pineapple one," I said. Coming up with "ananas à l'absinthe" was beyond me right now. "*Your* drink."

"Yeah." Yolanda frowned. "That occurred to me. The waiter. That damn waiter with the man bun, the creep. 'You were really good up there. You looked good, too,' remember how he said that to me?" She paced around the room, the spikes of her heels digging into her plush rug. "Yeah, I bet I looked good to him. Must've been a huge disappointment when you and I swapped drinks. I can't imagine he'd want to take you back to his place and do unspeakable things to *your* helpless body."

I was just as glad about that, but Yolanda clearly meant it as a cutting insult, and I couldn't figure out why she was being so cruel. "I'm sorry," I said. I wanted to placate her, to rewind back to the part of the evening when we were good friends. "I'm sorry I accused you of poisoning me again. And I'm sorry I said you tried to shove me in front of the train."

"Ah." Yolanda's voice softened. "No apology needed for that."

As soon as the words penetrated the fog in my head, it felt like an electric shock coursing through my body. "You really did that?"

"I did, yeah." Yolanda towered over me. "I saw you on the platform, and you were being an idiot by standing so close to the edge, and it occurred to me that if you fell in front of the train, it would make my life easier. So I gave you the teensiest little kick." Yolanda looked more gorgeous than she'd ever been, her eyes narrowed, her cheeks flushed with color, and I knew she was dangerous.

Her casual admission of attempted murder made me feel a little dangerous, too, but I had a huge disadvantage in that I was thoroughly messed up, both mentally and physically, by whatever had been in my drink. "I'll tell Daniel," I said. "This time he really will fire you." I'd meant it to sound vicious and intimidating, but it came out weak and ineffectual, like a little kid threatening to sic the teacher on the schoolyard bully.

"Danny will never fire me. Danny wouldn't dare." The ends of her lips curved up into a menacing smile. "He knows I'll destroy him, him and Niko both. I'll burn them to the ground. How well do you think Danny and Niko would do in jail? A pair of useless rich boys?"

I didn't understand what she was saying, but the gist of her words alarmed me. "What are you talking about? Why would they go to jail?"

"You don't need to know," she said. "All you need to know is, I've got job security. You don't."

She started to pace, stalking around the rug in her heeled boots, the sequins of her coatdress glittering in the low light. "That role should be *mine*." She was furious. "You've done nothing to deserve it. Why did Danny cast you? You're so plain and boring. The only advantage you have on me is your education, your precious *training*, and I'm sick of hearing about that."

I wanted to tell her that my training was the reason why I had a professional opera career, and I existed for opera. As much as she wanted the role of Barbarella, I wanted it just as much, and I'd done so much more work to be worthy of it. But I was growing more and more freaked out by her anger and her mounting loss of control, so I said nothing.

"You've had so many privileges, it makes me sick." It was a hiss. "Yeah, you had a bad childhood. Boo fucking hoo. So your movie-star mom thought her ugly daughter was disappointing. So your aunt's boyfriend hit you one time. Some of us got hit a lot more than that. Some of us didn't get some fancy boarding school to swoop in and give us hundreds of thousands of dollars' worth of voice lessons. God!" Her volume rose. "I didn't get any of that. I've done it all on my own. I've done everything I could, and I'm sick of everyone telling me I need to do *more*."

She was furious, she was an attempted murderer, and she hated my guts. It was time to get the hell away from her. I tried to get to my feet. "I'm sorry," I said. "I'll just go."

Yolanda shoved me again, just the smallest push, and once more I collapsed on the rug. "Fine," she said. "You can go. But first I'll tell you what I'm going to do. You made a big mistake tonight, running your mouth off about your past, because now I'm going to tell everyone all the ugly details. Every single person in the cast is going to know they're singing opposite someone who stabs people. How popular do you think you're going to be?"

My sense of outrage consumed me, fiery and agonizing. In a moment of weakness, I'd trusted Yolanda with my life story, and now she was going to use it against me. As when I'd attacked her on the stairwell after rehearsal, I moved before I could think about it, propelled by a strangely exhilarating burst of rage. I leaped to my feet and pounced on her, determined to hit her, choke her, claw out her eyes, rip out her hair, punch her in the face. "Don't you dare!" I shouted. "Don't you fucking dare. I'll destroy you, you psycho!"

I went for her face, but my hands clutched air. Shocked by my sudden attack, Yolanda nonetheless had the presence of mind to dodge out of my way, and in my compromised state, I couldn't change direction. I stumbled forward, careened into the wall, and crumpled in a heap near the door.

I tried to get up, but the room swirled around me, and I couldn't get my bearings. "You say you're going to tell everyone in the cast about my history, fine, I'm going to tell them all about you." I was panting for breath, and it was hard to get the words out. "Everyone's going to know about the eye drops and the subway push. The dead rat, too; I have photos." I thought Yolanda looked a little blank at the reference to the murdered rat, like she'd totally forgotten about doing that. Like she did so many shitty, destructive things in the course of an average day that it had slipped her mind entirely. "I'll bring down the opera if I have to, but I'm going to make sure the whole world knows that you're a psychotic asshole."

"Hmm. That would be a problem if I believed you," Yolanda said. She crouched beside me. "If I thought you meant it, I'd take steps to make sure you never opened your ugly mouth again. But the opera means too much to you. Face it, it's the only thing you have in your life right now, isn't it?"

"Yeah. Yeah, it is. You said I don't deserve the role, but that's bullshit, you're the one who hasn't earned it. I've worked my whole life for it, and you've done nothing!" I was gasping for air, my words coming out incoherent and strangled. "I'd rather burn everything to the ground than let you steal that role from me."

"That's the thing, though. I still don't think you mean it." Yolanda was calm, too calm, her expression serene and smug. "As long as you still cling to the hope that you'll be on that stage opening night, you won't do a damn thing to hurt the production. You'll let Daniel string you along and belittle your performance in front of the rest of us, and you'll try your best to be a good little girl who does everything he tells you to do, and it won't be enough. I'll be onstage, and you'll be watching from the audience."

The great burning hatred I felt for her was mixed with a sense of self-loathing, because she was partially correct: I'd been a good girl, obedient and disciplined, and I'd hoped that would be enough to allow me to hold on to the role. It had been a disastrous tactic. I should have fought from the start. That very first rehearsal, I should have gone above Daniel's head and called the police. I should have removed Yolanda from my life immediately.

"You tried to kill me," I said. "You're going to rot in jail. I swear I'm going to bring you down." I meant the words with all my soul, but they came out slurred and feeble. My vision seemed to be narrowing, too, everything around me growing smaller and blurrier, and with a sense of horror, I realized my burst of rage-fueled adrenaline had exhausted my sick body, and now I was on the verge of passing out.

Yolanda gave a huge theatrical yawn, covering her mouth with her hand. "If you haven't stopped me by now, you never will. But look on the bright side." She reached over and patted me on the cheek. I tried to move out of her way and ended up bonking the back of my head against the door. "The fact that you're a gutless loser is the only thing saving your life tonight."

I closed my eyes. My eyelashes felt wet against my cheeks. Damn it all, I was crying again. The burning anger was ebbing away, and I mourned its loss. I liked myself better when I was furious; I despised this weak, broken creature who lay helpless on Yolanda's rug.

I was only vaguely aware of Yolanda's hand grabbing my wrist and hauling me to my feet. "You can't sleep on my floor. That rug's been knotted by hand, and it's worth more than your life." She wrapped an arm around my shoulders and marched me into her bedroom. "Puke in my bed, and I swear to god I'll suffocate you with a pillow."

I found myself on my back on something soft; I felt her yanking off my boots. When I opened my eyes, I was surrounded by multiple shades of pink.

Yolanda's bed smelled like tea roses. I didn't know if she spritzed her bedding with perfume, or if she just used some kind of fancy laundry soap. I wanted to ask her about that, and I also wanted to warn her that I could make no guarantees that I wouldn't, in fact, puke in her bed, because it seemed like there was a pretty decent chance of that happening.

I also wanted to warn her of something else, something crucial. It occurred to me that someone had placed some kind of incapacitating drug in her cocktail right around the time her keys had vanished from her purse, and it seemed like there could be a connection there, a bad one, something that meant she was in danger, but then my mind clouded over with another wave of fog, and I forgot to say anything at all.

14

Acrimonious History

I woke up feeling dizzy and disoriented. I had trouble getting air into my lungs; my head pulsed in waves of agony, as though my brain wanted to burst through my skull. My memories of the previous evening were shapeless. How badly had I humiliated myself? What exactly had happened during that long, terrible night?

It was dark in the bedroom, and I didn't know if Yolanda was nearby. I flailed around in the general area where I thought a bedside lamp would be and knocked it over with a clatter. After setting it upright, I groped for the switch and turned it on.

As I remembered, Yolanda's bedroom was soft and feminine. I was the only one in the room. My stomach heaved when I sat up. Finding the bathroom before I vomited all over her nice bedding would be a good idea.

Puke in my bed, and I swear to god I'll suffocate you with a pillow. That was the last thing I remembered her saying. My stomach lurched again, more urgent this time, and I headed out of the bedroom.

The living room was dark, lit only by the glow of the bedroom lamp, but I could make out a mound of clothing on the floor beside the sofa, like someone had dumped out the contents of a laundry hamper. I squinted through the dim light and realized, with a growing sense of unreality, that the pile of clothes was Yolanda.

At some point after I'd passed out in her bed, she'd changed out of her sequined coatdress. She was clad in pajamas; they were surprisingly prim and girlish, made of white flannel with a nosegay print. She was curled into herself, the side of her face pressed against the rug.

I froze. I felt hollow and light, like my internal organs had been removed and replaced with nothing but empty space. I forced myself to step closer. I tried to say her name, but my mouth was dry, and all I could manage was a croak.

I crouched beside her. I touched her shoulder. "Yolanda?" My voice was a rasp, the loudest sound in the apartment.

The front of her pajamas was dark. I assumed it was a shadow, and then I saw the handle of what I guessed was a folding hunting knife embedded in the left side of her rib cage, and I realized it was blood. Blood formed a huge black splotch on the rug beneath her, messing up the symmetry of the pattern; I saw her right eye, open and cloudy, and I knew she was dead.

I remained in a crouch for a long time. When I stood at last, it took me forever to find my Birkin where I'd dropped it near the doorway, even longer to get out my phone, longer still to connect with the 911 operator. I didn't know Yolanda's address and couldn't remember the path we'd taken from the club, but the operator walked me through the process of finding a stack of junk mail on Yolanda's dining table and reading off the address printed on an envelope. I was still on the line when two uniformed officers arrived. Numb and disoriented, I made it down the stairs to open the front door.

I took them upstairs, and as soon as they saw Yolanda's corpse, they hustled me out of the apartment. When I asked if I could grab my coat and purse, they pretended they hadn't heard me. One of the officers, a compact woman with a helmet of short dark hair, held my elbow and marched me down the stairs and out into the cold night.

I balked when she led me to a patrol car parked in the bike lane and opened the back door. "Am I being arrested?" I asked, a note of panic creeping in. For a craven moment, I wished I'd just slipped out of Yolanda's apartment and hurried home so someone else could've found her body and reported her murder.

The officer gave my elbow a tug, indicating that I should climb into the back seat. "Just wait in here," she said. I must have looked terrified, because her face softened. "We need you out of our way while we secure the crime scene. Detectives will talk to you later."

She closed the door and left me alone. The back seat looked clean and reeked of bleach, the scent strong enough to make my nostrils tingle, like the interior had been blasted with some industrial-strength cleanser.

More police cars arrived, both sedans and SUVs; there were five or six of them, and they parked wherever they found space, blocking off the street, their swirling lights forming kaleidoscopic patterns on the windows of my temporary prison. Several of the newly arrived officers went inside Yolanda's building while one remained on the stoop, left behind to keep a vigilant watch on the front door. Shortly thereafter came the white medical examiner van, followed by an unmarked SUV filled with a gaggle of what I guessed were crime scene technicians, dressed informally in jeans and puffy winter coats.

The homicide detectives arrived last, a sleek matched set in dark suits and long overcoats. There were two: One was extraordinarily tall and looked like a retired supermodel, her jet-black hair scraped off her face and anchored in a thick ponytail, while the other was tanned and leathery and looked like he came from a family that belonged to a yacht club. The leathery man paused on the stoop to exchange a laughing word and a manly shoulder clasp with the officer guarding the door, while the tall woman ignored them both and swept into the building.

Alone in the patrol car, I wished I had my coat with me. The back seat was warm enough, but I trembled uncontrollably. The physical effects of whatever drug had been in my cocktail had largely worn off, though my head throbbed; I also kept forcing down sporadic waves of acute nausea. Vomiting all over the seat would only make this horror-filled night more uncomfortable. Now that I didn't feel quite so confused and spacey, though, I was keenly aware of my mounting panic. As unreal as it seemed, Yolanda had met a violent end while I'd been only a short distance from her, and it might be an uphill battle convincing the cops that I didn't know anything about how or why it had happened. Or who had done it.

Someone had come into the apartment in the middle of the night to murder her. Maybe Yolanda had opened the door and invited her killer in, or maybe it had something to do with those keys that had mysteriously disappeared from her purse. Or maybe someone else had a key . . .

A slim figure in a pale trench coat hurried up the stoop and was confronted by the uniformed officer, who stepped in front of the door and blocked his path. A few minutes of what looked like agitated conversation ensued. The new arrival fished his ID out of his wallet and handed it to the officer; while the officer scrutinized it, the new arrival turned to stare at the array of police cars with a look of incomprehension on his handsome face, and I recognized Leo. Leo, who was returning home from his night out, only to be confronted with grim news about his . . . neighbor? Tenant? What was Yolanda to Leo, anyway? My memories of everything that had happened in Yolanda's apartment slipped out of my reach whenever I tried to focus on them, but there was something there that suggested that Leo and Yolanda knew each other very well indeed . . .

You love all the things my mouth does for you. Foggy though my brain was, it managed to summon up Yolanda's mocking words to Leo. She'd said other things to him, too, things about Niko, and for all the outward intimacy of their dynamic, something acrimonious lay between them. Leo had been annoyed with Yolanda, maybe even angry, over something she'd done to him.

I was jolted out of my thoughts when the driver's-side door opened. The short-haired officer slid behind the wheel. Simultaneously, the rear door on my side opened, and I saw the leathery detective smiling down at me. His hair was a curly mix of blond and silver, and his eyes were a very pale blue, the color of ocean water close to a sandy shore. "Scooch over," he said, casual and friendly. I slid over, and he climbed in next to me, keeping the door open. He had my coat folded over his arm, with the fake Birkin bag dangling from his wrist. He held my driver's license up next to my face and grinned at me. "Hi, there. Katherine Margolis, I presume?"

"That's me." I said. It came out in an uncertain rasp; I coughed once to clear my throat.

"Nice to meet you, Katherine. Thanks for being patient. I know you've been waiting a long time." He tucked my license inside the Birkin bag and handed it to me in a bundle with my coat. He held up his badge, which hung around his neck on a chain. "I'm Detective Abernathy. That's Officer Reyes up front; she's going to be taking notes while we chat." Officer Reyes didn't look up or turn around, but she dipped her chin once while keeping her head bent over the screen of her phone, fingers tapping away, already transcribing our conversation. "I was hoping I could ask you some questions about tonight."

My heart hammered in my chest. "Do I need a lawyer?" I asked.

"No one ever *needs* a lawyer," he said with a small chuckle, like I was silly for asking. That was a self-serving lie, and it put me on my guard. "You can refuse to talk to me without one present, of course. But you might want to help me out right here and now so we can get this over with. Sound good?"

Back when I was twelve, after I'd stabbed Glen, I'd refused

to talk to the cops who'd interviewed me at the hospital, and consequently, they had treated me badly. I was traumatized and injured, barely able to speak through my newly wired jaw, and in their zealous efforts to ferret out the truth, they played mind games. They threatened me with prison, they accused me of being mentally unbalanced, they cracked crude jokes about my *Playboy* centerfold mom to see if they could get me to snap. Verbal tricks are fair game in police interrogations as long as they get results, I know that as an adult, but back when I was a sad, messed-up kid, their words had damaged me. Abernathy seemed genial, but I knew better than to trust him. Since he was steering me toward not having a lawyer present, I should've insisted on getting one.

But . . .

I grabbed on to his suggestion that we could get this over with quickly, that maybe I could wrap up my part in the night's horrific events and get on with my life. So I swallowed hard and said, "Sure. Okay," hating myself for taking the path of least resistance.

"Great." The pale eyes twinkled. "Can you tell me about the deceased? Let's start with her name."

"Yolanda Archambeau." I spelled it.

He nodded. "Occupation?"

"We're both opera singers." I hoped that sounded classy and impressive. Maybe Abernathy would assume a professional opera singer was likely to be civilized and law-abiding and therefore not the type to stab anyone to death in the middle of the night. "We're in rehearsals right now for a production. Yolanda's my understudy." Some pedantic part of my brain noted that I should use the past tense for Yolanda, but that seemed unthinkable. "I'm the lead."

"Congratulations." Abernathy didn't sound impressed, but at least he sounded affable. "What's the production?"

"*Barbarella?* It's a brand-new opera. It's based on the film."

It felt disrespectful to Astrid to even think it, but for the first time, I wished I were starring in something with more gravitas. "It's for a company called Brio."

His expression remained the same, but his eyebrows lifted in tandem briefly before settling back into place. "Brio? Is that what's-his-name's company, the Toska kid?"

Nothing he could've said would have surprised me more. While respectable enough, Brio was a minor player in the New York opera world. Abernathy sounded casual, but there were sparks behind those sun-faded eyes, and I had a sense that he was paying close attention now, scrutinizing subtle changes in my expression, my body language.

"Yes, it is. Daniel Toska is the artistic director. Do you follow opera?"

"Not in the slightest. I've never understood why anyone would listen to that stuff, sorry. I'm sure it's a flaw in my character." Abernathy winked at me. I wanted to ask him how he knew Daniel, but I didn't dare, and he slid into the next topic before I had a chance. "Walk me through how you found the body."

I didn't want to think about it. My stomach gave one of its abrupt lurches; I had to take a moment to stabilize myself, because it would shift this conversation onto a bad path if I barfed all over friendly Detective Abernathy. "I was asleep in the bedroom." Just talking about it put me back in that horrible moment. I felt myself start to shake again. "I got up in the middle of the night and didn't know where Yolanda was. I went to the living room, and . . . I found her."

"You were asleep in the deceased's bed?"

"Just out of convenience." Abernathy had sounded nonjudgmental, but I could feel myself blush. "I wasn't feeling well enough to go home. I live in Hudson Heights. We'd been at a cabaret club early in the evening." I had to stop and think about the name. "Chanteur Malheureux. It's just a few blocks from here. Yolanda was performing. When she was done, we ordered cocktails, and mine—it was Yolanda's cocktail actually, she ordered it, but we switched, so I was the one who drank it—must have had something in it."

Abernathy nodded at that, indicating he was following along. "What do you mean by 'something'? Do you mean your cocktail was drugged?" His interrogation style was conversational, like he and I were just making small talk and he had minimal investment in my answers, but I felt my nerves prickling with alarm, and once again I wished I'd had the guts to request a lawyer.

"Yes. I'm sure it was. I felt sick immediately after drinking it," I said. I was back in the club, swaying on my feet, Yolanda hustling me toward the door, arm around my shoulders so I wouldn't fall down. My hands, resting loosely in my lap, started shaking so much I had to clench them into fists to halt the motion. "I could barely walk."

"You sure you didn't just have too much to drink?"

"Absolutely not. I only had two cocktails." My credit card bill, which I felt certain Abernathy would check, would confirm my story. "Yolanda didn't think I could make it home on the subway, so she took me back to her place because it was closer. I passed out in her bed."

I was skipping over a lot of the story there, but if Abernathy didn't ask me directly, I wasn't going to mention the bad blood between myself and Yolanda. Earlier in the evening, I'd been hell-bent on exposing Yolanda's malevolent shenanigans to the world; now, in the wake of her brutal slaying, I wanted them buried forever.

"And that's how you managed to sleep through whatever happened to the deceased. Yolanda Archambeau." Abernathy looked thoughtful, his mouth twisted into a slight frown. He shifted around on the seat so he could face me with his whole body. "So who did this, Katherine? While you were asleep, who came into the apartment and stabbed your friend?"

"I don't know. But something weird happened earlier." I

swallowed hard. "When we came here from the club, Yolanda couldn't find her keys in her purse. One of her neighbors had a key, and he let us into her apartment."

"Yeah? Who's this neighbor?"

"His name's Leo. He lives across the hall. He's home right now; I saw him arrive a little while ago." I was aware that I was deliberately trying to deflect Abernathy's attention from me and onto Leo, which made me feel a little scuzzy. "He had a key ring with the keys to each apartment, so I guess he manages the building? Maybe he owns it."

Abernathy gave a quick glance toward the front seat, as though confirming Reyes was getting this all down, before turning his attention back to me. "You said she couldn't find her keys. Did they ever turn up?"

I shook my head. "She assumed they'd fallen out of her purse at the club. While she was performing, she stashed her purse in the green room, and someone could have taken them. Maybe it was the same person who spiked her drink. I think it could've been . . ." I stopped, realizing I was about to accuse a stranger of murder.

"Who do you think it was, Katherine?" Abernathy sounded patient, like nothing important hinged on my answer.

"There was this waiter," I said unhappily. "He was tall and skinny. Long dark hair that he kept in a bun. Yolanda thought he was creepy. He *was* creepy. After she performed, he complimented her on how pretty she was. When she realized I was sick, she thought he might have tried to slip her a roofie, not expecting us to switch drinks."

"We can check up on that easily enough," Abernathy said. "Do you know if Daniel Toska has ever been to the deceased's apartment?"

I'd expected him to grill me more about the waiter. The shift in topic took me off guard. "Daniel?" I looked at Abernathy, hoping his expression would give something away, but his face was a mask. "I don't know. I don't know why he would've, but . . . I guess it's possible. She's been dating his older brother. Niko."

"Ah, Niko." It was said softly, almost intimately, like Niko was one of Abernathy's oldest friends. "Now that's very interesting. Was she involved in sex work, do you know?"

All this lurching from subject to subject was making my head pound worse than ever. But I nodded and tried to follow his train of thought. "She models for this webcam site, Somebody's Baby. She uses the alias Carmen Callas."

Abernathy nodded, and it was hard to be sure due to his genial outer shell, but I got the sense he wasn't too interested in that. "How about prostitution? She ever do anything like that?"

I blinked in surprise. "Not to my knowledge," I said. "But I don't really know much about her."

I wanted to know why he was asking, if that was something he asked about all murdered young women, especially ones as beautiful as Yolanda, and I was trying to decide whether I found that offensive, but as soon as he'd broached the subject he dropped it, and the interrogation continued on along more conventional lines. In response to his straightforward questions, I told him the bits and pieces I knew about Yolanda's past and present. The sun rose while he grilled me, flooding the street with golden light. That was bad news, because it meant I probably didn't stand a chance of making it to rehearsal on time.

We were eventually interrupted by a new arrival, who crouched down beside Abernathy's open door and glared at us. It was Abernathy's partner, the tall woman. At her shoulder was one of the technicians, a young woman with spiky purple hair and Buddy Holly glasses.

The tall woman gave me a curt nod. "We need to get your fingerprints," she said to me. "They're dusting the apartment right now. Can you tell me everything you touched?"

Abernathy grinned at me. "This is Detective Khan, my partner. I'm the nice one; she's the mean one." Khan shot him a humorless look. Probably in her late forties, she was both beautiful and severe, with a strong, straight nose and formidable eyebrows. At a nod from Khan, the young technician leaned across Abernathy and, with a quick smile at me, took my hand and started pressing my fingers one by one onto the screen of a portable phone-sized device. I tried to ignore the surreality of it all and focused on Khan's request.

"I don't think I touched very much," I said. "I sorted through the pile of mail on her dining table to find her address when I called you, and I touched Yolanda, but only a little, just her shoulder. As soon as I saw that she was . . ." I stopped, the terror finding its way to my throat again, strangling me, and I desperately wanted a drink of water.

"Okay." Abernathy sounded compassionate, soothing. He turned to Khan. "Katherine believes someone put something nasty in her drink earlier tonight, and she's probably not feeling too well right now. I'm going to take her to the hospital, if you've got things covered here." He patted me on the shoulder. "Katherine, I'd like to take you to get a blood test, just so we can see what was in your drink. And while we're there, Officer Reyes can check you out physically."

That was ominous. "Physically, like . . . ?"

"Nothing to worry about." A reassuring grin. "It sounds like you had a pretty weird night, and we just want to check you for any injuries."

Ah. "Did Yolanda . . . How was she killed?"

Abernathy's eyes met mine, straightforward and serious, and I knew he knew why I was asking. He glanced at Khan, who answered my question in a brisk manner. "Medical examiner says she was stabbed four times." I remembered the blood on her chest and stomach, the knife lodged in her heart. "She managed to fight a bit; she's got some scratches and bruises on her."

And they wanted to see if Yolanda had fought me. Well,

good. I was uninjured, and surely that would be enough to rule me out as her killer. "I see," I said.

"You absolutely sure you slept through everything that happened, Katherine?" For the first time, Abernathy sounded wistful, like he'd wished my answers had been more helpful. "I have to imagine there was a lot of noise."

"I didn't hear anything. I'm sorry."

He seemed disappointed yet unsurprised. Presently, we took off in the patrol car, lights flashing but sirens off, Abernathy in front beside Officer Reyes, me still in the back, grateful I had my coat so I could huddle inside it for protection. We went to Mount Sinai, the same hospital I'd been taken to after Yolanda had poisoned me. In an examination room, a nurse administered a blood test, then took my temperature and blood pressure before handing me a little cup to pee into. While Abernathy loitered in the corridor, Officer Reyes instructed me to strip off all my clothes, underwear included, and gave me a polite yet thorough examination from my scalp to the soles of my feet. When that was done and I was once again dressed, Abernathy entered the room and smiled at me. "Okay, Katherine," he said. "That's all we need from you right now."

The tidal wave of relief left me drained. I'd half expected to spend the day in an interrogation room, or maybe a holding cell. Maybe I wasn't cleared as a suspect, but I wasn't under arrest, and that was a gift.

As soon as we headed into the hallway, though, I spotted a familiar face. It was kindly Dr. Makinde, who was striding down the corridor, his attention focused on his tablet. He looked up and spotted Abernathy, with his badge dangling from his neck, and Officer Reyes in her traditional NYPD uniform, and then his eyes met mine. I expected him not to recognize me, but he paused and said, "Ah! You must be here about the eye drops."

Abernathy halted. "What was that?"

Dr. Makinde looked from me to Abernathy and back to me.

"I thought you might be making a police report at last. Are you . . . ?" He trailed off, uncertain.

"What's going on here?" Abernathy sounded relaxed, but I could feel my skin burn, and I saw Dr. Makinde's friendly face tense up as he worried he'd made a blunder.

I could lie in front of Dr. Makinde. He probably wouldn't correct me, because I was pretty sure he couldn't disclose my medical history to the police without some kind of warrant. But Abernathy would follow up if he thought I was hiding something, and it would be better for me if he didn't discover that I was withholding information from him.

"I was hospitalized a couple weeks ago," I said. "Tetrahydrozoline poisoning." I took a deep breath, then came out with it. "It was Yolanda. She'd bought me a cup of tea, and I got sick, and later she admitted she put eye drops in it."

Abernathy stared at me. His affable expression had hardened.

"It was a prank. She didn't mean any harm," I said.

"So it sounds like you and the deceased had an acrimonious history, huh?"

"We'd only met that morning. It was the first rehearsal. She apologized, and we were friendly after that."

Only a thin, crackly layer of truth surrounded that wobbly ball of lies. I was acutely aware of how many uncomfortable facts about this case pointed right at me. Like the fact that Yolanda had repeatedly tried to kill me, and the fact that she'd posed an ongoing threat to my job security.

To say nothing of the fact that she'd been stabbed to death, and I'd stabbed someone in the past. Thanks to this chance encounter with Dr. Makinde, my rivalry with Yolanda was doomed to exposure, and that couldn't be helped, but I felt certain I should keep the details of my childhood buried as deeply as possible.

"Let's step aside for a moment," Abernathy said. His demeanor was newly grim. Ignoring both Dr. Makinde and Officer Reyes, he took me by the arm and steered me through the first open doorway, which turned out to be an empty examination room. He closed the door and turned his attention to me, and I saw, with a twist of my stomach, that the genial mask had dropped. He was furious.

"You've been lying to me, Katherine," he said.

"I haven't!" It sounded weak and unconvincing, even to my own ears.

"You didn't say one word about the victim trying to poison you."

He hadn't asked, but I had enough sense not to point that out. "It was just eye drops. She meant it as a joke; she didn't realize it would send me to the hospital. Like I said, we became friends after that."

"You didn't think that was something that might interest me?" It was hostile. As freaked out as I was in the moment, his change in demeanor came as a relief. I'd known his hail-fellow-well-met attitude was an act, designed to lull me into believing he was on my side. Now the act had been abandoned, and for the first time I was dealing with the real Detective Abernathy.

"No, I didn't, because it didn't have anything to do with whatever happened tonight." I liked how I sounded, strong and confident.

He was still holding my arm, and now he stepped closer, bending his head down so he could stare at me, his expression filled with unveiled contempt. "Don't keep things from me, Katherine. Don't even try it. Because now I'm tempted to take you down to the station just to see what else we can shake out of you."

I was back in that hospital room as a kid, the police investigators berating me for withholding information from them, even as the nurses tried their best to get them to leave me alone. I wanted to put up a spirited defense, but I was smart enough to realize that anything I said would make things worse. So I just swallowed and said, "I'm sorry. May I go now?"

Abernathy was silent, and I could tell he wanted a fight. "Get out of here," he said at last. "Officer Reyes will drive you home."

"There's no need," I said. "I can take the subway."

In truth, I would have loved to be driven to my apartment, even in the back of a squad car, because I felt exhausted and sick, and I wanted to get inside, lock my door, and crawl into bed. But I'd looked at the clock in the examination room, and it was now after nine. There was no way I could go home, because I was already late for rehearsal.

15

Stunned and Lifeless

Daniel was too controlled to yell at me when I arrived, but he was furious. He blocked my path as soon as I walked in, his body oozing tension. My castmates were seated on the edge of the stage or slumped in chairs in the first row of the auditorium, bored and irritated. At least there was no orchestra for me to inconvenience; the musicians weren't scheduled to join us until the afternoon.

"You're an hour late, Kit." Daniel's voice was flat. "We've been unable to do anything without you."

I'd never been late for a rehearsal in my life, and I had to fight the urge to burst into a flurry of apologies. "Can I talk to you alone?" I asked.

Daniel continued as if I hadn't spoken: "There was no point in going through the blocking without you. As soon as you knew you were going to be late, you should have texted. Yolanda isn't here yet either."

Instead of replying, I took him by the elbow and pulled him gently to the side of the stage. "Yolanda is dead." I said it softly so the rest of the cast couldn't overhear. "That's why I'm late. I've been with the police. She was murdered in her apartment last night. I was with her."

I had to stop talking. My throat felt parched. I needed a drink of water, maybe all the water in the world. ⸱

Daniel gaped at me, his features frozen in disbelief. He swallowed. "Yolanda's dead?"

The stage was too quiet. The cast couldn't hear us, but they saw our body language and probably sensed our shared horror, which spilled out of us like a physical force.

"Yeah." I forced a wave of dread back down into my stomach. "I wouldn't have been late otherwise."

"What happened?" It was a whisper.

"We went to a cabaret club last night, and someone drugged my drink. She took me back to her apartment, and when I woke up, she'd been stabbed in the heart."

Behind me, I heard a jagged inhalation of breath. Marla had silently joined us. "Yolanda was murdered?" She kept her voice low, but I could hear the horror in it.

I nodded. "It looks like someone stole her keys and entered her apartment."

Daniel's brown eyes looked black, like his pupils had swallowed his irises. "I feel sick," he said at last.

My dehydration was becoming incapacitating. My mouth and throat felt like they were coated with dust. "I need some water," I said. "I'm going to run to the drinking fountain and fill my water bottle, and then we can start the rehearsal, okay? I'm sorry I'm so late."

"Kit, we're not going to rehearse." Daniel sounded incredulous. "We can't . . . none of us can . . . I don't know if we can move on from this."

I gaped at him. "You mean the opera is canceled?"

"I don't know!" It came out as a bark, and I could sense everyone in the theater swiveling their heads toward us. Daniel inhaled and tried again, quieter. "I can't answer that right now. But . . . my god, does any of this really matter compared to what happened to Yolanda?"

"I don't know," I said. I sounded miserable. "But the show must go on, right?"

"We have less than two weeks until opening night, Daniel." Marla's voice was soft but firm. "Everyone is here. We need to learn the blocking." She placed a gentle hand on his forearm. "We need this rehearsal."

"We do, but . . ." Daniel looked crumpled. "But this changes everything. I'll have to let Niko know . . ."

"You should tell him as soon as you can," I said. "His name came up when the detectives talked to me, and they'll probably question him. It'd be better if he hears the news from you."

Daniel looked alarmed. "The police want to question Niko?"

"Because he knows Yolanda," I said. From the way Abernathy had reacted to Niko's name, there was something more to it, but I didn't know what, so I let it go.

Something occurred to me for the first time since Yolanda's death, a sad and ugly thought. "Yolanda has a daughter, back wherever she came from. She'll need to know what happened."

"She has a daughter?" Daniel's eyebrows raised. "The NYPD will handle next-of-kin notification, won't they?"

"Sure, but when you talk to Niko, could you ask him if he knows how to contact Yolanda's family? I don't like the idea of a kid out there not knowing her mom is dead."

"I'll ask him," Daniel said, but his tone was distracted, like his mind was going in many other directions. He glanced at Marla, then straightened up. "I'll tell the cast, and if everyone feels stable enough to proceed, we'll go ahead with rehearsal."

"Thank you, Daniel," Marla said. She gave his arm a reassuring squeeze.

While Daniel addressed the group, I slipped out the stage door and headed down the hallway to fill my water bottle. As soon as he made that announcement, everyone's attention would turn toward me, and I couldn't handle that right now.

Rehearsal was unbearable. Daniel had the right idea; we should have canceled. We were stunned and lifeless, zombies shuffling around the stage as Daniel tried to teach us our blocking. It was easier in the afternoon when the orchestra arrived; none of the musicians had known Yolanda, so no announcement was made, though I could see the word spreading via whispered conversations.

Every once in a while, the visceral horror of Yolanda's murder would pop into my brain while I was singing, and it shattered my concentration. My voice wobbled in ways it shouldn't, and twice I saw Marla, conducting from the orchestra pit, meet my eye and twitch her left pinky skyward, her personal shorthand for indicating that a singer is borderline sharp. My sense of pitch is very good. Not perfect; perfect pitch, or absolute pitch, is rare even in the opera world. Still, it was unprecedented for me to wander off the right note in a work I'd rehearsed as many times as *Barbarella*.

When we finished for the day, I slipped out of the theater and hurried home before anyone could ask me questions about Yolanda. The hallway leading to my apartment smelled like roasted chicken and onions, which reminded me that I hadn't eaten all day. During our lunch break, I'd gone upstairs to one of the practice rooms, closed the door, and sat on the floor, clutching my knees to my chest to form a small, protected ball while thinking about nothing in particular until it was time to join the orchestra on the stage.

Costas stuck his head out of his door as soon as he heard me coming. The chicken smell came from his apartment. Plenty of garlic. Maybe oregano. Heavenly.

"Police were here," he told me.

"They were looking for me?" I asked in alarm.

Costas shook his head. "For me. For your neighbors. For anyone who could tell them anything about you," he said.

That wasn't great. "Did they tell you why?"

"Your friend. The blonde, Marilyn Monroe. It's been on the news," Costas said. "Channel Four didn't mention you, but the detectives said you were there when it happened."

I didn't say anything. After a pause, he continued: "I told them about the fight you two had outside your door." His voice was gruff. "I didn't make more of it than it was, but I told them what I heard."

Not ideal, but probably inevitable. I just nodded. "I understand. I'm sorry they bothered you."

My stomach growled. I gave Costas an awkward nod in farewell and hurried to my own apartment.

It was stuffy, and it smelled like something was rotting in my kitchen. It smelled like death, which reminded me of the rat Yolanda had left on my doorstep. It was possible the police would get the idea to search my apartment, and right now I had a bloody steak knife wrapped in paper towels stashed beneath my sink.

I mulled it over. Destroying evidence in a police investigation was generally considered a dumb move, and there was a chance I'd make things worse for myself. Still . . .

I took out my phone and deleted the photos of the dead rat. The police could probably retrieve them, but only if they suspected there was something worth retrieving. I soaked the knife in a sink full of hot soapy water, scrubbed the serrated blade as best I could, then dried it and stashed it in my utensil drawer. When I'd thrown away the bloody paper towels, I felt a little better.

My tiny apartment still smelled bad. I went on a quick search for the source of the stench and found it in the cupboard. A mouse had eaten through the box of macarons Yolanda had given me, then expired in a pathetic heap beside it.

Why was the mouse dead? I'd trashed the macarons at first because I hadn't wanted to accept any food or drink from Yolanda after her trick with the eye drops. I'd fished them out, believing I'd been silly to think she'd try to poison me again. But maybe my first instinct had been the correct one.

I untied the satin ribbon and opened the box. The mouse had chewed a hole through the side. Five of the macarons were untouched; one was half eaten by the mouse in its final meal.

I picked up the chewed macaron and examined it. It was pale pink, with two layers of a light almond cookie sandwiching a thin layer of ganache. The top layer slid off in my hand, like someone had pried the macaron apart and stuck it back together.

There was grit on the pink ganache, a coarse blue powder. Maybe it was something innocent, like a dusting of colored sugar.

Maybe it was something ominous, like a dusting of rat poison.

My hands shook when I buried the box in the trash. As I disposed of the mouse corpse and scrubbed my cupboard, the tremor spread throughout my body until I was shaking all over. Yolanda had given me the tainted confections two weeks ago, and yet it felt like she'd reached out from the great beyond to attack me one final time.

It put me over the edge. I sat on my bed and sobbed, head pressed to my knees, hands knotted so tightly into fists that my fingernails sliced my palms. In deference to the thin walls, I did my best to smother my sniffles.

Still, it wasn't a surprise when I heard a knock. If my singing bothered Costas, surely he'd find my sobbing equally annoying. I considered ignoring him, and then I wiped my face on the sleeve of my shirt and answered the door.

Usually confident to the point of cockiness, Costas looked awkward, his broad shoulders hunched up to his ears. He carried a foil-covered plate in both hands. "Made too much for just myself," he said, his voice gruff. "Thought you might be in no mood to cook, so . . . it's just chicken and feta. Grilled potatoes, too." He handed it to me. "Leave the plate on my doorstep when you're done. Wash it first."

The plate was warm in my hands. I wanted to thank him, but I couldn't find the words, and he turned and retreated before I could pull myself together enough to reply.

16

III-Chosen Halloween Costume

Bright and early the next morning, as I was sipping tea with lemon and trying to clear my head of troubled thoughts about Yolanda, I received a text from Daniel. No message, just a link, which took me to a story at the *New York Post:* SEXY PAST OF SLAIN OPERA STAR REVEALED. This was their exclusive reporting, based on information from an unnamed source inside the NYPD. Prominently featured under the headline was Yolanda's profile photo from the Somebody's Baby website. She looked gorgeous and full of life, and it hurt to look at her.

I skimmed the article, then reread it carefully for the full details. Per the inside source, Yolanda had an arrest record: A year ago she'd been busted in New York for solicitation and booked under the name Donatella Fleming. I figured "Fleming" was a reference to superstar soprano Renée Fleming, just as her Carmen Callas alias had to be a reference to Maria Callas.

An arrest for solicitation. Huh. Detective Abernathy had made a good guess when he'd questioned me in the back of the police car.

According to the article, the police already had a suspect in custody. It was our waiter from Chanteur Malheureux; the *Post* had his mug shot, in which he looked sallow and scared, great swaths of his hair escaping its bun and dangling around his shoulders. His name was Kerr Nolan, and he was thirty-three; he had a police record for domestic violence, having once broken a girlfriend's arm at the elbow when he slammed her face first into the refrigerator during an argument. He was currently under arrest but not yet charged; a group of his friends had sworn he'd spent the night of Yolanda's murder partying with them after his shift at Chanteur Malheureux ended, but investigators were confident his alibi would collapse after a little digging.

I was mentioned in the article, identified by name as Yolanda's castmate and the unfortunate recipient of a drugged cocktail presumably intended for her. According to the *Post*'s source, my police-ordered blood test showed I had enough flunitrazepam—better known by the trade name Rohypnol—in my system to keep me unconscious at the time of the murder. Yolanda had guessed correctly: I'd been roofied.

I felt a little better after reading the article. It was good that a brutal murderer was likely off the streets, of course, but selfishly I felt relieved that the investigation might be wrapped up soon, and that I might be entirely out from under suspicion.

There was no morning block of rehearsal today. Instead, we were having our costume fittings. I had the first appointment. Brio's in-house costumer, Ana, was a wraithlike woman with long yellow hair worn in multiple braids and mandala tattoos running up and down her arms. She smelled of sandalwood and coffee, and she was all business as she laced me into a corset topped with a molded plastic breastplate that gave me golden boobs shaped like oversized snow globes.

Working in spandex, plastic, and vinyl, she'd made the corset herself, along with a matching pair of tight vinyl shorts that were strategically padded to give me the illusion of curvy hips and a perky ass. For footwear, she presented me with a pair of thigh-high white platform boots. She stood back, hands on her hips, and watched as I strutted around the costume shop, bending and twisting, raising my arms above my head, testing the costume for fit and flexibility.

"I want to increase the height on those," she said, gesturing to the boots. "Maybe an extra two inches. You have short legs, so we need to lengthen your silhouette." She looked up at me, her expression sharp. "You think you could manage that?"

There was already a four-inch platform; another two inches would be precarious. Still, if it looked good on the stage . . . "I'll practice," I said.

She nodded and leaned in to tug the hem of my shorts. This was the costume I'd wear in the first act; for the second, I'd change into a tight green dress covered with sequins. I'd also tried on a fur cloak, which I'd throw on over the corset for the scene set on the ice planet.

The doors to the main theater had been open when I'd arrived this morning, and I'd peeked inside on my way to the costume shop. The backdrops had been transported from the scene shop onto the stage, and I had a chance to see them for the first time, stylized renditions of multicolored spaceship interiors, icy planet surfaces, and decadent alien cities. I'd felt relief at the sight of them; they reassured me that, despite all the chaos and horror, the show would go on.

Daniel knocked on the open door. He looked exhausted and underfed, but that wasn't unusual for him; during the production of *Satyricon* he'd started out youthful and vibrant, and by opening night he looked like a corpse. "How's it coming?" he asked. He scrutinized me and frowned, which made me suspect I looked like a kid in an ill-chosen Halloween costume.

Yolanda would have looked like a goddess in this outfit. Hidden beneath the gold plastic snow globes, my underwhelming tits had plenty of spare room. Yolanda would have poured out over the top; she would have strained the seams of these shorts, no padding required. She would have looked voluptuous, fleshy, and very, very sexy.

"That's nice," Daniel said at last. "Looks good." He didn't sound like he meant it, and Ana twitched her right eyebrow, vigilant for any criticism of her craftsmanship. "Could we go higher with the boots, do you think?"

"I think it's going to work really well. Especially when I get the wig on," I said.

"I'm sure it'll be fine." He seemed weary. "How are you holding up?"

Yesterday's feeling of numb sickness had ebbed, and a façade of normalcy had settled over me. "I'm fine," I said. I wasn't sure I meant it. "Now that there's been an arrest, I'm looking forward to moving on from . . . all of that."

"Yes." Daniel sounded glum, like he didn't think there was much chance of moving on. I looked at him in concern. He kept staring at my face, then staring at the costume, and his expression was bleak.

Ah. It was a mercenary way of looking at it, but Yolanda's murder had solved two pressing problems for me: I no longer had to worry about her killing me, and I no longer had to worry about her stealing my role. But Daniel's problems still existed: He was still stuck with me in the lead, and he still viewed me as an underwhelming Barbarella. And now Yolanda wasn't around to step in and rescue his production with her beauty and sex appeal.

After Ana was done with me, I was free for the rest of the morning while my castmates had their own individual fittings, so I headed upstairs to the third floor and holed up in a practice room. Midway through my big aria, I was interrupted by a knock on the door. Before I could open it, Julie burst in. "Sorry to bug you, Kit. Have you seen Daniel?"

"Not since my fitting," I said.

"Maybe he ran downstairs for coffee. I'll check the café." Julie rubbed her arms and looked behind her, distracted. "Some detective is here to talk to him. If you see Daniel, tell him he's in his office, okay? I didn't want to leave him there, but he insisted." Before I could answer, she was already hurrying toward the stairs.

A detective. Abernathy, I was willing to bet. Why did he want to talk to Daniel? The suspect in custody—that waiter, Kerr Nolan—had no ties to Brio. A knot started to form in my stomach as I realized Abernathy probably wanted to question Daniel about me. Even though my blood test proved I'd been drugged, I could easily fall under police scrutiny again if Nolan's alibi held up.

Abernathy was in Daniel's office right now, and I was desperate to know why. It occurred to me that I might have a way to find out. The big window at the end of the corridor opened onto the fire escape right above Daniel's office. If Daniel's window was open, as it so often was . . .

The window frame was old wood, but I eased up the sash noiselessly. The window was opened and closed multiple times on a daily basis, as the fire escape was a popular hangout for actors rehearsing for one of the other productions taking place in this building; they'd slip outside for cigarette breaks, causing Daniel to gripe about the smoke that would drift into his office.

I climbed onto the wrought iron landing. Keeping my weight on the front of my toes, I crept down a few steps, then dropped into a crouch when I reached Daniel's window. It was double-hung, with the bottom sash fully open; I was hidden from view by the shade, which was pulled down over the top half. From my vantage point, I could peer into the office.

I was startled to see the back of Daniel's dark overcoat. He was seated at his desk, which came as a surprise, considering that Julie had been searching the building for him. He'd have to scrunch down and crane his head at a weird angle to catch a glimpse of me, but all the same, I kept myself frozen in my crouch, afraid to shift my weight even slightly in case the ancient steps decided to creak. It wasn't the most comfortable position, but my theater training had prepared me for this: All performers know how to remain perfectly motionless onstage for long periods of time. This holds especially true for those of us who've spent most of our careers at the back of the stage.

I squatted down as low as I could get, hoping to overhear some of his conversation with Abernathy, but he was silent. When he shifted in his chair, bending over his laptop to squint at the screen, hands on the keyboard, I caught a glimpse of fair curly hair. It dawned on me that it wasn't Daniel at all: Abernathy was alone in the office, and he was snooping on Daniel's laptop.

It was windy and freezing out on the fire escape, and the cold air billowing into Daniel's office must have annoyed Abernathy, because he abruptly swiveled around in Daniel's chair and scooted it over to the window. It was all I could do to remain frozen in place. If Abernathy got it into his head to look up, he'd spot me, and there was no innocent explanation for what I was doing here. Much to my relief, he yanked the sash down without glancing in my direction, then swiveled back around to face the laptop.

Noiselessly, I crept back up the fire escape to the third-floor landing, then retreated to the safety of the practice room. With the door shut, I felt secure enough to process what I'd seen.

Based on the questions he'd asked me in the police car as well as his curiosity about whatever was on Daniel's laptop, Abernathy clearly had some special interest in Daniel. Niko, too: I remembered the way Abernathy's attention had sharpened when I'd mentioned Niko. I took out my phone and started investigating.

A cursory google of the Toska brothers revealed no obvious red flags. I found a bunch of pieces on Daniel and his work with Brio, which told me nothing I hadn't already known. As to Niko, I came up with a five-year-old puff piece on a nightclub he had launched in Long Island City in partnership with a nightlife impresario with the faintly absurd name of Charlie Global. The piece included a photo of a grinning and likely shit-faced Niko posing with a gaggle of beautiful women; he looked like a version of his younger brother from some parallel universe where Daniel was sexy and fun. It mentioned that Niko was the eldest son of prominent developer Dorian Toska, past president of the Bronx Chamber of Commerce, who owned a cluster of valuable properties throughout the city.

So what was Abernathy's interest in Niko and Daniel? Did it have something to do with some past investigation? I couldn't find any connection online between Abernathy and the Toskas, but I did discover that Abernathy was apparently a relatively recent transfer to Homicide, following what seemed like a long and storied history in the NYPD's Criminal Enterprise Division; he was quoted in dozens of news articles about large-scale investigations into rings of smugglers and money launderers.

All of that seemed like it could be leading somewhere interesting. Even still, I didn't want to be anywhere in the building right now, just in case Abernathy decided he might as well interrogate me again as long as he was here. I grabbed my coat and my purse and headed for the exit.

I ran into Daniel on the front stairs. He was gripping a paper coffee cup in one hand, and he looked like death. "A detective is in your office right now," I told him.

He didn't even pause. He continued up the stairs. "I know. I just saw Julie's text."

As he moved past me, I made a fast decision. "Hey, Daniel?"

He stopped and turned his head to look at me without moving the rest of his body, in no mood for a chat. "I was out on the fire escape just now. I was just getting some air," I said. My cheeks felt warm at the obvious lie. "I happened to look inside your office, and the detective was sitting at your desk. He was snooping around on your laptop."

He turned all the way around to face me. "What?" He was alarmed, but more than that, he seemed genuinely baffled. "Because of Yolanda?"

"Maybe, but I doubt it," I said. "If it means anything to

you, this detective, Detective Abernathy, he used to work for another NYPD division. Criminal Enterprise."

The baffled look disappeared, and his face shut down. "Thank you for telling me," he said. It was cold and curt, and it was clear he didn't want any further discussion on the subject.

Too bad for him. I wanted a discussion. I wanted to make it clear that I'd just done him a favor and thus expected some form of quid pro quo, but I couldn't figure out how to phrase it. "I'm always going to do whatever's best for the opera, Daniel. You know that, right?"

"I know you will." Daniel's eyes met mine. "You've always been a team player, Kit."

It hung in the air, and I wanted to push the subject, make it explicit: I was helping him, so he should help me in return. He should admit I was his Barbarella; he should stop making me terrified of being replaced at any moment. But I didn't know how to get him to do that, and Daniel eventually turned away from me and continued up the stairs to the building entrance without another word.

I felt stupid. Yolanda would have pulled that off. Yolanda would have leveraged the information to extort an ironclad promise from Daniel that Barbarella was hers.

Danny will never fire me. Danny wouldn't dare.

Belatedly, for the first time since I'd woken up in Yolanda's bed, those words from the night of her murder came back to me. Not extortion, but blackmail: She'd been blackmailing Daniel and Niko, and that's how she'd known she'd never get fired from the production, no matter how much chaos she caused. I had no idea what damaging secret Yolanda had held over their heads, but I knew blackmail was a good motive for murder, and maybe I'd just done something very foolish by giving Daniel a heads-up that he should cover his tracks.

17

King Leopold

After our afternoon block of rehearsal had ended, I found myself wandering south on foot instead of heading for the train, acting on an idea that had been tickling in my head since yesterday when I'd realized Yolanda's kid would need to be told about her dead mother. I didn't remember exactly where Yolanda had lived, but navigation turned out to be intuitive, and before long I was standing in front of her apartment building.

It had three floors and six units. On the call box by the door, I saw a neatly typed label for ARCHAMBEAU beside the button for unit five. I didn't know Leo's last name, but there was a DE GRAAF in unit six, and "de Graaf" seemed like a fitting surname for poised, aristocratic Leo. I pressed the button.

Almost immediately, I heard a male voice, crisp and direct. "Yes?"

I leaned close to the intercom. "Is this Leo?" I asked.

There was silence. I continued: "I'm Kit Margolis. I met you the other night. I was with Yolanda when she lost her keys; you unlocked her apartment. May I talk to you?"

There was another silence, and then a buzzer sounded. With a click, the front door unlatched.

As soon as I entered the foyer, I felt nauseous. Impressions of that wretched night came over me: my sickness and confusion, Yolanda's anger and casual cruelty. I headed up the stairs, treading once more on that thick black carpet covered with gold fleurs-de-lis.

When I reached the top level, the door opposite Yolanda's unit swung open. Leo stood in the doorway.

He was as decorative as he'd been the first time I'd seen him. He was in a soft blue sweater, and his dark blond hair was swept off his sculpted face. His eyes were pale amber, almost gold. He observed me, his face impassive.

"You look much better than you did the other night," he said. "I'm sorry, I didn't get your name."

"Kit. Kit Margolis," I said. His expression was glacial; his body language was unwelcoming. "Yolanda and I knew each other from the opera we were both in. She was my understudy."

His face lightened. "You must be the one Niko mentioned. Your mother is the actress, correct? The one who was in all those terrible films." He smiled. "I'm sorry. That was a thoughtless thing to say about someone's mother."

He stepped back from the door. "Do you want to come in?"

The frostiness had receded, and surely it couldn't have anything to do with my awful mother. It must be Niko: Niko thought I was okay, so Leo thought I was okay as well.

Niko . . . Yolanda and Leo had discussed something about Niko during that long, horrible night, though if I tried to remember it, it slithered out of my grasp, like trying to grab a swimming fish with bare hands. "It's okay. Her films really *were* terrible," I said.

I followed him into an enormous living room. Leo's apartment was much bigger than Yolanda's, maybe three or four times the size. The street-facing wall featured a bay window on each end, bookending a large octagonal window divided up into diamond-shaped panes of leaded glass. His furniture was austere and masculine; I saw a lot of chrome-accented black leather. Above a black marble fireplace hung a huge unframed Basquiat, done in vivid lines and stark colors, angry shapes topped with a scribbled golden crown; of course it was a print, but I had a fleeting sensation that maybe, possibly, in these surroundings, it could be real.

Leo gestured toward a leather sofa, then waited for me to be seated before choosing an armchair across from me. He crossed his legs at the knee and settled back. "Niko forced me to watch one of your mother's films. I want to say . . . *Bikini Nurses?*"

"*Bikini Hospital,*" I said. "I didn't realize you and Niko were friends." That was disingenuous, but I had a hunch it might be better if Leo assumed I had no memory of his conversation with Yolanda. I couldn't remember the details, but things had been said that Leo hadn't wanted me to overhear.

"I've known Niko since our undergraduate days. He was my roommate in our freshman dormitory, and we got on well enough that we later found an apartment together in New Haven."

"New Haven" was coy. He and Niko were Yalies. "Did you meet Yolanda through Niko, or was it vice versa?"

"Niko met her first." There was a hint of reserve to it. He gestured around his apartment. "This was originally a private home, long ago. It's been in my family for generations, and when I started work in the city, my father sold it to me. I rent out the other units as a hobby." I nodded, having no idea where he was going with this. Maybe he was just seizing a chance to flaunt what I was beginning to suspect was immense familial wealth. "When Niko mentioned that Yolanda was looking for a place, I was able to help her out."

Fragments of the conversation between Leo and Yolanda popped into my head: *You love all the things my mouth does for you. I could lease your unit to someone who actually pays rent.* What were the details of their arrangement? Had Yolanda been sleeping with Leo in lieu of rent? Was Niko okay with that? I had questions, but there was no diplomatic way to ask them, so I kept quiet.

"What can I do for you, Kit?" Leo asked.

"Did you hear the police have someone in custody?"

"I read about that this morning." Leo smiled. He had a contradictory smile: It was stiff and closed-lipped, yet it somehow managed to seem warm and even charming. "I'm glad. It's good from the standpoint of justice, of course, but from a selfish perspective, I'm relieved to hear I'm no longer under suspicion."

It had, of course, occurred to me that Leo would be a suspect, since he clearly had a personal relationship with Yolanda as well as access to her apartment. Were it not for the arrest of the waiter, I wouldn't have boldly entered his living space to talk to him. "I know the feeling," I said.

"I imagine you do," he said, and it dawned on me that he'd very naturally considered me a potential murderer as well. "I went out to dinner with clients that night. We had a late reservation at Jean-Georges, and then afterward I met friends for drinks. I returned here to find a police officer guarding the entrance to the building. It was . . . alarming."

I didn't bother to mention that I'd observed his return from my vantage point in the back seat of a cop car. The less I thought about that night, the better. "Yolanda had mentioned to me that she has a young daughter."

Leo just nodded. "The cesarean scar. I asked her about it once. She said it was a boring subject."

"She left her kid with a friend, a former coworker. I want to make sure whoever is taking care of her daughter knows Yolanda is dead, and I want to make sure her daughter is going to be okay; I gather she relied on Yolanda's financial support." The corner of Leo's mouth twitched, like he thought I might be here to hit him up for a donation. "I'm trying to find anyone who knows anything about Yolanda's past."

Leo frowned. "Surely that's something the police will handle."

Daniel had said the same thing. "Probably, yeah. In any case, when the money dries up, I'm sure Yolanda's coworker will eventually figure out what happened. But . . ." I paused to give myself time to decide how much of this I wanted to explain to a stranger. "I don't know how to talk about this. I hadn't known Yolanda very long, and most of that time I didn't like her much. On the night she died, I actively hated her, in a way that I don't think I've hated anyone before. It's abhorrent to even think this, but sometimes I find it a relief that she's dead."

I stopped, thinking I might have gone too far in saying this to someone who might have been close to Yolanda, but Leo just nodded, his expression calm. "Go on."

"But there was something about her." One side of me wanted to do what the various traumas of my childhood had trained me to do: shut up and bury my darker and more painful thoughts. The other side, the side that had spilled my heart and soul out to Yolanda while under the tongue-loosening control of the Rohypnol in my drink, goaded me to continue, to make Leo understand why I owed this peculiar debt to someone I'd despised. "There are parts of me that I feel are missing, and Yolanda had all those parts, probably in too great a quantity. Maybe between us, we could have balanced out into one normal human being." My words tripped over one another as the chaotic thoughts in my brain spilled out of my mouth. "So now I feel like I owe her something, like maybe if I ensure her daughter is okay, that will make us even. Does that make sense?"

It didn't make sense, I knew that even as I said it, and I expected Leo to distance himself from the plain, awkward woman spouting heartfelt nonsense in his living room. My face burned, and I felt exposed; I couldn't have felt more mortified if I'd suddenly found myself sitting naked on Leo's expensive sofa.

But I'd seen a strange light flickering in Leo's eyes as I spoke, even though his face remained expressionless, and I had the curious suspicion that he might know exactly what I meant. His missing parts were probably wildly different from mine, but when I looked at him, so elegant and contained, I could nonetheless detect something fragmented about him.

"It does, in a way." The light had vanished from his eyes. He sounded polite yet distant again, and I knew he wasn't going to confide in me. "Something terrible happened to Yolanda while you were nearby, and you couldn't do anything to save her. Perhaps it's natural you'd want to save her child. But I'm afraid I know very little about her past."

He was retreating within himself, closing down. It was against my nature to push, but I'd exposed myself, and now I was going to push, damn it. I'd earned an answer. "When I first met her, she said she was from New Orleans, but I think that was a lie."

"Ah." Leo smiled, cynical and wry. "Well, she told me she was from Boston, but that definitely was a lie. I tried to talk to her about her favorite local spots, and she knew nothing about the city."

"Is that where you're from?"

He shook his head. "My people are from Sagaponack. But I lived in Cambridge while I was in graduate school."

His coyness about his high-end education was beginning to irritate me. "Harvard or MIT?"

He smiled, and it seemed more genuine this time. "Harvard. Business school. I would have made a terrible engineer."

"Did Yolanda have any close friends? Someone she might have told about her past?" I asked.

"Told the truth, you mean?" It was sour. We sat in silence while he gave the matter some consideration.

"Balenciaga is a possibility," he said slowly. In response to my look of confusion, he elaborated: "Niko and I had dinner with Yolanda and a woman named Balenciaga a few times. She seemed on easy terms with Yolanda, as though they knew each other well."

"You know how I could contact her?"

Another head shake. "I don't have her number."

"Would Niko?"

He took his time before replying. "I think that might be something you won't want to bother Niko about," he said.

"Why not?"

"Because . . ." For the first time, Leo seemed to flail. He glanced around his living room as though the answer lay somewhere among all the chrome and leather. "We're drifting into areas that aren't mine to discuss," he said at last.

"I just want to make sure her kid's okay," I said. "I don't want to cause trouble for you, or for Niko, or anyone."

"I don't think I can help you," he said. "I shouldn't have brought it up."

He seemed unhappy about turning me down, and that gave me a flicker of hope. But why was this causing him so much inner turmoil? I thought about it, and then I had it. Balenciaga. According to the *New York Post*, Yolanda had been arrested and booked under the name Donatella.

"I know Yolanda was busted for solicitation, if that has anything to do with this." I kept my tone neutral.

"Ah." The amber eyes focused on me. "And what are your feelings on that?"

"I haven't had time to think about it. I had reasons to dislike Yolanda, but her being a sex worker wasn't one of them."

Leo was quiet, and then he nodded. "If you're looking for Balenciaga, you can find her on Angels in the City. Do you know what that is?" he asked. When I shook my head, he continued: "It's an app. It's targeted toward busy young professionals. If you need a dinner date, or someone to go to the theater with you, or if you just want . . . companionship, it connects you with a top-shelf escort."

His use of the phrase "top-shelf" annoyed me, like he was comparing women to bottles of booze. "We're talking about prostitution, right?"

"Not at all. It's an escort service." He shook his head, lips pressed together, suddenly very prim. "Legally speaking, there's a world of difference."

It was a difference I couldn't parse, but I decided to move on. "And that's how you met Yolanda and Balenciaga. Through Angels in the City."

"Many of my peers use it." It was defensive. "It's a shortcut. Dating can be difficult, especially when you're . . . Well. I have money." He said it like a confession, like that fact could possibly come as a shock to me at this point. "When wealth is involved, a casual date can lead to nonviable expectations of a long-term commitment, and it can be a bit much when all you want is a single memorable evening. The app removes that pressure. It's not much different from any internet dating service, only the escorts are vetted carefully in advance."

"And it's legal?"

"As long as it's clear you're only paying for a woman's time, certainly." Leo shrugged, making the gesture seem elegant. "If, during the course of a pleasant evening, two consenting adults decide to take things further, that has nothing to do with the escort service. It's all perfectly aboveboard. Angels in the City cleared one point four million last year, and all that income was reported honestly and accurately." He smiled. "I should know; I handle their books."

Ah. "You're an accountant?"

"I'm a financial manager." He made the correction in a tone that suggested it mattered greatly, which I suppose it did; I wouldn't know. I filed my own taxes each year, and I planned on doing it that way until I someday managed to move up into a less underwhelming tax bracket.

"So if I were to try to contact Balenciaga . . . ?"

"I would suggest you download the app and set up a date."

My very own date with a sex worker. "It's probably pretty expensive, right?" I tried to sound light.

"It is." The thin-lipped smile returned. "Search for my profile on the app under Users and add me as a friend, and I'll apply a promotional code to your account. My username is 'kingleo-pold,' no caps or spaces."

King Leopold. Yolanda had called him that on the night she was murdered. "Thank you for your help, Leo." I rose to my feet.

Leo walked me to the door. He hesitated, hand on the knob. "You said you had some reasons to hate Yolanda?"

"She tried to do me harm," I said. "I gave her the benefit of the doubt, because she was so beautiful and magnetic, but it didn't turn out well."

"She was cruel to you on the night she was killed. I don't know if you remember," Leo said.

"I remember." She'd made a spiteful remark about my appearance in front of Leo. She'd been crueler after he'd left.

"She had a gift for making enemies." Again those lion eyes were fixed on mine. "And she was reckless. She couldn't prevent herself from retaliating against perceived threats, even when lashing out was likely to cause harm to herself."

I thought about the macarons she'd given to me, possibly laced with something nasty. If I'd eaten them and died, the trail would have led straight back to her. Maybe she'd been confident she could charm her way out of trouble. "I have an impolite question. You don't have to answer it," I said.

"Yes?" There was a new wariness in those eyes.

"How do you feel about her death?"

The answer was immediate. "Horrified. Gutted. Broken-hearted." He paused, and then said the word I'd suspected was coming: "Relieved."

I nodded. All of that was the truth. "Thank you for talking to me."

He opened the door. "I'm glad you're feeling better, Kit. Give my best to Balenciaga, if you see her."

I glanced back at him once when I reached the stairwell, and he was still standing in the doorway, watching after me, his expression unreadable.

—

Leo weighed heavily on my mind during my walk to the subway. He'd been lovely in some ways, friendly and unexpectedly helpful, but his reference to "top-shelf" escorts still rankled me, and if I thought about it, there was something grotesque about the ability to apply a promotional code on an app to get a free visit from a sex worker. I understood that many people viewed sex as a commodity, but that didn't mean I felt comfortable with the idea.

As I crossed Second Avenue, I passed in front of a grand old bank building, a churchlike structure of white marble with tall pillars in front and a crown-topped dome on the roof. Words were carved above the front doors: DE GRAAF BANK OF NEW YORK. A Walgreens now took up residence within, and I suspected the bank itself had been bought and absorbed by some conglomerate decades ago, but if Leo was any indication, it seemed the de Graaf family had held on to its riches.

18

First-Time Client

Later that night, safe in my apartment, I downloaded the Angels in the City app and created an account. I found Leo's profile—kingleopold—and added him as a friend; Leo and I weren't friends and never would be, but he had offered to do me an expensive favor, and I planned on taking him up on it. When I explored the app, I found myself staring at a series of well-lit, well-composed photographs of beautiful young women clad in formal evening attire smiling beguilingly at the lens. A separate section was devoted to male escorts; it wasn't extensive, but at least Angels in the City wasn't strictly confined to the purchase of women by men.

Angels in the City, it seemed from the marketing copy, provided attractive and cultured escorts to accompany clients to dinners, to business functions, to the theater, to the ballet, to the opera. Bookings were made in ninety-minute chunks, payable in advance via the website. There was no suggestion in the careful wording that intimacy would be involved or expected.

Balenciaga. There she was. She was Asian and probably in her early twenties, though her photo was expertly airbrushed to remove all signs of skin texture. She had long white hair, and she wore a white satin camisole over wide-legged black pants.

She sat on a love seat and posed like a fashion model, knees splayed wide, hands braced against her thighs, elbows jutting out at sharp angles. Her expression was challenging, but with a hint of humor in her raised brows and the faint curve of her lips.

I could make an appointment with Balenciaga, should I choose. I didn't know whether I did, in fact, choose, but I took a look at her calendar. Balenciaga was popular: She was already booked for the next three weekends, though she had a slot open for tomorrow night. While I was wondering whether this endeavor was madness, my phone beeped to alert me to a new message: Angels in the City user kingleopold had applied a ninety-minute promotional credit to my account. I took a deep breath and made an appointment for tomorrow.

For the first three appointments with any new client, the Angels did not pay visits to private residences, which was probably a good call in terms of escort safety. The app gave me the chance to choose a site for our rendezvous from an extensive drop-down menu of preapproved hotels, which were mostly higher-end chains.

I reserved a room for Thursday night at a business hotel near JFK, because a hotel within Manhattan would have torpedoed my monthly budget. I then booked my ninety-minute slot with Balenciaga for tomorrow and felt a small thrill of accomplishment when Leo's promotional credit was applied, showing my payable balance as zero.

I spent the rest of the evening convinced I should call off this whole operation. More than once, I sat on my bed with my finger hovering over the phone's screen, gearing up to cancel my appointment. I shouldn't squander my time hunting down Yolanda's kid; I needed to focus my energy on the opera. Despite my fumbling explanation to Leo, I knew I didn't owe Yolanda anything, not really.

But I couldn't let go of her, not just yet. In the brief time our paths had crossed, she had burned her way into my soul with her beauty and her vibrancy and her startling cruelty, and I knew I wouldn't have any peace until I discovered the source of her vitality. Something in her past had turned her into a glittering, fascinating force of destruction. Maybe if I tracked down the daughter she'd abandoned, I'd unearth some of her secrets.

By Thursday after rehearsal, I was a mass of nerves. What exactly does one wear to a sex-free hotel-room rendezvous with an escort? I eventually settled on a high-necked black dress that I'd last worn to the cast party for *Satyricon*, then donned my only pair of high heels, which were scuffed and frumpy. I applied a full face of makeup, then stared at my reflection in the bathroom mirror for a very long time. I looked like my mother, and that made me feel lonely and miserable, so I scrubbed my skin until it was red and shiny and headed out into the world with my face determinedly bare.

It was unlike me to fret about my appearance, but I'd spent the past few weeks in the company of absurdly attractive people, like Yolanda, Carlo, Roksana, Niko, and Leo, and unless Balenciaga's pictures on the Angels in the City app had been airbrushed into the realm of the fantastical, she fell into that category as well. I could feel strange neuroses beginning to take root in my psyche, wreaking havoc on my self-image.

I checked into the hotel room and wasted too much time channel-surfing through crap in a search for something watchable. I finally turned off the television and listened to *La Traviata* on my phone, lying on my back on the king-size bed, eyes closed, willing myself to unwind.

The landline on the bedside table rang, a soft electronic chirp that jolted me out of my music trance. A crisp female voice from the reception desk alerted me to the arrival of a Miss Balenciaga, and should she send her up to my room? I told her to go ahead.

I heard a knock on the door, a percussive pounding that

made me fear the police had arrived to bust me for hiring a sex worker. My hand fumbled with the security latch before I got the door open.

Balenciaga, petite as she was, had one hell of a loud knock. She grinned at me from the doorway. "Hiya," she said. "Kit?"

"Yeah." It came out as a weird croak. "Come in."

I stepped aside to let her enter, then closed the door behind her. My hand instinctively went to the latch, because that's what I did every time I closed a door in a hotel room, what with being a single female traveler. It dawned on me that maybe Balenciaga wouldn't appreciate being locked in with a client, so I left it alone. "You're Balenciaga?"

"The one and only," she said, and giggled. She wandered around the small space, peeking into the bathroom, behind the curtains, under the bed. Undoubtedly she was looking for bad surprises: a cop lurking in the shower stall waiting to bust her, a gaggle of drunk and horny men hiding in the closet. After confirming that she and I were alone, she looked at me and smiled again. "Well."

Up close, she was beautiful in a more grounded way than she'd looked in her retouched photos. Her hair was loose around her shoulders; it was a silvery shade of white, as in her photos, the color so consistent from roots to tips that I wondered if it was an expensive wig. She unbuttoned her long black coat and draped it over the back of a chair. Beneath it she wore a sleeveless silver top paired with black velvet pants and dangling crystal earrings. "Do you have anything to drink?" she asked.

"Oh. I don't. Sorry," I said. Damn it, I hadn't thought of that, and the room didn't have a minibar. "I can have something sent up?"

"That'd be great. I'd love champagne." She probably saw something in my face, and she laughed. It was a nice laugh, pitched to put me at ease. "I'm not trying to hustle you for a bottle of Dom. This place sells prosecco by the glass, and it's only like twelve bucks. But Diet Coke would be fine, too."

"Prosecco sounds good." My voice sounded foreign to my ears, thick, awkward. "I'll order a bottle."

"Cool. Thanks." Balenciaga had a small dimple in her chin that came out when she smiled. She glanced around the room. "Can I sit?"

"Please." She perched on the edge of the bed, legs crossed at the knee, leaning back, supporting herself on her arms. She observed me as I called the front desk and stammered my way through the order.

"First-time client?" Balenciaga asked.

"It's probably obvious, right?"

Balenciaga shrugged. "The agency always lets me know what I'm getting into. I know your name is Kit, and I know you're pretty nervous right now. And you know what, you don't need to be. You and I will drink a little bubbly, and we'll chat for as long as you want, and then we'll decide what our next step should be. Right?"

"I need to let you know . . ." I inhaled, then came out with it. "I have you here under false pretenses. I just want to talk to you. That's all."

"Sure. Whatever you want." Balenciaga seemed unconcerned. "Are you a journalist?"

"What? No, why?"

"I got one of those last year. A new client turned out to be researching a piece for *Esquire* on the history of call girls in New York and how they're becoming a relic of the past in the digital age, now that everyone has turned online for sexual gratification. It ended up being a really insightful piece; I was flattered to be included. But you remind me of him."

I was saved from answering by a soft knock on the door. I signed for the delivery of the prosecco, which came in a tin bucket filled with ice, accompanied by a pair of flutes. The room service waiter offered to pour it out, but I told him I'd handle the bottle myself, which turned out to be a mistake. The cork wouldn't budge no matter how hard I wrenched it; Balenciaga saved the day by taking the bottle from my hands and using both thumbs to ease the cork out of the neck with a soft pop. She handed the bottle back to me. It fizzed and over-flowed as I poured it out. I handed her a flute, wet and sticky. "Cheers."

She giggled as she accepted her dripping glass, but there was nothing mocking about it. "Cheers," she replied.

I sat beside her on the bed, and we clinked glasses and sipped. The prosecco gave me time to consider the best way to approach this. "I'm not a journalist, but . . ." I inhaled. "I wanted to talk to you about Yolanda Archambeau."

She paused, the rim of the flute touching her lower lip, which was glossy and beige. She lowered it and looked at me. "Do you have a badge you can show me?"

"I don't. I'm not a cop. I'm an opera singer. I knew Yolanda professionally. Did you hear about her murder?"

"I read about it online." Balenciaga was all business now, crisp and professional. "But how do I know you're not a cop?"

"I guess you have to trust me," I said. It was exactly the wrong thing to say; Balenciaga's eyes narrowed. "Look, I'm a singer. I'm performing the lead role in a new opera, and Yolanda was my understudy. I was asleep in her apartment the night she was killed."

Balenciaga examined me with a critical eye. "You look more like a cop than an opera singer," she said.

I didn't think I looked like a cop, but I knew what she meant about not looking like an opera singer. "I'm not glamorous like Yolanda was, but . . . look, this is me." I got out my phone and navigated to my professional website, which contained my CV, contact info, sound clips, and photos from past performances. The splash page featured a large color photo from a performance at Eastman in which I'd played the Nymph in Purcell's *Fairy-Queen*.

Balenciaga squinted at the photo, me in a gauzy pastel slip and tights, wildflowers woven throughout my tangled red wig. "That doesn't look like you," she said.

"I clean up pretty well," I said.

"Makeup helps a lot," Balenciaga said. She handed back my phone and squinted at my face.

My cheeks burned under her scrutiny. I shouldn't have jettisoned my initial impulse to try to look a bit more appealing; I should have adjusted my exterior so I could slip into Yolanda's enticing world. I took a drink of my prosecco to hide my nerves. Balenciaga's flute was already empty, so I poured her a refill.

"During the day, I work at the Sephora on Madison near the park," she said. "Makeovers are my specialty. Do you want me to show you a simple daytime look?" She rummaged in her purse, a big brown tote emblazoned with the Louis Vuitton logo in a repeating pattern, and extracted a black velvet clutch. She turned it upside down and dumped a bunch of high-end cosmetics and a set of brushes with rose-gold handles onto the bedspread.

"No, that's fine. I'm good," I said. "I just want you to tell me about Yolanda. Someone said you two were friends."

"Someone?" Balenciaga looked alarmed.

"Leo de Graaf. He gave me your name."

"Oh, *Leo*." That put her at ease immediately. "If it's okay with Leo, it's fine. But first of all, to be clear, I don't know anyone named Yolanda. I know that an opera singer named Yolanda got killed the other day; I saw that story in the *Post*. And I saw the photo that ran with the story, and I know the dead girl looks a lot like a girl I used to know in a professional capacity."

"What was her real name?" I asked.

Balenciaga shrugged. "Who knows? Real names don't get used much in this line of work. Aliases based on fashion designers are always popular. I know a Dior, a Dolce, and at least two Chanels."

Like Yolanda's webcam clients, Don José and the others, giving themselves opera-themed aliases as a way to feel closer to her. Yolanda's life had been a tangle of aliases and deceptions. "You mean your name isn't really Balenciaga?"

Balenciaga grinned at that. "Donatella. That's what she went by. Or at least the Donatella I knew looks a whole bunch like the dead girl in the *Post*. I worked with her a handful of times."

"You were friends?"

"I guess so. At least in the early days, we got along. We looked good together. She was heavier than me and had bigger boobs, but we were the same height and had similar hair color. Aesthetically we made sense as a pair, so if a client booked two girls and didn't specify who they wanted, the agency would sometimes send us both, if we were available that night."

I'd never thought about the aesthetic concerns involved in hiring sex workers in pairs, but it made sense. Yolanda and Balenciaga *would* have looked good together. "So you knew stuff about her? Like, her personal life?"

Balenciaga didn't answer. She dug through the mess of spilled cosmetics on the bedspread and came up with a pair of tweezers with long, pointy tips. "Can I at least do your brows? They're really bugging me. Two minutes, and I swear, you'll notice a world of difference."

"My brows are fine," I said. I had no idea if they were. At no time in my life had I contemplated my eyebrows.

"They're uneven," Balenciaga said firmly. "Brows are the frame that holds the artwork of the face. Every time I look at you, it's like I'm staring at a painting hung crookedly on the wall."

"What did Yolanda—Donatella—tell you about herself?"

"Let me do your brows, and we'll talk."

I was being extorted into getting my eyebrows plucked. Unbelievable. I figured it ultimately didn't matter what she did to my face; any damage could be fixed with stage makeup. "Knock yourself out," I said.

Her face brightened. "Awesome. Thanks." She kicked off her spike-heeled boots and sat cross-legged on the bed. Tweezers in one hand, she gripped my chin with the other. "Hold still."

"About Yolanda," I said.

"I don't know much about her." Balenciaga set to work with the tweezers, plucking with small, rapid movements, extracting hairs seemingly at random, switching between brows after every couple of hairs. It was alarming. I had the sense she was fully denuding my face. "We mostly met on business occasions."

"How long ago was this?" It was hard to concentrate on the conversation.

"Last time I worked with her was in the spring. First time was maybe a year ago? It could be a bit longer." Balenciaga leaned back a few inches, frowned, and resumed her attack.

"How'd she get the job?"

Balenciaga shrugged. "Probably the same way I did. I found the website and applied online. There's a link where you can fill out a form and attach photos or videos. I got called in for an in-person interview, and by the end of the day I was booked for my first client. Honestly, it was pretty much the same process as getting the job at Sephora."

"Do you like this kind of work?" I asked.

She frowned at me, then smiled. "Sorry. I'm just trying to evaluate the level of judgment in your tone. I get a lot of guys asking me that question, because apparently I'm supposed to loathe every minute but desperately need the cash, or else I'm doing this because I have low self-esteem or whatever. Honestly, I'm fine with doing this. I'm a people person, right? I know Donatella preferred camgirl work, but for me that's too impersonal. Guys you can't see ordering you to do stuff, like you're a character in a video game? Not my thing." She wrinkled her nose.

"Being a camgirl is probably safer than meeting clients in person, right?" I didn't know where I was going with this, but Balenciaga seemed willing to chat, and maybe something she said would give me insights into Yolanda.

"Sure, it can be, if you're careful about it. I don't think Donatella was ever that concerned with the safety aspect, though. She'd take basic precautions, like using a VPN so no one could track down where she lived, but then she'd brag to me about all the expensive gifts her clients would mail to her." Balenciaga rolled her eyes.

I fell silent, wondering how to phrase my next question without causing offense. Balenciaga saw something in my face and laughed. "I know you're thinking I'm kidding myself, because obviously escort work comes with its own set of dangers. But the agency does a good job of protecting us, like making all clients set up an account on the app. Knowing we have their credit card on file makes guys a lot less likely to misbehave."

Tweezers held in one hand, her attention still fixed on my brows, Balenciaga picked up her champagne flute from where she'd rested it on the nightstand and took a long drink. "This one time, a client got overly excited and tried out something we hadn't negotiated in advance, some tedious bondage scenario, and while I was in the process of extricating myself from the situation, I tore my rotator cuff. No huge deal, it was more annoying than frightening, and he apologized, but it pissed me off that he didn't listen to me. Like, that's a major no." She shrugged. "So I told Niko—if you know Leo, I figure you know Niko, right?—and boom, the client got his account canceled, just like that. And a few days later, he ended up with a broken arm. Right side, just like my rotator cuff. Whoops."

"Wait, what?" I jerked my head back in surprise.

Balenciaga made a little noise of irritation. She grabbed my chin and resumed her assault on my brows. "I don't know for sure that it had anything to do with what the guy did to me, not one hundred percent. But Niko seemed to want me to draw that conclusion."

"Why did you go to Niko about this?" I asked.

The question confused her. She paused in her task and stared at me. "It's just the way the agency works," she said. "I guess in a bigger organization, I'd go to my supervisor, or maybe the HR director or something. But Angels in the City doesn't have some elaborate corporate structure. We're encouraged to bring problems straight to the owner."

Ah, the owner. So Niko was at the helm of an escort service that had brought in a $1.4 million profit last year, with his close friend and college roommate handling the books. No wonder Niko had the cash to keep his brother's opera company afloat. Balenciaga didn't seem to realize she'd just handed me a small bombshell, and I thought it was time to move on to a new topic before it had a chance to detonate. "Did you know Donatella had a kid?"

"I knew she'd given birth." She winked. "Remember, I saw her naked a bunch of times."

"So she never talked to you about her daughter?"

"We didn't talk about our personal lives that much." Balenciaga's face was very close to mine as she mauled my eyebrows. She smelled good, but in a way that was a jarring blend of sophisticated and childish, like gardenias mixed with strawberry milkshakes. "Why are you asking?"

"She left her daughter in the care of a former coworker." I shrugged. "I want to locate the kid and make sure her caregiver knows about Yolanda's death."

Balenciaga sat back and lowered the tweezers. She moved my face left and right, up and down, looking at my brows from all angles. "Okay, wow, that's so much better. You want to look in the mirror?"

"Later," I said. I was terrified she'd left me with no brows at all. I was fine with looking plain, but I didn't want to look ridiculous. "First I want you to tell me everything you know about Donatella's past. Did she ever say anything to you about where she was from?"

"Sure." Balenciaga started replacing her makeup in her velvet clutch. "She said she grew up in Miami, but that was a lie. She was from Maine."

New Orleans, Boston, Miami, Maine. "How do you know?"

"I figured that out when she first started working for the agency. She'd talk about Miami, but I lived for a while in Miami Beach, and everything she said made me think she was full of crap. Anyway, we were pretty friendly at first, so we'd text each other sometimes. Early on, before she changed it, she had a phone number with a two-oh-seven area code. I knew that wasn't Miami, so I looked it up. It's Maine. The entire state." Balenciaga looked triumphant. "The way I figure it, no one has a Maine area code if they haven't actually lived there."

She had a point. "You said you were friendly with her 'at first.' It sounds like you soured on her."

"Yeah." She twisted up her mouth in distaste. "Okay, this goes back to Leo. I don't know if you've ever been to Donatella's apartment . . ."

"I have."

"Oh, right, you were with her when . . . Okay, so Leo is—was, I guess—her landlord. Although maybe that's not the correct term, because as far as I know, she never paid any rent. That started one night when Leo had us both over at his place. We were doing a Scotch tasting, which was actually *super* boring, but it seemed important to Leo, so I pretended to be enthusiastic. At one point in the evening, he took us on a tour of the vacant apartment across the hall. Apparently back in the day, his great-grandparents lived in that building, only it was a single-family home at the time. That apartment had been the nursery, and the live-in nanny slept there, so it had its own bathroom and kitchen. When the kids were grown, Leo's great-grandfather moved his mistress into the former nursery while he and his wife shared the master suite across the hall." She snorted. "Rich people, right?"

"Let me guess: Leo wanted to resurrect an old family tradition?"

"Right you are." Balenciaga pointed a finger at me and winked, like a game-show host congratulating a contestant. "He asked if one of us would like to live there. The thing was, I knew he really meant it for Donatella, because he was so clearly in love with her. Like, Leo's always so calm and sophisticated, and nothing ever seems to upset or surprise him, but sometimes I'd catch him staring at her, and he'd look . . . I don't know how to describe it. Like an orphan standing outside a big mansion, peering through the windows on Christmas morning while all the rich kids open their presents. Like everything he wanted most in life was so, so close, and yet forever out of his reach." Balenciaga snorted inelegantly. "Sorry. Champagne makes me corny sometimes."

"No, that makes a lot of sense," I said. So Leo loved Yolanda, desperately and hopelessly. If Yolanda hadn't returned that love—and I was willing to bet she hadn't, that she'd been incapable of it—maybe that would be enough to make Leo's outer shell of calm sophistication crack. If Kerr Nolan's alibi continued to hold steady, maybe Abernathy should start chiseling away at Leo's alibi next. "If Leo wanted the apartment for Yolanda, do you think he was including you in his offer to be polite, or because he liked the idea of the two of you competing for his affections?"

Balenciaga grinned. "You're good at this. Yeah, I'd say he wanted us to fight over him. In any case, I didn't think it was a great idea. On the one hand, free rent, yay! I live with my sisters in Flushing, and let me tell you, I'd love to have my own place. But on the other hand . . ." She exhaled, brow wrinkled.

"You didn't want to live that close to Leo?" I asked. Her flute of prosecco was empty, so I topped off her glass.

"That's not really it. Leo's cool; I like him. But I'm not entirely sure he knows women are actually human beings, if that makes sense."

"Because he pays for escorts?"

"Sure, but I'd be a hypocrite if I held that against him. No, it's the whole thing. Inviting escorts over to lecture us on the nuances of Scotch. Installing Donatella in his home for on-demand commitment-free sex. I'm probably overly sensitive, but I think I would have felt like a zoo exhibit if I'd been in her position." She shrugged. "But I saw no sense in snubbing him, and if you look at it in the right light, it was a generous offer. Of course I made a play for it, telling him how fun it would be to live right next to him."

"And Yolanda didn't like that."

"She most certainly did not." Balenciaga's smile was tight. "Even though he was always going to pick her, even though I was just going through the motions, she got offended. Only she didn't say anything to me. Oh, no. She just invited me on a shopping trip to Saks the next day and slipped a Prada wallet in my purse, which I didn't know about until I set off the alarm at the exit." The smile grew even grimmer. "I talked my way out of an arrest, but I have a lifetime ban at Saks now."

"She put poison in my tea when I criticized her singing," I said.

Balenciaga looked unfazed. "Well, that tracks," she said. She clinked her champagne flute against mine. "To us. For surviving Hurricane Donatella."

I kept at it for a while longer. I had paid for ninety minutes of Balenciaga's time, and I was determined to use it. I didn't learn much; if Yolanda had spilled any details about her past, Balenciaga didn't share them with me. We finished the bottle, and then Balenciaga was on her way, leaving me with a cheerful parting remark that, should I wish, I could submit a review of our encounter and leave her a tip through the Angels in the City app. As I closed and latched the door after her, I caught a glimpse of my reflection in the bathroom mirror. I couldn't fathom why I looked so startled, as though my encounter with Balenciaga had shocked me to the core of my existence.

It was the eyebrows. She'd tweezed them into high tapered arches, thus dooming me to look like everything in my life came as a surprise.

19

Unicorns and Rainbows

Since I'd paid for the hotel room, I'd planned to spend the night in it and head directly to rehearsal in the morning. Those plans were derailed twenty minutes after Balenciaga left, just as I was preparing to crawl into the bathtub for a long, hot soak. My apartment only had a shower, and I'd looked forward to the bath all day.

But it was not to be. I'd just kicked off my heels when my phone chirped. I didn't recognize the number, and as soon as I'd answered it, I wished I'd followed my impulse to ignore it.

"Hi, Katherine." Detective Abernathy sounded friendly and chipper. "Hope I'm not disturbing your evening, but I was wondering if you could come down to the precinct."

"Now?" I stared at the gush of hot water coming out of the tap. "I'm in the middle of something."

"Sorry about that. There's a new development. We'll talk it over when you get here." Something inflexible crept into the easygoing tone, and I knew this wasn't open for debate. "Check in at the desk when you arrive. You know where we are? By Tompkins Square Park. Half an hour?"

"It'll take me at least an hour. I'm out by JFK," I said.

"You're not going anywhere, are you?" It was sharp with alarm, like he thought I was skipping town.

"Not until the opera completes its run." Leaving the city would be close to impossible under the circumstances. I had daily rehearsals until opening night, and traveling ratcheted up the risk of exposure to cold germs and viral infections. Opera singers lead cautious lives while preparing for performances. "I'll be there as soon as I can."

"Great. See you soon," he said, then disconnected the call.

With one last look at the bathtub, I turned off the water and unplugged the drain. I changed from my dress into the sweater and slacks I'd packed to wear to tomorrow's rehearsal, then checked out of the hotel and traveled back into Manhattan.

At the precinct, Abernathy came out to meet me at the reception counter. I thought he seemed a little disconcerted by my new eyebrows, but he just shook my hand and thanked me for coming in on short notice.

"What's going on?" I asked, after he'd invited me into an interrogation room and offered me a seat. My impression of interrogation rooms was formed entirely from TV shows, so I was expecting something dingy, drab, and possibly gross, but this was clean and nice enough. Abernathy sat at a steel-framed desk; I was given an armchair across from him.

"You need any coffee or water? Just to give you a heads-up, we may be here awhile." Abernathy smiled, but I felt a ball of tension work its way up from my stomach to my throat where it sat in a lump. I shook my head, and he continued:

"There have been some developments, and we could use your help, Katherine." He looked older than I remembered, his tanned skin drained of color by the stark overhead light. "It's about your waiter at the club you were at that night. We've had him in custody, but it's starting to look like his alibi is pretty airtight. Barring the discovery of new evidence, we're going to have to let him go."

"So he's definitely not the killer?" I asked. I sounded a bit panicky.

Abernathy shook his head, though it wasn't quite a denial.

"I'll just say this: We're at the point where we need to focus our attention in other directions." He fell silent for a moment, his face examining mine, gauging my reaction to the news. Or maybe he was mesmerized by my eyebrows. "When you and I last chatted, you'd just been through one hell of a traumatic night. Now that you've had some time to bounce back, maybe there are more details you can think of to point us in the right direction, whether that's Nolan or somebody else." He smiled at me, friendly and jocular. "That doesn't sound too tough, does it, Katherine?"

Damn it, I was a suspect. "Sure, no problem," I said. I arranged my features into an expression of open and guileless honesty. "I don't think I know anything I haven't already told you, though."

"Why don't you let me worry about that?" Abernathy widened his smile, making his eyes crinkle at the corners.

"It's after eleven," I said. I tried not to make it sound like a complaint. "I guess you're used to working late hours."

"When there's an open case, my partner and I never stop working. Detective Khan is in the building right now, grabbing a nap on the sofa in the break room. But neither of us is going to get a good night of sleep until this puppy is off our plates." His smile began to look more calculated, and I felt a prickle at the back of my neck. "Not like being an opera singer, huh? Sounds like you guys have a pretty cushy schedule. I thought you'd be rehearsing for months, but it turns out you throw a show together in just a handful of weeks. And then there's only a couple of performances each weekend?" He shrugged. "From my perspective, that sounds like a walk in the park."

"Opera's not like traditional theater, or even musical the-ater," I said. "Giving a performance every night of the week is too hard on the voice. And the rehearsal time is short because singers learn the music in advance, long before the cast ever meets as a group. Many operas are old and well-known, so that also cuts down on the need for a long rehearsal period."

"That's not the case with this opera, though."

"No, it's brand-new. But I started learning my role way back in July, even though I was only the understudy at the time."

"That's right, you weren't the first choice." It was said lightly, but Abernathy's eyes scanned my face, ready to zoom in on any twitch or flinch. I didn't move, but I could feel my skin growing warm.

"No, I wasn't. The original lead had a conflict with her schedule in a Metropolitan Opera production. I'd been her understudy—in opera, we sometimes call it a cover—so Daniel promoted me to her role."

"And Yolanda Archambeau became your understudy. Your cover." Was I being sensitive, or was there a bit of disdain in his tone? "That decision turned out to be tragic for her, didn't it?"

I waited a few seconds before answering to make sure I could stay calm. "I wouldn't say that. There's nothing to suggest that being in this opera had anything to do with Yolanda's death. If it turns out someone was stalking her, for instance, they would have killed her even if she and I had never crossed paths."

"But you and Archambeau *did* cross paths." Abernathy kept his eyes locked with mine. "And it seems like that caused a lot of friction for both of you. You'd barely met, and she tried to poison you."

"She played a prank that backfired," I said.

"She wanted your job," Abernathy said. "And I don't mean to be offensive, but it sounds like plenty of people thought she deserved it more than you."

It was a struggle to stay composed. The silence had grown strained before I trusted myself enough to reply. "I don't think that's true," I said at last.

"You know the funny thing about this? When my partner and I first talked to various people involved with this opera, everyone told us nothing but unicorns and rainbows. Archambeau had been doing great, you were doing great, everyone got along. Sure, maybe the deceased had slipped eye drops in your tea, but everyone swore it was all in good fun." He shifted his chair forward. "Except for one person. Astrid . . . does she pronounce it the way it looks? Busk? The conductor lady?"

"Astrid's the composer, not the conductor." I cleared my throat. "What did Astrid say?"

"That your position in the opera was in trouble. That Daniel Toska was thinking about giving Archambeau your role, even though Archambeau had most definitely tried to poison you." He shook his head. "I guess the opera world is more exciting than I thought, because that all sounds like pretty crazy behavior."

The sense of betrayal caused a physical pain in my chest. I would have sworn Astrid liked me, but she'd thrown me to the wolves. Then I realized the truth: To almost everyone involved with the production, the opera was the only thing that existed right now, which meant completing a successful run took priority over seeing Yolanda's killer brought to justice. The production now hinged on me. With just over a week until opening night, there'd be no time for another performer to learn my role, and I had no understudy. Daniel and Marla and my castmates had misled the police not because they believed in my innocence, but because they'd rather share the stage with a possible murderer than see the opera canceled.

Except for Astrid. It would never occur to her to lie to shield me. Alone of us all, she'd be committed to the truth. If that meant her opera would never be performed, so be it.

"You seem like a smart woman, Katherine," Abernathy said. "Surely you picked up on the idea that nobody is all that happy with the job you're doing. Because it's starting to sound like everybody thought Archambeau had a better voice than you, that she was more suited to the role than you, that she was . . ." He shrugged. "I don't know, just a better fit."

"Prettier than me, you mean." I smiled, and tried my best to make it seem genuine. "Yolanda was gorgeous, absolutely. She would have looked great onstage. And she had a lovely voice.

But . . ." I chose my words carefully. "She wasn't a better singer. She hadn't had enough training. She made a fine understudy, but putting her on the stage in a lead role would have been a big risk."

"That's one way of looking at it, I guess," Abernathy said. "If I were in your shoes, though, I would have felt like my chances of performing that juicy leading role were fading fast. You're getting a little old to be playing an ingénue, aren't you, Katherine?"

"Yolanda and I were around the same age," I said. It sounded brittle to my ears. Abernathy was trying to provoke an emotional response, and I shouldn't take the bait. "Opera careers have a slow build. Mine is right about where it should be."

He raised his hands. "Hey, whoa, no offense. Obviously you know more about it than I do. I guess I hadn't realized you and Archambeau were similar in age. From her photos, she looked . . . well, you know what she looked like."

"Like I said, she was gorgeous." I stared at him. "Do you really think I wanted to kill Yolanda because she was prettier than me?"

"People have been killed for less," he said. "From what everyone says, this role was important to you, and you could see it slipping away. Archambeau had tried to hurt you before. Maybe you viewed it as self-defense, protecting yourself from another physical attack while also protecting your career. In any case, it wouldn't be the first time you'd stabbed someone, would it?"

I was silent. He knew. Of course he knew. The first time he'd questioned me, I should have told him about stabbing Glen, but I'd clung to the hope that he'd never find out.

"You haven't exactly been open and honest with me, have you, Katherine?" He seemed disappointed yet unsurprised. "I made a few calls to Michigan about you. I talked to your aunt and learned all about your youthful hijinks with knives. Don't you think that might have been relevant to our investigation?"

That wasn't great. I couldn't imagine my aunt having anything positive to say about her feral, furious niece. "No, I don't," I said. "What happened when I was a kid isn't relevant. I was a kid, it was self-defense, and there were no charges brought against me." My voice was tight with anger. "And I was unconscious when Yolanda was stabbed. I was drugged. You know that. Even if you think I have a motive, it would've been physically impossible for me to kill her."

"But it wouldn't have been impossible for you to work with her killer." Abernathy leaned across the table. "As near anyone can figure, Archambeau's keys disappeared from her purse in that club while she was performing. You could have taken them easily. Then you slipped the keys to an accomplice before sticking something in your own drink. You gave yourself an alibi by being unconscious while your friend crept into Archambeau's apartment and killed her."

"Who would this accomplice be?" I asked when I was able to form a coherent thought. "Is there anything about me to suggest I hang around with killers?"

"Killers? I don't know. But you do hang around with criminals, Katherine," Abernathy said. "It's not your first production with Brio. You can't tell me you don't know how it's funded."

Niko. Niko was funding Brio, and Niko ran a legal-on-the-surface-only escort service, and yeah, I suppose that made him a criminal. "I don't know anything about that," I said finally.

"Maybe you don't, maybe you do. Maybe Niko Toska came to you with a proposition. He's having some problems with a girl who used to work for him, one of his whores, and he knows that same girl has been causing problems for you. Maybe he's got a plan to solve both of your problems, and maybe you think that plan sounds like a pretty good idea."

I wanted to tell him not to call Yolanda a whore, but I realized he'd picked that word judiciously to offend me. He wanted to make me angry enough and frightened enough to lose control and say something incautious. It was working: I felt both angry and frightened. "I didn't kill Yolanda," I said. "Not on my own, and not with anyone's help. I wouldn't do that."

"I'm just throwing out some ideas, Katherine," Abernathy said. He smiled at me, friendly and open once more. "We're simply exploring some ways this whole mess could have gone down, that's all." He gestured at the mug on his desk. "I'm going to grab a refill. Can I get you a cup of coffee now? You look pretty worn out already, and I have to tell you, it'll probably be a long night."

I could only nod at him, feeling an overwhelming sense of hopelessness.

It was after four in the morning before Abernathy was finished with me. Our conversation had been long, ominous, and confusing; by the time he dismissed me with a cheery warning that he'd be in touch, I had no idea if his accusations were mostly a bluff, or if I was in danger of imminent arrest. My head throbbed, and I felt a smoldering resentment that I'd been denied my hot bath.

Rehearsal didn't start until nine, but I was much closer to the theater than I was to my apartment, and it would be heartbreaking to get all the way home and not have the option of staying there. Instead of going all the way north, I got off the train at Midtown and headed for the performing arts center.

The night was cold, and the wind bit my face. The double doors at the front entrance were kept bolted from the inside on nonperformance nights, so I walked down the alley, maneuvering around a bulky white van illegally parked by the side of the building, to enter through the side.

Daniel's key in hand, I glanced up. The alley door was directly beneath the fire escape, which meant Daniel's office was right above my head. His light was on, and if I tilted my neck, I could see the back of his head near the window, which meant he was working at this ridiculous hour. That seemed eccentric, but mounting an opera was a monumental task, and I didn't think Daniel had much of a life outside his work. That was something we had in common.

Once inside, I thought about stopping by the second floor to let Daniel know I was in the building. I didn't want to bother him, so I continued up the stairs to the practice rooms. The overhead lights on the third floor were off, but I could still see clearly from the street lights streaming through the windows at each end of the corridor.

In addition to a piano, the biggest practice room featured an ancient sofa, the upholstery worn to threads across the arms. I didn't bother turning on the light; before I could sing, I desperately needed a nap. I curled up on my side, my coat pulled over me like a blanket, and closed my eyes.

Exhausted as I was, my thoughts swirled restlessly in my head. Was I in danger of being charged with Yolanda's murder? Abernathy had made some barbed accusations, and I got the sense that he felt a fair amount of contempt for me, but now that I could think back over the interrogation, I refused to believe he genuinely thought I had conspired with Niko, of all the damn people, to murder my professional rival. If my hunch was right, Niko was the one in his sights, and Abernathy had wanted to scare me into revealing any damaging information about him.

It hadn't worked, not that I knew anything about Niko that Abernathy didn't already know. Out of a sense of self-preservation, I hadn't mentioned my encounter with Balenciaga and my subsequent discovery of Niko's connection to the escort service. Similarly, Abernathy hadn't tipped his hand as to why he considered Niko a suspect. Niko was shady, absolutely, but was he a killer? If Niko had killed Yolanda, did Daniel suspect or know what his brother had done?

I wished I could remember more of that night in her apartment, but my memories were murky. I remembered how my panic upon realizing I'd been drugged had subsided into passive acceptance as I surrendered to unconsciousness, the way the softness of Yolanda's extravagant bedding had surrounded me. I was back there now, comfortable and relaxed even as part of my mind alerted me to great danger . . .

My eyes flew open, and I was fully awake, heart pounding. An alarm clanged in the hallway, shockingly loud. I got to my feet and groped along the wall in the darkness until I found the switch, but the light refused to come on. I felt around the floor for my overnight bag, pulled on my coat, and ran out into the hallway.

I was hit by an acrid stench, and that solved the mystery of the alarm: The building was on fire. The corridor was filled with black smoke; I could barely see the windows at the ends of the hall.

I sprinted down the corridor. I threw open the window and scrambled out onto the fire escape. The cold outdoor air almost made me sob with relief. I hurried down the stairs as far as I could go; the metal steps stopped at the second floor, but from the landing outside Daniel's office window, I could easily drop onto the roof of the white van parked in the alley, then lower myself to the pavement.

But Daniel had been in the building when I'd arrived, and I was worried he might still be here. The fire could have started in his office, the smoke billowing up the center staircase to the practice rooms. I wanted to assume he'd already evacuated; I wanted to get myself to safety and call the fire department from the sidewalk. But . . .

On the platform outside Daniel's office, I pressed my face against the window and squinted into an inky void. It was much too dark to see if Daniel was still inside, but there definitely weren't any flames, which gave me a burst of courage. I could pop inside and quickly confirm that Daniel was nowhere around.

The window was closed but not locked, though there was

no obvious way to force it open from the outside. I pressed my fingertips against the glass as hard as I could, then pushed up. The lower sash shifted, just the tiniest bit, but it was enough. I wedged the tips of my fingers into the small gap I'd made and hauled the window all the way open.

Black smoke immediately billowed over me, great foul-smelling plumes of it, and I knew it could kill me if I wasn't careful. I turned my head away and took the deepest breath I could of clean night air, saying a mental thanks to my opera training for giving me extraordinary lung capacity. I wrapped my scarf around my mouth and nose and climbed through the window into Daniel's office.

The smoke was prickly and scorching; it seemed alive and sentient, and it surrounded me, attacking me from all directions. My eyes burned, and I could see nothing, so I squeezed them shut. Blind, I reached my hands out and grabbed the back of Daniel's empty chair.

I couldn't risk calling out for Daniel, because if I inhaled I'd get smoke in my lungs, so I simply dropped to the floor and groped about in all directions. I scrambled on all fours around the inner circumference of his small office, which reassured me that he wasn't lying nearby in a heap, unconscious or dead from smoke inhalation. His office door was closed; he'd clearly already left the building, which is what I needed to do immediately. My lungs screamed at me to breathe, and if I stayed any longer I'd suffocate.

I climbed onto the windowsill and crawled out onto the iron slats of the fire escape. A great black cloud of smoke came right along with me, so I hurried to slam the window shut. I yanked my scarf down beneath my mouth and nose and took in a deep gulp of air. I coughed, deep and wracking, and I thought my lungs were turning inside out. My face and my eyes felt scalded.

I glanced down. The headlights of the white van beneath me suddenly blazed on, which meant someone was inside it, maybe someone who'd noticed the smoke and the commotion directly above their parking spot. I tried to shout to get the attention of the driver, but when I drew in a breath, I coughed until I retched.

I could only see an indistinct blur through my burning eyes, but I heard the passenger door open, and then I heard male voices. Their words were low and indistinct, but it didn't sound like they were speaking English.

The beam of a flashlight hit my face, and I heard Daniel call up to me from the ground below: "Kit?"

I tried to answer him, which triggered another coughing fit. "Are you hurt? Can you lower yourself to the van?" Daniel asked.

I didn't try to speak again. Instead, I got to my feet, gripped the railing of the fire escape with both hands, and climbed over it. It was only a short drop to the top of the van, but my legs were unprepared for the landing, and I collapsed to my knees.

"Here." Daniel sounded very close to the side of the van. I felt a hand touch my boot. "I'll help you down."

I looked at him, but my eyes were too blurry to see much besides a dark-haired blob. The figure next to him looked like an amorphous white-clad shape. Unable to speak, I nodded in Daniel's general direction to let him know I understood before lowering myself down the side of the van.

He took hold of me, his hands first on my legs, then around my hips, and then he eased me the rest of the way to the ground. I was unsteady on my feet, and he must've been able to tell I was having difficulty standing, because he grasped my shoulders and held me upright. "What were you doing in there?" he asked.

"I was looking for you," I said. I started coughing again, but this time I got it under control. My throat felt like I'd been sucking on a lit charcoal briquette. "I thought you were in your office. I saw your light on earlier, and I wanted to be sure you made it out of the building."

"You were looking for me?" Daniel said, and it sounded teasing, almost flirtatious. Daniel was never a flirt, not under any circumstances. I pulled back out of his grasp.

"Oh. Not you," I said to Niko. "I was looking for your brother."

20

Entrepreneur

"Danny's fine," Niko said. "He's nowhere near this place."

"I thought you were him," I said, or tried to say, and then I started coughing again.

Niko frowned in concern at my cough. "Sit in the van," he said. "You look like you're about to collapse."

He took my arm and guided me toward the van. As my eyesight returned to normal, I saw that the side door was marked with the logo for some business called Dragusha Electronics, which had an address in the Bronx. I pulled away from him. "We need to call the fire department," I said through another paroxysm of coughing.

"There's no fire. Just a lot of smoke." Niko sounded cheerful. He reached into my overnight bag, which was still slung over my shoulder, and fished around in the contents. I wondered what that was all about, but then he pulled out my water bottle, unscrewed the top, and handed it to me. "One thing I know from Danny is that singers always carry water," he said.

I took a swig. Swallowing was painful, but the water eased the burning dryness in my throat.

"Here." He took the bottle back, then soaked a large white handkerchief and handed it to me. "You have ash and stuff on you."

I dabbed at my face. My skin stung, and the handkerchief turned gray from soot.

"Danny complained to me about some wiring problems in his office. So I called this guy right here, this is Teodor, he's a licensed electrician, and we told Danny we'd take a look at it early some morning when the theater was closed, so we wouldn't disrupt rehearsal." He patted Teodor on the shoulder. Teodor, who was tall and hulking with thinning blond hair and a formidable scowl, glowered in response. "We arrived too late, though. When we got here, smoke was pouring out of an electrical outlet, so we bailed. This is a cool old building, but it's a dump; I keep telling Danny he needs to move Brio someplace nicer. What were you doing here in the middle of the night?"

I ignored his question, distracted by the gaping holes in his story. Why wouldn't Daniel ask the building management to fix his wiring problems? If the fire had already started by the time Niko arrived, why had I spotted him sitting at Daniel's desk?

I could still hear the clang of the alarm from inside the building, and surely that would attract the fire department soon. Teodor glanced up at the fire escape and said something in a language I couldn't identify. His tone was sharp, and he made an impatient gesture toward the street. Niko responded in the same language, his manner easygoing and placating. Teodor snorted at whatever he'd said, then slipped past me to walk around the van and climb into the driver's seat, glaring at me all the while.

"Kit." Niko touched my arm to get my attention. "What were you doing here?"

I felt a spark of fear, and suddenly I was aware of an urge to give Niko the most innocuous explanation possible to explain my presence. This, fortunately, happened to be the truth. "Daniel gave me a key so I could use the practice rooms whenever I want," I said.

Niko pursed his lips, mulling this over, and then he relaxed.

"It's not even six in the morning. Danny's got to be impressed by your dedication," he said. He frowned in concern as I stifled another cough. "Hey, the night air can't be doing you any good. Hop in. We can drop you anywhere you want."

He opened the passenger door and gestured for me to climb in. I saw a laptop on the seat, and I spotted that asinine OPERA IS MY ARIA OF EXPERTISE bumper sticker.

"You swiped Daniel's laptop and started a fire in his office to cover for it, didn't you?" I asked. The words popped out of my mouth as soon as they entered my brain.

"Of course not. I grabbed his laptop on the way out to protect it from damage." His face was bright and open, and he was lying. "Come on. Let's not loiter in this alley until daybreak." He took my arm again, and this time I felt genuinely frightened. I yanked it out of his grasp.

"I'm not going anywhere with you," I said. My voice went high and sharp, but I was glad I sounded more resolute than terrified.

"Kit . . ." Niko smiled at me, placating and friendly.

"Touch me again, and I'm shouting for the cops." He was between me and the alley exit, and he could easily overpower me. At that hour, I couldn't be sure anyone would hear if I yelled for help.

Frustration crept in around the edges of Niko's friendly demeanor, and then he relaxed and smiled again. "You don't need to be scared of me," he said. "There's an all-night diner around the corner. The Constellation. You know it?" He waited for me to nod. "Go there and wait for me. I'm going to say goodbye to Teodor, and then I'll meet you in a few minutes. I think I need to explain some things."

My first impulse was to tell him I wasn't going to meet him anywhere, and then it dawned on me that I should agree to his suggestion and seize the chance to get away from him. "Fine," I said. I nodded curtly and moved past him and Teodor, ready to run if either grabbed me.

"Kit." Niko spoke softly. I glanced back at him. "You will meet me, right?"

"Sure," I said, and started coughing again. "Sure. I'll be there."

I meant it as a lie. I meant to head straight for the nearest subway station and go home. Or maybe first I'd give Abernathy a call to update him on this ominous turn of events. As soon as I exited the alley, though, I saw the awning of the Constellation, and I reconsidered. It was a well-lit public place with plenty of witnesses. And I genuinely did want to know what Niko had to say for himself about his actions tonight, because there was at least a chance it had something to do with Yolanda's murder.

Even at this early hour, the diner had a healthy smattering of customers: white-collar employees grabbing coffee before a long day in the office, MTA workers fueling up on pancakes after slogging through the night shift, lonely souls who had nowhere to go and too much time to kill. I took a seat on a turquoise vinyl stool at the counter, which was pink laminate with gold flecks. The sole worker, balding and heavyset, came over, coffeepot in hand. His brow furrowed at the sight of me, which reminded me that I probably looked like hell.

He didn't comment on my appearance. "Coffee?"

"Tea, if you have it. With honey," I said. "Is there a restroom?"

He grunted and slid a key across the counter to me. It was attached with wire to the handle of a metal flour sifter, thus greatly decreasing the odds of anyone pocketing it. He nodded toward the back of the diner.

"None of my business, kid, but are you okay?" he asked.

There was a spark of genuine concern behind his gruff exterior, and that made me think I might have an ally. "I'm meeting a guy here," I said. "It might be fine, or it might be a problem. If it looks like I'm having trouble . . ."

I half expected him to tell me to take my trouble elsewhere, but he just nodded, as though requests like mine were commonplace. "Got a baseball bat behind the counter and the

Midtown South Precinct on speed dial," he said. "Your guy gives you trouble, give me a shout."

I nodded my thanks, then found my way to the restroom, which doubled as a janitorial closet; I maneuvered around a mop and bucket to reach the sink. The mirror was cloudy with age, but it gave me a general idea of what I looked like, and it wasn't pretty. I soaked a paper towel in warm soapy water and set about scrubbing myself clean.

When I stared at myself, I looked deeply shocked, maybe traumatized, and then I realized that was just the damage Balenciaga had inflicted on my poor defenseless eyebrows.

Upon my return, my tea was sitting on the counter, a sturdy plastic mug of hot water with a tea bag and a honey packet resting on the saucer beside it. Niko, seated in a booth against the far wall, raised his hand in greeting. I hesitated, then collected my tea and slid into the seat across from him.

"I hoped you'd show up. I wasn't sure you would," he said.

"I wasn't sure, either," I said, or tried to say. I was interrupted by another coughing fit. I didn't like that cough. What if the smoke had damaged my throat or, worse yet, my vocal cords? What if I wouldn't be able to perform in *Barbarella*? What if the damage was permanent; what if I'd never sing again?

Niko kept staring at me, his expression very intense. "You changed your hair since the last time I saw you," he said.

"It's just covered in soot right now."

"No, you look different. You look even more like Tonya Margolis." He grinned. "You lied about that. I know she's your mom. No way she isn't."

I didn't bother answering. I dunked the tea bag in the water, added the honey, and sipped without waiting for the tea to steep. The warmth immediately soothed my throat. "I look different because I got my eyebrows tweezed earlier this evening. Or last night, I guess." I looked at him, wanting to see how he'd take this. "By Balenciaga."

His brows raised. "Balenciaga," he said at last. "Did Yolo introduce you to Balenciaga?"

I shook my head. "Leo suggested I contact her."

"Oh, you met Leo? Isn't Leo amazing? I love that guy," he said, suddenly enthusiastic. "But I don't get why you needed to meet with Balenciaga."

"I don't get why you needed to set your brother's office on fire and steal his laptop."

He smiled. I suspected he knew he had a great smile, wide and charming, and he was whipping it out strategically to put me at ease. "You've got the wrong idea," he said, his voice filled with warmth and affection, like I was one of his favorite people in all the world. "I didn't do any of that."

"A couple days ago, I told Daniel that I saw one of the detectives investigating Yolanda's murder looking on his laptop. Tonight, you set fire to your brother's office and stole his laptop." Nobody was seated in the booths on either side of ours, but I kept my voice down. "Seems like there's a connection."

"I don't know what to tell you." Niko looked especially attractive right now, almost angelic, the picture of baffled innocence. "Obviously I didn't do anything like that. It happened just like I told you."

This conversation wasn't going to be helpful. Niko had no reason to tell me the truth and probably a lot of reasons to maintain his string of denials. I considered threatening him with the police, but that seemed like an escalation I might regret. If Niko had killed Yolanda, he could decide I needed to be silenced. For the first time since the alley, I felt a jagged spike of fear. My mug clattered against the saucer when I tried to set it down with shaky hands. At the counter, the server shot a glance in our direction. His expression was unbothered, but he was keeping an eye on us, and that restored my confidence.

If I couldn't threaten Niko, how could I get information out of him? Could I bribe him? He was infatuated with my terrible mother, and maybe that could be useful. Maybe I could promise him an autograph, or even a phone call; my mom had no time for me, but I thought she'd probably make time for a handsome and wealthy young man with a crush on her.

But my mother wasn't there. I, on the other hand, was. For the first time since sitting down in the booth, I smiled. I tried to make it both friendly and bewitching; I tried to make my eyes sparkle with promise.

"Tell me something, Niko," I said. I rested my chin on my hand and gazed at him, keeping the smile on my face. "Both your brother and Yolanda have talked to you about me, haven't they? What did they say?"

He smiled. "They told me you're a damn good singer."

"That's a diplomatic answer." I giggled. Giggling does not come naturally to me, but I tried to remember the sound of my mother's giggles in the behind-the-scenes video of her *Playboy* Playmate photo shoot that she'd pop in the VCR whenever we had company over, or the way Yolanda had giggled, musical and light, when Daniel had praised her at our first rehearsal. "It's true, though: I *am* a damn good singer. But I imagine they also told you I was boring. Obedient. Single-minded in my devotion to opera." I trailed my free hand through my hair, sweeping it casually out of my eyes before sliding my fingers down the side of my neck and along my shoulder. This was one of my mother's signature moves that she'd trot out for all of her onscreen seduction scenes. She'd taught it to me when she was coaching me for an audition for some Disney Channel show when I was nine.

The move had not been a hit with the casting directors, I'm delighted to report, but it seemed to work some magic on Niko. He sat back, and his eyes opened a little wider.

"I do agree with one of their assumptions," I said. I made sure to maintain the sparkle in my eyes, the mischief in my voice. "Your brother's opera is my whole life. For instance, I'm pretty sure I just caught you in the middle of a highly illegal act of arson, and do you know the only thing I was worried about? That the smoke might have damaged my voice." I tapped two fingertips lightly against my throat.

Niko looked genuinely upset. I was spitefully pleased to see he looked guilty, too. "Oh, wow. Is your voice okay?"

"It'll be fine." I knew that to be true; the honey and hot water had already relieved the swollen and scratchy feeling, and my cough had vanished. "If I thought I could no longer sing, I'd be dissolving into hysterics right now. But my point is, I'm living for Daniel's opera these days, and I would never do anything to jeopardize it. You know what that means?"

"Tell me." Niko seemed transfixed by me. His approval was gratifying; whenever I thought of the way my clumsy attempt at flirting had repelled handsome Patrick, the apartment hunter, I felt mortified.

"It means I want to keep the police far, far away from anything to do with the opera. And that means keeping them away from Daniel, and keeping them away from you." I kept my gaze fixed on Niko's face. "Okay?"

Niko nodded. "Okay," he said. "Okay. I understand that."

"All I want in return is for you not to treat me like I'm a toddler. You can do that, can't you, Niko?" It was almost a purr. "Why'd you steal Daniel's laptop and set fire to his office?"

He looked like he was going to deny it again, and then he dipped his head in a gesture that seemed like some sort of concession. "'Fire' is an overstatement," he said. "Teodor just made the wiring smolder inside the wall. A bit of smoke, enough to activate the alarm system, but totally harmless."

The smoke could have killed me, but Niko had no reason to think I'd been in the building, or that I'd barge into Daniel's office in a misguided attempt to rescue him. "Why'd you do it? Because of the police investigation?"

"I'll answer your questions, but you need to go first." Niko folded his arms and leaned over the table. "Why were you talking to Balenciaga?"

I considered my options, then went for honesty. "Yolanda had a daughter," I said. "You probably knew that, right? A former coworker has been raising her, but I don't even know what city they're in, and the daughter should know her mom is dead. Leo said Yolanda was friends with Balenciaga, so I asked her about Yolanda's past."

Niko's eyes widened. "Yolo had a kid?"

God. I was almost certain Niko had seen Yolanda naked. "You really didn't know?"

He shook his head. "You're trying to find the kid? That's all?"

"That's all."

He mulled this over. "So if you talked to Balenciaga, I assume you know . . ." He trailed off.

"That you're a . . ." I gave a cute little frown. "I don't know what I should call you. Do you consider yourself a pimp?"

"Please." He looked wounded. "I'm an entrepreneur. Angels in the City is registered as a corporation, all of our escorts are licensed for this kind of work, and all income, including tips, is reported in full to the state and to the IRS. We're one hundred percent legitimate."

"That's what Leo said, too," I said. "And yet Yolanda got arrested. Was that while she was working for you?"

Niko winced. "Yeah. We've been in operation for two years, and we've only had one arrest, and of course it was Yolo." He rolled his eyes. "We have a protocol in place to make sure our escorts don't wander into legal snares. It's drilled into them: Take things slowly, start with small talk, get a feel for the situation. If anything seems fishy, they know they're supposed to immediately bail."

"And Yolanda didn't do that?"

"She had a date with a Broadway casting director who turned out to be an undercover cop." He shook his head affectionately. "This guy, he'd even set up a fake LinkedIn profile listing all his credits, which he showed to Yolo. He claimed to be casting a revival of *Sweet Charity* and thought she had the right look, and when she told him she could sing, he swore he could get her a meeting with the director." He grinned at me. "She was a smart girl, but that blew through her defenses. She went right for his pants and offered to show him how great she'd be in the role, and he whipped out his badge. The charges were dropped, because my lawyers argued it was entrapment, but even still, it was bad. We'd done everything we could to fly under the radar of law enforcement, and . . ."

"And Yolanda put you on the radar," I said. That would cause Niko some aggravation, but it surely wouldn't motivate him to kill Yolanda, and in any case, her arrest was a year ago. "Is that why Detective Abernathy is on your tail?" I scrunched up my lips into what I hoped was a sexy pout. "When he asked me about Yolanda, he didn't seem to like you very much."

"That guy." Niko snorted. "No, he's got a bug up his ass about me for other reasons. Ignore him."

"He used to work for some other NYPD division, right? Criminal Enterprise, is that right? I looked it up. That's organized crime."

"Yep. I know."

"Prostitution doesn't fall into that division, does it? That's Vice Enforcement."

"Yep. I know that, too." Niko seemed like he was enjoying this conversation, but he also seemed like he wasn't going to be too chatty about his possible connection to organized crime, so I shifted gears.

"That guy with the van tonight. Who was he?"

"Teodor. He's great. He's a licensed electrician." A licensed electrician who was apparently cool with setting electrical fires. "He does some work for my father."

"What language were you two speaking?" I asked. I tried to look fascinated. "I speak a bunch of languages, Italian and German and Russian and French, and I didn't understand a word you were saying."

Niko pursed his lips, and for the first time, he seemed reluctant to answer. "Albanian."

Ah. "I see."

"No, you don't." He laughed. "My father is a *businessman.* Albanians in New York, everyone automatically jumps to organized crime, right? That's not the case, not at all. My father is a property developer. He's a past president of the Chamber of Commerce. He's *totally* legitimate." I'd already gleaned from this conversation that Niko's definition of legitimate differed from mine, but I nodded anyway. "He was born and raised in Tirana, and he still has close ties to his roots. We have a summer home near Porto Palermo. He's done well for himself, so people here go to him for favors, and he goes to them for favors. Thanks to my dad, I know guys like Teodor, but . . . I mean, I also know the mayor."

I was primed to disbelieve anything Niko told me, but this seemed plausible. "Why is Detective Abernathy so interested in Daniel's laptop?"

"Because Detective Abernathy has too much time on his hands." Niko had very pretty eyes, huge and dark brown, and he used them to maximum effect. He gazed at me soulfully, like I was his treasured confidante. Probably he was used to hearts melting at his gaze. My heart remained intact, but I decided it was time to trot out another giggle in agreement. "Nothing on that laptop should—*should*—be problematic, but if the cops look too closely into Brio's finances, it could raise awkward questions. So . . ." He shrugged. "Danny's office gets damaged in a thoroughly unsuspicious electrical fire, one that's just big enough to cause a bit of smoke and chaos, and his laptop disappears. Maybe an inattentive firefighter left the building unlocked, who knows? Point being, if the NYPD gets a notion to search Danny's office, the laptop's not there, and there's nothing Danny can say or do that might incriminate himself. That's good for Danny, good for me, and good for Leo."

I straightened up. "Wait. What does Leo have to do with this?"

"He handles Brio's books. You know he's a financial manager?"

"I've heard," I said. "Would those books hold up under investigative scrutiny?"

"I mean, maybe?" Niko shrugged. "I had to shift around some money from some of my other enterprises, and god knows Brio could always use an influx of cash. Opera is not exactly a profit-making juggernaut."

"You just told me you reported your income honestly, Niko. You told me that like five minutes ago."

"Sure, but I was talking about Angels in the City. That's not my only business."

I stared at him. "What else are you into?"

"This and that. *Things*. It's fine." He waved a dismissive hand. He looked like an altar boy, innocent and pure.

"What kinds of *things*?" Somewhere along the way I'd dropped the giggles and the gooey eyes, but now that Niko had started talking, he seemed unwilling to stop. I felt some concern for my own safety—what if Niko decided he'd told me more than he should?—but I was learning some intriguing stuff. To keep Niko going, I rested my chin on my hand again and gazed at him adoringly. "This is all very interesting."

He thought for a moment. "You know how there are things you can't do in Manhattan that are perfectly legal if you hop a tiny bit down the coast to Atlantic City? I'm bringing a piece of Atlantic City into New York, that's all."

"You're running a casino?"

"I'm disrupting the traditional business model of unlicensed gambling dens," he said. He beamed at me, proud of himself, and I realized Niko's need to boast outweighed his sense of discretion. Niko was going to wind up in jail someday. "I partner with nightclubs and restaurants and event venues. Particularly ones with hidden back rooms or basements; old speakeasies are ideal. And then I run pop-up casinos. I make it a super luxe experience. I've flown to Macao and Monte Carlo to study the world's greatest casinos, and I've adapted that aesthetic for a young, sophisticated crowd of Manhattanites. We bring in world-class party planners and mixologists, we recruit top dealers from Vegas and Reno and Atlantic City, we spread the word through an aggressively curated mailing list, and for a couple of days, maybe a long weekend, it's the hottest ticket in the city. A successful weekend can clear fifty grand or so, and I can't exactly report that, can I? It shows up in Brio's books, so it's not like I'm cheating the government out of money."

"How tight is your dad with the mayor?" I asked.

"They've lunched. Why?"

"I'm just wondering how hard the city will come down on you after your inevitable arrest."

"I liked this conversation better when you were flirting with me." He grinned, and it dawned on me that I shouldn't make the mistake of assuming Niko was a complete fool. Once again, I felt a prickle of danger.

"Do you think any of your side hustles had anything to do with why Yolanda got killed?" I asked. Niko's expression darkened, so I found myself hastening to explain. "I don't mean that you did anything to her, just that she might have found herself in danger from whatever you were into. You know how she was; she was a magnet for trouble."

Niko shook his head emphatically. "Yeah, but no way would I ever have done anything to endanger Yolo. I loved her. I was absolutely crazy about her."

"Even considering the arrangement she had with Leo?"

"I could live with that. I knew she was never going to be entirely mine." Niko sounded a little exhausted and helpless, and I liked him better that way. He seemed less glib and more like a real person. "I never asked for or expected anything more than she wanted to give."

He stared beyond me at the battered jukebox near the entrance. Silent since I'd walked in, it had just begun to play "House of the Rising Sun." He closed his eyes and swayed his head in time to the music. "Ever since Danny told me about her death, I have these white-knight fantasies where I burst into her apartment and save her in the nick of time. I know it's stupid, but there it is." He opened his eyes, and he looked older and wearier. "She was amazing, right? She was crazy, but she was a goddess."

He left soon after that. I stayed in the diner through multiple rotations of customers, ordering a second cup of tea and some dry toast when the counter guy slipped the check under my saucer. Just after eight, I received a curt text from Daniel telling me that the morning rehearsal was canceled due to a small fire in the building, and that he'd update us after the FDNY inspection to let us know if we could meet in the afternoon. I read his text, wondering how much Daniel knew or suspected about the cause of that fire. Afterward, I remained in the booth, sorting through my jumbled thoughts.

Niko was probably a savvy businessman, but he was also reckless. He'd talked too much about things he should have kept to himself, wanting to impress me by boasting about his illicit activities. He reminded me of the guys my mom used to date when I was a kid, handsome young idiots who talked a big game about their exciting in-the-works Hollywood deals, all of which ultimately amounted to very little. I'd liked her boyfriends, mostly, just as I mostly liked Niko. I disapproved of him, and I'd never trust him, but he made for an entertaining conversation partner.

Was I being naïve, though? Niko was a man who'd lost the love of his life, or someone he'd thought was the love of his life. I believed that, but I wasn't certain he wasn't somehow responsible for her death. Niko had set Daniel's office on fire just to swipe his laptop. Covering up his financial shenanigans was one thing; I didn't approve, but I also didn't really care. But could it be linked to Yolanda's murder? Had she gotten herself involved in something she shouldn't have, and had Niko—or Daniel, for that matter—killed her to prevent her from bringing dark secrets to light? Did Daniel's laptop contain evidence of the murder that Niko wanted to destroy?

Should I call Abernathy right now and spill the beans about my rendezvous with Niko?

I couldn't decide, so I sat and drank more tea, feeling relieved that the pain in my throat was a distant memory. Everything was terrible, but at least my voice would be fine.

21

Box Seats

Daniel texted all of us in the afternoon to meet him at the Bradwell Theatre, a couple of blocks south of our performing arts center. The main stage at the Bradwell was large and grand, with a double balcony and four box seats; thick velvet drapes flanked the ends of the stage, while gargantuan chandeliers dangled from the ceiling above the auditorium seats. On that big stage, we ran through *Barbarella* without sets or costumes or an orchestra, each of us doing the best approximation of our blocking that we could manage in this new space.

It was ragged. The rehearsal was littered with missed cues and missed notes. As for myself, I made no mistakes, but I felt bone-tired from stress and lack of sleep, and I could sense that exhaustion bleeding into my performance despite my best efforts to boost my energy levels. Our first technical rehearsal was scheduled for Monday, and then opening night would be one week from today, and at the moment, it didn't seem like we'd be ready.

After we'd finished, Marla noted my lack of vim and vigor with what seemed like worried disappointment; Daniel didn't say anything at all about my performance, which I found ominous.

We'd all assumed this change in location would be a one-day-only kind of thing, but at the end of rehearsal, Daniel assembled us in the front row of the auditorium and dropped a bombshell while standing in front of the empty orchestra pit.

"We can't go back into our theater," he said. "The building failed the FDNY inspection. Management just told me it'll be closed to the public through the end of the year."

Next to me, Jerome shifted in his velvet seat. "Why won't they let us inside?" he asked. "Our stage wasn't affected by the fire, was it?"

Daniel shook his head. "There was no structural damage to the building. But my office wall had to be dismantled so inspectors could look at the wiring, and in the process the asbestos insulation was exposed."

"They removed the asbestos over the summer," Carlo said, his voice indignant. "That's what our delay was all about."

I didn't like Carlo much, but I shared his outrage. The asbestos, we'd been assured, was a problem of the past.

"Only from the walls of the main stage," Daniel said. Any remaining life had seeped out of him. His button-down shirt was rumpled; his sweater vest sagged. "Management did that as a stopgap measure, figuring it would be too expensive and disruptive to tackle the whole building at once. But now, in order to replace all that old faulty wiring, the asbestos on each floor must be removed."

I felt a vicious stab of fury, which was focused right at Niko. In his half-cocked effort to cover his ass, he'd screwed us all over.

Daniel tried to smile. "There *is* a bright side," he said. He gestured around the theater. "This is a wonderful facility. It's almost double the size of our space. We can draw a bigger audience, and we might need those extra seats. Interest has been high in the production since . . . well, since all the news coverage." He flushed, as though it occurred to him that crowing about how Yolanda's brutal murder would boost ticket sales might be unseemly.

I mulled this over, wondering whether this could be viewed as a net good for the production. Transferring all the pre-assigned seats of current ticket holders to a new venue and informing all patrons of the change in location would be messy, but at least our minimalist sets and backdrops wouldn't require much retooling to fit this larger space. And as ghoulish as it was, Daniel was right: We *could* sell more tickets now, to match pace with the heightened interest. Overall, this disruption would probably work out fine.

But Daniel was still speaking: "This leads me to the next issue." He closed his eyes and dipped his head down, like he'd been overtaken by a wave of exhaustion. He straightened up, squared his shoulders, and looked straight at us, and I realized he'd been bracing himself to deliver news we didn't want to hear. "Today marks one week until opening night. From what I saw today, that's not enough time. As long as we're already forced to make major changes, I'd like to seize the opportunity to take as much time as we need to do this right."

My gut felt tight. I didn't know anything, not really, but I *knew.*

"We're going to reschedule our performance dates?" That was Claudette, and she sounded as wracked with anxiety as I felt. I suspected I had more reason than she did to feel like the world was about to come crashing down.

"I think that might be best," Daniel said. "If we push back our production calendar by two weeks, that will give us plenty of time to work out all the remaining kinks. Instead of opening in one week, we'll open the third Friday in November. We'll have four weekends of performances as before, and we'll wrap in mid-December." He didn't bother asking if we had any conflicts. The opera came first, and we'd shift our schedules around accordingly.

"Is that necessary, though?" Carlo asked. "We weren't *that* bad today, were we?"

"I think it's for the best." Daniel sounded gloomy yet inflexible.

"There are matters I still need to discuss with Marla, but my office will email the new schedule to all of you as soon as we finalize it. I know this isn't ideal, but I appreciate everyone's patience."

Daniel fielded questions for a bit longer, but at that point I had already zoned out and thus paid no attention to what everyone was saying; I had only a vague awareness that my castmates were unhappy, and that Daniel was equally unhappy. Me, I was apoplectic. Since that first rehearsal, I'd been terrified of doing the wrong thing because I was afraid Daniel would take Barbarella away from me. I'd done everything right, and now he was going to snatch the role from me anyway.

Two weeks. I knew what that meant, and it was infuriating. It was also freeing, because that sick knot of dread that formed in my stomach at the close of every rehearsal while I waited to hear what criticisms Daniel had about my performance had vanished at last. It had been replaced by a great burning anger, and I welcomed it.

Time must have passed while I sat in my seat, feeling the rage consume me, because all of a sudden the auditorium was empty, save for me and Daniel. I was still seated, and Daniel was still standing in front of the orchestra pit, and now he was staring down at me, his expression a curious mixture of defiance and caution.

I got to my feet at last, picking up my coat and the Birkin bag. "A two-week extension, huh, Daniel?" I said. I barely recognized my own voice, thick with scorn. "Just in time for Roksana to wrap up *La Traviata*. Were you planning on cutting me on opening night, or were you going to do me the favor of letting me know ahead of time?"

If he was startled by my uncharacteristic sarcasm, he hid it well. "I was going to tell you on Monday, actually." He'd never sounded so cold, so brutal, so prissy. "I'll call Roksana this weekend and see if she can start coming to rehearsals next week.

Even though she's still wrapping up her run, at least some of her mornings should be free."

I thought of Roksana lightly disparaging *Barbarella* to me in the hallway outside the rehearsal room. "So you don't know if she even wants the role back."

"It doesn't matter whether she wants it. She's contractually obligated to do it. We stepped aside because we understood the Met took priority, and we had other options, but now . . ." He hunched his shoulders in a tiny and infuriating shrug. "We're out of options."

"That's ridiculous. You have me, and I'm a perfectly good option. I'm a *fantastic* option," I said. "Roksana probably hasn't even looked at the score in months."

"She workshopped the role with Astrid for weeks. She just needs to learn the blocking, and she'll be ready to perform," Daniel said stiffly.

He was right, damn it all. Once an opera singer learns a role, they know it for life. After a rehearsal or two to sort out her blocking, Roksana would be ready to swan onto the stage in my platform boots and my vinyl corset. "What does Marla say? Is she on board with your decision?"

"Not entirely," he said. It was a begrudging admission. "You've shown improvement in recent rehearsals. We've both noticed that; Marla in particular has been impressed. She believes it would be simpler to keep you, but she'll accept my judgment." He saw something in my face and hastened to speak before I could reply. "I'm not saying you're doing a bad job. Not at all. But Roksana is the total package, and I have to think of the greater good of the production."

I was silent, not trusting myself to speak. Daniel cleared his throat. "You'd be on hand as her cover, of course. Depending on her schedule, we may be able to give you a performance or two. For instance, she might have travel plans over Thanksgiving weekend."

I burst out laughing, even though nothing about this situation was funny in the slightest. "Oh, screw that," I said. I spoke without thinking, but the words felt *good*. If I was fired, I was fired; I was pretty sure there was nothing in my contract that could force me to stick around to cover a role I'd lost. "Screw that *so* much. If you bump me, you'll never see me again."

Daniel's brows knitted in disapproval. "Earlier this week, Kit, you told me that you always would do whatever's best for the opera."

"Yeah. Let's revisit that conversation, shall we?" I laughed again. There was a demented note to it, and Daniel was starting to look alarmed by my rare and dangerous mood. "I did tell you that, didn't I, right after I'd told you the cops were interested in your laptop. And then you got spooked that they might discover the dirty casino money that Niko and Leo had dumped into Brio to wash it clean, so you told Niko about our conversation. And then Niko got the *brilliant* idea to set your office on fire to give him an excuse to swipe your laptop." I couldn't stop laughing, great peals of it coming out of my body, wild and crazed. "So I guess that's on me in a way, because if I'd kept my mouth shut, our old stage would still be available, and you'd have to find some other excuse to boot me from the production. But yes, you're absolutely right, I did say I'd always do whatever was best for the opera."

Daniel had looked cadaverous at the start of our conversation. Somehow, now, he looked even worse, his skin turning gray before my eyes at my mention of Niko. "How do you . . . I don't know what you're talking about," he said. It was feeble.

I ignored him. "You can't guilt-trip me now about the best interests of the opera, because I've had its best interests at heart from the beginning. No one can possibly say I haven't. But maybe, just maybe, it's time I start looking out for my own best interests. Which, honestly, don't seem to overlap much with yours."

"I'm not following anything you're saying, Kit." Daniel was trying to sound calm and authoritative, but he was flailing. "You've made some wild accusations about Niko, and I don't know—"

"I'm going to stop you right there, Daniel." I enjoyed watching him flounder more than I should. "I heard all this straight from Niko himself. We went out for tea, right after he torched your office. I was in the building when he set the electrical fire, did you know that? Did you know that I rushed into your smoky office because I thought you might need rescuing? I think Niko felt kind of guilty about that, because he was pretty quick to answer my questions. I know a *lot* now, Daniel. I know so, so much."

Daniel started to stammer out some outraged denials, but I couldn't hear him over the giddy roar in my ears. Sometimes rage has a noise, overwhelming and yet soothing, like the crash of ocean waves on the shore during a squall. It had felt fantastic to wallow in that wild burst of fury, but I sensed that now it was time to pull it back inside myself. If I gave my anger free rein for too long, I would say things I could never take back. I could inflict irreparable damage to my professional reputation, if I hadn't done that already.

To calm myself, I tilted my neck back and looked up at the ceiling, so vast and so impressive, at those gigantic chandeliers, at the ornate double balconies and the box seats. This theater was much nicer than our smallish, rudimentary opera house back at the performing arts center. We only had a single balcony and no box seats . . .

Box seats.

Yolanda's mysterious conversation with Leo on the night of her murder popped into my head. At the time, I hadn't understood what she was talking about. Now, though . . .

Is Niko still mad at you for blabbing to me about the box seats?

I cut Daniel off in the middle of whatever he was saying,

talking right over him. "I know everything about what you and Niko have been up to," I said. "I even know things Niko didn't tell me. I know about the box seats."

"What?" I wasn't imagining the alarm in Daniel's face.

"On the night she died, Yolanda told me about the box seats." Daniel didn't need to know that wasn't quite the way it had gone down. "Leo was desperately in love with Yolanda, and he mentioned the box seats to impress her. She probably coaxed it out of him, because she liked knowing everyone's secrets, because sometimes she could use them for her own gain." I thought of Yolanda on the night of her murder, threatening to tell everyone in the cast about how I'd stabbed my aunt's boyfriend. "And she ran to Niko, armed with that knowledge."

"I have absolutely no idea what you're talking about."

"You told me you cast Yolanda as a favor to Niko, but that's not the whole story, is it? You cast her because she was blackmailing you about the box seats. That's why you made her my understudy, right?"

"I made her your understudy because her audition impressed me." Daniel sounded very proper and refined, like he had regained firm control over the conversation, but I could see he was unsettled. Scared, even.

"Feel free to stop lying to me at any time, Daniel," I said. "Remember, I know everything now. It *was* blackmail, wasn't it?"

He was ready to deny it, and then he nodded once, curt and wordless. I felt a swell of satisfaction at the confirmation of my guess. "Over something Leo told her about how Brio was funded, right? Something involving box seats?"

"When Yolanda heard about *Barbarella*, Niko asked me to let her audition." Backed into a corner, Daniel had no real choice but to answer me. Now that he had started talking, though, I had the sense it came as a relief to him, like he was anxious for the chance to spill out the whole sorry tale. "She wasn't formally trained, so I said no; I didn't want to waste anyone's time, hers included. Soon, though, she began to pester him about the box seats, dropping hints to the effect that she could cause us both a great deal of trouble." He frowned at the floor, unable to meet my eyes. "So I changed my mind. She came in and auditioned, and she was much better than I had any reason to expect. That was fortunate."

"Yeah, that sure was fortunate." It was dark and venomous, and Daniel lifted his head and stared at me, as though surprised I could have any objection to his decision to cast Yolanda. "So what's the deal with the box seats?"

I thought he was going to refuse to answer. Instead, he let out a helpless sigh. "Just a way to balance the books. It was Niko's suggestion," he said quickly, and I knew from the way he said it that if scrutiny of Brio's finances ever became too intense, Daniel would immediately sacrifice his brother to save himself. "Brio used to receive a great many cash donations from wealthy and anonymous opera lovers. Leo suggested that those donations might attract suspicion due to their sheer volume, so Niko came up with the idea of selling box seats."

I was starting to see where this was going. "You sold box seats. For an opera house that *has* no box seats," I said.

"Right. But our ticket records say otherwise," he said. His mouth twisted into a grim smile, and I had the impression that Daniel didn't like himself very much these days. "For every performance Brio puts on, a healthy chunk of our box office take comes from in-person cash purchases of what I would characterize as wildly overpriced box seats."

No wonder Niko didn't want Daniel's records to fall into the hands of Abernathy, who was still eager to see the downfall of the influential yet shady Toska family, even though he'd transferred to a different division.

Daniel cleared his throat. "Kit, I have to ask what you plan to do with this information."

Good question. "I'm pretty sure I know what Yolanda would do in my position," I said. "She'd take this information and leverage the ever-loving fuck out of it."

"So you're going to blackmail me." Daniel sounded resigned.

I can't be 100 percent certain, even in hindsight, but I think for a moment, for a long, intoxicating moment, I was going to say yes. The role of Barbarella was right in front of me, shimmering and radiant, and it would have been so easy to pull a Yolanda and grab it by any means possible. I knew information that was damaging to Daniel, possibly devastating, and I could use it to force him to admit the role was mine. I knew it, and he knew it.

"Early this morning, I told your brother that your opera was my whole life, that I was willing to excuse all kinds of illicit behind-the-scenes behavior to make sure I was on that stage opening night." I met Daniel's eyes, hoping I could convey to him the gravity of what I was saying. "Even a week ago, that would have been the truth. But I was lying to Niko, because I wanted him to confide in me." I gave a long, weary sigh, suddenly aware of my exhaustion. It was difficult to get my thoughts together, but I knew this was the most important thing I would ever say to Daniel.

"I love this opera, Daniel. I love playing Barbarella. And I know you disagree, but I think I'm damn good in the role. I hope I someday play this role on a stage; I hope it's *your* stage, but I'm not going to blackmail you to ensure that. I want to earn it." I was tired, so tired, and yet at the same time something was burning inside me, and I needed to let it out. I was afraid I wasn't explaining this well, and it seemed so, so important to get it right. "I'm not blackmailing you. I'm simply reminding you that I've worked my ass off for you and for this opera. I'm reminding you that I've done you favors. I'm reminding you that I'm great at this role, even if I'm not as glamorous as Yolanda or Roksana. And I'm putting you on notice that if you place a call to Roksana, I'm gone. I'm not going to go through the indignity of being her cover, just so I can prove I'm a good team player."

"The New York opera world is a small place, Kit. Word

spreads fast about problematic singers." Daniel had regained some of his spirit; his words were laced with menace.

"I'm sure it does." I shrugged. "I'm curious to see how fast it spreads about problematic directors."

We stared at each other, at an impasse. The silence dragged out, and after a long while, I started to give some serious thought to simply turning around and walking out of the theater, never to return. And then, like a bolt from the blue, I saw the way past our stalemate.

"Why don't you put it to a vote?" I asked. "We'll keep the technical rehearsal on Monday. All you have to do is delay your plan to call Roksana this weekend." I gestured at the stage. "Watch me on that stage, in full costume, with the sets in place and the orchestra in the pit, and then you and Marla can decide whether I stay or go. If it's a tie, bring in Astrid to see what she says. If, between the three of you, you still can't see me as Barbarella, call Roksana on Monday night and tell her the role is hers."

Daniel's expression was impossible to read. I continued.

"The cast doesn't want the two-week delay; I can't imagine Marla does, either. Or you, for that matter." I shrugged. "So today's rehearsal was ragged and messy. It happens; you know that. We've been through a lot this week, and none of us were at our best. Remember *Satyricon*'s first dress rehearsal, when everyone was so nervous and exhausted that half of us forgot our lines? And yet we still managed to bring it all together by opening night. Why don't you see if we're better on Monday at the tech rehearsal?"

He was silent, so silent, for such a long time that I began to wonder if he'd even heard me. Maybe he was so lost in his dark thoughts about blackmail and money laundering that he hadn't even processed anything I'd said. At long last, though, he nodded.

"Okay," he said. "Show up here on Monday morning. We'll see what happens."

"Thank you," I said. I sounded calm, but I felt grim. I was relieved by this last-minute reprieve, but I was aware of how dangerous it would be to let my hopes rise too high. If Daniel was set on getting rid of me and bringing back Roksana, he'd do his best to do exactly that, and I couldn't rely on Marla and Astrid to ally themselves against him.

Back home in my apartment, I had time to think about how reckless I'd been and how badly I'd behaved. I didn't regret anything I'd said, but I knew I'd acted in an unprofessional manner; after all, it was a director's prerogative—indeed, it was a vital part of the job—to replace performers who weren't working out. All of Daniel's decisions had been made for what he believed was the good of the opera. Just because I disagreed with his decisions didn't mean he'd been wrong.

But I was so tired of Daniel, and so tired of being made to believe I was a disappointment.

Box seats. If only Yolanda hadn't found out about the box seats; if only she hadn't gained that valuable piece of leverage over Niko and Daniel. She'd come close to ruining everything for me, and even though she was dead, I still hated her for that.

But there'd been something about Yolanda I couldn't dismiss. She reminded me of a classic opera heroine sprung to life, bold and vivid and far too dramatic, and people had lost their heads over her. Leo had spilled the beans to her about his involvement in illicit activities because he thought it'd impress her, and Niko had pulled strings to get her the *Barbarella* role. Daniel had known she hadn't had sufficient training, and yet he'd seen his dream Barbarella in her. If Yolanda hadn't been killed, he would have replaced me with her at some point before opening night, I was certain of that. Next to her, I was as unsubstantial as a shadow.

I wanted to sob and scream about how unfair this was. Instead, I went to the fridge and got out the bottle of champagne

Yolanda had given me as a peace offering. I'd meant to save it until the end of the run when I could toast myself in triumph.

I popped the cork, after once again examining the cage and foil for signs of tampering, because: Yolanda. I splashed champagne into a coupe glass, one of a pair I kept on a high shelf in a half-empty kitchen cabinet. The glass was sticky with dust from disuse.

Yolanda had probably used coupe glasses every day of her short life. She probably drank champagne as often as I drank hot tea with honey.

Yolanda, Yolanda, Yolanda. Yolanda, who'd buried her heart in an iron casket, only to have it turn to ashes. I couldn't remember where that line had come from—a half-remembered poem? A song?—and then I had it. Chanteur Malheureux. Yolanda's voice, filled with passion and sorrow.

I hummed the line to myself. I plunked it out on my keyboard with one hand, the other hand clutching the coupe glass, and tried to recall as much of the melody as I could. I sang along, hoping more of it would come to me. The song was haunting and melancholy, and right now it suited my mood.

I got out my phone and tried to look it up, typing fragments of half-remembered lyrics into a search engine and sifting through results that didn't seem to have anything to do with what I was looking for. I found one result for that exact phrase, *buried my heart in an iron casket*. It led me to a streaming video.

As soon as the video started playing, I knew I'd found the song. Whoever had uploaded the video had transcribed the lyrics in the description field; the video looked like footage of a performance at a small club, and it had been uploaded over five years ago.

The uploader didn't know the title, either. I read her description: *really good singer at the lonely lady in old port last night, this song made me cry, dunno what it is, i cant find anything about it but i love it lol.*

In the video, the song was sung by a curvy redhead in a sequined tank top and skintight jeans. She held a microphone in one hand and kept her other arm draped over the top of the upright piano, which was being played by a stunning dark-skinned woman dressed in a gold lamé tunic. As the redhead sang, I started singing along with her, feeling my way through the melody, enjoying the tune, enjoying the singer, who was performing it beautifully, infusing the words with meaning. She was almost as good as Yolanda . . .

Well, holy crap.

I was singing a duet with Yolanda. Five years ago, a red-haired Yolanda had sung this song in a club in . . .

Old Port? Was that a town?

A quick search showed it was a neighborhood, actually, in Portland, Maine. Per Balenciaga, Yolanda once had a phone number with a Maine area code.

More searching. The Lonely Lady was a lounge near the Portland waterfront. From online reviews, it seemed like a dive, but it was known for attracting good local performers. Blues, mostly, and some jazz. Definitely no opera.

I watched the video again and again. I drank more champagne. Yolanda looked fleshier in the video, chestier, though that might be the camera angle. Five years ago, she might've been pregnant with Violet. She looked gorgeous.

So now I knew: Yolanda was from Portland, Maine, or she had lived there at one time, or had at least performed there. Maybe she'd worked at the escrow company there, if what she'd told me was the truth, and she'd left Violet behind with a coworker while she headed to New York on her own.

It was Friday night. Portland was a five-and-a-half-hour drive from Manhattan. I could rent a car first thing in the morning and drive up there, then spend the day looking for Violet. I'd come back early on Sunday, in plenty of time for Monday's tech rehearsal.

A lot hinged on being at my very best at that rehearsal,

well rested and focused, and a substantial part of me thought I should abandon this reckless plan and spend the weekend badgering Gerard for as much extra coaching as he could give me. In any case, I wasn't supposed to leave the city without permission; Abernathy had explicitly told me that during last night's interrogation.

But I was going to leave anyway. Maybe the champagne was making my decision for me, but I knew it in my soul: I was going to head up to Maine in the morning, find Yolanda's kid, and uncover the buried secrets of someone I'd admired and despised.

22

Vortex of Bland Perfection

I'd never been to Maine, and given more time, I would have chosen a more picturesque route so I could enjoy the fall foliage. Instead, I zipped along the interstate in my cheap little rental car. I hadn't driven in years, ever since moving to the city, and sitting behind the wheel surrounded by wide-open space was a pleasant sensation. It felt freeing.

This was a stupid endeavor. I'd realized that in the morning after I'd sobered up from the champagne. This was a waste of money, to say nothing of valuable rehearsal time, and it would probably come to nothing. But I remembered that electric stab of excitement I'd felt when I'd recognized Yolanda in that video, the giddy feeling of discovering something unknown to anyone else, and I wanted to indulge that feeling to its natural end.

In Portland, I could find out who Yolanda really was and where she'd learned to sing like that. Maybe I could find out why she'd turned into such a rotten yet compulsively attractive person. I could track down her daughter and make sure she was doing okay.

When I arrived in town, I headed straight for the Lonely Lady, where I was greeted by darkness punctuated by the neon glow of beer logos and a pervasive smell of fried fish. We were in that nebulous zone after lunch but before happy hour, so the place was mostly empty, apart from a pair of guys in heavy canvas jackets sitting at the bar who looked like they might live there. I hadn't eaten, so I ordered haddock from the bartender along with a beer that I didn't want but felt I should get, because it didn't seem like the sort of place where I could ask for a mug of hot water and a wedge of lemon without being mocked. The bartender was old and leathery, but when I asked him how long he'd been working there, he said he'd only started over the summer, which meant he'd be no good for my purposes. I asked about the owner, and he pointed in the direction of a corner booth, where a woman sat by herself, reader glasses on, leaning close to the screen of her laptop. I took my beer over to her and asked if I could talk to her for a minute.

She looked up. She was somewhere in her fifties, with deep lines on her face. She shoved the reader glasses down her nose so she could look at me. "Grab a seat."

I slid into the booth across from her. She looked wary, like she was afraid I wanted to register a complaint about her establishment. I had a cover story all prepared, an alternate version of events that didn't include the phrase "brutally murdered," so I launched into it.

"I'm trying to locate a friend. We were in an opera together. I lost track of her, and then I saw her online in a video that was filmed here." I'd noted the platform stage along the back wall and the upright piano covered with a checkered vinyl tablecloth for protection. "This was a few years ago, but do you know if she still lives in town?"

I held out my phone with the video playing. The woman didn't look at it at first. She kept her eyes locked with mine, as though trying to suss out if I had any nefarious motives. She glanced down as Yolanda started singing. The sound quality wasn't great, but even so, the soulful voice that streamed out of my phone still sent chills down my spine.

The woman stared at the screen. She shook her head, and I felt a twinge of disappointment. "I don't know her. We have multiple performances each week, and after a while they all run together," she said. "But you could always ask Opal."

"Okay, great," I said. I took a quick glance around the bar. "Does she work here?"

The woman tapped the phone. "Opal Cazenave. The pianist." The beautiful woman in the gold lamé tunic. "She's a vocal coach. That girl is probably one of her students. Opal brings them in to perform whenever we don't have another act booked."

"Do you know how I can contact her?"

"I'm sure she has a website. I'd start with that. She probably doesn't have too much free time right now, though. She's in the middle of performances."

"Where does she perform?" I asked.

"Right now, she's at the Tate Theater. They're doing an opera." The woman closed her eyes, as though searching her brain for the name. "*Die Fledermaus*. That's it. I saw it on opening night. Opera is emphatically not my kind of music—no offense, I know you just mentioned you're a singer—but I couldn't take my eyes off Opal. She's a born performer." She laughed, loose and easy. "I'm biased, though. Opal is an old, old friend. I've known her ever since she was Harry."

I stared at the woman, trying to make sense of that last statement. "Since she was hairy?"

"Harold. I went to my prom with Harry Van Allen. Not as boyfriend-girlfriend; he and I were a pair of dorks in the jazz choir. No one wanted to date us, and he was just my smart, funny friend with a crazy talent for music. After graduation, he went off to some school in Paris and performed his way across Europe, singing for kings and queens, and somewhere along the way, Harry became Opal. Though to hear her tell it, she was Opal all along, it was just the rest of the world that hadn't known it." She grinned, which dropped decades off her and made her look like a high school kid delighted by the success of her talented friend. "Opal moved back to Portland about ten years ago, still doing her thing. She might've made some changes to her outer shell, but she's still got that amazing voice."

I nodded. Trans performers in professional opera are rare but not anomalous, and in any case, opera has a long-established history of gender fluidity: In bygone days, female parts were sometimes sung by castrati, and many popular operas feature trouser roles, which are male characters performed by a soprano, mezzo, or contralto. I was tempted to spill all this knowledge to the woman, then realized her interest in opera was limited, and besides, she'd already told me everything I needed to know.

I checked into a budget hotel, where I took a moment to purchase a seat for that night's performance of *Die Fledermaus* at the Tate, upgrading my ticket to include a post-performance reception with the cast members. I showered and changed into clean black pants, a beige wool sweater, and the same black boots and coat I'd been wearing all fall. I looked presentable yet drab, even with the fake Birkin bag hanging off my arm. I scrutinized myself in the bathroom mirror and wished that I'd packed some clothes with a bit more pizzazz. I thought about Yolanda showing up to *La Traviata* in silver and sequins. Sequins weren't quite my style, but it was dawning on me that I had no style at all. In terms of appearance, I was a void.

My mood was gloomy when I arrived at the theater, but it lifted when the curtain rose. It was an excellent production. *Die Fledermaus* is an opera I know backward and forward, so I had to restrain the urge to move my lips along with the libretto. Opal played Rosalinde's spouse, a gender-flipped Gabriel von Eisenstein, singing in a magnificent tenor while dressed in a long gown adorned with ruffles and bows, and she was marvelous. The woman at the Lonely Lady had claimed Opal had sung in Europe for kings and queens, and I'd assumed that was hyperbole, but now I could give it some credence. Opal had a voice suited for royalty.

To my eyes, Opal was the star, though the entire ensemble was strong. Except . . .

I paid special attention to the young and lovely soprano playing the flirtatious little chambermaid, Adele. She had a meticulous voice, clear and precise, and her facial expressions were bright and easy to interpret, and yet she was a great sucking black hole in the middle of the stage, an absolute abyss of charisma; during her performance of "Adele's Laughing Song," a crowd-pleaser of an aria that should have been a slam dunk, I found my eyes roving around the stage, waiting for Opal to sing again.

And then it dawned on me, terribly and inexorably, that while I'd been hung up on concepts like sexy/unsexy, charming/charmless, attractive/plain, *this* was what Daniel and Marla had meant about me. I was this soprano, trained and talented and doing everything correctly, yet adrift in a vortex of bland perfection. Sitting in my seat in the darkened auditorium, I felt my face burn bright with shame. There's nothing more humiliating than realizing you actually kind of suck at something you've long considered one of your great strengths.

The opera ended, and I stood and clapped with everyone else when Opal took her bow, because while the entire production had operated at a high level, Opal had earned an ovation.

The post-performance reception included wine and hors d'oeuvres. I accepted a glass of water, wanting to keep my head clear, and waited for the performers to emerge.

Opal was surrounded, immediately and deservedly, by fans and well-wishers who thronged about her and showered her with praise. She was still in her costume, and she was gorgeous, even with the exaggerated layer of stage makeup on her skin and the sweat that soaked the hairline of her curled wig. I waited in the mob, heart beating, and I couldn't tell if that was because I might be close to finding out secrets about Yolanda, or because Opal was a star and I was a brand-new fan.

Opal turned her attention to me at last, and I was ready. "You were wonderful," I said quickly. "You were the best Eisenstein I've ever seen."

Opal took my hands and pressed them between both of hers. She smiled. "Thank you so much."

She released my hands and seemed ready to turn to the next guest, but I whipped my phone out, the streaming video loaded up. "I'm an opera singer in New York, and this woman, this former student of yours, was my understudy. I wondered if I could talk to you about her."

I could see a faint flicker cross Opal's face at the request, as though she was exhausted from a long performance and knew she'd have to maintain an outer façade of lively bonhomie for a while longer, which would be difficult enough without strangers sticking their phones in her face and asking her to watch online videos. But she graciously looked down at the screen, then froze.

She gently circled my wrist with one long, slim hand and brought the phone up closer to her eyes. When she looked at me, for the first time the stage illusion had cracked, and she looked middle-aged and weary. "Ah, that one," she said. "What did she do this time?"

"She's dead," I said.

A moment frozen in time, and then the side of Opal's mouth twitched. "Excuse the silence," she said. "I had to censor my first dozen replies to that, because my momma in heaven would be disappointed in me for speaking ill of the departed." She looked me in the eye, her expression calm. "She was your understudy? Did she pull an *All About Eve* on you? Steal your role and steal your man? Or did she go full-on *Showgirls* and push you down the stairs?"

"No stairs. Just an oncoming subway train." Opal's eyebrows twitched upward at that, and while my reply had taken her by surprise, I could tell she believed me.

This wasn't a conversation we should have in public, and there were others vying for Opal's attention. I spoke quickly. "I'm returning to New York in the morning, but I really would like to speak to you. When you're done here, could I take you to dinner?" After a performance, I'm always ready to devour everything in sight.

She shook her head, the coiled ringlets of her wig bobbing around her shoulders. "After this, I want to go home, crawl into pajamas, and pour myself a large glass of wine."

Very understandable, and I was in no position to argue. I tried to think of a non-pushy way I could convey the importance of my request, but before I could make my case, Opal spoke again. "Stop by my home in an hour. I can give you twenty minutes. Do you have a pen?"

I didn't, but I had my phone, and I entered Opal's home address into it. "Thank you," I said, but Opal had already turned away, clasping the hands of her next admirer, accepting their praise with calm grace.

23

Glitter and Be Gay

Opal lived in a pale mauve town house in a neighborhood called Munjoy Hill. A painted sign dangling above her wraparound front porch featured her name in gold calligraphy, along with the designation VOCAL COACH. I rang the doorbell, and Opal answered.

She'd shed her costume and stage makeup, of course, though she hadn't gone quite as far as pajamas; she was dressed in a soft white hoodie and matching wide-legged pants. Her head was shaved, with only a soft fuzz on her scalp. She held a glass of white wine in her hand and smiled at me, though she looked a bit tentative. "I didn't get your name back there."

"Kit Margolis. I should have introduced myself."

The smile widened as she ushered me inside and closed the door behind me. "An opera singer named Kit?"

Opal's home was dramatic, with violet walls patterned with flowering vines painted in copper, the wallpaper peeling at the top near the crown molding. She motioned for me to take a seat on a sofa with a carved wood back. "I go by Katerina onstage," I said.

Opal laughed. "That's more like it. Wine?"

"Please," I said. Opal headed into her kitchen while I scoped out the gilt-framed posters of past productions hung on her walls: She'd performed in *Figaro* at Staatsoper Berlin, in *Tosca* at La Monnaie in Brussels.

Opal handed me a glass. The wine was sweet, cold, and thick. "Thank you for agreeing to meet with me. I know you must be exhausted," I said.

"Not at all. I'm dying to learn more of the tragic fate of our mutual friend Kimberly." Opal's tone was flippant, but I sensed she was using flippancy to disguise something deeper, maybe painful. She sank down next to me and folded up her long legs beneath her, one arm resting on the carved back.

"Kimberly? Was that her name? I knew her as Yolanda Archambeau."

"A fine opera name. I approve." Opal sipped her wine. "Kimberly Stubbings. Obviously she'd need to change that."

She was quiet. I thought it was best not to crowd her thoughts, so I sipped my wine and waited.

At last, she let out a weary sigh. "She was in an opera with you? You said New York? Which company?"

"Brio? It's small. We're in the Tammany Performing Arts Center in Midtown."

Opal nodded slowly. "Brio. They're interesting, aren't they? I remember reading something a while back. An opera based on . . . was it *Charlie's Angels*?"

"That's the one. Yolanda and I were in an opera based on *Barbarella*."

Opal gave a small cough, like she'd been consumed with the urge to giggle in the middle of a sip of her wine. "Well. That's either going to be dreadful or fabulous. Which is it?"

"The opera itself is fabulous. Our production of it could go either way. Opening night is next Friday."

"I remember the film well. You're playing Barbarella?" There was no judgment in Opal's voice, but I found myself flushing.

"Yes. And Yolanda was covering the role." I smiled, trying to seem loose and relaxed. "You're probably thinking Yolanda—Kimberly, sorry—would be a more natural fit for the part."

"Don't assume you know what I'm thinking." It was light. "I won't say appearance doesn't matter, but of all the criteria that make one right for a role, it should be given the least weight. I can't imagine Strauss had someone who looks like me in mind when he wrote the role of Gabriel von Eisenstein."

I'd had those thoughts before, about the relative unimportance of appearance on the list of reasons to cast a singer, and it felt good to have them confirmed by an authority like Opal. "We're supposed to start performances next week, but since Yolanda's murder, we've had some big setbacks, and our production schedule is in doubt."

"Murder." Opal looked pensive. "You didn't mention that part, though it's a logical enough end for Kimberly. You didn't do it?" It was teasing, but her eyes watched me closely.

I shook my head. "She was stabbed to death. I was with her at the time, though."

"Goodness gracious." Opal's eyes widened. "Were you hurt?"

I shook my head, suddenly aware that I didn't want to talk about it, couldn't talk about it. "I was asleep at the time. Drugged," was all I managed to say about that night. My throat closed up; I drank more wine, a large swallow, to lubricate it enough to continue speaking. "Yolanda was a complicated person. I didn't like her very much, but in some ways I found her fascinating."

"Really? I always found her fairly simple. Duplicitous, of course, but in an obvious way." Opal rested her wineglass on her folded knees. She looked impossibly elegant. Suddenly and fiercely, I wished I could be Opal, unwinding in her beautiful and comfortable home after her onstage tour de force.

"I met Kimberly . . . oh, probably six years ago now. She had an office job in town. I want to say it was in real estate, but I'm not sure that's right. She was bored with work and wanted something more out of life. She'd been a star soloist in her high school choir, she said, so she asked me for music lessons."

I nodded to let Opal know I was following along. It was dark, the room lit with multiple candles arranged on the marble coffee table in front of us. They cast soft pools of light up to the ceiling, which was tiled in squares of embossed copper.

"She'd had lessons before, musical theater and jazz and cabaret performance, and she wanted to continue in that vein. I said fine, we could do some of that, but my specialty is classical music. Opera. She was willing to learn. And she was very good."

"She had a beautiful voice," I said. "And you trained her well."

Opal shrugged. "I did what I could. But learning opera through two lessons a week . . ." She closed her eyes and pinched the bridge of her nose, giving her head a small shake. "Even though she was also practicing on her own, that's not nearly enough, not for the level of ability I sensed she wanted. I had difficulty convincing her of that, though. Frankly, I'm not sure she ever comprehended it."

I thought of Yolanda's conviction that she'd perform onstage at the Met someday. "Why do you dislike her so much?" I asked.

She wrinkled up her mouth in a sour twist, like she'd just eaten something unpleasant. "Because she was rotten at her core. I'm sure she had a bad childhood or something terrible in her past, but she was spoiled and cruel, always trampling over others to grab whatever she wanted and lashing out if she couldn't get it."

Opal sighed and leaned back into the sofa. "I raised my rates. She'd told me she was struggling, so I'd given her a very good deal, the same deal I give to other students who have trouble making ends meet. With Kimberly, I wasn't sure it was worth it. She had a stable desk job with benefits; she had designer clothes, a sporty little Miata, all the signs of someone doing well for herself. She went to New Orleans for Mardi Gras. She went to Miami for two weeks, then chartered a boat to the Caribbean with some friends and spent her winter break resort hopping. Lord knows I don't begrudge a girl any of that, but I didn't think I needed to throttle my income to allow her to live out her tropical fantasies. So when she returned, I told her I could no longer offer her the discounted rate. She threw a tantrum. She told me I was extorting her, that I was a washed-up old fraud, that I should be nicer to her because she'd be famous soon."

She rolled her eyes expressively and took a long drink of her wine. I thought of Yolanda's outburst on the day we'd met when I'd criticized her skills, right before she'd poured her eye drops into a cup of tea and handed it to me.

"I told her I could no longer teach her. The next day, the cops came to visit me. Someone had anonymously reported that I'd been grooming young boys, pupils of mine. That I'd molested them."

I felt a sick pit in my stomach. "I'm sorry," I said. It was inadequate.

"I'm a Black trans woman. If the wrong police officers had been sent to investigate, I could have ended up dead. Everything considered, it's surprising I didn't get arrested, my hard-earned reputation destroyed." Opal shook her head, fast and irritated, like she was shaking away bad memories. "None of that happened. I was born in Portland. I grew up in this neighborhood. Both my parents taught in the public school system for decades; the officers who spoke with me knew my family. Perhaps more to the point, I had no young students I could possibly have been grooming; I don't give lessons to children. Kimberly knew that, of course, and I've told myself that she might have viewed it as a prank, nothing that was likely to damage me. But I'll never forgive her for that. Never."

She looked at me. "So when you say she tried to shove you in front of a train, I have no trouble believing it."

"She also put eye drops in my tea. I was hospitalized. It could have caused organ failure; I'm lucky it didn't," I said. "She killed a rat and left it on my doorstep. She probably slipped poison in some cookies she gave me." My words came out faster and faster, now that the emotional floodgates were opened. "She did it because she wanted my role, but she didn't even have to do any of that, because the director liked her better anyway. This is my first big chance, my first lead, and everything has gone wrong. Even though she's dead, the role is probably still going to be taken from me."

My line of logic was starting to get tangled, because it wasn't Yolanda's fault that Daniel was going to replace me with Roksana. That was all my own doing, thanks to my inability to be interesting onstage. Opal stared at me like she was trying to make sense of my word salad. "Who's taking it from you now? It can't be Kimberly, not anymore."

"No. The director isn't happy with my performance. He's bringing in someone with more experience. She's sung on the stage of the Met, so she's a great choice. But my heart is breaking."

"What's wrong with your performance?"

I considered the best way to explain it. "*Die Fledermaus* tonight. I don't want to disparage the singer, but . . . Adele?"

Opal nodded, very slowly, and I could see she was on my wavelength. "You're Adele?"

"I've had the training. I can sing. I think I had a good amount of natural ability to begin with, and years of study and practice have honed it. I can act. But I'm like your Adele. Somehow it's not enough, and I don't know why."

"Will you sing for me?" Opal uncurled her body and planted her legs on the floor, suddenly crisp and professional. "Right now. Stand up. Sing something for me. Anything."

I was used to following the instructions of vocal coaches without needing to be coaxed, so I set my glass down on her coffee table, rose to my feet, inhaled, and immediately launched into "Glitter and Be Gay" from *Candide,* one of my audition standards. I was singing a cappella, and I hadn't prepared for this, but that hardly mattered; especially for a spur-of-the-moment performance after half a glass of wine, I was in good voice. I hit every note, even the song's tricky trio of high E-flats. No small feat, especially without a warm-up. Perfection.

But perfection wasn't enough, was it?

When I finished, Opal applauded softly, beating the long fingers of one hand against the palm of the other. "Brava, Katerina," she said. "That was beautiful."

"It lacks soul, doesn't it?"

Opal shook her head, but it wasn't a denial. "Soul is a subjective concept, and I often find it not very helpful. Is that what your director told you?"

I nodded. "I lack soul, I lack charm, I lack connection with my audience. I'd interpreted it to mean I lack sex appeal, but after studying your Adele tonight, I think it's something different."

Opal smiled. "I think you're not feeling the music to the extent you should, perhaps because you find the prospect of surrendering to your emotions too frightening. Your facial expressions line up perfectly with the feelings conveyed in the song, but none of it is reaching your eyes. You sing it without believing it."

"You could be right," I said cautiously. "But what can I do about it?"

"In your case? I'd suggest therapy." It was blithe, and it stung, but Opal eased the sting with a smile. "I don't mean that cruelly. I don't know you, but I would guess you've been through some things in your life that have made you want to walk a very direct and narrow path. Emotions scare you, so you hide them somewhere deep, and then when you perform, you struggle to keep them safely buried."

She gestured at me. "Shoulders back. Chin up. Let's start this again. 'Glitter and Be Gay' from the top, only sing it as though you're gutted to the core about losing the *Barbarella* part. Sing it as though this is the last time you'll ever sing again. Sing it as though you've been told you'll never be cast in another role. Sing it while feeling that loss."

"Glitter and Be Gay" is not a song about loss; it's a song about taking a secret, shallow delight in material possessions. But Opal seemed to know what she was doing, so I launched in again without complaint.

Yolanda. I thought of Yolanda stifling a yawn at my first rehearsal. The realization that Daniel preferred Yolanda to me. My inability to interpret what Daniel wanted from me in the role. His open desire to replace me with Roksana. I'd had my chance at success, and now that chance was gone.

I felt anguished. Emotion threatened to drive my voice higher, and I worried I was going sharp. Those high E-flats weren't as good this time; I didn't hit them as cleanly. It was a terrible idea to let real emotion creep in. This was wrecking my voice, which was the only thing of value that I owned.

I ended. Opal's face was unreadable. "Again," she said. "This time you're scared. You're terrified. Whatever happened when Kimberly was murdered, you said you were there. I won't ask you for details, but I will ask you to remember it. 'Glitter and Be Gay,' only in great terror."

I hesitated. "I think I went sharp last time," I said.

"You did. You should've." Opal sounded firm. "Go sharp sometimes. Not in performance, of course, but don't be afraid to go sharp when you practice. You're so hung up on being in constant control that you've placed a barrier right at the point you consider perfection, and you don't know what it feels like to go a little bit past it." She must've seen the skepticism on my face, because she chuckled and shook her head. "Don't look at it as letting imperfection creep in; look at it as reaching a new level of perfection. But you'll never know how to find the right path to that level if you don't occasionally overshoot it."

I hated this. I hated this experiment, but I was so used to doing whatever a vocal coach told me to do that I followed her advice and started singing once more. I thought about the hazy drugged terror of the night Yolanda was killed, when I woke, sick and confused, to find her body on the floor. I thought of Yolanda lying in a crumpled heap, blood staining her expensive rug, and the memory brought with it an almost delirious sense of horror. I felt like I was screaming out the song, my volume swelling, my pace quickening, and I could only hope the residents of the neighboring townhome had thick walls, because I was loud, and I was terrifying. The E-flats were there for me, incredibly, and I felt scared and angry and embarrassed and triumphant, and when I finished, Opal applauded, loudly and genuinely. She rose to her feet, gripped my arms with both hands, and gave me a small shake.

"Yes," she said. "Katerina, yes. That is where you need to be."

I couldn't speak. I thought I might burst into tears. Opal could probably see that, because she picked up my wineglass and placed it in my numb hand, then guided me back down to the couch.

"Do that," she said. "Feel that level of passion within whatever emotion *Barbarella* calls for—joy or fear or lust or anger, whatever it is—and your director will have no further thoughts of replacing you."

I took a swallow of my wine, feeling a stabilizing warmth through me. "Thank you. Thank you very much. I hope you're right."

"Of course I am. I've been doing this for years," she said, and I loved how casual she seemed, like in her mind the matter was already settled: I was Barbarella now, and that was all there was to it.

She let me sit in silence while I finished my wine. "Another glass?" she asked.

I shook my head. "I should go. You promised me twenty minutes, and I blew past that long ago."

"Was there something about Kimberly you wanted to ask me?" she asked.

Oh. The purpose of my visit. Right. "Before talking to you, I didn't know her name, or where she came from. I don't think the police know," I said. "She once told me she'd left behind a kid. I came to Portland to make sure her kid's okay."

"Her daughter. Of course. The daughter came later, after I'd already cut ties with her. I coached her through her pregnancy, but I heard about the birth from mutual friends." Opal was pensive. "I don't know anything about her. But I imagine Corey could tell you."

"Who's Corey?"

"The child's father. Corey's a musician in town. Jazz and blues, mostly. He's very talented, though he doesn't have his head screwed on straight enough to do much with his gifts. We've all got our demons, but Corey's are stronger than most." Opal smiled, and it was clear that whatever Corey's story was, Opal liked him and wished him well. "He wrote that song you played in that video, the one Kimberly sang. He's a good enough songwriter to make a go of it professionally, but I can't imagine he'll ever make that happen. But he loves—loved— Kimberly, and I'm sure he's in his daughter's life in some way, even if nobody would be foolish enough to give him custody."

"Do you have a way to contact him?"

Opal had to think about that. "Possibly. I ran into him downtown over the summer. He looked like death, strung out on lord knows what, but at least he had a place to stay. He asked me for cash; I didn't feel like giving my money more or less directly to his dealer, but I got an address from him. Dropped off a box of food. I threw in some soap and toothpaste and deodorant, because it seemed like he might be short on all of those things. Clean socks."

"You kept the address?"

Opal got up and rummaged around in a drawer in a table by the entryway and finally produced an address book. "This is where I went. Some nice girl answered the door and said she'd make sure he got my package. I can't tell you if the address is still good; this was maybe five months ago, and I don't think anyone should count on Corey to maintain a stable living situation."

She handed me the address book, open to a handwritten entry for Corey Floyd. I took a photo of the page.

"Thank you. I won't keep you any longer." I picked up my coat and my purse and faced Opal. "I don't know how to thank you. Both for the information and for your help."

Opal's eyes darted to my coat, my sweater, my slacks, my sensible boots, and I saw her frown. She looked at me, her expression unreadable. "You want to thank me? Give me your coat."

I had no idea what she meant. "I'm sorry?"

"Your coat." She gestured at it. "Leave it with me. I'll give you a replacement."

I hesitated. My coat was thoroughly unremarkable. Opal's shoulders weren't very broad, but her arms were longer than mine, and she was much taller than me, and I doubted it would fit her well. "I don't understand."

"Your coat is terrible." Opal smiled. "Or it's boring, at least, and Katerina, if you've learned nothing else tonight, it's that you can't afford to be boring. One minute." She withdrew into the back hallway and disappeared, leaving me to stare down at my coat and wonder whether it was actually terrible.

She came back with a great deal of black fabric draped over her arm. She handed it to me, and I felt feathers under my fingers. I straightened it out.

It was a long velvet frock coat, lined in satin, with a smattering of feathers sewn around the collar. It wasn't black, I now saw in the soft lights, but a very dark green. Opal gestured at it. "I bought it at a Paris flea market in a burst of optimism that it would fit, and it emphatically does not. I've hung on to it for years because I couldn't bear the thought of surrendering it to eBay. Try it on."

It was large on me, but not absurdly so, and it fit me well

at the waist before flaring out to my knees. I buttoned a small straight line of abalone buttons and faced Opal.

She surveyed me critically. "The color is good on you. Hoop earrings, I think, would go best with that haircut. Gold. They don't have to be expensive, but keep them in good condition. If you get the drugstore kind, throw them out as soon as they tarnish. Plum lipstick, as dark and creamy as you can stand. Your eyebrows are already sublime; whatever you do to them, you must keep it up." She stood back, folded her arms over her chest, and assessed me. "There. You're Katerina now, not Kit. Be Kit on your own time all you want, but at rehearsals, to make an impact on your director, Katerina must dominate. Does that make sense?"

It didn't, but it did, and I felt as though Opal had given me some key puzzle piece that I'd been missing for too long, a piece that might prove more valuable to me than my new knowledge of Yolanda's true identity.

24

Kimberly Stubbings

The address Opal had given me was on a shabbier block in her own neighborhood. The paint was peeling on many of the homes; chain-link fences surrounded dead lawns. I pulled the green velvet coat tighter around myself and wished I hadn't agreed to Opal's impromptu exchange. The coat was gorgeous, but I was freezing; my wool coat may have been terrible, but it had been warm.

It was just after eight in the morning. From the little Opal had said about him, it didn't sound as though Corey was likely to be an early riser, but after spending the night in the hotel, I wanted to get back on the road to New York as soon as I could.

The house I was looking for turned out to be tiny, just a cottage, with faded red paint and cracked cement steps. I rang the doorbell, and a young woman answered. She was short and cute, with brown skin, tight curls, and a snub nose. She wore a short-sleeved button-down shirt with the logo of a convenience store embroidered on the pocket; from inside her house, I could smell coffee. She held the door open a few inches, the warped screen door still a barrier between us, and looked at me, unspeaking and unsmiling.

"Sorry to bother you. I'm looking for Corey Floyd?" I gave her a friendly smile.

"Why?" She didn't seem hostile, but she also didn't seem likely to let me inside without a good reason.

"I have bad news about a friend."

"Which friend?" Her eyes narrowed a bit, like she knew Corey's friends and didn't like any of them.

It took me a second to remember Yolanda's real name. "Kimberly Stubbings?"

Her expression didn't change, but she blinked twice, rapidly. There was a long silence, and then she opened the door wider. "Then you want to talk to me."

I followed her inside. The interior was small and disorganized in a comfortable way; I found myself in a combination living room and dining room, featuring a sagging sofa, an armchair, and a pasteboard folding table covered with empty cereal bowls and juice glasses. Two small girls, one little more than a toddler, the other school-age, lay on their bellies on the carpet, watching a cartoon on a shared tablet. The woman crouched between them and addressed the older girl: "Laura, can you take Violet to her room and get her dressed? We're leaving for Grandma's house in fifteen minutes."

Violet. That was the name of Yolanda's daughter, and unless it was a more popular name than I thought, this woman had to be Yolanda's former coworker.

Violet was cute and chubby, with messy hair and juice-stained pajamas. She beamed at me as she rose gracelessly to her feet, accepting my presence without question. "Hi," she said.

I have no finesse with kids, none at all, so I said hi back and gave her a stiff wave, feeling awkward.

The other girl, Laura, was more reserved around strangers. She shot me a wary glance from behind a tangle of dark curls, then took Violet by one hand and led her into the back of the house. The woman waited until we heard a bedroom door close before she turned back to me. "What's this about Kimberly?"

"You might want to sit down," I said. "This is a bad story."

The woman looked blank at that, and then she shook her head as though clearing it. "Sure. Yeah. Take a seat. Look, do you want coffee? I have to leave for work soon, but I can give you a couple of minutes."

"I'm fine. Thank you." I sat down on the sofa, shifting a small stack of picture books and an empty juice box to the coffee table. The luxurious velvet coat seemed wildly out of place in these cheerfully grubby surroundings. The woman sat next to me. "My name is Kit Margolis. I came here from New York looking for Kimberly's family. Someone told me Corey might be staying here." I gestured down the hallway. "That was Kimberly's daughter? Violet?"

She looked like she didn't want to answer, and then she relaxed. "The small one's Violet, and the other is my daughter. Laura. Same daddy, Corey. I'm Trae. Kimberly and I used to work together."

"At an escrow company?"

She nodded, and I felt a dull surprise that something Yolanda had told me about her past had actually turned out to be true. "Access Title and Escrow, out in Scarborough. Two years back, Kimberly left Violet in her car seat on my front steps with a note pinned to her coat saying she'd be back in a couple of days. She called me a week later and told me it'd be longer than that, maybe months. That was the last I've heard from her." She shook her head. "Two damn years."

I tried to remember everything Yolanda had said at that wine bar after we'd seen *La Traviata*. Seemed like ages ago; it shocked me to realize it was just last week. "She said she'd burned a few bridges when she left."

Trae smiled without humor. "Usually Kimberly had a flair for exaggeration, but in this case I'd say she's downplaying it. Bitch burned whole *lives* when she left."

"Yours included?"

"Oh, yeah. Well, I mean, it turned out okay." She looked around at the comfortable mess, at the breakfast dishes and the pile of picture books I'd placed on the table. "Violet and Laura and me, the three of us make a good team. Violet is a doll, most of the time, and Laura loves her little sister. But when Kimberly got Access shut down, I lost my good job and my benefits, and since then I've been doing whatever I can while looking for something better." She tapped the convenience store logo on her shirt. "My momma lives in town, and she can look after the girls whenever I need her, so it's working out all right, but it sure would have been nice if Kimberly had stepped up and been a responsible parent."

"She sent you money, though, right? Cash every month?"

"She told you that?" She sounded grimly amused, and I felt embarrassed for accepting one of Yolanda's lies without question. "Once, right at the start, I got a FedEx envelope filled with bills, just under a grand. And then a few months later I got another one. That time it was maybe two hundred bucks. But that's been it. No calls, no texts, no emails, nothing."

"What happened at your workplace?" I asked. "Why'd it get shut down? She told me she had an affair with your boss?"

Trae nodded. "Joel. He was our chief escrow officer. Joel Tierney," she said. "He and Kimberly were sleeping around, even though he was married. At first it was fine, whatever, not my business. It got awkward, though, because they were not especially discreet about it. They'd keep running off to New York for quote-unquote business trips, leaving me to look after Violet and field a bunch of increasingly unamused calls from Joel's wife. She stormed into the office once and had a huge shouting match with her husband, right in front of all of us, so Joel finally promised to call things off with Kimberly." Trae gave me another tight smile. "I thought Kimberly would probably just quit after that, but that wasn't enough to satisfy her need for drama. So instead, she picked the nuclear option."

"Which was?"

"We handled the escrow for all these huge real estate transactions, mostly sales of office buildings and apartment complexes. Turns out Joel had been siphoning off tiny bits of money from each sale. Kimberly knew all about it. Maybe she was in on it with him from the start; I didn't know a damn thing until the cops raided our offices, which was just a *super* fun day for everyone there, myself included. They took Joel away in handcuffs, and that was the end of my career in the exciting world of escrow."

"Kimberly tipped off the cops?"

"She sure did. But not before she cleaned out Joel's secret bank account. It had maybe a hundred grand in it, which was a nice little cash bonus for her. Then she dumped Violet on my steps and skipped town."

"What happened to Joel?" I asked. Throughout her short life, Yolanda had left ruin in her wake wherever she went.

"He's in jail for embezzlement. Judge gave him a five-year sentence," Trae said. "I can't say he didn't deserve it, but if this were a fairer world, Kimberly would be there with him." For the first time, she sounded nakedly resentful.

"I take it you and Kimberly weren't friends?" I asked.

"At one point, I thought we were cool." Trae scrunched up her face, like she'd smelled something unpleasant. "I guess she trusted me enough to leave her child with me, so there's that. But no, she's not someone I could ever call a friend." Something bitter crept into her voice, the same bitterness I'd heard from Opal when she was recounting the way Yolanda had casually tried to destroy her life.

"She did something shitty to you, didn't she? I mean, apart from leaving her kid with you?" I asked. Trae looked surprised and maybe a little suspicious, so I smiled. "She did something shitty to me, so I was just wondering."

"Yeah, well. Okay, you asked about Corey." Trae exhaled. "Corey and I were together for a long time. *Years.* Corey had his problems, tons of them, but at heart there was something sweet about him. And we had Laura together, and I'm never going to be unhappy about that. So one fine day I introduced him to my funny, gorgeous, talented coworker, Kimberly. She could sing like an angel, and Corey wrote music fit for angels. Sounds like a great partnership, right?"

"Until Kimberly ended up pregnant with Violet?"

"Until Kimberly ended up pregnant with Violet." Trae nodded slowly. "I kicked Corey out, obviously, and he and Kimberly got a place together, and for a while they seemed happy. It made things pretty damn awkward between me and Kimberly at work, especially since she'd drag Corey with her to work-related social events, but I'm a grownup, so I got past it. And then the way Corey told it, before she even gave birth, Kimberly got tired of him. She kicked him out and started screwing around with Joel, who was good-looking and lived in an expensive house, and even though he was married, he probably struck Kimberly as a more attractive long-term prospect than Corey. Corey had nowhere to go, so I let him crash here whenever he wanted." She shrugged. "We weren't together, not anymore. He was a cheat and a junkie. But he was my daughter's daddy, and it was nice for Laura to have both parents around."

"And Kimberly?"

Trae nodded, like she figured I could guess the next part of the story. "Outwardly, Kimberly seemed cool with it. I mean, she'd kicked him out, right? I assumed she was happy with whatever she had going on with Joel and didn't give a damn about me and Corey. But the week Corey moved back in with me, someone swatted us."

It took me a moment to work out what she meant. "Like . . . SWAT team, swatted?"

"Uh-huh. Someone called the cops and told them some drug addict on a delusional rampage was holed up with a gun and hostages inside this house. SWAT team came and burst down the doors and threw me and Corey on the ground, with Laura screaming and crying in her bedroom the whole time. Nobody got hurt, apart from some pretty traumatic memories, and it was cleared up fast, but . . . I mean, that could have been bad. Fatally bad. I don't know for absolutely sure it was Kimberly, but . . ."

"But you know Kimberly," I said.

Trae nodded. "But I know Kimberly."

"Kimberly's dead," I said. It didn't seem like Trae was the type who would need me to break the news gently. "She was killed in New York last week. I knew her a bit, enough to know about Violet, and I wanted to make sure Violet was doing okay."

"Violet's fine. Violet's great." Trae sounded defensive, but I believed her. I knew the warning signs of troubled households, and I saw none of them here. "But what happened to Kimberly? How was she killed?"

"She was murdered. Stabbed to death. They haven't caught whoever did it." I left it at that. I saw no benefit to explaining how I fit into the picture. After last night's conversation with Opal, I felt raw, like I'd exposed too much of myself to a stranger.

Trae was staring at me, her eyes very large and dark, and her face was unnaturally still, like she'd just suffered a profound shock. I was starting to think I should have broken the news of Yolanda's murder more gently, and then she spoke. "Okay, that's weird," she said. "Because Corey was stabbed to death a month ago."

It came as a jolt. I had noted her use of past tense throughout our conversation whenever she'd mentioned Corey, but I'd assumed that was because her ex was no longer a part of her life. "Christ. What happened to him? Do you think there's a connection?"

"Who knows? It doesn't seem likely, though, does it? The world's a violent place." Trae's words made sense, but I saw the small furrow in her brow, which indicated to me that she wasn't entirely convinced of what she was saying. "They haven't caught whoever did it, but Corey was spending most of his nights out on the street, whenever he wasn't crashing on my couch. Cops are working on the theory someone stabbed him before rolling him for whatever cash or drugs he had on him, and knowing Corey as I did, I think that sounds about right. Still, though . . ." She shrugged. "It's a weird coincidence."

It was probably no more than that, but I thought at the very least it was a coincidence worth exploring. "Do you know if Kimberly and Corey kept in touch after she left Portland?" I thought that was a long shot. To my surprise, Trae nodded.

"I asked Corey once if he knew where she'd gone." For a moment, she looked younger and more optimistic. "I want to adopt Violet. A family court gave me temporary custody, but I'm always terrified someone's going to take her away from me. I wanted to find Kimberly and get her to help me make Violet legally mine. Corey said he had no idea where she was, but when I pushed him, he told me that Kimberly had emailed him shortly after she left town."

"Did she tell him where she was living?"

"He said she refused. She thought he might try to find her if she let him know which city she was in, which . . . yeah, I can see him doing that. Corey and I always got along pretty well, and for a long time I think we were probably in love, but whatever he felt about me was nothing compared to what he felt about Kimberly. He was obsessed with her. He wrote her dozens of songs, really beautiful ones. He would've happily died for her." Trae's smile looked tight and bitter again, and I wanted to tell her I knew how she was feeling. It was easy to suddenly turn invisible when compared to Yolanda.

So Corey couldn't have told Yolanda's killer where she was living. A small, flickering flame of thought that had ignited in my mind—that Yolanda had been murdered by someone she'd wronged in her past, someone who'd also murdered Corey after finding out where she'd gone after fleeing Portland—was quickly extinguished. However, Trae wasn't done talking.

"Corey was desperate to see Kimberly, so she gave him a link to some damn titty site where she was showing her worldly treasures for money. She told him he could watch her online and chat with her there." Again that tight smile; I felt guilty for making Trae dredge up what were obviously unwelcome memories. "Corey always needed money from me, always. I knew better than to give him cash, so I gave him two hundred on a prepaid Visa about a month before he was killed. You know how he spent it?"

"Chatting with Kimberly on the titty site?"

"What an awfully good guess." Trae shook her head. "Can you believe that?"

I thought it over. If Corey had told someone about Yolanda's Somebody's Baby account, that person could have chatted with her under an alias. Balenciaga had said Yolanda was careless about her personal safety. Like that post office box she kept to receive gifts, for example: Anyone who knew that address would know she lived in the greater New York City area. New York was a big place, but once her killer was in the city, maybe he could've figured out where she lived. Maybe he trailed her from the post office when she went to pick up her gifts.

But who would have done that? Was it even remotely logical to assume Yolanda's murder was related to Corey's murder? I thought there was a chance of it, at least: Two violent stabbing deaths in a month seemed significant. Could be a coincidence, but I felt a tingle at the back of my neck telling me there was a connection.

"Trae, if anyone you know was likely to murder Kimberly, who would it be?"

She frowned, and I thought she might demand to know what my interest was in this matter. "I guess Joel is the obvious choice," she said at last. "He was crazy about her, like he almost ruined his marriage for her, and she stole his money and put his ass in jail. But he's still got three years to go on his sentence, so he's out. Maybe it's his wife. Linh." She spelled it. "She's Vietnamese, I think. I met her a few times. Each year Joel and Linh would host a big Christmas party at their home, and she was always very nice to me, even when she was furious about her husband's bad behavior. But when Kimberly called me after she skipped town to make sure I was cool with keeping Violet for an undetermined amount of time, she said she'd been forced to leave because her life was in danger. She said Linh tried to murder her."

"Wait. What?"

"I know." Trae gave me a half smile. "Kimberly had that effect on people, right? Joel and Kimberly went to a big escrow conference in New York together, and whatever Linh saw in her husband's credit card bill after that trip made her think the two of them had been up to no good, which I guarantee you was absolutely the case. According to Kimberly, Linh was waiting for her in the parking garage in her big honking Land Rover when she was leaving the office, and she tried to run her down. Knocked her to the pavement and gunned the motor when she got back up. Kimberly told me if she hadn't managed to run to the stairwell in time, she would have been dead."

That was an interesting twist. Yolanda had frozen on the stage at Chanteur Malheureux. She'd told me she'd been startled because she thought she'd seen someone she didn't want to see. I'd assumed she was lying to cover up a burst of stage fright, but maybe she'd caught a glimpse of Joel's wife in the crowd. Maybe Linh had slipped the drug in Yolanda's cocktail—my cocktail—then trailed us back to Yolanda's apartment, after stealing Yolanda's keys from her purse backstage.

But that was only a wild theory, and I didn't know what I could do with it. I'd come to Maine to learn everything I could about Yolanda and make sure her kid was fine; now I knew about Yolanda's past, and I knew Violet was better off with Trae than she ever would have been with Kimberly Stubbings. I was done here. I should get in the rental car and drive back to New York.

I had been silent for a long time, staring into the distance, thinking. When I snapped back to the present, Trae was staring at me, her expression strange. She cleared her throat. "Hey, I need to get ready for work . . ."

"You've been a lot of help. I appreciate it," I said. "I'm glad you're taking good care of Violet." I thought about leaving it at that, but there was one more thing I needed. "You said you used to go to parties at Joel and Linh's home. Do you still have that address?"

"I do, yeah," Trae said slowly. She took her phone out and started flipping through her contacts. "But do you really think Linh . . . ?"

She didn't finish it. I shook my head. "I don't know," I said. "But I think it's worth checking out."

She passed me her phone, and I set about copying the home address of Joel and Linh Tierney into my own phone. She sat in silence, watching me, and then asked, "Who are you?"

It was blunt, and I could see it had just now dawned on her that she'd done a lot of talking to a complete stranger who'd popped up on her doorstep with bad news about an old nemesis. "You said you knew Kimberly, but are you a private detective or something?"

"Just an opera singer," I said. I handed her phone back and got to my feet. "Thanks for your help."

25

Wedding Photo

The address Trae gave me for the Tierney home was in an upscale neighborhood called Back Cove, which looked pleasant and inviting, the enormous trees still hanging on to their multicolored leaves well into fall. I drove through winding streets of large, graceful homes, catching occasional glimpses of the waterfront of the namesake cove. Along the way, I made a quick detour to a drugstore, because it had dawned on me that, in this rare instance, my unmemorable appearance might lead me into trouble. If Linh Tierney had indeed been at Chanteur Malheureux, she might have noted Yolanda's drab friend. Even if she didn't remember the particulars of my face, the arrival on her doorstep of a nondescript creature asking uncomfortable questions about her husband's ex-flame might alarm her, if she had indeed traveled down to New York to murder the ex-flame.

I was unused to shopping for makeup, so I tried to remember Opal's off-the-cuff recommendations and fulfilled them as best I could. I picked up lipstick in a deep shade of plum, plus a dark eyeliner pencil and a cheap pair of gold hoop earrings. In the front seat of the rental car, I gave myself a fast and dirty makeover in the rearview mirror. In the end, I thought I looked a bit silly yet undeniably more memorable, especially while wearing the gloriously over-the-top velvet coat. Surely no one would recognize me as the mouse who'd hung out with Yolanda on the night she was murdered.

Maybe this was a reckless endeavor, but I had my reasons. If Yolanda's killer had come out of her past, I would clearly need to tell Abernathy everything I'd learned in Portland. But I wasn't supposed to leave New York, and I certainly wasn't supposed to be off conducting a renegade amateur investigation into Yolanda's murder, and there was a strong possibility I could get into serious trouble for this. Abernathy didn't like me, and he'd be furious about my unsanctioned out-of-state travel, unless I could hand him some solid evidence pointing to Yolanda's killer. My plan was to knock on Linh's door, posing as an utterly oblivious out-of-town stranger looking to get back in touch with an old friend who used to work for Joel Tierney. I'd seize the chance to scrutinize Linh's reaction to my unexpected mention of Kimberly Stubbings; I was willing to bet I could tell if I was chatting with Yolanda's killer. If I thought Linh was guilty, I'd contact Abernathy immediately and tell him all about my suspicions. If not, I'd slink back into New York and hope my absence had gone unnoticed.

Linh Tierney lived in a white three-story home with a steeply gabled roof, located on a tree-filled corner lot. A Land Rover was parked in the driveway in front of the two-car garage, which lent credence to Trae's story about Linh running Yolanda down. I reminded myself to be on my guard.

When I rang the doorbell, a dog barked behind the closed door, loud and angry. The door opened a few inches, the chain lock still on. I saw a young Asian woman dressed in what looked like surgical scrubs, her hair tied up in a messy topknot. Her expression was equally balanced between friendliness and natural caution around strangers. "Hi," she said. "What's up?" She touched the collar of the scariest-looking dog I'd ever seen, a one-eyed pit bull with an ear missing, its face divided by a long pink scar, who stood by her side, staring up at me with a petulant expression on its face.

At the sight of the woman, I realized I was on the wrong track. Measuring from her scuffed-up Crocs to her topknot, Linh had to be a few inches under five feet; I'd be shocked if she weighed over a hundred pounds. If Yolanda had been found dead in the bed beside me, stabbed to death while still asleep, maybe I could believe Linh had done the deed. But Yolanda had been tall and strong and healthy, and she'd confronted her knife-wielding killer in her living room; barring a streak of wild luck, I didn't think there was any way this petite woman could've stabbed Yolanda multiple times, attacking from the front, ending with a blow directly to the heart. Even unarmed, Yolanda would've defended herself, and I was willing to bet she would've won.

This would likely be a waste of time, but as long as I was here, I figured I might as well go through with it. "I'm looking for Joel Tierney?" I asked.

The young woman snorted. "You can stand in line. But I have to tell you, I don't think there's going to be much left of him after his parole officer gets to him."

Parole officer. "You're Linh Tierney?"

"It's Linh Phan, actually. I've been divorced for a couple of years." The pit bull tried to slide past her out the partially open door; without taking her attention away from me, Linh patted it firmly on the collar. At her touch, it stopped moving and stared up at her. "What do you want with Joel?"

"He's been paroled? I'd heard he was still in jail."

"Paroled in August, cleared out his bank account and dropped off the face of the earth in September. Every couple of weeks someone from the Department of Corrections drops by to see if I'm hiding him in the garage or whatever." Linh frowned at me. "Is that you?"

I shook my head. Linh scrutinized me, and I realized how

incongruous I must look in this nice upscale residential neighborhood, dressed in velvet and feathers. Linh seemed to reach the same conclusion, because she grinned. "You don't look it," she said. She was probably about my age, but she had a smattering of freckles across her nose that made her look like a teenager. "But if you knew Joel was in jail, why are you looking for him here?"

"I'm here under false pretenses." Linh's eyebrows twitched up at my confession, but she didn't seem alarmed. "I actually wanted to talk to you about Kimberly Stubbings."

"One of my favorite subjects." It was ironic. "You want to come in? That's a fabulous coat, but you look like you're freezing."

If Linh turned out to be a murderer, accepting her invitation would be a bad move. But she seemed only darkly amused by my mention of Kimberly Stubbings, and it seemed like she might be willing to talk about her.

She closed the door to take off the chain lock, then opened it wide. I hesitated, not out of any particular wariness about Linh, but because the pit bull was blocking my path. Linh gave it an affectionate pat on its muscular flank. "Just nudge past Flower, and she'll get out of your way. She's a sweetie to people I like. It's only people I don't like who have to worry."

"Good to know. Hi, Flower." I lowered my hand to her snout, and Flower snuffled against it. When I patted the top of her head, Flower butted up against me, leaning into my touch, tilting her head up to gaze at me with liquid eyes. She trotted beside me, anxious for more pats, as I followed Linh into the house.

"My name is Kit Margolis," I said. "I was a friend of Kimberly's in New York."

"Kimberly has friends? Go figure." Linh snorted again. "Sorry. I'd say she's not my favorite person, but I'd be underselling our whole dynamic." She padded in her Crocs toward the open kitchen. "Can I make you some coffee? I'm drinking chamomile tea, because I just got off the night shift and it's past my bedtime, but the water's still hot."

"Tea would be lovely." Linh's house was nice; her furniture was heavy and good quality and looked expensive. Flower wasn't the only animal in residence: A huge tank filled with colorful fish took up a good chunk of the far wall, and a fluffy white cat glared at me with magnificent green eyes, then jumped off the arm of the chesterfield sofa and stalked out of the room. "Are you a doctor?"

"Veterinarian. I work at the twenty-four-hour emergency clinic." Linh poured hot water over a tea bag. I watched her movements carefully to make sure she didn't slip anything else into the mug. She passed it to me and gestured for me to take a seat on the sofa. "So . . . Kimberly?"

The mug was delightfully warm in my hands, which had become numb with cold just from standing outside Linh's home for a couple of minutes. I loved Opal's coat, but the weather was only going to get colder over the next few months; I might have to relegate it to the back of my closet until spring. "Kimberly's dead," I said.

Flower flopped to the carpet at Linh's feet, resting her big scarred head on her front paws. She raised her nose to look at me, like she sensed the vibe in the room shifting, and Linh leaned down to give her a reassuring pat.

"I wish I could feel bad about that." Linh sounded thoughtful. She picked up her own mug from a coaster on the coffee table and took a long drink of her tea. "I know I should, like I'm sure there were people out there who loved her and will miss her, and I guess I feel bad for their loss, but she was *such* a crappy human being." She shook her head. "So what happened to her? Why are you here to see me?"

Hard to know where to even start. "Kimberly and I were in an opera together. She was my understudy."

Linh smiled. "You look a lot more like an opera singer than

a parole officer," she said. "You said New York? Are you anyone I should know? Like, in the opera world, are you famous?"

No one had ever asked me that before. I shook my head. Linh looked disappointed.

"You look like you could be famous," she said. "I hope that's not a weird thing to say."

It *was* a little weird, but it was also unexpectedly flattering. I could feel my face growing hot with embarrassment, but I felt happy that she thought I looked dramatic, or maybe even a little glamorous. In any case, she thought I looked like I belonged on a stage.

I cleared my throat. "Since her death, I've been looking into Kimberly's past. I came up here to find whoever was taking care of her daughter and to let her know that she's dead."

"I hope you didn't think that was me." Linh looked horrified at the idea. "I knew Kimberly had a kid, but I have no idea who's looking after her."

"No, I found the daughter. She's fine. But . . ." This was harder, since it would probably drift into areas Linh had every right to feel sensitive about. "I heard about Joel for the first time this morning, and I guess I had some questions for you. Kimberly was murdered. She was stabbed to death in New York last week." Linh's eyes opened very wide, but she said nothing, so I continued. "They don't know who did it. Today I found out that her daughter's father was stabbed to death here in Portland last month."

"Oh, wow." Linh looked shocked but not overwhelmed by this blast of violent news. "You're talking about Corey, right? I don't know his last name. The musician? Kimberly brought him here to our Christmas party once. He was a mess, but he seemed like an okay guy. Are their deaths linked?"

"I don't know. But when Kimberly left Portland, she changed her name and cut ties to her past, except she kept in touch with Corey." I was still thinking this through, even while I was speaking. "If someone wanted to hunt down Kimberly but didn't know where to look, they could have gone to Corey to get that information out of him . . ."

"By *someone* you mean Joel, right?" Linh's expression sharpened, and it was hard to tell what she was thinking. "What you're saying is, you think Joel killed Corey and Kimberly."

"Until I arrived on your doorstep, I thought Joel was still in jail. I thought it might be you, actually." I saw Linh's eyebrows rise all the way up her forehead in surprise, so I hastened to explain myself. "It was a theory that made more sense before meeting you."

"You thought I could be a murderer? A *double* murderer?" Linh seemed both outraged and tickled at the thought.

"I hadn't met you!" I said. "But I'd heard from someone who knew Kimberly that you tried to run her over once."

Linh laughed, shocked. "Reverse that. She ran *me* over."

Unbelievable. I'd fallen for another of Yolanda's many lies. This one had been filtered secondhand through Trae, but even still, it shouldn't have caught me. "What, really?"

"You knew Kimberly was sleeping with Joel, right?" Linh asked. "Joel and I had a good run, for the most part; I thought he was cute and charming, and I'm pretty sure he thought *I* was cute and charming. Our marriage was solid. And then Kimberly started working in his office."

She kicked off her Crocs and sat cross-legged on the sofa. Flower took that as an invitation to jump up and snuggle between us, propping her big drooling jowls in Linh's lap. Linh scratched Flower behind her good ear, her attention still fixed on me.

"I knew they were flirting, and I was okay with that; Joel was a flirty guy, and I knew Kimberly was with Corey. I knew they were raising a baby together, so I stupidly figured she was off the market. But then Joel went to New York on a long weekend for some escrow trade association convention." Linh pressed the fingers of one hand to her temple and rubbed, like the topic had given her a sudden headache. "I found out from one of his coworkers that Kimberly had gone with him, which was something he had somehow neglected to tell me. Must've slipped his mind, right? They'd shared a suite. He insisted nothing was going on between them, but to keep me happy, he swore he wouldn't spend any more time alone with Kimberly."

"He didn't keep that promise?"

"He sure didn't. I had suspicions, so I asked his coworkers a few questions. Turns out most of the office knew the two of them were sneaking around. Like, the *interns* knew about it. Anyway, another convention came up, and he went off to New York again. Alone, he swore to me. Kimberly had ended things with Corey by this point, and I was *super* suspicious. Joel and I kept our finances separate, but I knew the password to his computer, so . . ."

"You snooped," I said.

Linh nodded. "I snooped. I figured he gave up the right to privacy the first time he cheated. I checked his bank account while he was gone and saw him racking up all these crazy charges, four-star hotel suites and thousand-dollar bottles of wine at nightclubs, and I knew he was with her. *Knew* it."

I felt awkward, silently listening to Linh's tale of spousal betrayal. It seemed like Linh was experiencing some catharsis by talking about an uncomfortable subject with a stranger, so I decided to keep quiet and just let her talk while gleaning everything I could about Joel Tierney from her recollections of the past.

"When he got back from New York, I went a little nuts. I stormed into his office in the middle of the day and had it out with both Joel and Kimberly. I told Joel he could pack up and move out, and he pleaded with me to give him another chance. He promised me in front of Kimberly that he'd end things with her, and I told him I'd think about taking him back." Again that tense smile. "So then as I was leaving my shift at the clinic that night, someone in a stolen Ford Explorer tried to run me over in the parking lot. I dodged in time to avoid becoming a messy splotch on the pavement, but the car knocked me to the ground before speeding away. My memories of getting hit aren't too clear, but I think I remember catching a glimpse of Kimberly in the driver's seat. No proof it was her, but . . ."

"You're sure."

"Yeah. I'm sure. One hundred percent." Linh exhaled. "My right femur snapped when she hit me. My leg still aches if I remain standing for too long. I have a job that keeps me on my feet for most of my shift, so whenever it starts hurting, I think fond thoughts about Kimberly."

I'd noticed earlier that she walked with a slight lurch when she'd moved around the kitchen fixing my tea. "You must know Joel better than anyone. Do you think it's possible that he . . . ?"

"Killed Kimberly? Killed Corey, too?" Linh considered my question. "While I was recovering in the hospital, Joel's office was raided. Police got an anonymous tip that he'd been embezzling funds from clients. By the time I was cleared to go home, he was out on bail awaiting trial. I was with him when he found out from his lawyer that Kimberly was the one who'd betrayed him."

Wrapped up in her narrative, she'd stopped stroking Flower. Flower stared at her indignantly, then turned her attention to me, dropping her heavy, wet head on my leg. I nudged the folds of my velvet coat out of the path of her slobber and stroked her behind her good ear.

"He had a secret bank account, and she'd talked him into giving her access to it, which was absolutely *brilliant* on his part, of course. They had this grand plan to accumulate all the money they could, then run away to New York and start a new life together. He was going to run a fancy casino, and she was going to perform in it. Like a nightclub act. Instead, she wiped him out, called the cops, and skipped town."

Fancy casino. "He told you all of this?"

Linh shook her head. "I pieced it together later. He'd sent her emails, which I still wish I'd never read. God, he was *obsessed* with her. He loved me, maybe, but he worshipped her in a gooey, fervent way, like he was a teenager and she was his favorite pop idol." She shuddered. "Anyway, when he found out she'd been playing him, he lost it. It was the scariest thing I've ever been through; I'd never seen that side of him. He demolished the living room." She pointed at the fish tank. "That's a new tank; he knocked over the one we used to have, and it shattered on the ground. Most of my fish ended up dying, not that he cared about that. I had this really nice glass coffee table that I'd had since college, and he picked up one of our dining room chairs and used it to smash it to smithereens. He punched holes in the walls. He broke windows, and he kept screaming that he was going to kill her."

Her voice started to quaver as she talked. Her living room was warm, but she wrapped her arms around her body like she was freezing. "Flower freaked out because she assumed he was going to attack me, and I'm not so sure he wasn't. I thought Joel might kill me, and I thought Flower might kill Joel, so I hobbled on crutches into the master bedroom and barricaded myself inside with Flower, then called the police. His bail was revoked, obviously. I started divorce proceedings while he was in a jail cell awaiting trial." She made some disgusted noise deep in her throat. "Should've done that as soon as Kimberly came into his life."

I wanted to make some appropriately soothing reply, but my mind was caught on something she'd said earlier, something that seemed of urgent importance. "You said Joel planned on running a casino in New York?"

She nodded. "That had been his dream for years. He'd told me about it earlier."

"In New York, though?" I asked. "Not Vegas, or Atlantic City?"

"New York. It had to be New York." She was very firm on this. "They have secret casinos there; we went to one on our honeymoon. It was illegal, like it was literally in the back of this building in Chinatown, and we had to know a password, which he got by paying to join some top-secret mailing list. I thought it would be seedy and maybe scary, but it was actually pretty glamorous."

With a twist in my gut, I thought about Niko telling me all about the time, expense, and skill that went into planning his pop-up casinos. He'd studied the world's greatest casinos; he'd recruited the best workers. He'd made it a luxurious experience.

"It honestly wasn't my thing—I was in New York for Broadway shows and carriage rides in Central Park—but Joel went crazy for it," Linh said. "He got along great with the guy who was running it, like they became instant bros. He wanted to invest part of his retirement fund into this guy's whole plan. Later he got the idea that we should pack up and move to New York so he could go into business with this guy. I talked him out of it, but he kept bringing it up from time to time." Linh looked at me, her expression sour. "I think he always resented that I stopped him from living out his stupid dream."

I cleared my throat. "The guy who ran the casino. Do you remember anything about him?" Filled with dread, I realized that Niko might be right at the center of Yolanda's murder. I felt distraught. I'd found myself sort of liking Niko after I'd talked to him in the diner. I'd assessed him from all angles then and decided he was unlikely to be a killer, but perhaps my instincts were wildly off base. Perhaps I'd believed his lies the way I'd believed Yolanda's.

Linh shook her head. "He was just a guy. Average looking, middle-aged. Smooth talker, very friendly." She wrinkled her brow, giving the matter some thought. "He had a weird name."

"Niko Toska?" The description didn't sound much like Niko, but the combination of illegal New York casinos and Yolanda couldn't be a coincidence, damn it all.

I felt a rush of relief when she shook her head. "No. It was something ridiculous, like a cartoon superhero. Like . . . Tommy

Universe. Something like that." She looked like she wanted me to help her come up with the name, but I had no idea where she was going with it. Her expression suddenly brightened. "Charlie Global! That was it."

I'd come across that name recently, and it took me only a couple of seconds to remember the context. I'd seen it in an online article: Charlie Global and Niko had been business partners in a nightclub a handful of years back. I tried to piece together all this information. Joel Tierney had wanted to move to New York so he could become partners with Charlie Global in an unlicensed casino. Yolanda had visited New York with Joel at least twice, and it was well within the realm of possibility that she'd met Charlie Global at that time. I'd assumed Yolanda had met Niko through Angels in the City, but Yolanda could easily have met Niko earlier at one of his clubs or casinos. When Yolanda fled to New York with Joel's money, she could have turned to Niko for help establishing her new life. It didn't mean Niko was involved with her murder, but it might mean he knew her killer.

Linh was looking at me expectantly, waiting for me to speak. "Do you have a photo of Joel?" I asked at last.

"Sure." She seemed unsurprised by the request. She got up and walked across the carpet. The fish tank was placed on top of a long walnut sideboard; she rummaged around in one of the drawers beneath it and came up with a photo in a slim silver frame. "I deleted all our pictures that we'd stored online, but I held on to the physical copy of our wedding photo. I'm not entirely sure why. I guess it's nice to remember that at the start, our marriage wasn't as awful as it was by the end." She passed the frame over to me. "It'd probably be healthier if I just got rid of this, but . . . that's Joel."

She sat down next to me on the sofa again. I held on to the picture frame with hands that had suddenly gone numb. In the photo, Linh was radiant in a high-necked sleeveless wedding gown; Joel was dressed in black tie. His smile was wide and flawless; his sandy blond hair was almost the color of his deep and even tan.

"Whenever I start thinking I was an idiot for ever marrying him, I remember how damn good-looking he was." She glanced down at the photograph, a half smile on her lips. "Handsome, isn't he?"

He was. I'd thought he was handsome when I'd seen him standing in the doorway to Costas's apartment, and once again when I'd tried to flirt with him while he was sitting at the bistro table outside my building. Joel Tierney was Patrick, my next door neighbor's prospective sublessee, and I had no clue how it had happened, but it seemed entirely likely that I had led him straight to Kimberly Stubbings.

26

In the Mouth of the Wolf

As soon as I was back in New York, before entering my own apartment, I knocked on Costas's door. I'd made excellent time on the drive from Maine. While usually a precise, cautious motorist, I'd kept edging up the speedometer on my rental car, ticking it higher and higher the closer I got to the city, feeling an urgency that I had trouble containing. I was jittery yet exhilarated: I'd solved Yolanda's murder. I might not have any proof, but I felt convinced that Joel Tierney had extracted Yolanda's Somebody's Baby alias from Corey before killing him, then tracked Yolanda to New York and murdered her. But he'd tracked Yolanda to *my* apartment, specifically, and it seemed important to figure out how that had happened.

Costas was in the middle of cooking his dinner. When he opened the door, I was greeted by a fragrant blast of roasting lamb. He looked amused by my appearance, the showy velvet coat and what were probably greasy, smeary remnants of makeup by now, so I rushed to speak before he could make a wisecrack. "Do you remember that guy who wanted to sublet your apartment? Patrick?"

Costas folded his arms over his chest. "The one you scared off with your dead rat? That the guy you mean?"

"That's the one," I said giddily. "I saw him in the neighborhood two weeks ago and chatted with him a bit. I wondered if he gave you any way to contact him." Costas looked suspicious, so I supplied an innocuous explanation for my interest: "I thought he was cute."

"Well, good for you. It's about time you put yourself out there a little more." Costas's glance at my fancy coat was laced with meaning, and I thought he seemed pleased. "But you're out of luck with that guy. He left me his number, but when I tried to follow up, it rang at some laundromat in Harlem. I figure the rat must've killed any enthusiasm he had for this place, so he gave me a phony number."

"You said he was sent to you by the building management, right? You think someone in the rental office would know how to reach him?"

"Could be. He never mentioned who he'd talked to. I spotted him in the hallway near your door and asked what he was doing. You know I like to look out for you, a single girl living by herself."

I knew he liked to snoop in my business. Perhaps he sincerely viewed that as the same thing.

"He told me he'd heard about a vacancy on this floor. I'd talked to Julio in the rental office a few weeks back to see if I could sublet without violating my lease, and he said it would be all right as long as the sublessee passed a background check. So I figured management sent him over."

If I called the rental office, I was willing to bet no one there had ever seen or heard of Patrick, because he didn't exist. But Costas had dropped an interesting tidbit of information: Joel had been loitering outside my door the night the bloody rat had been left for me. I'd assumed it was a gift from Yolanda, and even though Niko had given her an alibi, that still seemed well within the realm of possibility. But maybe Yolanda hadn't left the rat after all; maybe it had been from Joel. Maybe he'd trailed Yolanda to my apartment when she'd stopped by to present me with gifts and insincere apologies, and maybe he'd assumed she'd lived here. Maybe he'd left the rat as a warning for her.

"You want to join me for dinner?" Costas held the door open wider. "Leg of lamb with baked eggplant. There's plenty."

It smelled good, and I was tickled that Costas now regarded us as being on drop-by-for-dinner terms, but I had other things on my mind. I begged for a rain check and headed for my own apartment.

I knew I needed to call Abernathy—I should have called him from Maine, in fact, since I had crucial information that could help him apprehend a killer—but nerves kept getting in my way. While my news about Yolanda might temper the anger he'd feel at my unsanctioned travel, he'd still be annoyed, and if I fumbled my approach, I could end up under arrest. This would be an inopportune time to wind up in police custody, because I had a high-stakes battle to keep my role in *Barbarella* scheduled for tomorrow morning.

So I delayed calling Abernathy out of a mixture of gutlessness and selfishness, and thus I missed the opportunity to gain the upper hand: He called me first. I had to steel myself before answering. "Great timing, Detective. I was just about to call you."

"What are you doing in Maine?" It was a growl.

"I'm not in Maine," I said. I sounded chipper and blithe, which probably wasn't the best approach, since he clearly already knew what I'd been up to.

"Don't lie to me, Katherine. I'm not in the mood."

"I'm already back in the city. It was just a fast trip," I said. "Listen, I have—"

He cut me off. "A trip you had no business making." It was cold, ominous. "I should arrest you for leaving the state during an active murder investigation."

"I think I know who killed Yolanda." I'd wanted to build up to this after first establishing a meticulous case for my conclusions, but instead I blurted it out with no finesse, desperate to derail his thoughts of arresting me.

"Joel Tierney?" As soon as Abernathy said that name, I fell silent. Apparently I wasn't as many steps ahead of the authorities as I'd assumed.

"A young lady named Linh Phan called the precinct a little while ago suspecting that her ex-husband might have murdered Yolanda Archambeau. Seems you popped up at her home this morning and made some bold claims along those lines."

I paused, taking this in. I couldn't possibly hold it against Linh that she'd gone to the police; indeed, it was the responsible course of action. She'd just found out her ex was a likely double murderer, and there was no conceivable reason for her to sit back and expect the stranger on her doorstep to handle the situation appropriately. But I felt uncharitably peeved that I'd been robbed of the chance to expose a killer.

Abernathy was still talking: "Come down to the precinct and tell me all you know about it."

That last interrogation, right before the fire in Daniel's office, had lasted most of the night; this one might go even longer. Hell, there was a better than even chance he'd let me sit in a holding tank for a day or so to punish me for skipping town, and I had the most important rehearsal of my professional career in the morning. At tomorrow's tech rehearsal, Daniel would decide whether to keep me or get rid of me, and if I was under arrest, that would simplify his decision. "I can't make it tonight."

"I'm not asking, Katherine."

"I'll come in tomorrow morning," I said. "Bright and early."

I'd withheld information from Abernathy before, but now I was nakedly lying to him. Tomorrow morning I'd be at the Bradwell Theatre, and with a lot of luck, Abernathy would have no idea where to find me.

"Tomorrow's a Monday. Won't you have a rehearsal?" It was caustic.

"Our theater is shut down through the end of the year," I said. I forced myself to sound relaxed, because if Abernathy suspected how high the stakes were for me, he'd leverage that knowledge against me. "Rehearsals have been postponed until we find a new venue. There was a fire in the building."

"Yeah, I may have heard a little something about that." Abernathy gave a dry chuckle. "Funny timing, that fire."

"Are you looking for Joel Tierney now?" I asked. "Did his ex-wife send you a photo of him? Because I've got one if you need it." I'd taken a picture of Linh's photo from their wedding day.

"I have it. There's an APB out on Tierney." That was a relief. "But I've got a lot of questions about your role in this. Come in now."

"I'll see you tomorrow," I said, and disconnected the call. I turned my phone off, because I was pretty sure Abernathy would keep calling throughout the evening, and then I tossed a few things into an overnight bag and headed out the door.

I wouldn't say Gerard was thrilled to see me on his doorstep, but he limited himself to a single long-suffering sigh before inviting me in. "Did the boiler burst in your apartment building again?"

"Just avoiding the police," I said. "I think they might want to arrest me."

"I'm harboring a fugitive, then. How delightful." He glanced down the corridor in both directions, like he genuinely thought the police might be hot on my trail, then closed it and locked it behind us. In his voluminous smoking jacket, he was an immensely comforting figure, and I had to restrain a highly uncharacteristic impulse to give him a big hug. "They don't honestly think you had anything to do with what happened to that poor girl, do they?"

"No. They're on the right track now." I hadn't met with Gerard in the week since Yolanda's murder, though I had called him twice to give him cursory updates on the whole grim situation. "But I think they suspect I've been withholding information from them."

"You, keeping things to yourself? I'm shocked," he said. I followed him into the living room. "The sofa is yours, my dear. Linens are in the hall closet; you know where to find them. I plan on sleeping late, so try not to make too much noise when you leave in the morning." He frowned at me. "It's your technical rehearsal tomorrow, isn't it? Are you ready?"

"I am," I said. I was. I felt it. Felt it in my bones.

He nodded in approval. "You look ready." On his way out of the room, he paused and glanced over his shoulder at me. "In bocca al lupo, Katerina."

In the mouth of the wolf. The phrase was an old opera superstition, akin to telling a performer to break a leg: He was wishing me good luck.

I bowed my head in thanks. "Crepi," I responded, completing the ritual: *May it die.*

I worried at first that I wouldn't be able to sleep, wracked with worries about a looming arrest and tomorrow's high-stakes rehearsal, but Gerard's sofa was a big plush affair, covered in aubergine velvet and topped with furry cushions; I could stretch out to my full length. I dropped off immediately and woke up feeling refreshed.

I arrived at the Bradwell Theatre at the leisurely hour of eleven. The prop, scenery, and lighting crews had arrived earlier to set up; we would all—singers, orchestra, crew—spend the rest of the day and likely well into the night piecing together a performance, replete with starts and stops, with every technical element in place for the first time. In the costume shop, Ana helped me into the vinyl corset with the magnificent gold plastic breastplate. I had to lean against the wall for support while she zipped me into the thigh-high boots.

My castmates milled about in various stages of dress. In

his giant feathered wings and loincloth, his bare chest oiled down to showcase his ripped abs, Carlo looked both sexy and angelic; when he smiled at me and asked how I was doing, he didn't seem like he could possibly be the same dirtbag who'd flaunted the photo of Yolanda in the sushi bar. I thought I detected some genuine concern in his query, which meant Julie had briefed him on my precarious position; he knew the stakes of this rehearsal.

Daniel found me in the makeup room, where Veronique was instructing me on the proper application of black winged eyeliner. My hair was slicked back and pinned close to my scalp; my shining and glorious blond wig rested on a foam mannequin head in front of me. When Veronique moved off to tend to Claudette's face, Daniel stood behind me and scrutinized my reflection in the mirror. He looked like a wraith, doom radiating from his pores.

At last, he let out a short, tense sigh. "Well, Kit," he said. "I hope it goes well for you today."

"It will." I sounded calm and confident. I turned around in my chair to face him. "It's a good production, Daniel. You've got an amazing cast. Everything's going to turn out fine."

I thought the gloom in his face lifted fractionally, as though he appreciated the sentiment even if he couldn't bring himself to agree with it. "I suppose we'll find out soon enough."

I spoke before he could turn away. "Hey, can you tell Niko I need to talk to him?"

His brow creased. "Why?"

"Just tell him. There are some things about Yolanda he should know."

"Such as?"

"It wouldn't mean anything to you," I said, and I saw Daniel's eyebrows twitch in surprise at my rudeness. It might be a dangerous strategy, but in the face of Daniel's current morose apathy, bossing him around seemed like the best way to get him to follow instructions. "Just tell him to contact me, okay?"

He looked unsettled, and I thought he was going to grill me about my intentions, but then Veronique asked him a question about Claudette's hairstyle, and he moved on from me.

It was almost three before the rehearsal actually began. I'd warmed up by myself in an empty dressing room, then again with the rest of the cast onstage. I'd explored all corners of the theater, familiarizing myself with our new performance space. I'd brought a thick, heavy book, because tech rehearsals always feature a tremendous amount of downtime, but I didn't get around to opening it. Mostly I paced back and forth in my platform boots, getting used to my daunting new height while learning how to move without wobbling, and tried not to let my thoughts get stuck on anything I'd learned about Yolanda in Maine. This afternoon was all about Barbarella.

The orchestra launched into the overture. The heavy curtain was drawn back for the first time, and there I was, in the center of the stage.

The opera opened with my duet with Claudette, and I was transported back to that first rehearsal, my first unfortunate encounter with Yolanda. I thought about everything Opal had told me, and I opened myself wide and let myself experience the music. This was a song of bravery and triumph, and I gave myself permission to feel both of those things.

I felt a wild burst of foreign emotion, and it took me a long time to identify it: It was optimism, tinged with the kind of exhilarating happiness I hadn't experienced since Yolanda waltzed into my life. Now, though, I had reason to be optimistic. I'd solved a murder, practically—maybe even a double murder. Maybe tomorrow Abernathy would arrest me for obstruction or whatever, but I found it hard to care, just as long as I was out of jail by opening night. I beamed at the thought: Opening night was Friday, and now I knew I would be on that stage, because right now I was spectacular, and Daniel would be a reckless fool to dismiss me. Across from me onstage, Claudette saw my smile and grinned in reply, wide and genuine.

As anticipated, the rehearsal was long and murderously slow, filled with hiccups and delays and disasters of all definition, but my buoyant feeling lingered. When we reached my aria at the climax of act 1, I sounded magnificent. I felt like I radiated sound and light, a celestial being made incarnate; I felt alive and dynamic and sensuous. When I reached my final note, Marla pressed her hands together from her lectern in front of the orchestra, her right hand still clutching her conducting baton, and bowed to me.

And then there was Daniel, rising up from his seat in the auditorium, his bound score held between both hands. His brow was furrowed in concern. My heart stopped, because as marvelous as I knew I'd been, he looked morose. He'd agreed to my demand to put it to a vote, and I felt there was a good chance Marla and Astrid would combine forces against him, but if I hadn't been able to win him over today with the performance I'd just given, I knew he'd never be happy with me in the role.

He frowned at my boots, his attention fixed on them, and I felt a sense of despair: Here, at the moment of truth, he couldn't even meet my eyes. He snapped his fingers to get the attention of Ana, who'd been standing in the wings: "Do you think we could go even higher with the boots? One more inch? Kit's legs still look short from the audience."

Ana shrugged and nodded, and Daniel turned his attention back to me. Finally, he met my eyes.

"Katerina," he said. "If you sing like that on opening night, we're going to have a superb run."

Someone—Carlo, I think—burst into applause and whoops, and then the rest of the cast joined in, and then I was surrounded by a sea of jubilant cheers. Everyone had known or had guessed the stakes for me today, and everyone was overjoyed that I passed this test; their support made my heart expand, my rib cage suddenly too narrow to contain it.

We took a lengthy break to prepare for act 2. I wriggled

into the green sequined dress I'd wear for the remainder of the opera, then returned to the auditorium. I intended to grab my book and find a quiet corner where I could read, but then I saw a familiar figure in the last row of seats. I wobbled my way down the aisle in my preposterous boots and slid into the seat beside Niko.

He grinned at me. "You know who you look like?"

"Tonya Margolis?"

He shrugged. "I was going to say Yolo, actually. In that wig, you two could be sisters."

I didn't look much like Yolanda, even with the big, bouncy blond wig, but I knew what he meant. I was painted and padded to Yolanda-esque levels of desirability; it wasn't real, but I bet it looked great onstage. A cynical part of me suspected my modified appearance probably had done as much to change Daniel's mind as my rejuvenated performance. Maybe that was too harsh, though; maybe I wasn't giving Daniel enough credit. In any case, it didn't really matter: At last, at long last, the role was wholly mine.

Niko shifted in his chair. "Danny said you wanted to talk to me?"

"I need to know how you met Yolanda," I said. "Was it through Charlie Global?"

His eyebrows raised at the name. "What do you know about Charlie?"

"I know you two were in business for a while. I found that online," I said. "That can't be his real name, can it?"

"It's Charlie Globa, actually. G-L-O-B-A. It's Russian. But the autocorrect on his phone kept adding an L whenever he'd send a text, so at some point he just decided to go with it." Niko grinned, though his expression was wary. He wriggled around in his chair so he could face me.

"Charlie was my mentor," he said. "Back when we were running our nightclub together, he'd just started experimenting with pop-up underground casinos, and that seemed like both a lot more fun and less of a grind than what we were doing. So I paid him what I guess you could call a franchise fee and followed his example."

"You had to pay him?"

He shrugged. "Token of respect. It could have otherwise been interpreted that I was stealing his business by placing myself in direct competition. He still gets his cut off the top, just to ensure there are no hard feelings." Niko sounded as relaxed and easygoing as ever, but there was something dark around the edges of his expression, and I knew there were parts of his world that I didn't want to know much about. "Anyway, when I met Yolo two years ago, she was picking up some freelance work as a hostess at one of Charlie's places, serving drinks to high rollers."

"She came to town with money," I said. "She stole it from her boss. Maybe a hundred grand. She'd worked at an escrow company, and her boss was embezzling."

"The money wouldn't have lasted long," Niko said. "She had expensive tastes. When I met her, her lifestyle was burning through her savings, so she needed cash. I was just getting Angels in the City up and running, and when she learned about it, she wanted to give that kind of work a try. But seriously, Kit, why are you asking about Charlie?"

I brought out my phone and passed Linh's wedding photo to him. "The guy is Yolanda's former boss. His name is Joel Tierney. Does he look familiar to you?"

Niko shook his head, his attention on the screen. "Should he?"

"I was in Portland yesterday. Maine. It's where Yolanda came from." Niko had seemed mildly interested in our conversation before, but now I sensed I had his undivided attention. "I met the woman in that picture. She was married to Joel Tierney, but he was having an affair with Yolanda. He was obsessed with her, in a life-destroying kind of way. It sounds like their relationship was an absolute shit show."

"Typical Yolo, in other words," Niko said.

"Very much so. When Yolanda swiped that money from Joel, she also tipped off the police about his financial crimes and got him sent to jail. He's out now, and his parole officer has lost track of him."

Niko looked up from the phone and stared at me. He didn't say anything, but there was an intensity in his eyes.

"According to the ex-wife, Joel knew Charlie Global and had this dream of going into business with him. He probably took Yolanda with him to Charlie's casinos during trips to New York. When Yolanda went on the run, I think she turned to Charlie for work when her money started running out, and that's how your paths crossed." I inhaled. "Here's the important thing: I saw him in New York. Joel Tierney. I saw him twice in the days leading up to Yolanda's murder. He was hanging outside my apartment one night after Yolanda came to visit."

Niko still held my phone lightly with both hands, and though he seemed calm, his fingers were trembling. "This guy Joel," he said at last. His voice was tight. "He's the one who killed Yolo?"

My throat was dry. I had to swallow before replying. "Yes." It came out as a whisper.

He didn't look up. He passed my phone back to me while still staring at his lap, like he didn't want me to see whatever was in his face right now. I wasn't sure I wanted to see it, either.

"I think there's a good chance Charlie Global knows where to find Joel. I don't think Joel came to New York just to kill Yolanda, though I'm sure that was his main goal. Since he skipped parole, he's a fugitive. He can't return to Portland, so I'm betting Joel would have approached Charlie about his dream to go into business with him." I cleared my throat. "Will you introduce me to Charlie?"

A reflexive headshake, still without looking up. "You shouldn't go," he said. "You shouldn't get involved in this. I'll ask him."

"I *am* involved in this." At the sound of something new in

my tone, something hard and hollow, Niko looked at me at last. "Don't cut me out, Niko. You wouldn't know about this if it wasn't for me."

He stared at me, his expression impossible to read, and I thought he was going to refuse. Eventually he nodded. "Tonight?"

On the stage, the musicians were settling into their places in the orchestra pit, which meant it was almost time to start the second act. "Rehearsal's going to go late."

"Doesn't matter. Charlie's a night owl. Text me whenever you're done, and I'll pick you up here." He was still holding my phone, so he opened my contacts list and entered his number. He frowned at me. "Wear that outfit."

I glanced down at the green sequined dress. "This is a costume," I said.

"Yeah, but it's a *good* costume. You look great. Perfect for Charlie's establishment. Wear it."

"Are you serious? They'll never let me take it out of the theater."

"Sure they will. I'll talk to Ana right now. It's Ana, right? In the costume shop? I'll tell her to let you borrow it tonight as a favor to me."

That was a little grand of him, and Ana wouldn't love having her boss's brother order her to bend some well-established rules. But Niko probably had good instincts as to what I should wear, and I had the sense that tonight would be, in some respects, a performance. I might as well show up in costume.

27

Boyfriend Material

After Niko talked to her, Ana was cool with loaning me my costume for the evening at the end of our murderously long rehearsal, though she made me pinky swear that I would return it to her with no rips or stains and with all sequins still attached. In place of the platform boots, she scrounged up a pair of spike-heeled gold sandals from the theater's costume shop; they were reckless footwear for a chilly October night, but they looked great with the dress. As soon as Veronique heard I was going out for what she assumed was a fancy night on the town, she insisted on redoing my makeup. She firmly nixed my idea of wearing the Barbarella wig, then set about fluffing up my short locks, wielding a curling iron like a magic wand to turn my hair from straw into gold. Both women fussed over me, willingly extending their long day to prettify me.

At first this made me uncomfortable, even miserable. Makeovers had always been my mother's way of telling me I was a disappointment. Even when makeovers are meant with kindness, there's an insult at their core: Someone has deemed your outer shell inadequate.

But tonight was a performance. Practical Kit Margolis would be out of place at an unlicensed gambling den, but Katerina

Margolis, opera diva on the trail of the murderer of her one-time rival, would readily visit one in the course of her investigation. Ana and Veronique were using their skills to help me prepare for my role, and it would behoove me to be grateful, gracious, and cooperative.

At one point while fussing over my face, Ana warned me in a low voice that Niko might be fun for an evening, but I mustn't mistake him for boyfriend material. The idea of dating Niko left me speechless with a kind of intrigued horror.

When I texted Niko that I was ready, he arrived at the theater in a chauffeured town car. I wore Opal's velvet coat over the sequined dress while carrying the fake Birkin. Niko, clad in a dark suit, took my arm and helped me into the back seat, then nestled in beside me.

"I called Charlie and told him we want to talk," Niko said as the town car crawled through night traffic. We moved across the Manhattan Bridge, Brooklyn glittering on the other side. "He's expecting us. What's the plan?"

"We ask him if he's been in touch with Joel. The police have an APB out on Joel, thanks to his ex-wife; if Charlie can give us an address, I can pass it along to them."

Niko frowned. "Charlie won't want his name linked to this."

"I figured that. You probably don't want yours linked, either," I said. "When I contact the police, I'll keep you both out of this." I wasn't sure how to pull that off, but I'd been making a habit of withholding information from Abernathy, so I might as well continue.

"Don't worry about protecting me from Detective Abernathy," Niko said. He smiled at me. "I don't care about tangling with that guy, just as long as we get the asshole who killed Yolo."

The latest incarnation of Charlie Global's traveling casino turned out to be in Dumbo. The car let us out in front of a stretch of renovated factories and old warehouses; Niko led me past a string of upscale wine bars and vintage shops into a long alley just off of Washington, which opened up into a large T-shaped area. The entire top of the T was taken up by an unused loading dock for an abandoned warehouse. It didn't look like we were in the right place, but Niko seemed to know what he was doing. We climbed up the steps of the loading dock to a concrete platform, and Niko rapped his knuckles against an unmarked metal door.

An enormous bald man opened it. His massive upper body strained the seams of his suit jacket; his neck was the size of my waist. He grinned when he spotted Niko. "Boss said you might stop by tonight."

"Good to see you, Tomás," Niko said. They shook hands. "Let him know I'm here, will you?"

Tomás ushered us inside, and we moved through a concrete corridor into the makeshift casino, which seemed to be modeled after an upscale hunting lodge. The walls were covered in what looked like mahogany paneling; a taxidermied lion head hung high on the wall above what had to be a fake malachite fireplace. The gaming tables were made of leather-topped wood and seemed authentically vintage; I spotted a battered wooden roulette wheel that looked like an antique.

The curved bar near the entrance was overseen by a gorgeous bald woman dressed in sharply tailored tweed. Niko steered me over to her. "Do you like martinis? Manon makes the best in the city." Manon smiled at him and bent to her task. She poured out our martinis from a silver shaker into long-stemmed glasses and garnished each with a trio of pearl onions on a gold toothpick. Niko passed me a glass and raised his own. "To Yolo," he said.

I hesitated, then touched the rim of my glass against his. "To Yolanda," I said.

"You didn't like her much," Niko said. It wasn't a question.

I was about to point out that Yolanda had tried to kill me, but that was nothing he didn't know. "I think she was vindictive and destructive. I was intrigued by her, but no, I didn't like her."

Niko looked unhappy. "She had a rough childhood," he said. "She never said much about it, but I got the impression that was at the core of her behavior."

On the night Yolanda died, I remembered how fiercely she'd resented what she'd seen as my privilege: the boarding school that had rescued me, the music education that had given my life purpose. She'd been bitter and spiteful, but she hadn't been wrong. Maybe without those things, I would have wound up like Yolanda, and maybe with the aid of a safety net, Yolanda would have wound up like me.

My thoughts were interrupted by the arrival of a dark-haired man, who slid beside Niko and clasped him on the shoulder. Niko beamed at him. "Charlie! Good to see you." He gestured at me. "Charlie, this is my friend Kit."

"Katerina," I said grandly.

Maybe twenty years older than Niko, Charlie was short and slight. Perhaps to compensate for this, he dressed to grab attention: His double-breasted suit was a startling shade of blue, and he accentuated it with a wide necktie patterned with thick gold stripes. He clasped my outstretched hand in both of his, and for a second I thought he might kiss it. "Katerina. Lovely to meet you. I hope you're enjoying my little spot here." He glanced at Niko. "Somewhere private to talk?"

At Niko's nod, Charlie guided us through the crowd to a cozy dark corner, which was shielded by hanging velvet drapes. The place wasn't packed, but it was well populated. Charlie's clientele mostly consisted of men in expensive suits, many of whom looked something like Niko or Leo: rich and young, in possession of too much money, always in pursuit of new ways to lose it. Charlie steered us toward a circular library table. When we were seated around it, he turned his attention to Niko. "I wanted to tell you, I'm sorry about Yolo. They haven't caught the guy?"

Niko dipped his head. "Not yet."

"That's why you're here tonight, though, am I right?" Charlie leaned across the table, his stare hyperfocused on Niko, friendly yet intense.

"What do you know, Charlie?" Niko sounded careless, but I could see the way his fingers tightened around the stem of his martini glass.

"You called this meeting." Charlie made a little gesture with one hand to indicate that Niko should go first. Niko glanced at me.

"Show him that picture," he said.

I fished around in the Birkin bag for my phone and found Linh's wedding photo. I held it up so Charlie could see it. "You know the guy?" Niko asked him.

Charlie glanced at the screen, frowned, and returned his attention to Niko. "Sure. Yeah. I know the lady, too, though I only met her once," he said. "Joel. From somewhere in Maine, but he bought his way onto my mailing list, and sometimes he'd come down here on the weekend to have a good time. Once with the lady in that picture, then two or three times with Yolo. Only she went by something else back then. I forget what."

"Kimberly," I said. "Kimberly Stubbings."

"Kimberly, sure." Charlie nodded at me. "Anyway, I liked them both. They were good customers. Lots of fun, big spenders, and Kimberly was a beauty. Joel and me, we got on from the start. He floated the idea of someday going in with me on one of my enterprises, and I thought that sounded like an okay idea. Kind of like I did with you, Niko, the way I took you under my wing." He gave Niko's wrist an affectionate pat. "He seemed smart, ambitious, eager to learn. He wouldn't do me much good up in Maine, so I gave him my number and said we'd talk if he ever wanted a change of scenery."

Niko listened in silence, nodding to show he was following Charlie's narrative. He seemed calm, but there was an off-kilter energy buzzing off him that started to infect me. I began to feel anxious, like I was anticipating an explosion but didn't know when or where it would detonate.

"Maybe two years ago, Kimberly looked me up, only she was now calling herself Yolanda. She'd moved to the city to be a singer, and she needed a job." Charlie grinned. "She wanted to sing in my clubs, torch songs, blues, stuff like that. She had a hell of a talent, but I don't have much use for singers. I liked her, though, even though she had a crazy knack for causing drama, so I put her to work serving drinks. When I inquired about our mutual friend Joel, it was clear there was some bad story there, so I wrote him off. That's where you came in," he said, nodding at Niko. "It was around that time that you swooped in and stole her away from me." He winked to show there were no hard feelings.

"No one could make Yolo do anything she didn't want to do. You know that, Charlie."

"That's true enough, my friend." Charlie clasped Niko's shoulder affectionately. "Anyway, Joel got in touch with me maybe six weeks ago. I met him for dinner in the city. He was looking for a change of pace from whatever he'd been doing, real estate or whatever, so he'd made the move to New York. He asked about going into business with me. He had some cash, thirty grand or so. Small peanuts, so I said no, I'm not looking for a partner. He said he was willing to bartend, deal cards, bounce drunks, whatever I needed, just as long as he could hang around and learn all he could from me."

Charlie thought about his next words. "I didn't like him as much this time around," he said at last. "Whenever we'd met before, I'd been impressed by his polish, by his drive. There was a desperation about him now that turned me off. He was way too eager. He kept flattering me, laying it on thick, and I got the sense he was just saying whatever he thought I'd want to hear so I'd give him a job. I didn't want to be an asshole, though, since he was clearly down on his luck. I told him to keep his money, and I'd give him a call if I thought of some way he could make himself useful."

"Did you tell him where he could find Yolanda?" I asked. Niko frowned at me, like he thought that was too direct.

Charlie shook his head. "He asked about her, and I said I'd heard nothing. I knew Yolo didn't want anything to do with him anymore, and I respected that. When I saw in the *Post* that she'd been killed, I thought there was a chance it was him, but . . . I mean, you knew Yolo, Niko. The list of people who might've wanted to do her some harm was probably not short."

Niko furrowed his brow. "You might've told me, Charlie."

Charlie nodded. "Maybe, sure. But I'm getting to that. When you called tonight and said we should talk, I figured it was about him. I figured I might've made an error in judgment by not saying anything to you, so I made it right."

"What have you done?" Niko was almost finished with his martini. I hadn't taken more than a couple sips of mine; it was strong and cold, but after my drugged drink on the night Yolanda died, I seemed to have lost all taste for cocktails.

"I called him after I talked to you and said he should come in tonight and work the tables. Said I was short on staff. Promised I'd make it worth his while."

My stomach flipped. Niko sat straighter in his chair. "He's here now?"

Charlie shook his head. "Nah. He's driving in from Paramus, got a place there. He's been doing some kind of crummy-sounding gig work. Delivery driving. I told him to finish his shift; I wouldn't need him until midnight. I figured that way you and I could have a chat first and see what needs to be done about this."

"Thank you, Charlie," Niko said. His voice sounded newly solemn, almost formal. "I appreciate this."

Charlie shrugged. "My pleasure. You get a chance, maybe tell your dad I helped you out?" He gave Niko a long, hard stare. "I guessed right, didn't I? Our man Joel killed Yolo?"

Niko just returned the stare. Charlie nodded, eyes still locked with Niko's. "So what are we going to do about this?"

Niko still didn't answer. Making very precise movements, fighting to keep himself under control, he drained the last few drops of his drink, set his empty glass down on the table, and leaned over and plucked my still-full martini out of my hand. He gathered up my coat and purse from where I'd draped them over the arm of my chair and handed them to me. "First, we need to say goodbye to Kit. To *Katerina.*"

He had me on my feet, bundling me into my coat and hustling me through the crowd to the door before I understood what was going on. "Niko, what—"

"You need to get out of here," he said. "You said you saw that bastard hanging around outside your apartment. He knows what you look like. It's almost midnight, and by the time he arrives, I want you far from here."

"He won't know it's me," I said. "I look completely different. I'm literally wearing a costume right now. *No one* would recognize me."

He paused in his movements and stared at me, his hand still lightly gripping my arm. "I would," he said.

He might, but that was only because he thought I looked like my mother. I wanted to tell him that, but he continued hurrying me toward the exit without giving me a chance to speak. Tomás held the door open for us, and Niko swept me straight through it. He half pulled me down the stairs leading from the loading dock, and I worried I'd break an ankle in the stupid heeled sandals. "Go home, Kit. This is dangerous for you."

I started trembling with adrenaline, my heart beating so fast that I found it hard to breathe. "Come with me. We'll call the police."

Niko shook his head emphatically. "No. Absolutely not. I'm not sending the cops here. You don't want to do that, either. Charlie wouldn't like it at all, you have to trust me on that."

"Then when Joel shows up here, have Charlie send him home. The police can arrest him in Paramus. We'll leave Charlie entirely out of it."

"Kit, no," Niko said. He was firm. "This is a gift. We've been handed an easy way to deal with this."

"What's going to happen?" I asked, as if I didn't know.

"Charlie did me a huge favor by asking that asshole to come here. I think it's a good idea to make the most of it."

Well, hell. Niko had spontaneously formed a grand plan to kill Joel to get revenge for Yolanda, and whatever way that turned out, it would be a catastrophe for everyone involved. "This is a bad idea, Niko."

"Just go home. Go to sleep. You've got rehearsal in the morning. I promise I'll tell you everything later about how this turns out." He placed his hands on my shoulders lightly, then bent down and kissed me on the forehead. "Go."

He turned and hurried up the stairs to the platform, where Tomás was still holding the door open for him. And then he was gone, and I was standing in a dark alley at night, alone.

This was horrible. This was in large part my fault for being too cowardly to talk to Abernathy, and for thinking that asking for help from Niko, a reckless wild card with known criminal ties, was a sound idea. My options sucked: I could send the police here and invite the wrath of Charlie Global and create problems I was unequipped to handle. Or I could go home and try to forget about this while Yolanda's murderer walked into a death trap. Some cold and vicious part of me thought that was the better option. Surely whatever Niko and Charlie had in mind for Joel counted as justice, of a sort.

Joel was coming in from Paramus. He'd be driving, which added a special set of obstacles in New York; traffic could be murderously slow, and he'd have precious few choices of places to park. Charlie had told him to show up at midnight, and he still had about ten minutes to go, but I was willing to bet Joel— down on his luck, on the run, low on options—wouldn't want to risk messing up a shot at making a good impression tonight. He'd give himself plenty of time to get here, which meant he'd try to arrive early. He could be here already, killing time in his car, waiting until midnight to make his entrance.

I found the nearest public parking lot on my phone, a tiny

space tucked beneath the Manhattan Bridge. I'd head over there to do some quiet reconnaissance and see if I could spot him. If he was there, I'd call the police. Despite Niko's concerns, I felt confident Joel would never recognize me—after all, he'd failed to recognize me at first when I'd approached him at the bodega outside my apartment building, and he'd almost surely been waiting there for me, hoping I would lead him to Yolanda. If necessary, I'd intercept Joel and somehow prevent him from entering Charlie's casino until I could summon the police.

It wasn't much of a plan, but it felt better to commit to something than to remain in a state of miserable indecision. I started walking along the sidewalk, teetering in my stupid heels, heading toward the bridge.

28

Opera Girls

My trajectory intersected with Joel's a block from the parking lot. He was striding down the sidewalk, heading in the direction of Charlie's casino, and I was so deeply mired in anxious worries about whether I'd messed things up beyond repair that I went blank at the sight of him. I spotted his sandy hair and his camel coat, and then I stepped right into his path with no strategy in mind.

Joel, whom I was having difficulty not thinking of as Patrick, looked startled and a bit suspicious when I accosted him, and I had to reassure myself that Niko's concerns were groundless: Of course he didn't recognize me. In heavy makeup and a flashy outfit, I looked vastly different from how I'd looked on our prior encounters, and here in Brooklyn, miles away from my Hudson Heights apartment, he'd have no reason to connect me with the drab girl who'd hung around with Yolanda. The trick now was finding a way to grab his attention.

I'd tried to mimic Yolanda when I'd flirted with him outside the bodega, and it had failed, probably because I was no Yolanda. Thinking back on our brief conversation, I realized his interest in me had evaporated the second I'd mentioned that we held our rehearsals at the Tammany Performing Arts

Center. After he'd lost Yolanda's trail at my apartment, I'd help-fully put him back on track, and then he had no more use for me.

But now I had to stop him from continuing on to Charlie's, and I also had to stick with him until I could summon the police. Flirting with him seemed like a decent enough option, but if I tried the same approach as before, trying to imitate Yolanda's seductive playfulness, it likely wouldn't work any better than it had outside the bodega. Worse, it might jog his memory of that encounter.

Instead of trying to bewitch him with my feminine wiles, I opted for wide-eyed innocence, transforming myself into a tipsy and helpless sequin-clad naïf trying to navigate her way through the mean streets of Brooklyn. "Excuse me, sir?" I asked. I pitched my voice higher and made it breathy in a way that would have given Gerard a coronary from outrage if I ever tried it during a lesson. I opened my eyes as wide as I could and tried to channel the spirit of a wounded fawn. "Do you know how I can get to the A train from here?"

His suspicion faded as soon as I opened my mouth and squeaked at him, and now he looked benevolent yet smug, like he was glad the wounded fawn had the sense to turn to a strong, worldly man like himself for answers. "Hang on a sec-ond," he said, and brought out his phone. He squinted at his screen, then glanced around to orient himself. "You want the High Street station. It's just that way." He pointed straight down Washington.

I added a dollop of visible distress on top of my helplessness. "Is it far? I don't know this area. My friends and I took a car here. We went to a bunch of places and got separated, and now no one's answering my texts."

"It's pretty close. A few blocks." Joel smiled at me. He was handsome, I'd remembered that from my earlier encounters with him, but more than that, there was something likable and appealing about him. He had a warm smile and soft eyes; viewed objectively, I could see why Linh had fallen for him. Viewed subjectively, I despised him. When he smiled, I remembered the way I'd felt when I'd found Yolanda lying in a cold bundle on her blood-soaked rug. "Do you think you can find it from here?"

"Are you going in that direction?" I asked. "Could you walk with me?"

He frowned and glanced at his wrist. In the light of the streetlamps, I caught a flash from the wide gold band of his Rolex. Had to be a fake, a good-quality one, like the Birkin bag on my arm; if what Charlie had to say about Joel's current prospects was true, he would've pawned a real one by now. I could see him calculating whether escorting me would make him late for his appointment with Charlie. Evidently he concluded he'd have time, because he smiled. "Sure. No problem."

At least Joel was a well-mannered murderer, going out of his way to help a lone woman make it home safely at night. I wobbled along beside him as we headed down Washington. He gave a solicitous glance at my feet. "You doing okay in those shoes?"

My feet were too frozen now to feel much pain from the way these sandals were forcing all my body weight onto the tips of my toes. "Fine, thank you." I flashed him a cute smile. "Do you live in this area?"

I was making aimless small talk, my mind fixed on figuring out how to play this. If I spotted a police car, that would be ideal; I would scream and wave my arms and force them to stop, at which point I could explain that Joel was a double murderer. It'd be messy, but Abernathy had said there was an APB on Joel, and that should help untangle the mess with a minimum of fuss. Failing that, I'd insist that he escort me all the way down to the subway turnstile. Once inside the station, I'd grab the attention of the nearest armed transit cop. It was vital to wait for the right moment; I couldn't be reckless. I had no idea whether Joel was carrying a weapon tonight, but I'd seen Yolanda's corpse. I knew what he was capable of.

"I have a place on Park Avenue," Joel said. I knew that was a lie—Paramus is a long way from Park Avenue—and yet when he said it, it seemed plausible. His demeanor was genial yet polished, radiating a kind of laid-back affluence, like success came easily to him, and I could see why Charlie Global had at one time contemplated mentoring him. "But I love coming into Brooklyn. It's got so much character."

I don't know what I would have said in reply, because as we were passing beneath the Brooklyn-Queens Expressway, I stepped wrong on the pavement, and the golden spike of one of my heels snapped clean off. I pitched forward, and I had to grab Joel to prevent myself from taking a header on the sidewalk. "Oh no!" I said in a cute-baby wail, remaining firmly in character. "My shoe broke."

Joel stooped down and gallantly picked up the detached spike. He handed it to me. "Sorry about that. That's going to hinder walking," he said.

It would. Removing both shoes would make it easier, but cold weather aside, my strong fondness for personal hygiene made me balk at going barefoot on a New York sidewalk. "I'll manage," I said, and gave a sad giggle.

"Here." Joel slipped his arm in mine to support me. I tried my best not to recoil at his touch. Everything about me wanted to jerk out of his grasp, but that would be out of character for the flighty, helpless creature I was embodying right now, so I clutched his arm and let him help me limp along the underpass. The Birkin bag was dangling from my wrist, and it was awkward to have it in the way while Joel was holding that arm, so just as we'd reached the little grassy park on the far side of the underpass, I switched the bag to my other wrist. Joel glanced down to see what I was doing, and before I knew what was happening, he'd grabbed me by the front of my dress, bodily dragged me off the sidewalk and across the grass, and slammed me against the stone wall supporting the expressway.

Taken entirely by surprise, I'm ashamed to report that my very first thought was some desperately confused hope that Joel hadn't torn my costume, because I didn't want Ana to think I was the kind of person who would violate a pinky swear to return it in pristine condition.

He braced me against the wall with one strong forearm across my sternum, leaning in and pressing hard and painfully enough to make me worry he'd cracked some bones. With his free hand he fished around in the pocket of his camel coat and produced a folding hunting knife. I'd seen the handle of a similar knife sticking out of Yolanda's chest. He worked it open one-handed and held it near my face. "How'd you find me?" It was a snarl, his handsome face contorting in rage.

I froze, horrified to my core at how fast and shocking his reaction had been. I'd slipped up and tipped him off as to my identity. "How'd you know it was me?" I asked. I'd shed the helpless-baby persona, but my voice still came out high and breathy with fear.

He didn't answer. Instead, with the knife still near my face, he released the pressure on my chest and lowered his arm to yank the Birkin bag off my wrist, and for a nonsensical moment, I thought I'd misunderstood the situation. Maybe he hadn't recognized me after all; maybe he just wanted to mug me. He held the bag by its base with one hand and dumped it upside down. One violent shake, and my keys and phone and wallet tumbled onto the grass. He thrust the bag against the wall near my head and slashed at the lining with the knife, keeping the elbow of the arm holding the knife against my throat to hold me in place, and suddenly I knew what he was doing. When he turned the bag over again, a small white plastic disc bounced onto the grass beside my wallet.

That had been tucked inside the sloppily sewn inner seam

I'd noticed when Yolanda first handed the bag to me. The final pieces of how Joel had found me, and why he'd assumed Yolanda lived in my apartment, fell into place, so smoothly and so obviously that I wondered why I hadn't seen them before. "That was a pretty good plan," I said, struggling to sound cool and collected despite my panic. "You snuck a GPS tracker into your present for Yolanda. Too bad she brought it straight to me after she picked it up from her post office box. It never made it to her apartment. Tough luck for you, right, Don José?"

His face was too close to mine. The gentle handsomeness had vanished, and now he seemed feral. I could smell his sweat. "How did you know about that?"

Overlooking the significance of the Birkin bag was perhaps a forgivable mistake, but as an opera singer, I had no excuse for not making this connection earlier: Yolanda's Somebody's Baby alias was Carmen, a legendary opera heroine who gets stabbed to death in a deranged fit of possessive passion by her onetime lover, Don José. I fought down the chagrin I felt about missing that and forced myself to assume an outer façade of unbothered swagger. He'd tossed the Birkin bag aside, and now the knife was near my face again, and I doubted he'd have any hesitation about sticking it in my chest. But he was curious about what I knew, and I planned on keeping it that way.

"I know everything about you, Joel. The NYPD knows everything about you. There's an APB out on you right now. *Everybody* knows about sad, angry Joel Tierney, the lovesick loser who deluded himself into thinking Kimberly Stubbings, of all the damn people, could actually care for him." It was generally considered a bad move to deliberately piss off a knife-wielding murderer, but I had a crazy theory that this was the correct tactic to use on him. I needed to keep him right at the brink of losing control without pushing him over; I needed to keep him enraged, because if he wanted to argue with me, he'd have to keep me alive for that. I forced myself to smile at him, and this time I really did channel Yolanda, making it as cruel and as gloating as I could. It was the smile she'd given me while explaining how she was going to ruin my reputation among our fellow cast members. "She showed you how much she cared, didn't she? She stole all your money and sent you to jail."

It was midnight, and we hadn't passed many people on the sidewalk, but New York never sleeps, and sooner or later someone would walk by on their way to the subway, or someone in a passing car would catch a glimpse of us in the darkness and decide to investigate, and I really wanted that to happen before Joel decided to stab me to death. The longer we kept arguing and the longer he felt the need to explain himself, the better my chances.

"It wasn't the damn money," Joel said. Furious as he was, his voice quivered, and he sounded like he was on the verge of tears. "If she'd just stolen the money from me, I could have forgiven her. She didn't need to call the police. I treated her like a goddess, and it wasn't good enough for her. She ruined my life. I couldn't let her get away with that. You need to understand, I loved her. I *worshipped* her."

"You and everyone else. Stand in line, Joel. I met Yolanda for the very first time less than a month ago, and since then I've run into a whole slew of guys who felt that exact same hopeless, obsessive, stupid love for her that you did. She didn't care about any of you. You know what Yolanda told me when she dumped that purse off on me? *Maybe the next handbag he buys me will be in a color I actually like.* That's what she thought of your gift. That's what she thought of men in general: useful for buying her *things*, but not worth an attachment."

"That's not true," Joel said. "Kimberly and I had a special connection." There was hurt in his eyes, intense and desperate, and I marveled at Yolanda's ability to worm her way so deeply into his psyche that it had obliterated any sense of proportion or logic.

I felt a surge of contempt for Joel as the truth dawned on me:

He hadn't killed Yolanda because she'd stolen from him and sent him to prison. He'd killed her because she'd rejected him.

"Sure. That's what you thought. And when you found out it was all a lie, your ego couldn't handle it. That's why you hunted her down and murdered her," I said. "Corey Floyd too, right? You made him tell you how you could find Yolanda, and then you killed him to cover your tracks."

"I killed him because he was unworthy of Kimberly." It was a hiss. "He was a junkie. He was a ridiculous mess. He was living on the streets. He wasn't good enough for her. He never was."

"And yet she had a child with him. And yet she kept in touch with him after she'd burned every other tie to her past." I shook my head sadly. "I don't know, Joel, it sounds to me like she was a lot more into him than she ever was into you."

"She loved me," he said. "She was crazy about me."

We were going in circles. Joel's brain had short-circuited, and all he could do was insist that Kimberly Stubbings had loved him despite ample evidence to the contrary. He'd confessed to murdering her and to murdering Corey, and I suppose it was good that it was out in the open, but he'd soon realize he had nothing left to say.

I saw a shadow on the sidewalk and a blur of movement out of the corner of my eye, and then I heard the unmistakable click of a hammer of a gun being cocked back. Niko had emerged from nowhere to stand behind Joel and press a snub-nosed revolver to his temple, and his presence was so unexpected that I thought I was hallucinating.

"Let her go," Niko said. He sounded calm, considering the circumstances. "Lower the knife and step back."

Joel turned his head to look at the new arrival and flinched when the gun was pressed to his nose. "Who the fuck are you?" he asked. The knuckles wrapped around the knife handle near my face went white as his grasp tightened.

"I'm the guy who's going to kill you," Niko said. It was a

melodramatic statement, but he kept his voice steady, and I thought he probably meant every word.

Joel ducked, pivoted, and slashed the knife at Niko in one seamless move. It caught Niko across the chest in a long arcing motion, and I saw a line of bright red. Niko howled in pain and shock, and then Joel dove at him, knocking him to the grass. The gun flew out of Niko's grasp, skidded down the grassy slope, and came to rest on the sidewalk.

I went after it. After one step, I realized I couldn't run in these shoes, not with one heel missing and the other heel sinking deep into the grass with every step, so I dropped down and crawled, hiking the sequined dress up and out of the way of my knees. Niko and Joel were rolling around together on the lawn, wrestling for control of the knife, two dangerous lovesick men desperate to kill each other over a dead woman who probably hadn't cared much for either of them. Joel retained possession of the knife, and he stabbed it down at Niko, who deflected the blade with his open hand, howling in pain as the blade sliced through his palm.

For a panicked moment, I realized I'd lost track of the gun, which was lying somewhere on the sidewalk in the darkness, and then my groping hand touched the barrel. I'd never fired a gun, but I'd held one onstage in college while playing Marguerite as a chain-smoking gangland moll in a reimagined production of *Faust* set in 1920s Chicago. There'd been a weapons master on set, and at the time I'd thought his detailed lessons had been unnecessary, since the gun we'd used onstage was only a realistic prop, but now I was wracking my head to recall everything he'd taught us. The first step should be to check to make sure the gun was loaded, but my hands were shaking, and I couldn't figure out how to swing open the cylinder. Niko had already cocked it—it was a small mercy that the gun hadn't fired when he'd dropped it—so all I would need to do was pull the trigger.

I stood in a fighter's stance, spine straight, feet shoulder-width apart, knees slightly bent, which was not at all easy to do in my broken, unbalanced, stupid sandals. I held the little gun raised and steady in both hands, my finger not yet on the trigger. Still locked in their mortal battle, neither Niko nor Joel were paying one bit of attention to me. "I have the gun!" I shouted. "Put the knife down, or I'll shoot!"

The noise of the nearby expressway drowned me out, and I don't think either of them heard me. Niko, on his back beneath Joel, happened to look up, and his eyes went very wide at the sight of me; Joel, sensing something had changed, glanced back over his shoulder and saw me.

A frozen moment, and then Joel leaped to his feet and pounced at me. I drew on my last remnant of knowledge from my gun training—*always fire at center mass*—and I aimed as best I could at the middle of Joel's body. I pulled the trigger.

The gun was pretty dinky, and being inexperienced with such things, I hadn't expected much of a recoil, but it knocked me backward. I staggered around, only narrowly managing to keep my balance. The noise the shot made was deafening, drowning out the expressway, the enraged shout from Joel, and the blood roaring in my ears from the realization that I'd just fired a gun with the intent to kill.

For a while, everything was confused and surreal. I think I entered a short-lived fugue state, because I still can't remember much about the moments immediately after firing the shot. When I came back to reality, I was still holding the gun raised and ready, though it was aimed at nothing in particular. Joel was on the ground, crumpled; I remember thinking he looked surprisingly small, the way Yolanda had looked when I found her body. Niko crouched next to him, peeling his fingers back to work the knife out of his grip, and Joel bellowed something incoherent into the grass and tried to shove him away with one flailing arm, and that was when I realized Joel was still very much alive. My best aim, as it turns out, was pretty miserable, and as close as Joel had been to me, I'd hit him in the shoulder, not the chest.

Joel's hunting knife now in his possession, Niko got to his feet. He looked pale and sick, and the front of his white shirt was splattered with blood from where Joel had slashed him across his chest. I was still pointing the gun in front of me, so he very prudently approached me from the side. "Kit. Give me my gun," he said.

His words penetrated the static-filled haze in my brain, and I lowered the gun. On the grass, Joel tried to wriggle up to his feet, but couldn't seem to make it work. "You came here to shoot him," I said to Niko.

"I had absolutely no idea he'd be here tonight. You know that," Niko said.

"You brought a gun."

"I always carry it," he said, which was something I sure wished I'd known before I'd proposed this evening's adventure. But he sounded tired, no longer filled with vengeful fury, and even though I knew Niko had it in him to do something profoundly stupid, at the moment he was exhausted and wounded, and the window for reckless action had closed. "Give it to me."

I passed the gun to him, thankful to be rid of it. "What are you doing here?" I asked him.

"I was looking for you," he said. "I chickened out. I told Charlie to get Joel's address and send him home, and we'd have the police handle the rest, just like you suggested. I think Charlie is gravely disappointed in me." He managed a ghastly smile. "I was hoping to catch up with you before you reached the subway."

Niko trained the gun on Joel, who had worked his way up to his knees. Joel bent his head to the grass and clutched his shoulder with both hands while making odd agonized gasps and gurgles. I looked at him and felt only a muted relief that I hadn't killed him.

Niko swayed to the side, like he was close to collapsing. It would do us no good if he fainted, so I slipped one arm around his waist and held him close against me to keep him on his feet. I needed to call 911, but my phone was lost somewhere on the crumpled, blood-splattered grass, and I couldn't let go of Niko, and anyway, I heard sirens now, coming closer, no doubt attracted by the noise of the gunshot. My ears were still ringing.

Now that the terrifying part had passed, the whole situation had an aura of hyperreality to it. Niko and I had reached the dramatic climax of our very own opera, one filled with crimes and louche behavior involving sex workers and mistresses, gangsters and blackmail, stabbings and poisonings and vengeance, and the curtain was about to fall. I immediately felt guilty for that flight of fancy, because the man on the ground had murdered two people, and despite the crazy rush of adrenaline that was causing me to see the world in a heightened and dreamlike way, this wasn't a stage.

"Don't say anything when the police arrive," Niko said. His voice was weak, but his eyes glittered with excitement. "Just tell them that this asshole murdered Yolo and tried to kill you, and leave it at that, okay? Let my lawyers do the talking."

Under the circumstances, it didn't seem like bad advice. "Am I going to make it to rehearsal tomorrow, or am I going to be in jail?"

"You'll make it. I promise you that. I give you my word of honor." Niko sounded noble and self-sacrificing and ridiculous. His body felt very warm as he leaned against me. He laughed, soft and weak.

"You know who you looked like with that gun?" he asked. "Your mom. *Savage Rage Two.* You know the ending, when she guns down the man who murdered her fiancé? God, I had such a crush on her in that film."

"Never saw it," I said. His cologne was something outdoorsy, the scent of spruce forests and mountain rivers. I found it incongruous because Niko was such a creature of the city, but it smelled good right now.

"That's a crying shame," he said. He patted my shoulder. "I'll come over some night and we'll watch it together."

I thought that sounded like a frankly terrible idea, but I said nothing. He was starting to babble, probably from pain and blood loss and the remnants of what must have been a wild adrenaline spike during his battle with Joel, and I knew I shouldn't pay much attention to anything he said.

He laughed again, and it sounded a little unhinged. "Opera girls," he said. "I can't stand opera, do you know that? But apparently I have a thing for opera girls."

I couldn't think of a reply. "Ana will kill me if you get blood on this dress," I managed to say at last.

The sirens drew closer, getting louder and louder.

29

Iceland Is Lovely in January

"I don't want to make you nervous, but you should know we sold out." That was Daniel, sticking his head through the door of my dressing room. "I just heard from the box office. Every seat is gone."

I looked up. "Wow. Okay, thank you for telling me." Sold out. It shouldn't have come as a surprise; I knew tickets had sold briskly all week, thanks to the frenzy of news articles about the capture of Yolanda's murderer. Even still, I felt a giddy rush. I'd never performed in a sold-out show before.

Niko had been as good as his word. I'd made it to rehearsal the next morning, groggy from a night of police questioning but in decent spirits. To Ana's relief, my costume hadn't needed repairing, despite the previous evening's adventures. Since then, I'd been questioned a couple of times throughout the week, both about everything that had gone down in Brooklyn and about Yolanda's murder. A detective from Maine had even driven down to the city to ask me a handful of questions about Corey's murder; I hadn't been able to help her much, but it was good to know authorities were making the effort to link it to Joel. Abernathy had been easier to tolerate when I had a duo of high-powered lawyers—Niko's lawyers, really, but they were smart and ferocious and seemed to have my best interests at heart—at my side telling him exactly which questions I would and wouldn't answer. Joel was currently in custody, no chance of bail, and all was right with the world.

Daniel glanced around my dressing room. "Pretty flowers," he said.

"Aren't they? The yellow roses are from Roksana," I said. I'd found them in my dressing room when I'd arrived at the theater. It had been an unexpected and gracious gesture from her. There were peonies from Gerard, too; Daniel bent down to smell them, and I wished he wouldn't, because I didn't want him to notice the signature on the card stuck into the lavish arrangement of dark red roses in the tall vase behind them. Those had come from Niko. Niko was an impulsive guy with a penchant for big gestures, so I didn't want to read too much into it, but I thought there was a decent chance he'd developed a crush on me as a result of our emotionally charged evening, a prospect I found mostly dismaying, yet a tiny bit intriguing.

Daniel took a deep breath. "Thank you for your patience," he said. "With . . . everything, I suppose. You've worked very hard. I want you to know I appreciate your efforts."

"Thank you." I smiled at him, warm and conciliatory, and right now it was hard feeling much resentment toward him.

I'd already decided *Barbarella* would be the last time I worked for Brio. It was a practical decision, not an emotional one. Daniel had given up on me too early on; it had been little thanks to him that I'd been able to claw my way back into my role. While I seemed to have risen in his estimation as a performer, he and I simply weren't a good team. It would be best for both of us if I looked elsewhere for future work.

Plus I had a hunch Brio wouldn't be around much longer. *Barbarella* might very well become a hit, but Niko's zany financial hijinks would come to light sooner or later. Maybe their father's influence would keep Niko and Daniel out of jail, but

Brio would collapse, and I wanted to be far away by the time it happened.

On his way out of the dressing room, Daniel brushed past Astrid, who slunk into my room and leaned against the wall near the door. She stared at me in silence as I put the finishing touches on my stage makeup. Finally, she spoke. "Contrary to what people may say, Iceland is lovely in January."

I stared at her, our eyes meeting in the mirror. "I'm sure it is."

"Ice and snow, of course, the same as New York. But it is beautiful. You would come up in January and stay through February; that should do it. Reykjavik is very cultured. Our museums are well worth visiting. You will enjoy it there."

I turned around in my chair to face her. "Why am I going to Iceland?"

"To workshop with me. I have an idea for a new opera." Behind her glasses, her gray eyes glinted. "*Red Sonja.* You know *Red Sonja*?"

"It was a film, wasn't it?" I remembered the poster, something with sword-wielding barbarian queens and muscle-bound hunks. It looked like something my mother would have desperately wanted to star in.

"A comic book as well. It is the comic book that serves as my primary inspiration." She nodded at me. "You must be my Sonja. My warrior."

I stared at her in surprise. "This would be for Brio?" I asked cautiously.

Astrid shook her head. "The Icelandic Opera. We are in negotiations now. I won't press you for an answer until the end of this run; after *Barbarella,* you will have other offers, and maybe mine will seem small by comparison. But I would like you to consider mine, please."

"I will," I said. "Absolutely, I will. Astrid, thank you so much," but she just nodded and slipped out of the room before I could get too mushy in my burst of gratitude.

The Icelandic Opera. A role in a brand-new opera, one tailored to my strengths as a singer and a performer . . . I stared at my reflection in the mirror for a long time before returning my attention to fixing my face.

A soft knock on my door alerted me to Marcus, our stage manager, giving the performers our five-minute call. We all took our places, moving silently past one another in the near darkness, spectral figures in our outlandish costumes. I'd spent so much time that week walking around in the tall vinyl boots that by now, despite the ludicrous extra height Daniel had urged Ana to add to them, they felt as comfortable as bedroom slippers.

I had butterflies in my stomach, oversized and enthusiastic ones. When the curtain rose, my life would change.

I thought about Yolanda, how this opening night would likely have been hers if her past hadn't caught up to her in such a violent and tragic way. Even though she'd wished me ill, I was aware of a debt to her. Maybe I'd keep in distant contact with Trae, and maybe when Violet was older, if she'd inherited or developed any of her mother's gift for music, maybe I'd make sure she had the opportunities for professional training that Yolanda had missed. But that was a long way off. What mattered was this moment here, right now.

The orchestra struck up the opening notes of the overture. I took a deep breath and cleared my head of all thoughts of Yolanda.

The curtain rose.

Acknowledgments

Thanks are due to my agent, the great Kerry Sparks, for her knowledge, insight, and enthusiasm. I'm also in the debt of everyone at my agency, LGR, with a special nod to Rebecca Rodd for handling all matters relating to my books while Kerry was on leave.

Caitlin Landuyt originally acquired this book but left Knopf before she could edit it. I'm deeply grateful to Morgan Hamilton for stepping in as my new editor. In addition to being a delightful human being, Morgan has been a smart, stabilizing presence; her shrewd insights helped me shape the story in new and stronger ways.

Thank you to my production editor, Melissa Yoon, and her team for their work copyediting my words. In addition, there are many others at Knopf who worked behind the scenes to make this book as strong as it could be; they all have my sincere gratitude.

I wrote the first draft in the Eulalie and Carlo Scandiuzzi Writers' Room at Seattle's Central Library. Thank you to Linda, Richard, and Bridget at the Seattle Public Library for supervising the Writers' Room Residency program that allowed me the use of that beautiful space, and to the reference librarians who

ACKNOWLEDGMENTS

helped me to hunt down information about the world of opera in the course of my research. My heart belongs to public library systems, and Seattle has one of the very best.

Thank you to my sister, Ingrid, for reading the manuscript and telling me it was good when I most needed to hear it.

A Note About the Author

Morgan Richter is the author of *The Divide*. A graduate of the Filmic Writing Program at the University of Southern California's film school, she has worked in production on several television shows, including ABC's *America's Funniest Home Videos* and E! Entertainment Television's Emmy-winning comedy series *Talk Soup*. She is an avid popular culture critic and the author of *Duranalysis: Essays on the Duran Duran Experience*. Richter currently lives in Seattle.

A Note on the Type

This book was set in Minion, a typeface produced by the Adobe Corporation specifically for the Macintosh personal computer and released in 1990. Designed by Robert Slimbach, Minion combines the classic characteristics of old-style faces with the full complement of weights required for modern typesetting.

Typeset by Scribe
Philadelphia, Pennsylvania

Designed by Michael Collica